THE MONEY THE MOB AND WALL STREET

THE MONEY THE MOB AND WALL STREET

A Novel by Harry Brooks

Library of Congress Control Number:		2015901457
ISBN:	Hardcover	978-1-5035-3887-0
	Softcover	978-1-5035-3888-7
	eBook	978-1-5035-3889-4

This novel is a work of fiction. All of the characters, events, and places are products of the author's imagination and in no way are intended to represent any real-life incidents. Where the author uses the names of public places, personalities, celebrities, politicians, publicized events or alludes to them, they are used only to dramatize and to establish a time frame and point of reference. With the exception of making reference to a publized event that actually has taken place and is a matter of public record this story is not intended to depict any true story about any one person or financial institution.

Print information available on the last page.

Rev. date: 02/18/2015

To order additional copies of this book, contact:
Xlibris
1-888-795-4274
www.Xlibris.com
Orders@Xlibris.com
672840

As Always to Joan

PREFACE

THIS WAS THE first day of the trial. The date was March 10, 2004, almost a year to the day since the defendants had been arrested. Normally in these types of trials, the gallery is filled with the average curious citizen who has nothing better to do. Instead on this day, there was row after row of suits—expensive lawyers eager to observe a long-awaited case, one that could influence the outcome of a handful of civil suits pending across the country. There were no ceiling fans whirling to beat the heat like in the movie, *Inherit the Wind.* This was an average federal courtroom in the federal building in downtown New York. The first several rows of seats were reserved for the associates of the federal prosecutor and defense team, each of them with his pad and pen prepared to take notes and then pass them on to either the defense lawyer or the federal prosecutor.

The jury was made up of four middle-aged white women who looked like the average housewife, all wearing flower-print dresses, two elderly black men, each with a full head of white hair, and six assorted black women of different sizes and shapes. It looked like a pew in a Baptist church somewhere in Harlem. Since the judge would not allow any cameras in the courtroom, the coverage from both television and the print media was sparse. The trial was listed on the federal docket as USA v. AA Financial Corp., its officers, and coconspirators, et al. Wade Simon was seated in the front row between his two attorneys. His face was expressionless. He was dressed in a thousand-dollar Brooks Brothers suit and looked as if he were waiting to accept a "Man of the Year Award."

The judge in this trial, the very righteous and sometimes cantankerous Honorable Walter J. Hodges sat in his lofty seat, waiting for the bailiff to announce the case. Once he did, the Honorable Walter J. Hodges spoke, "Good morning, everyone. Before the federal prosecutor and the learned defense attorney make their opening statement, I would like to remind the jury that what they will say in their opening statements should have no bearing on the verdict that you will ultimately reach at the conclusion of this case. Your decision will be based solely on the evidence presented during the course of these proceedings. During the course of this trial, you are going to hear about a maze of convoluted, boring, tedious financial transactions from both sides. I have instructed both sides to attempt to cut through the mountainous heap of acronyms and obfuscations in explaining to you what this case is about and cut to the chase. I do not expect this case to draw a great deal of media publicity; however, that doesn't distract from the importance of these proceedings."

It was easy to understand why this case would not be prime meat for the media. Both the government's case and the defense were very complicated. The defense lawyers' main line of argument was going to be that the corrupt Wall Street institutions, with the extreme complexity of their infrastructure, were the real culprits in this case. And the prosecution, in order to win a conviction, would have to prove that the defendants in this case actually did exploit these loopholes. Unless either side came up with some surprises, this was going to be a long, boring trial.

Seated in the last row in the courtroom, a very attractive woman dressed in a tailored suit and wearing a large brimmed hat and dark sunglasses sat listening to every word the judge said. She watched the federal prosecutor and his team and also the defense attorneys as they talked amongst themselves and scribbled notes on long yellow legal pads. She also looked at each of the jurors, trying to get a sense of what they were thinking. Impossible.

Then it was time for the lawyers to make their opening remarks. The federal prosecutor, a tall, slender man dressed in a conservative three-piece suit went first. He wasted no time in expanding on what the judge had said about the complexities of the case. He apologized to the jury for the "hellishly dull maze of convoluted, difficult to understand, and boring financial transactions" they were about to spend weeks hearing about. He only spoke for about thirty minutes, closing with, "This case is about right and wrong. It is about lying and cheating. Although the aspects of our financial institutions and banking system are complex, the fraud perpetrated here by the defendants and their associates is very clear and easy to understand. Cities, towns, and millions of honest American citizens all across this great country of ours were lied to and cheated out of hundreds of millions of dollars by defendants. They in fact introduced organized crime to Wall Street and thereby attempted to corrupt our entire financial system." The defense attorney stood and objected to the accusation that their clients brought organized crime to Wall Street. The judge warned the federal prosecutor to be careful as to his accusations. He would give him a lot of latitude, but he would not tolerate unfounded claims and told him to stick to the case at hand.

Then it was time for the defense attorney to speak. When he walked over to the jury box, he had an engaging smile as he looked at each juror. His face was suntanned, and there was not a hair out of place. He was well over six feet tall and looked like he might have played football in college. Before he started to speak, the man in the Brooks Brothers suit seated in the front of the courtroom turned around and looked at the woman sitting at the back of the courtroom. He smiled, made a pistol out of his index finger and thumb, pointed it at the prosecutor then snapped down his thumb and mouthed the word "click." The woman smiled and gave him a thumbs-up.

CHAPTER ONE

Fourteen Years Earlier, 1990, Las Vegas, Nevada

"One hundred..."
"Two hundred..."
"Three hundred..."
"Four hundred..."
"Five hundred..."

THE MAN COUNTING the money was Morris Simon. His hands were clammy, and you could see the sweat running down the sides of his face. He finished counting the money and slowly pushed the crumpled bills to the opposite side of the desk. Seated on the other side of the desk was an ominous-looking man by the name of Carmine Mastoria. He was forty-five years old, prematurely gray, and with the face of a predator. He looked like a successful businessman—but actually he was a con man, loan shark, and bookie who had ties to one of the organized crime families in Chicago. He was not sweating; he was simply staring at the man who had just painfully counted out the $500. He had a face that looked like it was chiseled out of stone. He looked at the five $100 bills that Morris Simon had pushed across the desk to him. He fingered the bills as if they were garbage and said in a cold intimidating voice, "What the fuck is this? Are you trying to insult me, Morris?"

"No . . . of course not Carmine."

"Well then, tell me what this shit is." And with that, he swatted the $500 so that three of them fell on the floor. Morris bent over to pick them up when Mastoria said, "Leave them."

"What's the matter, Carmine? Why are you so pissed off?"

"Why am I pissed off? You come to me last month and tell me you need three large. I ask you what for and you tell me there is a poker game at the Trop with a couple of dead money guys. It's a walk in the park, you say. Carmine, you will have your money back in a week, you say. So do I give you any grief? No, I give you three large, and I tell you it's gonna cost you three bills a week for the juice. No problem, you say. That was six weeks ago. The juice is three bills a week, and if I count this shit offering here, it makes a total of $800 that you will have paid in juice. That leaves you about $1,000 short and still counting, and you want to know why I am pissed?"

In banking circles, they call it usury. In the garment industry, they call it shylocking or loan-sharking. The wise guys call it "juice." They lend you a hundred and call it a small. They lend you a thousand and call it a bone or a large. It costs a hundred a week of vigorish or juice to borrow a large. You can't pay the juice and at the same time make a payment on the loan. You borrow a large; you pay it back in one lump sum. When you can't make your payments, that's when the wise guys own you. They want favors. If you can't pay or grant the favors, that's when there comes a day that the juice man's collectors pay you a visit. You don't ever want that to happen.

"Carmine, tell me how long we been doing business?"

"To fucking long Morris you're a degenerate gambler, and worse than that, a fucking liar. Take off your pants, Morris."

"What?"

"I said take off your pants. What, are you deaf too?"

"Carmine, come on . . ."

"I'm not gonna tell you again, Morris. Take off your goddamn pants."

Morris slowly dropped his pants to the floor and just stood there.

"Okay, now take off your shorts."

"Carmine, give me a break!"

"Your shorts Morris, take them off!"

Morris dropped his shorts and stood there, balls naked from the waist down.

Carmine walked around the side of the desk and looked down at Morris's penis. "So this is what you are screwing me with how about that?"

"Jesus Christ, Carmine. Give me a break."

"You already said that Morris," then Carmine turned away and walked to the leather couch on the other side of his office, at the same time waving his arms in disgust. "Okay, okay, put your goddamn clothes back on and come over here and sit down."

"I have some good news for you. I paid off Jimmy, the bookie you been using downtown. You owed him four grand plus the juice. So now you owe the money to me. Counting everything, you now owe me just about ten grand, give or take a couple bucks, and the clock is ticking."

Morris just stood there, his pants still down around his ankles.

"Now the real good news, Morris, is that I have a way for you to clean up what you owe me. Everything, the three large plus what you owed Jimmy and all the juice."

Morris pulled up his shorts and pants, walked over to the couch, and sat down next to Carmine. He knew whatever Carmine was about to say was not going to benefit him. Carmine never did anything for anybody without getting payback.

Carmine put his hand on Morris's knee. "So tell me, how is that son of yours doing?"

"Wade?"

"Do you have more than one son?" Carmine said sarcastically.

"Wade . . . he's fine."

"I understand he is quite a basketball player. He was high scorer for UNLV last year, wasn't he?"

Morris had no idea where this was going, but he didn't like it. "Yeah, matter of fact, he was. I didn't know you were a basketball fan, Carmine."

Carmine got up, walked back to his desk to get a cigar, then leaned on his desk and smiled at Morris. "I'm not a basketball fan, Morris. I'm a basketball better. There is a difference." Carmine lit his cigar then walked back and sat in the large wingback chair opposite Morris. He puffed on his cigar and looked at Morris. "Monday night, UNLV plays Duke for the championship. Is that right, Morris?"

"I'm not sure, Carmine. I think so."

"You think so. Don't you follow your own kid's games? What kind of a father are you?"

Morris knew Carmine was playing with him.

"UNLV is a ten-point favorite. If they win by less than ten points, I can make a lot of money. You understand what I'm getting at, Morris?"

Morris stood up. "Jesus Christ, Carmine, you're not asking me to . . . ?" But before he could finish, Carmine stood up and looked at him with cold, evil eyes. "I'm not asking you a fucking thing. I'm telling you. I want your kid to shave the points. You do that, and you're off the hook for what you owe me. Either that or you pay me back the ten grand by noon tomorrow, your choice, one or the other."

"Carmine, why are you busting my chops like this? Have a heart."

"I do have a heart, Morris, but I use it at home for my wife and kids. This is business. In business, I use my brain and my balls. And another thing, don't you ever fucking raise your voice to me again, you Jew bastard."

Morris sank back down on the couch, a beaten man.

CHAPTER TWO

LIKE MOST CITIES, Philadelphia, the "City of Brotherly Love," is made up of many different neighborhoods. There is center city with the Gothic structure of city hall, the Union Club, a private republican club, which up until recent years was restricted, and of course, all of the high-rise office buildings. There is South Philly, which is predominately Italian and famous for Pat's Steak House and Giordia's Soft Water Ice. The Irish Catholics dominate the neighborhood more commonly known as "K and A," named for the two main cross streets, Kensington and Allegheny. The area in the greater northeast is called Oxford Circle and is home to the white middle class. North Philly is where you will find most of the city's black population. Overbrook Park is inhabited primarily by middle and upper class Jewish families who look down their noses at the Jews who live in Oxford Circle.

Then they have the neighborhood called Strawberry Mansion, with the greenery of Fairmount Park on one side, the famous Philadelphia Zoo on the other side and surrounding communities ranging from the indigent to the affluent. The social boundaries of Strawberry Mansion are more like transparent membranes than walls. In 1945, this was the neighborhood where Morris Simon was born and raised. Strawberry Mansion was a neighborhood where people actually knew and cared about one another. And contrary to most of the other neighborhoods in Philly where ethnic groups lived together, the Mansion was a melting pot.

One of the most famous landmarks of the Mansion was Champs Gym. Many a Philadelphia boxer trained there, fighters like Ike Williams, Joey Giordella, Bob Montgomery, and Gil Turner. Next door to Champs Gym was Gil's Pool Hall. That's where Morris Simon spent most of his time when he wasn't working, playing cards, shooting craps, or at the bar owned by his good friend, Abe Cohen. Morris's father owned a small men's shop on the corner of 31st and Montgomery Avenue. When Morris finished high school, he reluctantly went to work for his father in the men's store. He hated it. He would rather play pool, play cards, shoot craps, or bet on the horses. He was a compulsive gambler. But what was worse was that he was an unlucky, bad, compulsive gambler.

Morris met the girl he would eventually marry, Ann Gold, in high school. She thought he was a very cool guy. Even while still in school, Morris knew a lot of the neighborhood wise guys, and that impressed her. She would have been better off if it hadn't impressed her. They were both just twenty years old when they decided to get married. Both sets of parents told them they were too young. But Morris wanted to move out of his parents' house, and Ann thought she was pregnant. They were both right. Their only child, Wade, was born in 1966.

By the time Wade was twelve years old, he was as streetwise as any grown up in the neighborhood. On the streets and back alleys of the Mansion, he came up with his own philosophy, his view of the world. He knew there were givers and takers. He lived in a neighborhood where he saw the big kids take from the little kids, where the wannabe wise guys took from the schmucks who were either too weak or too dumb to fight back. He learned early in life about prostitution, alcohol, corrupt police, and gambling.

Wade was a gifted mathematician with an intuitive sense of numbers. He would often watch some of the older kids shoot craps in Gil's Pool Hall, and he was able to calculate the odds in his head. It was there that he learned an indelible lesson about gambling and life. "There's no such thing as a lucky gambler. There are just winners and losers. The winners are those who control the game . . . all the rest are suckers." He also came to grips with the fact that crime and corruption were no mere by-products of the economy and politics but rather a cornerstone. That was pretty damn smart for a twelve-year-old.

In school, where he excelled, he acquired the nickname, "Wade the Wiz." He used to drive his math teacher crazy. When she was writing a column of numbers on the blackboard, he was adding them up in his head and had the answer by the time she was finished. At home, when his father would leave the racing form lying around the house, Wade would read it and figure out which horse had the best chance of winning the race. The next day, he would look at the race results, and more times than not, he had picked the winner.

When he started tenth grade at Blaine High, he was already six feet tall and weighed 160 pounds. The basketball coach encouraged him to try out for the team, and in his sophomore year, he was made the starting guard. That was the same year his mother and father got divorced. Ann Simon could not continue to put up with her husband's gambling and drinking. Morris's father passed away shortly after Wade's bar mitzvah, and Morris took over running the men's store. It didn't take long for him to force the store into bankruptcy. Wade wanted to quit school and help support his mother. She worked at a grocery store in the neighborhood as a cashier, and Wade hated the fact that she had such a difficult life. However, she insisted he stay in school. His parents were only divorced a year when his mother remarried. Of all people, it was to the owner of the grocery store. The local joke was that it was cheaper for the owner to marry her than pay her to be a cashier. In the meantime, Wade's father went from job to job and continued to gamble. Although Wade saw him fairly often, and his father attempted to maintain a relationship with him, Wade had very little respect for him.

In his senior year, Blaine High School won the city championship, mainly due to Wade's play. His basketball coach convinced him to apply to several different colleges, telling him he was sure he would be offered a scholarship. However, Blaine was not a hotshot basketball school, so very few of the major colleges recruited their players. As it turned out, the only offer he received was from the University of Nevada Las Vegas. Although his mother had reservations about his going to Las Vegas, she didn't want him to pass up the opportunity of going to college. So she decided he should accept the basketball scholarship to UNLV.

By this time, Morris Simon owed money to just about every bookie in the Mansion. He was also into some of the small-time wise guys in South Philly. Over the past few years, he got smacked around pretty badly by some of the people he owed money, but for some reason, he was always able to bounce back. He would have a good win, pay off one guy, bullshit another guy, and just kept "dancing." When he heard that Wade was going to UNLV in Las Vegas, he decided it was time for him to get out of Philly. He would get a new start in a place where they had legalized gambling, Las Vegas. How fucking smart was he? He waited until he knew that Wade was settled in at school, then sold what little furniture and other shit he owned and set out for Las Vegas.

Wade's mother had called her son to give him a heads up about his father moving there, "Don't worry mom I will handle it," Wade said, knowing that at some point there would be problems. How could there not be?

Wade was only in Las Vegas two months when his father called him.

"You will never guess where I am, kid. I'm here in Vegas. I got in a couple of days ago. I wanted to get settled before I called you. I rented myself a furnished place down by the airport, and wait until you hear this. I got a job in the men's store at Caesar's Palace. How great is that?"

Wade wanted to say, "Not so great"

He knew his father was a bad gambler and the worst place in the world for a bad gambler is Las Vegas. But he was still his father, what could he do?

They agreed to meet for dinner that same night.

CHAPTER THREE

FOR THE RECORD, Benjamin "Bugsy" Siegel did not create or build Las Vegas. There was a town there with people long before he arrived. However, if it wasn't for him, that is all Las Vegas would have been, a town with some people and a couple of small gambling joints with sawdust on the floor. There is no argument that Las Vegas is the story of incredible courage and of desperation, of tragedy and heroic deeds, of injustice and of compassion, the rich and textured story of everyday men and women who turned a dusty railroad town into the entertainment capital of the world. But none of this would have been possible if it wasn't for what is commonly called the mob, organized crime, and the Mafia.

Gambling has always been an important business for the Mafia. From card games to betting on horses, to fixing championship fights, to probably the most lucrative aspect of gambling, sports betting. Up until the time the Mafia infiltrated Las Vegas, with the exception of their casinos in Cuba, all of their gambling operations were illegal. When Bugsy Siegel and Meyer Lansky decided to build the Flamingo Hotel in Las Vegas, their timing could not have been better. Up until that time, American tourists looking for a place to go where they could gamble, see gala floor shows, and dine in fine restaurants went to Cuba. During the reign of the corrupt Batista regime, where the Mafia was more than welcome, casinos were plentiful, and their profits were huge. Then Fidel Castro's revolution swept Cuba, and the mafia was ousted. Looking to replace what they had in Cuba, the Mafia turned to Las Vegas.

It didn't take long before The Flamingo Resort Hotel and Casino became a cash cow for Lansky and the New York Mafia families. By the mid-fifties, the Chicago Mafia families joined their New York counterpart in Las Vegas. They started with three casinos: The Stardust, The Desert Inn, and The Riviera. By the early 1960s, the New York and Chicago Mafia families owned ten casinos between them. It wasn't long before Mafia families from all over the country were building casinos in Vegas. Meyer Lansky became concerned that the increased competition would affect the profits. He was also concerned about one family trying to take over from another family, so he organized a "combine." He proposed that all of the families would share in all of the profits. After some fierce negotiations between the various families, a deal was reached that would give each family an interlocking share in one another's casino and hotel. By the time the lawyers legalized the deal, it was nearly impossible to tell who owned what, and that was just fine with Meyer Lansky. Whatever happened was that everyone got a piece, and the piece was large.

When Wade arrived in Las Vegas in 1985, large corporations had begun to take over ownership of the casinos. It was the start of a new era. Mega resorts and casinos were being built and financed by both Wall Street and some of the nation's major banks. There was a wide scale attack on Mafia casino interests in Las Vegas by the F.B.I., forcing them to sell to legitimate owners. However, the Mafia had no intention of leaving Las Vegas. They found other ways to make money in "Sin City." Escort services, laundry companies, casino valet parking, and food supply companies became the Mafia's new sources of revenue.

Las Vegas. There is no other place in the civilized world like it. Over fifty million people journey to it every year. Only Mecca inspires as many pilgrims. And Las Vegas knows its visitors and caters to them. Though strangers, they are familiar. What makes this city so unique, so derivative, and in the end, so exemplary? As nowhere else, people come to Las Vegas seeking something with a self-consciousness and intensity, if not desperation, that has always set the city apart—diversion, entertainment, money, escape, another chance, a last chance, another life if only for a few hours, days, maybe even forever. But in Wade Simon's case, he didn't come to Las Vegas for any of those reasons. He came to Las Vegas for a college education. Little did he know his education would include a lot more than what they taught at UNLV.

CHAPTER FOUR

WADE AGREED TO meet his father at an Italian restaurant off the strip. Although he hadn't seen him in several months, he really wasn't looking forward to having dinner with him. His father was at the restaurant when he arrived. His father got up from his chair and was about to hug him; Wade simply extended his hand and said, "Nice to see you, Dad, how you been?"

"Great. This is some town Las Vegas. How is school?"

Both of them were more than uncomfortable.

"Okay. I lucked out and got a nice guy for a roommate. He is from Chicago."

"Jewish?" his father asked.

"Why, what difference does that make?" Wade was irritated at the question.

"No, of course, it doesn't make any difference, I was just asking."

"Well if you must know, he is Italian. I'm sure you will get to meet him. His name is Louie Santino."

"Did you say Santino?"

"Yeah why?"

"Well there is an Angelo Santino in Chicago who has been in the papers lately. Is he related?"

"I don't have a clue. Why was he in the papers?"

Wade's father leaned across the table and said, "Something to do with organized crime and the stock market, not really sure what."

CHAPTER FIVE

BORN ANTONIO ANGELO Salvatore Santino, Angelo "The Boss" Santino came to the United States with his family in 1935. He was ten years old. Like a lot of other Italian immigrants, they settled in New York on the Lower East Side. The neighborhood was an Italian ghetto. It had the reputation of being one of the toughest areas in New York. The streets were narrow, and the Italian immigrants lived in crowded tenements. They lived elbow to elbow in squalor and poverty. Angelo spoke very little English, so he struggled in school. After only two months of going to school, he decided he would learn what he had to on the streets of New York's Lower East Side. It didn't take long before he joined a gang, and at the age of eleven, he was robbing stores and getting some of the other kids to pay him protection. One day, a couple of Irish kids from a nearby neighborhood beat up one of Angelo's former schoolmates and stole twenty cents from him. Angelo told the other the kids in his neighborhood, "If you don't want some of those Irish pricks coming into our neighborhood and stealing your money, pay me, and I will protect you."

When he was fifteen, he was caught robbing a hat store and was sent to Juvenile Hall for six months. While he was there, he met a kid named Skinny Lenny. Skinny worked for Vito Genovese, who at the time was the unofficial crime boss of New York's Lower East Side. Skinny told him, "When you get out of here, you come see me, and I'll introduce you to Vito Genovese. He'll show you how you can make some real money, not the penny-ante shit you're doin'."

Angelo took Skinny's advice. After being released from Juvenile Hall, he went to see Skinny and met Vito Genovese. Vito liked him. He told him he could come to work for him. During the next three years, he graduated from robbing old men and neighborhood stores to hijacking trucks, selling cigarettes with illegal tax stamps, and where necessary, being an "enforcer." By the time he was eighteen, he was Vito's right hand man. In 1943, Vito Genovese asked him to go to Chicago and help his good friend Tony Accardo. Tony was Al Capone's former bodyguard. He had just been made acting boss of the Chicago family after Frank Nitti was sent to prison. Genovese knew Accardo needed men he could trust and thought this would be a good opportunity for both men. Although Angelo would have preferred to stay in New York, he agreed to go to Chicago. It ended up being the best thing that could have happened.

Two years later, when Tony Accardo was made the permanent boss, Angelo was made underboss. He was now a made man, a capo to be feared and respected.

At age twenty, Angelo was one of the youngest men ever to rise to such a high position in the organization. Lucky Luciano was only twenty-one when he became the underboss in the Maranzano crime family in New York.

During the fifties, the "outfit," as the F.B.I. called it, was at the peak of its power. Supreme in Chicago, their gambling and vice activities included clubs and casinos on Rush Street in the heart of the old North Side cabaret district in Cicero, as well as in Calumet City. The mob had moved from running prostitutes on the street to striptease clubs and call girl services. They ran floating crap games and paid off city officials, so it really didn't make any difference where they operated their gambling activities. With Meyer Lansky's help, Angelo invested in one of the casinos in Cuba, and when Castro threw the mob out of Cuba, Meyer Lansky helped Angelo get a foothold in Las Vegas. In 1960, Angelo started his own "family," and over the next decade, he amassed a fortune of several hundred million dollars. Equally as important, he became one of the most powerful and respected capos in organized crime circles.

The 1970s were tough on the Chicago crime families. Off-track betting cut into their bookmaking operations. The state lottery cut into whatever action there was in numbers, and pressure on corrupt unions intensified. There were also ethnic and political changes in Chicago that limited the mob's opportunities. Angelo decided it was time to legitimize as much of his money as possible. He needed a front, a respectable business. In 1975, Angelo's attorney introduced him to a man by the name of Albert Kline, the executive vice president at one of New York's largest brokerage firms.

"You two should have a lot in common," Angelo's attorney told him.

It didn't take Angelo long to discover that his new acquaintance was in the same business. They were both crooks. The difference was that Kline had a large office in a high-rise office building on Wall Street, wore a three-piece suit to work every day, ate lunch at the Bankers Club, and had received several humanitarian awards. To quote the famous line at the end of the movie Casablanca, "This was going to be the beginning of a long (and very profitable) friendship."

Financial or white-collar crimes, as some people call them, are nothing new. The story dates back before the United States was the United States. Back then, the original thirteen colonies printed their own currency, and it worked very well, turning the young America into a powerful growing economy. However, the bankers of Europe saw this as a threat to their deeply cherished religious belief that the gods intended for the bankers to have all the wealth of the world. So, the Bank of England lobbied King George III to impose the Currency Act on the colonies, which forbade the colonies to use their own money and instead required them to borrow their lawful tender from the Bank of England at a high rate of interest. They really didn't give a shit about the average person; their only concern was how much money they could make.

It took only a couple of years for this scheme to reduce the formerly prosperous and productive colonies down to the poverty and unemployment level typical of London as depicted in the literature of Charles Dickens.

While the state-run American schools teach that the revolution was about the Stamp Act and the tea tax, it was the rage created by the enforced impoverishment of the Currency Act that fueled the rebellion. Unfortunately, the new American bankers were not much better than their predecessors.

By 1811, the owners of the First Bank of the United States had become rich while ruining the lives of ordinary Americans. Thomas Jefferson wrote in part,

> "Everything predicted by the enemies of banks, in the beginning, is now coming to pass. We are to be ruined by the deluge of bank paperwork and the greed of the bankers themselves. If anything, they have imposed a burden on manufactures and commerce with their swindling profits and misuses of the trust the American people have placed in them."

Albert Kline introduced Angelo to a whole new world of crime. The world of corporate crime, of bank fraud, stock market manipulation, crimes that didn't require the use of guns or back alley rendezvous.

He explained to Angelo that not all white-collar crimes are committed by dyed-in-the-wool thieves. In a lot of cases, the motivation is simply greed. There are legitimate businessmen, lawyers, stockbrokers, and bankers, who when the opportunity presents itself, cross the line. For example, there is insider trading when a corporate executive leaks proprietary information to his friends or family. There are attorneys involved in mergers and acquisitions who buy the stocks of one of the companies during the negotiations, knowing the stock will go up after the merger is completed. Then, of course, there are payoffs and bribes in exchange for leaked information. That is a little more serious. However, what he was proposing to Angelo was not as simple as those things. He had experimented with some much more complicated and serious types of illegal financial manipulation. What he was proposing had the potential of generating hundreds of millions of dollars. What he needed now was someone with money to help finance his scheme.

Both corporate fraud and illegal Wall Street dealings involve billions of dollars in losses every year, not only to the financial institutions themselves but also to individual investors and stockholders. And while Albert Kline and Angelo were plotting how they could combine their efforts to share in this billion dollars, the SEC was in the process of suing F. D. Roberts Securities Inc., a New Jersey boiler room, and one Dominick Fiorese, who was reputed to be associated with organized crime for manipulating a microcap stock. It did not deter Kline and Santino from forming an alliance that would ultimately generate millions of dollars for them. The first part of their plan was to open their own brokerage firm on Wall Street. Santino said to his new partner, "Meyer Lansky once told me the penalty for a small crime is usually the same as for a big one. Small-time crooks steal small. That's not my style." Albert Kline had no problem with that philosophy.

CHAPTER SIX

WHEN WADE RETURNED to the dormitory at UNLV after having dinner with his father, he was still thinking about what he asked him, "Is your roommate related to the Angelo Santino who has been in the news?"

His roommate Louie Santino was lying on his bed, reading.

"So how was dinner with your father?"

Wade had previously told Louie that he and his father were really not that close. Thinking back, Louie never spoke about his father. As a matter of fact, he never spoke much at all about his family, other than the fact that they lived in Chicago.

"Dinner was okay," Wade answered. "Like I told you, we're not very close, so after the first couple of minutes, there's not much to talk about." Then he decided he had to find out if as a matter of fact his roommate was related to the person in the news. "How about you and your dad, Louie, you guys close?"

His roommate put down the book he was reading and looked at Wade. "I don't know, I guess you could say so. My father was forty-one when I was born, but he was old school Italian, well you know what I mean."

Wade smiled. "Yeah, I guess so." Then he decided to just go for it. "Louie, can I ask you a personal question?"

His roommate sat up on the side of his bed and stared at Wade for a couple of seconds before answering. Then when he did answer, Wade almost fell down.

"Look, Wade, when they assigned us to room together, I was going to tell you, but I decided against it. If it's a problem, just tell me, and I will arrange for a different room."

"What the hell are you talking about?" Wade said.

"You said you wanted to ask me something personal. I assumed you wanted to know if it's true that I'm gay. Well it is true. I am gay. That is what you were going to ask, isn't it?"

That's when Wade almost fell down.

Louie Santino was tall and handsome. He had a bronze-like Las Vegas suntan, a kind of hypnotic baritone voice, and in no way was he at all feminine. There was no way in hell that he could be gay. Or could he?

"Holy shit Louie. That is not what I was going to ask. What made you think that?"

"I don't know, maybe it's because it's been on my mind. I like you. I don't mean like a gay guy, Wade, like a friend. The couple of months we have roomed together have been great. And I didn't want you to hear it from somebody else."

Wade just looked at him.

"I'll arrange to move out as soon as possible."

"Don't be crazy. I mean, you caught me off guard, but don't think for a minute that I have any problem with you being . . ."

"You can say it, Wade . . . gay!"

"Okay . . . gay. There I said it."

"That is what you are saying now, Wade, but . . ."

Before he could finish what he was saying, Wade instinctively walked over to his roommate who was now standing beside his bed and put his arm around him. "No fucking way you are moving out. And just so there is no confusion, I am not gay. I like you too, not as a gay guy, just as a guy."

"Then you better stop hugging me," Louie said, and they both started to laugh.

"So now that you know I'm gay, are you still going to walk around naked?"

"Don't fuck with me." Wade laughed. "Tell me. Is this a secret or what? I mean, do many people know?"

"Well it's not something I want to advertise. And by the way, just so you know, there is a guy that I have been seeing. Does that make you uncomfortable, Wade?"

"Of course it doesn't."

"Is this going to be a problem with you and the guys on the basketball team?"

"Hell no, why should it? First of all, it's none of their damn business."

"Okay, so now that we got that out of the way, what is it you wanted to ask me?"

After what had just taken place, Wade was embarrassed to ask his roommate about Angelo Santino.

"C'mon, Wade, what is it?"

"Well when I was having dinner with my father, he asked me if you were related in any way to . . . to . . . to Angelo Santino."

Without hesitation, Louie Santino said, "He is my father."

Wade had no response.

"Sit down, Wade. I want to tell you a little bit about my family."

Wade held up his hand. "No, that's not necessary, Louie."

"I think it is, Wade. First off, your father probably asked because my father has been in the news lately."

Wade simply nodded.

"To be perfectly honest with you, Wade, I know very little about my father's past. We were a very traditional Italian-American family. My father was involved in a number of different businesses while my mother was a housewife and mother. Of course, we lived in a very affluent neighborhood, surrounded by a lot of my father's friends. Everyone knew my dad, and even as a young child, I could sense he was important. When he entered a room, the energy changed. People would rush over to shake his hand and kiss his cheek. He made time for all of them. I remember hearing stories where he lent money to this one or that one, where he paid off the mortgage for a widow when her husband died, all kinds of stories of extreme generosity. One day when I was about ten years old, which was just about the time he became involved with AA Financial, which by the way is the reason he has been in the news, he sat me down in the kitchen. He told me I would probably start hearing some things about his life. Some of it would be true. A lot would be stories that people made up. He wanted to explain it to me the best way he knew how.

"He told me how a group of men in the 'old country' formed a secret society and vowed always to protect each other and their families. In order to do that, sometimes it meant breaking the law. He went on to tell me that when he came to this country as a poor immigrant, there was no such group to protect his family or the other poor immigrants. He said because of that, as a young man, he had to find a way to get by on his own in this country. That is when he joined forces with other young Italian immigrants, and they formed a group similar to the group in the old country. When he told me about the group here in America, it didn't sound like something that was bad or wrong. It was nice to know we had friends that would look after us if we needed it.

"My mother is a shy, quiet woman who married my father when she was only nineteen years old. I don't think she ever went out with any other boys. She was and is the perfect wife. She is an old-fashioned, loyal, and steadfast 'stand by your man' kind of woman who doesn't ask any questions. I went to a private school. Mostly it was children of wealthy lawyers, doctors, and businessmen. That's when I began to realize how different we were. For starters, my father didn't seem to fit in with the other fathers. He was not into sports or group activities. And my mother never attended any of the parent-teacher meetings. The funny thing is I was okay with that.

"Of course, growing up, I knew about the Mafia. They were the ones involved in murder and racketeering and all that kind of stuff. I was either too young or too naive to reconcile that gangster image with my father. But the truth of the matter is for a long time, he was living two lives, the one with us and the one that involved his business. Over the years, I heard stories of violent mob crimes, but I never associated my father with them. However, just recently when the Mafia boss Paul Castellano was murdered, my father was mentioned in the story as being one of his associates. My mother told me that when my father was very young, he had friends that were considered less than desirable, and because he is Italian, the F.B.I. assumes he is Mafia. She also told me that when he was a teenager, he was sent to Juvenile Hall for some petty crime. My father never talks about those days.

"Now as I mentioned, for the last ten years, he has been the largest stockholder in AA Financial Group, a very well-respected Wall Street brokerage firm. Over the years, both the SEC and some other federal agencies have investigated him in an effort to force him out, but they have been unsuccessful. And as I said, the reason he has been in the news lately is because the New York Times has been running a series about mob activity on Wall Street. They claim that Mafia crime families are switching increasingly to white-collar crimes with a focus on smaller independent Wall Street brokerage houses. And because AA Financial falls into that category, they are once again trying to dig up things from his past that link him to organized crime to force him out."

Wade listened in amazement.

"You know, Louie, I was raised in a neighborhood in Philly where there were bookies, con men, wannabe wise guys, you name it. There was a guy I went to school with whose father was supposed to be connected. But it didn't matter to me or the other guys in the neighborhood. So I know what you're talking about. Louie, it makes no difference to me if your old man is connected or not. It's none of my business. I appreciate you telling me this, and you can be sure it goes no farther."

"I appreciate that, Wade."

The two men shook hands and knew their friendship was solid.

"Okay, pal, you got my whole life story. You now know I'm gay, and my father is probably connected. What can you tell me about your family that will top that?"

"Besides the fact that my father is a compulsive gambler, and he decided to move to Las Vegas and my mother got remarried to the guy who owned the grocery store where she worked, nothing."

CHAPTER SEVEN

THE FRESHMAN YEAR passed quickly. Between his studies and playing basketball, Wade had little time for anything else. He dated a couple of girls, but nothing serious. Louie spent a lot of his free time with his "new friend" off campus. Wade met him and didn't like him. More than that, he didn't trust him. He was only a couple of years older than Louie and worked at the MGM Grand in the VIP check-in suite. Louie had met him at a gay bar in downtown Vegas.

Wade went back to Philly for Thanksgiving. His father wanted him to stay in Vegas and spend Turkey Day with him, but he opted to go home. His mother came to Las Vegas over Labor Day weekend, but that was the only time they saw each other since he started college. His father had already changed jobs twice in the six months he was in Las Vegas. He was now working in one of the casinos downtown as a doorman.

Louie invited Wade to spend Christmas with him in Chicago. At first, Wade hesitated, telling his friend he didn't want to impose. Louie asked him if it was because of his father.

"Absolutely not, just that its a holiday, and I don't want to impose."

"You're coming," Louie insisted. Finally, he accepted. Wade had never asked Louie if his parents knew he was gay. As their plane was landing at O'Hare in Chicago, he decided to find out.

"Yeah, they know," Louie said when Wade asked him. "It's a little difficult for my father, you know all that Italian macho shit, but my mom is very supportive."

"Must be difficult for you?" Wade offered, trying to understand.

"Sometimes, but it's really not that bad. I think you will like my parents, basically they are good people." Wade simply smiled. Louie added, "That is, if my father doesn't shoot you!"

"Very funny," Wade added.

When the two boys reached the baggage claim area, Angelo's driver was there waiting for them. Louie introduced Wade, and by that time, their luggage arrived. The driver took the bags off the carousel. When Wade offered to help, the driver told him he was fine, and he didn't need any help. Wade was sure he didn't. He looked like an ex-heavyweight fighter, medium height, very muscular, and had a nose that appeared to have been broken more than once. If he was a fighter, Wade was sure the guys he fought looked worse than him. The driver ushered them outside and into a long black limo that was parked next to a sign that read "No stopping or parking anytime—Fire Zone." Standing beside the limo was an airport security guard. After Wade and Louie got in the limo, Wade saw the driver hand the security guard a hundred-dollar bill. The guard thanked him. The driver got in the limo, and Wade was on his way to meet Louie's parents

The ride from the airport to the Santino mansion—and it was a mansion—was about forty minutes. The house was located in the suburbs of Chicago reserved for homes of at least $5 million or more. Or at least, that is what Wade assumed. When they arrived at Louie's house, Angelo's driver pushed a button in the limo, and a large iron gate swung open. Wade could see the TV cameras at the entrance and again along the driveway that led to the house. The main house was located on ten acres of ground, far enough back so that you could not see it from the street. The greenery and shrubbery looked like something out of a movie set. When the limo pulled up to the front of the house, a very large stone-faced man dressed all in black was standing between two very large marble statues of lions. Wade thought to himself, if Louie's father wasn't Mafia, then he was either the pope or the president?

"Wade, say hello to Mario." Mario was the man dressed in black. "Mario, this is my roommate at school, Wade." Mario simply nodded. Wade wondered whether or not he had killed anybody yet today. Probably not, it was still early. The man in black took the suitcases from the limo, exchanged a few words with the driver in Italian, and then he asked the two boys to follow him into the house. Wade thought to himself, "*Is this all for real?*" Louie's mother was waiting for them when they entered the house. She was not at all what Wade expected. She was very pretty. She was in her early forties, dressed conservatively but very stylishly. She was not wearing very much jewelry, but you could tell that what she was wearing was expensive. She did not look like what Louie had described as the typical Italian wife.

"Mom, this is Wade." Louie's mother extended her hand. Wade took it and then leaned over and kissed her on the cheek. She smiled and said to her son, "I like him already."

"Where's Dad?"

"He is in his den on the phone he'll be out soon." No sooner had she finished speaking when a tall, good-looking man came in from another room. Angelo Santino was in his early sixties. He was six feet tall and weighed almost two hundred pounds. Even at his age, he still had a barrel chest and broad shoulders. He had a swarthy complexion and piercing black eyes. He had a full head of pure white hair combed straight back. Wade understood immediately what Louie meant when he said that when his father entered a room, the energy changed.

Louie introduced Wade to his father. "It's very nice to meet you, young man. Louie has spoken of you often. You are from Philadelphia, yes?"

"Yes. sir I am." Wade felt like he was in the principal's office.

Louie's mother interrupted. "Let the boys freshen up before dinner, Angelo, then we can all visit, and you can show Wade the stables and the rest of the house."

Wade thought to himself, "*The stables?*"

"Of course," Angelo said, and with that, he shook Wade's hand and left.

Louie's mother escorted the two boys upstairs to his room. "I am sure you will be comfortable here," she said, pointing to the bed in the room. Louie started to laugh.

"What's so funny?" his mother asked.

"Mom, Wade is not my lover. He is my roommate at school. He sure as heck doesn't want to have to share a room here when he has to put up with me all year at school."

"Oh . . . I thought . . . I am embarrassed now," Louie's mother said.

Wade liked her. "I am flattered, Mrs. Santino, that you thought I was good enough for your son."

The three of them laughed. The tension was gone. Wade wondered how it would have gone if Louie's father was in on this charade. "*Not well*," he thought.

The rest of the holiday visit went well. Wade felt Louie's father warm up to him a little bit more than when they were first introduced. Maybe Louie's mother told him that Wade wasn't his son's lover. Wade figured the old man probably wouldn't shoot him, at least not this Christmas.

Since Louie and Wade didn't have to be back at school until the tenth of January, Louie's parents convinced the boys to stay and spend New Year's Eve with them. They were planning a large party at the house and told the boys they would enjoy meeting some of the invited guests. Wade was a little hesitant, but once again, Louie convinced him. As it turned out, during the week between Christmas and the party, Wade discovered Louie's father to be much friendlier. He took the boys to a Chicago Cubs game, where they sat in the owner's box, attended the grand opening of a restaurant of one of his friends, and spent several nights just sitting around talking. He was also very proud of his stable of four horses. He told Wade he originally bought them to race but decided he would rather just keep them as riding horses.

Angelo was very tuned into what was happening in the country, business, politics, and the economy, and he discussed these things with Wade at great length. Never once was there any mention of organized crime or the SEC investigating him in an effort to oust him from AA Financial. In fact, he never mentioned AA Financial until the day before the party when Angelo made it a point to tell Wade that Albert Kline, the CEO of AA Financial was going to attend the party, and he wanted Wade to meet him.

"I know they hire interns at AA during the summer," he told Wade. "Might be an opportunity for you to land a summer job and be close to home."

Wade was surprised at his interest.

CHAPTER EIGHT

ON THE FLIGHT back to Las Vegas, Wade told Louie that Albert Kline had offered him an intern job for the summer.

"Are you going to take it?" Louie asked.

"I am considering it. What do you think?"

"I think it would be great. Who knows, you may decide to be a stockbroker someday. By the way, you do know that I'm planning to go with my mom to Italy for about six weeks this summer."

"Yeah, I know you were talking about it. I didn't know it was a done deal."

"So that would work out. You can work at AA for most of the summer, go to Philly for a couple weeks, and by that time, I'll be back from Italy. Another thing and I don't want any shit about it."

"What?"

"Next semester, I'm renting an apartment. We had to spend the freshman year at the dorm, but that's it."

"So?" Wade said.

"So what all that means is that we will still be roommates, but not in the dorm, but at the apartment I'm renting. I already spoke to a realtor in Vegas, and she has a couple real nice two-bedroom apartments lined up not too far from school."

"Hey, Louie, I don't know that I can afford . . . ?"

"That's what I meant when I said I didn't want you to give me any shit. It's my apartment, and I'm paying for it. End of story. When you become rich and successful, you can pay me back."

"I don't know, Louie . . ."

"Will you stop with that I don't know, Louie' crap already. Now let me get some sleep. Wake me up when we get to Vegas."

CHAPTER NINE

ONCE THE BOYS were back at school, they each fell into their own routine. Wade met a girl who was from Philly, and they started to date pretty regularly. Between dating, attending classes, and playing basketball, it didn't leave him much time for anything else. He did, however, manage to have dinner with his father at least once a week. His father was still working as a doorman in one of the downtown casinos, and according to what he told Wade, he was holding his own as far as his gambling was concerned.

Meanwhile, Louie broke up with the man he had been seeing and was now involved with a student, Gary Roberts, who was from Los Angeles. Although Wade had no problem with Louie being gay, he had to admit he felt strange when Louie brought Gary to the apartment. Louie and Gary were into designing and decorating and talked about starting a business together when they finished school. There was no doubt Louie would have to come up with the seed money. Wade thought to himself, "*Do gay guys also marry for money sometimes?*"

Wade liked living in the apartment that Louie rented a hell of a lot better than living in the dorm. He had decided to take the job offer from Albert Kline to work as an intern at AA Financial during the summer, and he was looking forward to seeing his mother more often. Albert Kline had given him the name of a woman at the firm to call in the event he accepted the job. When he called her, she said the firm had a one-bedroom apartment on the top floor of the converted brownstone that was their office building, and Mr. Kline said he could live there during the summer. Once again, Wade was overwhelmed at the generosity and could only attribute it to the fact he was a friend of Angelo's son.

Being so busy made the time go by quickly, and before they knew it, it was May, and classes were over for the summer. Wade and Louie said their good-byes. Wade was going to New York to work for AA Financial, and Louie was flying to Chicago to meet his mother and then go on to Italy. Wade could tell that Louie didn't want to leave his friend Gary for such a long period of time. He felt badly for him.

The girl Wade had been dating was going back to Philly for the summer. He told her he would try to get to Philly on the weekends, and she told him she was looking forward to it. She also said she would try to come to New York at least one weekend. As it worked out, they only saw each other a couple of times during the summer. She hooked up with an old boyfriend in Philly, and Wade simply lost interest. He hoped that Louie had better luck with his love life.

CHAPTER TEN

WALL STREET IS an eight-block-long street running west to east from Broadway to South Street on the East River in Lower Manhattan in the financial district of New York City. Over time, the term Wall Street has become a metonym for the financial markets of this country as a whole, even though some of the country's largest financial firms are not physically located there. Wall Street is the home of the New York Stock Exchange, the world's largest stock exchange by market capitalization of its listed companies. Several other major exchanges have or had headquarters in the Wall Street area, including NASDAQ, the New York Mercantile Exchange, the New York Board of Trade, and the former American Stock Exchange.

One of Wall Street's most famous symbols is the Charging Bull statue, which represents a "bull market," a constantly rising market. It might sound strange, but many young people come to Wall Street expecting to make the world a better place. This is partly the fault of the recruiters who tempt college seniors with promises of real-world responsibility and rhapsodies about socially responsible investing. But that is just wishful thinking. Albert Kline made it very clear to Wade before he invited him to join his firm. He said, "We're not here to save the world. We exist for one reason, and one reason only, and that is to make money!"

There is no way in God's world that Wade could have known that Angelo Santino and Albert Kline had picked him to be Albert's successor. Both men knew that someday Albert would either want to retire or just get out, and there was no one in the firm that was completely in the loop. Albert had devised a system in which some of his brokers knew some things, but no one broker knew everything. They had decided that Wade was a smart, good-looking young man who had all of the smarts to do what Albert was doing. He was a math major, which made him exceptional with numbers. He was streetwise, having grown up in a neighborhood in Philly where he was exposed to hustlers, con artists, and the like. Louie had spoken to his father often about Wade, and when Angelo met him, he immediately liked him. The fact that he was a star college athlete gave him an additional pedigree. Time would only tell if, when Wade learned what it was they wanted him to do, it was in his "wheelhouse," so to speak.

AA Financial's offices were housed in a converted large brownstone located on the corner of Broad and Beaver Street about a block and a half south of the New York Stock Exchange. On the first floor, there was the traditional brokerage house sales office. There was a receptionist, twenty stockbrokers who spent most of their day on the phone, two runners who took the orders from the broker to the floor manager, a floor specialist who constantly monitored the ticker tape, and a cashier. All of the mail was opened by the cashier no matter how it was addressed. She removed all checks or money orders before forwarding the mail. Albert Kline's office was on the second floor. He had a secretary and two assistants. There was also a large conference room on the second floor. The mail room, copy machines, and supplies took up the third floor, and on the top floor was the small apartment where Wade was going to live that first summer. The apartment was completely separate from the offices. There was a separate entrance from the outside, different phone lines, separate utilities, and it even had its own mail address.

At the end of his first day at work at AA Financial, Roger Clayman, the floor manager, called Wade into his office.

"So tell me, Wade, how was your first day?"

"It was fine, Mr. Clayman. I didn't do very much, kinda felt like I was in the way, actually. There is a lot going on here." The floor manager smiled. "Please, Wade, call me Roger."

Wade just nodded.

"I can understand how you feel. Actually all I want you to do for the first couple of days is watch, listen, and learn from the brokers as they go about their day. Become familiar with the lingo of the street. Let me tell you a little bit about the stock brokerage business. There are basically three different types of brokerage houses. There is the full service brokerage firm, which offers their clients a complete package of investment services. They recommend securities, research a particular issue, and provide financial advice, and if the client is important enough, they will wipe his ass."

Wade smiled. The man had a sense of humor.

"Then there is the discount brokerage house. This is a relatively new animal. While a discount broker can offer a wide range of services, they are not allowed to give investment advice.

"And thirdly, there is the limited products firm that specializes in a limited number of securities products. Of course, that is a quick overview. But for now, that will at least give you some idea as to the different types of brokers.

"So where do we fit in? Really we are a hybrid. If you ask one of our brokers, he will tell you he is a financial trader. That means we buy and sell shares, bonds, and assets for investors, including individuals and banks. We make prices and execute trades. Our objective is to maximize assets and minimize financial risk, never losing sight of the reason we are in business, and that is to make as much money as possible. Although we do buy and sell common stock for our clients, we specialize in the sale of corporate bonds and IPOs. We work with municipalities, helping them raise money by floating bond issues. We also work with banks who want the municipalities to use their bank to hold the money."

"Now I realize this is only a summer job for you, but hopefully you will like the business and consider joining us after you graduate."

"Well it is certainly something I will consider," Wade said.

"Good. You know, Wade, I would not want to mislead you. Although you can make a lot of money in this business, it takes a lot of hard work in the beginning. Of course, some newcomers get lucky or have great connections and make a big score. But the vast majority of new brokers spend endless hours on the phone, finding new clients with sufficient assets to invest. I see by the look on your face you are thinking, 'what am I getting myself into?'"

"No, not at all, just trying to digest it all."

"Well the upside is we here at AA Financial have a lot of very successful clients who have allowed our brokers to earn in the high six figures."

That brought a smile to Wade's face.

"Now Mr. Kline has told me you are a friend of the family, and although he doesn't want you to receive special treatment, he would like to see you succeed. So with that, I will let you go. I wish you good luck this summer and want you to know my door is always open."

Wade left the office a little bit confused. *"A friend of the family. What was that all about?"* He had the feeling there was something going on that he didn't know about. Did Louie know? Or was he just being a little bit paranoid?

By the end of the first week, Wade recognized how easy it was for someone to get rich in this business. He listened as the brokers closed deals on the phone and gave him some of the slips to take to the floor manager. Every so often, he would glance at the paperwork he was carrying and see where the broker made several hundred dollars of commission on one transaction. He made up his mind right there and then that he was going to learn all he could about the stock market, notwithstanding that he still had the feeling there was something going on that was "not for publication." For the most part, the stockbrokers were too busy to pay much attention to him. However, there was one broker, Joe Cantor, who was only a few years older than him, who he ate lunch with a couple times. Joe was from upstate New York. He had been with AA for about six months. The third week that Wade was there, Joe invited him to go to a party with him. The odd thing about Joe was that he was always asking Wade questions about what he was doing there like he was the new person and Wade was the veteran.

"I've been seeing this girl pretty steady, Wade. She lives on the Upper East Side. Her family has money. Actually that is how I met her. I sold her old man some bonds that have appreciated almost 20 percent, plus they pay a nice dividend. So one day, he invites me to have lunch with him and his daughter. It seems she had just broken up with some guy, and her old man wanted me to meet her. It was a little awkward at first, but the funny thing is we hit it off right away. That was about two months ago. Anyhow she is having a party, and I am sure there will be some single girls there. You need some R and R, buddy."

So Wade agreed to go. That was where he met Albert Kline's daughter, Brenda. Joe was as surprised as Wade that she was at the party. It seems that she just started working at Doubleday, where Joe's girlfriend Sally worked, and like Joe invited Wade in the hopes he would meet someone, so did Joe's girlfriend do the same thing with Brenda Kline. When they were introduced, the first question Wade asked her was, "Are you related to Albert Kline?"

"He is my father."

Wade remembered that when he asked Louie if he was related to Angelo Santino, he got the same answer, "He is my father." He decided that he'd better stop asking that question.

She had long hair and was built just the way Wade liked, tall and thin. Her eyes were green and complimented her oval face. She was very pretty.

"I understand you work for my father," she said.

"Well you can say that. Actually I'm an intern just working for the summer. I'm still at school. And you?"

"I just graduated from Vassar, and now I work at Doubleday."

"Well excuse me," Wade said with a smile.

"It's not as fancy as it sounds," she said. "Vassar is not much different than most colleges. When I told my father I wanted to be a writer, he got me a job at Doubleday. Sometimes it's not too bad having a father with some pull." Wade liked her. She was down to earth. No bullshit.

Before the night was over, Brenda gave Wade her phone number. "Call me," she said, "We can meet in the city for dinner or something. I know you don't make much money. We can go Dutch treat." She was okay.

During the next two months, they saw each other no less than twice a week. Sometimes they would meet in Manhattan at a movie or a restaurant. A couple of times, she took him to an art gallery. What he enjoyed most was when he would go to her apartment on the Upper East Side. She would either make dinner or they would order takeout and then watch TV, listen to music, or just hang out and talk. They never got past the petting stage. It's not that he didn't want to; it was just that it wasn't happening. Then one night, Wade asked her if her father knew they were dating.

"Why do you ask?"

"I don't know, poor boy from Philly, still in school, dating the boss's daughter?"

"Get over yourself, Wade. First of all, you're not a poor boy from Philly. Well on second thought, maybe you are." They both laughed.

"Yes, as a matter of fact, I did mention to my father that I was seeing you and that we were planning to get married."

"You told him what?"

"Wade . . . Duh!"

She did have his sense of humor.

"Okay, you win, sorry I asked."

"Really I did tell him we were dating, and all he said was that you were a nice young man. Shows how smart he is."

"Very funny Brenda."

Then two weeks before Wade was due to leave to return to school, something very strange happened. Roger Clayman the floor manager called Wade into his office.

"Wade, AA is taking a company called Petro Electronics Public. We usually don't get involved in this type of company, but Mr. Kline is a friend of the company's founder, and well anyway, Mr. Kline has decided to give all of AA Financial employees a bonus of some of the shares. The stock will come out at $5 a share. It will start trading in two days. In your case, you will own one thousand shares when the IPO is completed."

"Wow, that's great. I don't know what to say."

Somewhat sarcastically Roger said, "A simple thank you will do." Wade got the impression that Roger thought Albert Kline was giving him special treatment. After all, he's just a summer intern, and he is getting stock in a new issue. Wade wondered if it had anything to do with the fact that he was dating his daughter Brenda.

Two days later, the stock came out at $5, and before noon, it shot up to $15.25. Trading was halted by the floor commissioners. The exchange announced that so many buy orders were coming in that they could not handle them. Finally, an hour before closing, the stock reopened at $20.15. It kept going up and closed at the end of the day at $36.35. Wade was ecstatic. He had just made over $36,000. Before leaving the office, he asked Roger Clayman if he should sell his shares.

"Absolutely not I want you to just hold them. When the stock hits $75, then you can sell."

Wade looked at him like he was crazy. "How do you know it is going to hit $75?"

"I know. Now I'm busy. I'll see you in the morning."

The following day, the stock opened at $35 and closed at $47.

Two days later, the stock was $74.50. Roger called Wade into his office. "You can sell your stock at the end of the day tomorrow," he told him. Wade simply said, "Thanks!"

The following day, the stock opened off $2. However, by the end of the day, the price was $76.10. Wade told his friend Joe to sell his shares.

He had just made over $76,000. He could not believe it. Two days later, the stock dropped to $41. By the time he was ready to go back to school, the stock was $7. It was then that Wade was sure there was more going on at AA Financial than he knew about.

The night before Wade was to leave to go back to school, Brenda made dinner for them in her apartment. After he helped her clean the kitchen, she took him by the hand into her bedroom. She sat on the end of the bed and held his hand.

"Wade, I'm not a virgin." Wade started to say something, but she stopped him.

"I had sex with the guy I broke up with before I started dating you. He was the only one."

"Brenda, that's not my business."

"Yes, it is. I really like you, Wade. But you're going back to Las Vegas, and I'm in New York. I don't know if we will ever see each other again, and I want to make love with you before you leave."

Wade bent over and kissed her. "And I like you, Brenda, very much. I always liked older women." She laughed. "I'm only two years older," she said as she stood up and put her arms around his neck. That night, they made love several times, neither of them knowing if this was to be the first and the last time they would enjoy each other's passion.

Before he left, he wondered if he should tell her about the stock her father had given him but decided against it. On the plane ride back to Vegas, he could not stop thinking about her. He also thought about the $76,000 he had made without lifting a finger. That was all in New York. Unfortunately, Las Vegas and New York were three thousand miles apart.

CHAPTER ELEVEN

IN 1975, WHILE Angelo Santino and Albert Kline were planning to form their own brokerage company and embark on a scheme that would earn them millions of illegal dollars, the Mafia was already well entrenched on Wall Street. And even though the authorities were investigating some of the brokerage houses as well as some organized crime figures, Santino and Kline were not at all concerned. Angelo was convinced that Albert Kline's plan to scam millions of dollars was infallible.

During a televised interview in 1970, both law enforcement officials and financial regulators admitted that the mob's influence on Wall Street may be even greater than they once supposed. They claimed there was evidence that the mob had expanded their reach from penny-stock scams into sophisticated NASDAQ schemes. They said that "mob brokers" have been able to skip from one scam to another unscathed by regulators. An F.B.I. spokesman said, "The white-collar crimes being committed by organized crime on Wall Street are characterized by deceit, concealment, and a violation of trust and are not dependent upon the application of physical force or violence. The crimes being committed by organized crime fall under the heading of corporate fraud and they include false accounting procedures, money laundering, fraudulent trades, insider trading, kickbacks, misuse of corporate Funds, and individual tax violations."

He went on to explain that through the manipulation of financial data by "the mob," the share price or other valuation measurements of a company can be artificially inflated. This results not only in significant losses to investors but can also potentially cause immeasurable damage to the overall economy. It also affects investor confidence, thereby causing financial damage to legitimate brokers. In the canyons of lower Manhattan, one can find members of organized crime, their friends and their associates. How large is their presence? No one—least of all regulators and law enforcement—seems to know.

Over the years, none of this had gone unnoticed by Angelo Santino. Many of his friends and associates were already involved in Wall Street long before he hooked up with Albert Kline. The only reason he didn't follow in their footsteps was that the right opportunity had not presented itself. That he had not ventured into Wall Street scams didn't mean he wasn't involved in a different type of financial scam. He and a group of his associates were running illegal casino games in Connecticut. They had bribed an official at the state's largest credit union to give them access to stacks of pre-approved credit loan applications. They then used them to extend instant money to tapped-out players. Word quickly spread that immediate cash was available to players. Of course, the interest rate was considerably more than if they had borrowed from the credit union. Not satisfied with just scamming the players, Albert and his group began using the credit union to underwrite their illegal gambling business. Of course, they never repaid the credit union and eventually the credit union declared bankruptcy and went out of business. The irony of the whole thing was two of the top officers of the credit union were charged with conspiracy and sent to jail. Albert and his associates were never mentioned.

However, the scheme proposed by Albert Kline now allowed him to get in on the big money from Wall Street. And so in 1975, AA Financial Corporation was born. Santino put up the money, and Albert Kline was the front. He was a respected Wall Street broker with years of service. He had received numerous awards not only from Wall Street but also from civic organizations. He was on the board of directors of several charities and belonged to one of the most prestigious country clubs on Long Island. But like Angelo said, the one thing they had in common was that they were both crooks.

CHAPTER TWELVE

DURING THE EIGHTIES, Las Vegas began to suffer an identity crisis. The slow but inevitable departure of the mob and the era of Regan conservatism put a damper on the shining star of the desert. The fire at the MGM Grand, which killed more than eighty people surely didn't help. Even the showrooms that once featured stars like Elvis and Sinatra were attracting fewer people. Then like a shining knight on a white horse, Steve Wynn rode into town in a Rolls Royce and with Wall Street money began a resurgence of the Las Vegas strip. Wynn gambled big time. With $630 million of junk bond money, he started construction on a hotel-casino that would eventually change the course of history of Las Vegas. It would be called the Mirage. It was fronted by five-story waterfalls, lagoons, and lush tropical foliage—not to mention a fifty-foot volcano that dramatically erupted regularly.

However, all of this had nothing to do with Wade. He had his own problems. Between studying for classes at school, playing basketball, trying to maintain a long distance relationship with Brenda, which by the way was not going well, and paying off his father's gambling debts in an effort to keep him from getting his legs broken, didn't leave him much time to be concerned with the Las Vegas economy, at least not until the start of his junior year at UNLV.

It was 1988, and Wade had almost two summers under his belt working at AA Financial, and although he didn't completely understand the inner workings of Wall Street, the brokerage business fascinated him. Then one day, Brenda's father invited him to lunch at the New York Athletic Club. It was a week before he was due to return to school. After some small talk, Kline told him he knew that he and his daughter were no longer seeing each other. He told Wade he was sorry and hoped they could work it out. He liked Wade.

Wade could tell his relationship with Brenda was in trouble shortly after he started work that second summer. He had decided to rent his own apartment instead of staying in the apartment on the top floor of AA. Brenda found him a furnished apartment in the village, and with the money he had made the previous year from the stock deal, he was able to afford it. The first two weeks that he was in New York, Brenda spent the weekends with him in his apartment. Then one Friday night, she said she couldn't see him that weekend. She told him she was going to Cape Cod with some friends from college. Wade didn't think too much of it. However, it wasn't too long after that she told him that she had been dating one of the publishers from Doubleday that she met several months ago, and as a matter of fact, that was who she went to the Cape with. Wade was caught totally off guard. He thought they had something special. However, after they talked it out, Wade understood. It was very difficult to sustain a relationship when he was in Las Vegas and she was here in New York. They really tried to make it work. She went to Vegas a couple of times for a long weekend, and he came to New York whenever he had a break from school and basketball. Evidently it wasn't enough to keep it going. They both admitted they cared for one another, but the three thousand miles that separated them made it very difficult.

Kline asked Wade, in view of what happened between him and his daughter, if he intended to come back to AA Financial the following summer.

"I really don't know. I like the business and have considered your offer to come to work full-time after school, but I just don't know now."

Kline understood.

"Tell you what," he said. "There is a small brokerage firm in Vegas that does the same kind of work that we do, underwriting municipalities. The president is a good friend of mine. We have done some business together in the past. He also deals in junk bonds. Do you have any idea what junk bonds are, Wade?"

"Not sure that I do."

"They are bonds that have a credit quality rating below BBB. That is below what the Street calls an acceptable investment grade. The reason for that is because there is a greater risk of default. And because junk bonds have a greater risk of default, they pay a higher rate of interest to compensate the investor for taking the risk of buying the bonds. Think about it like a person's credit score. People with a poor credit score are charged a higher rate of interest when they borrow money or try to get a mortgage. It is the same concept. The higher the risk the greater the return."

"Is all that legal?" Wade asked.

"Of course it is. Michael Milken from Drexel Burnham is the guy who invented junk bonds. Where do you think Wynn got the money to build the Mirage Junk bonds""

"Anyway, here is what I have in mind. Why don't you stay in Vegas the next two summers, and I will arrange for you to work at Vegas Investment Associates, my friend's brokerage house. It will be good experience, plus it's something for you to do while you're still in school. It will help to keep us connected, and when you finish school, I'm hoping you will come to work for us. What do you think?"

"I think it is pretty damn hot in Vegas in the summer."

"Find a place that's air-conditioned." Both men laughed.

At the same time that Albert Kline was explaining junk bonds to Wade the SEC was in the process of looking into allegations of insider trading by Michael Milken and Ivan Boesky. As part of his plea bargaining, Boesky implicated Milken in several illegal transactions, including insider trading, stock manipulation, fraud, and stock parking (buying stocks for the benefit of another). While all of this was going on, Wynn was building his hotel with the $630 million Milken supplied to him from the sale of junk bonds. The investigation by the SEC would eventually lead to a lawsuit by the SEC against Drexel Burnham and ultimately their bankruptcy in 1990. But none of this deterred the mob or Albert Kline and Angelo Santino from continuing their illegal activities on Wall Street.

Junk bonds were destroying the central financial system of the country. Milken's junk bond operation at Drexel Burnham Lambert Inc. was nothing short of a deadly threat to the entire American financial system, more so than what the mob was doing on Wall Street.

CHAPTER THIRTEEN

THE SEASONS SLIPPED by in the haze of the bright lights on the Vegas Strip, and before Wade knew it, it was 1990. A lot had happened in the last two years. Notre Dame beat West Virginia for the college football championship. The Berlin Wall was no more. Egypt, Iraq, and Jordan formed a common market. Inflation increased to 5.1 percent less than two years after "Black Monday," the day the New York Stock Market suffered the biggest loss in fifty years. The prime rate of interest soared to 11 percent, and in New York, Drexel Burnham Lambert, filed for bankruptcy law protection. In spite of what was happening in the financial markets, Steve Wynn was still preparing to open his Mirage Hotel and Casino. Albert Kline's company, AA Financial, was having one its best years, and Vegas Investment Associates, the brokerage company in Las Vegas where Wade was working, had gone from dealing in junk bonds, the money raised to be used to build more casinos in Las Vegas, to owning a small piece of one. Wade had learned enough about the stock market to know you were supposed to be squeaky clean to have a brokerage license, so how could a brokerage company also be a casino owner? Sometimes one and one don't equal two.

Wade and Louie were both looking forward to graduation. Louie was still involved with his friend Gary Roberts. About a year earlier, Gary moved in with Louie. Wade offered to move out and find his own apartment. Louie wouldn't hear of it.

"What's the big deal? Gary will share my room. Look at it this way, Wade, he is a terrific cook, he irons and does windows."

Wade laughed. He and Louie had really bonded. He was happy that he found somebody.

After graduation, Louie and Gary planned on opening a design company in Los Angeles. Louie already had a commitment from his father to fund the start-up.

As far as Wade was concerned, he now had two options after graduation. He had the offer from Albert Kline to move to New York and go to work for AA Financial or stay in Las Vegas and go to work at the new casino his firm had helped finance. They offered him the position as vice president of financial management, whatever the hell that meant. The hotel was scheduled to open in about three months. He thought he owed it to Albert Kline to tell him about the Las Vegas offer. Surprisingly Kline told him it might not be a bad idea for him to stay in Vegas for a year or two. "There is a lot you can learn working in a casino that can be of help when you come to work for me," Kline told him. "My offer is always on the table," he added.

But right now, Wade's focus was on the upcoming basketball game in five days against the number three seed Duke, for the national championship. The press was having a field day promoting the seventh and pivotal game. "Good vs. Evil; East vs. West; Tobacco Road vs. the Strip; Grits vs. Glitz; Bookworms vs. Croupiers." You name it the press had a slogan for it. And to add to the hype, Jerry Tarkanian, the UNLV coach, had just settled a lawsuit with the National Collegiate Athletic Association for an estimated $370,000, a lawsuit that had been festering for almost thirteen years. When the press interviewed Tarkanian earlier in the week and asked him if winning the championship would be a vindication, in view of his alleged harassment by the NCAA, he answered, "Ask me again after the game!"

Although the UNLV Runnin' Rebels had just about the best college basketball team ever assembled, they did not get the respect they felt they deserved. They had the mentality that it was them against the rest of the world. Coach Jerry Tarkanian had the reputation of taking inner-city kids who had trouble in high school getting passing grades or kids that had some "baggage" when no other coach would touch them. The press portrayed the Runnin' Rebels as a bunch of roughneck thugs, hoodlums, and street kids playing indoors. The players also resented the way the NCAA continually dogged their coach. The real bottom line was these were just a bunch of young kids who loved to play the game.

Wade had just finished basketball practice when he received a telephone call from his father.

"I need to see you as soon as possible, Wade. It's really important."

"What's the matter? Tell me."

"Not on the phone. Can you meet me at the diner on Flamingo Road?"

"Yeah, I guess so how soon?"

"Can you be there in about half an hour?"

“I wish you would tell me what—” His father interrupted him before he could finish.

“I’ll tell you when I see you.”

About twenty minutes later, Wade arrived at the diner in his convertible Jag, the one he bought with some of the money he made on the stock deal at AA Financial three years before. His father was already there. Wade was a familiar face at the diner. Besides going there with some of his teammates, he would often have dinner there with his father. When the counterman saw Wade come in, he hollered, “Hey, Wade, how you doin’? We gonna beat them fags from Duke on Monday?”

One of the customers also recognized Wade as he walked past him. “Kill them bastards on Monday, kid. I’m bettin’ a yard on you guys.”

Wade nodded and smiled. Here at the diner, he was a minor celebrity. He saw his father sitting in a booth at the back of the diner, looking like he had just lost his best friend—that is if he had a best friend. Wade sat down, and quickly the waitress came over with a coke and two menus. Wade thanked her and looked at his father.

“What’s going on?”

“I’m in a lotta trouble.”

“So what else is new?”

“No, Wade, for real, this time it’s serious, and, and . . .”

Wade looked at his father and waited.

Finally, his father asked him, “Does the name Carmine Mastoria ring a bell?”

“I’m not sure maybe? Isn’t he some connected guy here in Vegas or something?”

“More than something he is probably the biggest bookie in Vegas.”

“I don’t think I’m going to like what I’m going to hear.”

“I’m sorry, Wade, I really am. You see, I owe this guy ten grand and . . .”

Wade shouted, “You what? You owe a bookie ten grand? Are you out of your freakin’ mind?”

“Wade, please keep your voice down. Let me explain.”

Wade sank down in the booth, a little ashamed for being so loud. The counterman could hear them and yelled, “Don’t be too hard on the old man, Wade. We all owe the bookies in Vegas.” That brought some laughs from the few customers in the diner. Wade faked a smile and waved at the counterman then asked his father, "What the hell is going on?"

After Morris Simon explained to his son what happened at Carmine Mastoria's office several hours earlier, Wade simply sat there staring at his father, until finally, he whispered, "Are you actually asking me to shave points in the championship game on Monday?"

"No of course not, I would never ask you to do a thing like that."

"Then what are you asking?"

"I thought maybe you could, you know, maybe you could lend me some money so I can get this guy off my back."

"You just told me he wants the whole ten grand by tomorrow. So what do you mean by lend you some money?"

"Well what I was thinking was, I know you made all that money on that stock deal couple years ago, and I was thinking maybe, shit, Wade, I don't know what I was thinking. I'm sorry I said anything. This is my problem, and I'll find a way to handle it."

Wade looked at his father. He was a broken man. On the one hand, he felt sorry for him, and on the other hand, he was angry. Sorry won out. "Look, Dad, I got about fourteen grand left. It's in a savings account in First National. It's too late now, but I can go to the bank the first thing in the morning and get you the ten grand so you can pay this guy off."

"No, Wade. I can't let you do that."

"You don't have a choice, Dad. Meet me at the bank at nine o'clock."

CHAPTER FOURTEEN

WHEN MORRIS SIMON called Carmine Mastoria to tell him he had his money, he was not totally surprised. He hadn't become as powerful as he was without being resourceful. Morris Simon walked into his office at 10:30 a.m., an hour and a half before his deadline. Mastoria was a very hard, stern-looking man. You could tell his mood from the set of his jaw. When he looked at you, it seemed as if his thoughts were focused exclusively on your future. He did this to make people feel uncomfortable in his presence, and it worked. He puffed the long, thick cigar crunched between his teeth. Even when he spoke, the cigar never left the center of his lips. Morris walked over to the couch where he was sitting and handed him a large manila envelope.

"It's $10,000, Carmine, just like you said."

Mastoria took the envelope and tossed it on the table beside the couch.

"Don't you want to count it?" Morris said with a smirk. He was feeling pretty cocky at this point.

Mastoria's smile sent a chill up Morris spine. "No, I don't have to count it. I am sure there's ten grand in there, but that doesn't change anything."

Morris grew pale. He slowly sat down in the same chair that he sat in the day before when Mastoria had given him the ultimatum "Either pay the ten grand or have your kid shave the points!"

"What are you talking about, Carmine? What do you mean it doesn't change anything?" Morris was now sweating and finding it difficult to breathe.

Mastoria took a long puff from his cigar and leaned forward. "Let me ask you something Morris, do you know what a cooler is? I don't mean the kind you carry soda in. I mean a casino cooler."

"I think so . . . I'm not sure."

"Well back in the day, the Vegas casinos used to hire guys who were known to bring bad luck. Losers, guys like you." Morris was both angry and embarrassed.

"These guys would walk around the casino and look for a hot table. When they found one, their job was to 'cool that table.' By that, I mean, when a player got lucky and was on a roll at a table, the cooler would go to that table and start to play. Invariably the winning streak ended. The table got cold. That's what you are, Morris. You're a cooler. If you didn't have bad luck, you wouldn't have any luck."

"Carmine, I don't follow you. What has all that got to do with our deal?"

"I'm just trying to point out to you how unlucky you are. You see, our deal, as you call it, has had a twist. Guess who just happened to call me late yesterday afternoon?"

Morris simply shrugged his shoulders

"Johnny O from Philly, you remember Johnny O, don't you, Morris?"

"Johnny Omatto the bookie called you. Why?"

"He wanted to lay off some of the bets he has been taking on the game Monday night. Now is that a coincidence or what? Well one thing leads to another, and he asks me if I know you. He knows you like to bet the games, and he also knows your kid plays for UNLV, so he is just being sociable. Then he tells me the story about how you stiffed him out of five grand when you left town."

"That's bullshit, Carmine, I never stiffed him."

"That's not the way he tells it, Morris."

"Well he's a goddamn liar, Carmine. I had bet with him for years and always paid up. About six months before I left Philly, I had a couple of big football parlay bets with him. I remember he told me I screwed up the bet, and I hadn't won what I thought I did. We really got into it but agreed to wait until the football season was over to resolve it. We always used to settle up at the end of the season. Well at the end of the football season, he tells me I owe him $6,500. I go crazy. I show him all the betting records I kept during the season, but they don't match up to his. We go back and forth, and he starts to smack me around a little.

"I know some of the guys from downtown, so I tell them what happened and they agreed to talk to him for me. The bottom line is we settle for me owing him $1,500, which I gave him before I left."

Mastoria got up from the sofa, walked over to his desk, and picked up a sheet of paper. "Johnny O tells a different story, Morris. As far as he is concerned, you still owe him $5,000. Now if you want to figure in the vig over all these years, well it looks to me like you now owe him a hundred grand."

Morris jumped up from the chair, about to say something, when Mastoria held up his hand. "Relax, Morris, I'm here to help you. I made a deal with Johnny O to buy your note, at a considerable discount to me, of course. However, that doesn't change the fact that you now owe all of that money to me. So you see, Morris, we are right back to where we were yesterday."

Morris pointed to the envelope on the table. "What about the ten grand?"

"What about it?"

"You're not going to keep that too, are you?"

Mastoria puffed his cigar and laughed. "No Morris, of course not. I'm going to donate it to the Jewish Charity for Asshole Gamblers!" Then he laughed out loud. "Morris, you are a born loser. You are a cooler!"

Morris could feel the anger boiling over inside, and without thinking, he lunged toward Mastoria, who stepped aside and tripped him. Morris fell against the desk and cut his head. Mastoria looked down at him in disgust. "Get up, Morris, and go in the bathroom and clean up that cut. Then get the hell out of here, and go see your kid. Tell him to make sure UNLV doesn't cover."

Morris looked up at the big man standing over him and wished he had a gun. Not so that he could shoot him, but so that he could shoot himself. He really had no will to go on.

CHAPTER FIFTEEN

WADE SIMPLY SAT and listened while his father relayed what happened earlier in the day at Mastoria's office. They were sitting in the same booth in the diner on Flamingo Road, where less than twenty-four hours ago, Wade's father told him he needed $10,000 to pay off his gambling debt. Now he was talking about a hundred thousand dollars.

"You might as well be talking about a million dollars," Wade told his father.

"I know, Wade, I know."

Just about then, Louie walked into the diner. He saw Wade and his father, stopped to say hello to someone sitting at the counter, then walked over and sat down next to Wade.

"Fancy meeting you guys here. What's up?" Then quickly he realized there was something going on between Wade and his father, and it didn't appear to be anything good.

"Hey maybe this is a bad time, I'll grab a seat at the counter." He started to get up.

Wade grabbed his arm and told him to sit back down. "We're just going over some family stuff. No big deal."

Louie looked at Wade's father then back at his friend. "You're full of shit, Wade. What's the matter?"

Wade thought for a minute then asked his father if he could talk to Louie alone. He suggested that his father go home and sit tight until he called him. Reluctantly his father agreed. After he left, Louie once again asked his friend what was going on.

When he told Louie the whole story about his father and Mastoria, all Louie could manage was, "Jesus H. Christ!"

"Do you know who this Mastoria guy is?" Louie asked. "First of all, not only is he one of the biggest bookies in Vegas, but he is also very much connected. How the hell did your old man ever get involved with him?"

"Good question, Louie. You tell me."

"For Christ's sake, Wade, with all the sports betting places here in Vegas, why the hell was he betting with a bookie, and of all people, with somebody like Carmine Mastoria?"

"Well I can tell you the reason he was betting with a bookie. When you place a bet at any of the betting parlors, either in one of the casinos or at one of the other sports books around town, you put up the money at the time you make the bet. They don't extend credit. You pay when you bet, and you collect if you win. With a bookie, my father was able to bet on credit."

Louie just shook his head. "I see what you mean, Wade. Once you start betting with these guys, they got you hooked. You just keep getting deeper and deeper in the hole!"

Wade looked at his friend for a moment and then put his hand on his arm. "Louie, I need to ask you a favor."

"Anything you want Wade you know that."

"Do you think your father can do anything to help get my old man out of this jam?"

Louie looked at his friend and thought to himself, *"Man, this is really some favor!"*

CHAPTER SIXTEEN

OVER THE YEARS, the Chicago "outfit" earned the reputation of being the most organized crime group in America. Their legacy of corruption, political control, gambling, and even of murder and mayhem had its origins in the Windy City long before Al Capone and his ruthless gangs of bootleggers. The outfit was a coalition of extortionists, narcotic traffickers, vice merchants, and corrupt labor union leaders. The Chicago outfit also had a strong foothold in Las Vegas. The Tropicana was owned by Frank Costello and managed by the Chicago mobsters' front man, Lou Lederer. The Riviera was licensed to Ross Miller and Bernie Nemerov, both Chicago bookmakers, and the Desert Inn was managed by Moe Dalitz, also a Chicago mobster.

Starting in the late seventies, illegal gambling in Chicago was controlled by Tony Accardo. He took control of gambling in the city by installing a sense of fear and loathing among his rivals. Once he controlled this part of the outfit's activities, he set out to apply modern business practices, the same way that Myer Lansky and Lucky Luciano did years before him.

Together with Louie's father, Angelo Santino, they set up a network of betting parlors, floating crap games, and independent bookies. They got a piece of anything that had to do with illegal gambling in Chicago.

Carmine Mastoria went to work for them when he was nineteen years old. At the ripe old age of only twenty-five, he received approval from Tony Accardo to set up shop on his own in Las Vegas with the understanding that Tony received a piece of all his action. In return, Accardo provided him with "muscle" in the event that he needed it. There were times a better left town owing Mastoria money. Accardo's people had a way of finding the better and collecting.

Although Louie's father left Accardo in 1975 when he partnered with Albert Kline, they remained friendly over the years. When he called his old friend and explained the favor he needed, Accardo didn't hesitate for a minute. "It's done," he said. To expedite the favor, he sent Bobby Francisco, the man who ran his illegal gambling operation on the Chicago West Side, to Las Vegas to talk to Mastoria. This was a very touchy situation. He didn't want to simply call Mastoria and tell him what to do. He wanted to find a way to explain it to him so that he wouldn't feel like he was being pressured. Although had he chose to just call him, there was no way Mastoria could have turned him down. But he thought it was better this way.

Bobby Francisco was just over six feet, with broad shoulders and the physical appearance of an athlete. His dark green eyes were piercing, and although his nose was a bit long, it seemed to fit his long, narrow face. He had an engaging smile a certain vitality an aggressive self-confidence that the women in his life found sexy. He was the only man working for Accardo who had attended college. And while in college, he played basketball. He was the perfect person to send to Las Vegas to talk to Mastoria.

CHAPTER SEVENTEEN

BOBBY'S PLANE TOUCHED down at McCarran International at 10:30 a.m., on the morning after Mastoria had told Wade's father, "Either come up with a hundred grand or tell your kid to shave the points!" He went directly to the baggage claim area, where there was a uniformed limousine driver from the Sands Hotel holding up a sign that read, "BF." The driver took Bobby's bag and escorted him to the limo parked outside the baggage claim area. Mastoria's office was located in a strip mall that he owned, about a half mile from the Sands. He had converted one of the stores into two offices. One was for his assistant, and the other larger office he kept for himself. Bobby gave the driver the address and told him after he dropped him off that he didn't have to wait. He would take a cab to the Sands when he finished his meeting. The driver offered to return to pick up Bobby and take him to the Sands, but Bobby said that was not necessary.

Accardo had made all the arrangements for him in advance. A suite comped at the Sands, a limo to and from the airport, and $1,000 in chips in case he decided to play in the casino. Although Las Vegas was cleaning up their act as it related to the mob, some things just didn't change.

Accardo made the decision not to tell Mastoria in advance that Bobby was going to Las Vegas. The plan was for Bobby to call him from the airport and tell him he was simply taking a couple days of R and R in Vegas, and Accardo suggested he see him while he was in town. He thought the element of surprise had its advantages. However, when Bobby called Mastoria, the Las Vegas bookie knew he was full of shit. You just don't "happen to be in Vegas," and if Accardo told him to stop in and say hello, something was up. So much for the advantage of the element of surprise!

The two men had only met once before, and that was in Chicago about five years ago. When Bobby arrived at Mastoria's office, he received a warm welcome. It was like two guys playing chess, each waiting for the other to make the first move. They looked like two really nice guys, just sitting around talking about getting laid the night before.

But that was not the case. They may have appeared to be two normal guys, but they were both part of a different culture. Everybody had a job to do in the organization, whether it was gambling, murder, burglary, blackmailing someone, or in this case, convincing one of the others to do things his way. The question of whether something was right or wrong never entered a mobster's mind. That question always got buried early. Out of a desire to get ahead in the organization, it remained buried. Some guys who worked for the outfit might tell themselves they did what they did for their boss, or they did it because they had no choice. That was all bullshit. They did it because they wanted to.

Finally, Mastoria broke the ice.

"So tell me, Bobby, what are you really doing in Vegas?"

Bobby smiled. Mastoria was no dummy.

"Believe it or not, Carmine, I am here to save your ass."

"Is that a fact? I didn't know my ass needed saving."

"That's the problem, Carmine. Sometimes we never know when our ass is in trouble."

"Okay, Bobby, enough with the crap. What's goin' on?"

Bobby didn't waste any time, he got right to it. "Tony feels you are making a mistake by thinking that if this kid Wade Simon shaves some points, UNLV won't cover in the game on Monday."

"Really, and what makes him think that?"

"Me."

"I beg your pardon," Mastoria said as he got up to get a cigar. Bobby could tell he was becoming agitated. "What makes you think you can come into my town and tell me how to run my business?"

"I'm not trying to do that, Carmine. I played basketball in college, and I still follow the game. I know these teams. UNLV is a powerhouse. They will win with or without this kid."

"What makes you so goddamn sure? I hear around town this kid is the star on the team."

"Trust me, Carmine. That's not true. I agree he is good, but they got this kid Larry Johnson who is 6'7" and goes at least 250 pounds, who is a monster. He can throw down three pointers like it's nothing. UNLV has the most underrated backcourt in the league. They got two kids, Anderson Hunt and Greg Anthony, who can play with anybody. I've been following them this season, and I've never seen kids play like this. It's scary just watching them. If any one of these guys foul out, they got kids sitting on the bench who can come in, and the team doesn't lose a beat."

Mastoria puffed on his cigar and looked at Bobby Francisco.

"What's your angle, Bobby?"

"Whattayou mean, what's my angle? I told you, Tony don't wanna see you get hurt."

"All of a sudden, Tony doesn't wanna see me get hurt. I don't buy it, Bobby. There's something else goin' on."

Bobby thought for a minute.

"I respect you, Carmine, and I am not going to lie to you. There is something else going on, but that still doesn't change what I just told you. UNLV is going to win, with that kid or without him, and believe me when I tell you they are going to cover, and then some."

"You gonna tell me what it is?"

"Tony owes a favor to somebody who doesn't want this Simon kid to have to shave points. And like I said, it wouldn't make any difference even if he did."

"And the kid's old man, what about him?"

"Tony wants you should wipe the slate clean with him. You got the ten grand he owed you. One other thing, Tony would appreciate it if you didn't take any more bets from him."

"You guys sure know a lot about my business."

Bobby didn't answer.

"How about the money I give to Johnny O? Am I supposed to eat that?"

Bobby smiled. "Carmine, I said I was going to be honest with you. I expect the same from you. Why don't we stop trying to bullshit each other and get to the point."

"What the hell are you talking about?"

"The deal you made with Johnny O was to give him $2,500 after the game, as long as you won your bets. You didn't give him anything up front. The fact that you're asking Wade's old man for a hundred grand is not up for discussion."

"How do you know that? You telling me Tony called Johnny O? What does that make me look like?"

"I am sure Tony didn't say anything to embarrass you. Look, Carmine . . ." With that, Bobby reached into his jacket pocket and pulled out an envelope and handed it to Carmine. "There's five grand in there for the Johnny O deal. You can do whatever you want with it."

Carmine thought to himself that while Tony is in a giving mood, he might as well see what else he could get. He looked into Bobby's eyes. They were expressionless. Was this it or was he leaving something on the table? After a few silent moments, he said, "Let's suppose I lay off the kid's old man. What's in it for me?"

"That's it, Carmine, plus what I just told you. Don't bet on UNLV not covering. That information alone is worth a hundred grand."

"Too late. I booked a lot of bets the other way. If UNLV covers, I stand to lose a shitpot full of money."

Bobby thought for a minute. He and Tony had talked about this, anticipating Carmine would bring it up. "I know Tony will appreciate you going along with this, and he doesn't want you to get hurt. We can lay off most of your action around Chicago, so you should be okay. Then you can take bets going the other way and still make money."

"Does anyone else know about this? I mean I wouldn't want it to get around that I let somebody off the hook so easy?"

"This is between you and me and Tony."

"You seem pretty goddamn sure of yourself about these kids at UNLV, Bobby."

"I am, Carmine. Tell you what, let's you and I bet $100 on the game. I'll take UNLV and give you fifteen points, not ten. That's how sure I am."

Carmine couldn't help liking the guy. "Okay, tell Tony we have a deal."

Flying back to Chicago, Bobby thought about all the fuss that had been made about this kid being asked to shave some points. "*What's the big deal? It's not murder; it's not like you beat up somebody's kid. Jesus Christ, it's not even being a communist. Its part of the American system, let the better beware.*" Oh well that wasn't for him to decide. He did his job, and that was that.

CHAPTER EIGHTEEN

WHEN HE RETURNED to Chicago, Bobby called Tony Accardo. Tony called Angelo Santino. Angelo called his son, who in turn called Wade.

"Everything is okay, Wade. I just spoke to my father, and your old man is off the hook. And you can go play basketball and score a hundred points if you want. One thing, though, your father can't go around town blabbing what happened. Tell him to just forget about the whole business. And another thing, he can't place any more bets with Mastoria."

"Talking about placing bets, how about my ten grand, Louie?"

"That's down the toilet, pal. Sorry."

"Yeah, I figured that. Really didn't expect to get any of that back. Look, Louie, I'm sure you know how much I appreciate what you and your father did. I don't know how I can ever thank you."

"As the boys say: Forget about it. So tell me, how is practice going? You guys ready for the big game?"

"As ready as we'll ever be. Are you still planning to drive to Denver with Gary?"

"Yup, as a matter of fact, when I hang up from you, we're going to get something to eat and then take off. If you're finished practice, do you want to meet us at the diner for a quick bite?"

"No. Think I'll take a pass, Louie. I want to call my father and give him the good news."

"By the way, is your old man planning to fly to Denver for the game?"

"As far as I know, he is. You guys have a safe trip. See you in Denver."

After talking to Louie, Wade called his father and told him what Louie said. Although he was happy that he didn't owe any money, and Wade wouldn't have to shave any points, he was pissed that he couldn't bet with Mastoria anymore. Mastoria was right. Wade's father was a born loser.

When Wade asked his father if he was going to the game, he wanted to know if there was any way he could fly out with the team on the charter. Wade explained that space was limited, and the coach had already turned down requests from other players wanting to take family members on the charter. His father told him he would try to get there. Wade thought to himself, *No good deed goes unpunished.*

The game was being played at the McNichols Arena in Denver on Monday night at eight o'clock. The UNLV team left for Denver on a chartered flight on Saturday morning. This is how the championship game begins, with a two-hour plane ride to the play-off city. College athletes, like the pros, fly a lot, and it is not as glamorous as it is cracked up to be.

And a college basketball team does not travel light. In addition to the players, there are the coaches, the trainers, several public relations people, a secretary, the equipment manager, plus all of the team's equipment. Teams are much more comfortable when they play at home in their own stadium. They know the quickest route to the arena, and their pre-game routine remains the same. Flying to a different city can create all kinds of problems. Just getting on the plane can become a challenge. Think about the numerous possibilities for delays. The bus to the airport is late; the charter arrives late; some of the players may not be on time; for some reason, not all of the team's equipment gets on the plane, or there is a foul up about who is on the charter. Any one of these things can make getting to the game a disaster. And even if everything goes as planned, the players have a lot of downtime to think. Be introspective, analyze their game, reread the play book, or if they are lucky, take a two-hour nap. And strange as it may seem, in some cases, the bonding with teammates can be torn apart. With so many different egos confined to a small place, inevitably personality issues will arise. But when the charter arrives in the play-off city, and the players get off the plane, any problems that may have arisen are soon forgotten. The bus ride to the hotel, the crowds at the hotel, some cheering some booing, the hullabaloo in the hotel lobby, all of this adds to the excitement of the game. At this point, the players are ready. All that is left is to play the game.

CHAPTER NINETEEN

IF IT'S MARCH, it's time for "March Madness" to take center stage. It's an invigorating time, commencing at postseason conference tournaments and climaxing at the final four, then of course on April 9, the championship game, in this case between UNLV and Duke. The NCAA tournaments are an American tradition that sends millions of fans into a synchronized frenzy each year. It is the concentrated hype of sixty-eight teams vying for college basketball's biggest prize, a national championship.

The fanfare leaves memories etched indelibly in the mind. One can't possibly forget some of the past on-court excellence stemming from North Carolina's triple-overtime win against Wilt Chamberlain-led Kansas, to Villanova's stunning upset of Georgia. Off the court, it's difficult to forget watching scalpers maneuver, the press asking the players stupid questions and the coaches trying to keep calm, while inside they can't wait to play the game. The great moments in sports don't arrive gradually. They just happen, in what seems like one unforgettable soaring second. So it was to be when the Runnin' Rebels of UNLV, met the Blue Devils of Duke. Nobody could really predict what was going to happen; it just happened.

The "establishment" has a way of dealing with those that seem to "buck the system." Years ago, it countered the braggadocio of then heavyweight champion Jack Johnson with police harassment. It attempted to douse the spirit that burned in the souls of Olympic champions John Carlos and Tommie Smith with corporate racism. And then there was "Broadway Joe" Namath, the American Football League antiestablishment, shaggy-haired quarterback. The NFL flat out said they didn't want that type of quarterback playing in their league. So it was with Jerry Tarkanian's two-decade battle with the NCAA. They resented his style of coaching and the way he recruited players. They alluded to the fact that the UNLV players were all thugs and incompetent, ignorant, uneducated, and didn't belong in the same arena as the Blue Devils of Duke. In the end, the question would be, "Were the bad guys gonna play ball? Were they really that good?" On the night of the game, as the UNLV players got off the bus and made their way into the McNichols arena, an ESPN reporter pushed a microphone in front of Larry Johnson's face and asked, "How do you feel about all that has been said about your team and the coach?"

Larry Johnson pushed the microphone aside and said, "Hey, man, we're just here to go to school and play ball and enjoy the ride."

This was the era of ESPN, right up the alley for a team that was full of in-your-face highlights. They were the biggest show on the Las Vegas strip. However, for all the brashness that oozed from their pores, the Rebels style of play was good, clean, entertaining basketball. The mistake was for those who mistook Larry Johnson's gold-toothed grin as a weakness.

When Duke showed up on Monday night in its characteristic bridesmaid's veil—the Blue Devils being zero for eight in Final Fours—Tarkanian's swifter, stronger, and more confident legions were dressed to kill. The key for UNLV was Larry Johnson, who in only thirty minutes on the court contributed twelve points, eleven rebound's, four steals, two three-pointers, and one extraordinary flip-behind-his-back-while-lunging-to-the-floor save of a ball about to go out of bounds. When Wade Simon fouled out with about six minutes left to play, he later told the press—in jest—that Johnson's play was so physical and rugged that he fouled him out even though he's his teammate.

After the game, Duke's forward, Christian Laettner, told an ESPN reporter that he had never seen such a punishing perimeter defense as that of UNLV. "We couldn't get the ball past the hash marks," he said, adding. "And on offense, they beat us off the dribble, on the run and every other which way for open shots. It was scary. They engulfed us. We didn't just lose. They beat the hell out of us."

In all, the 103-73 win by the Runnin' Rebels was the biggest blowout in the history of the championship game. It was not just that UNLV became the first team to score one hundred or more points in the final. Or that it won by the largest margin ever. That was mere offense in a game where their defense was really the story.

At one point in the game, Duke's skinny freshman guard, Bobby Hurley, was simply overwhelmed. Harried surrounded by UNLV players, he tried to throw the ball inbounds and instead overthrew everybody, and the ball hit one of the players in the humbled Duke band.

Among some of the stories that would be told about the game in the years to come happened just before UNLV took a 47-35 lead at intermission. Duke sophomore Brian Davis made an attempt to slap high fives with Laettner, missed, and instead smacked his teammate in the face. It was that kind of night for the team from Durham, North Carolina.

In Chicago, Bobby Francisco was watching the game on TV in his apartment. When the game ended, he called Carmine Mastoria in Las Vegas. When Carmine answered the phone, Bobby simply said, "You owe me a hundred bucks," and hung up.

CHAPTER TWENTY

IT WAS 1993. Wade sat in his office on the second floor of the Moon Glow Hotel and Casino, looking out of the window at the lights on the Las Vegas strip. He was reflecting on the past three years. When he was originally hired as the vice president of finance at the casino, he thought it would be nothing more than a "job-title position." However, within a couple of months of being hired, he was given all sorts of responsibilities, and now three years later, he was second-in-charge and reported directly to Jeffery Wilson, the CEO. And in about an hour from now, he had to make the biggest decision of his young life.

Things were much easier in 1990 after winning the NCAA championship. Back then, he was on a real high. The entire UNLV team was. They received all sorts of special privileges, including the seniors not having to attend any more classes until graduation. Lunch was free for the team at the diner on Flamingo Road, and the girls were plentiful. After graduation, Wade decided to go to Philly for a week to visit with his mother. While he was in the East, he went to New York to have dinner with Albert Kline before starting work at the Moon Glow Casino.

Once again, Kline made it very clear that he hoped Wade would eventually come to work for him at AA Financial. While he was in New York, he called Brenda and invited her to have a drink with him before he met her father for dinner. They agreed to meet at a small bar near the New York Athletic Club. Wade arrived first and waited at the bar. He had just ordered a drink when he heard a women's voice call his name. He turned around, and there she was. She walked toward him with a certain grace that seemed effortless. He noticed immediately that her hair had been cut shorter, and on any other woman, it might not work, but on Brenda, it added to her beauty. She was dressed in a dark blue suit that did nothing to hide her shapely figure. Her legs were long and inviting, and he couldn't help remembering the first time he saw her. She looked even more beautiful today. She greeted him with a warm hug.

"Wade, it is good to see you. I am glad you called."

He felt a wonderful delight; there was no other word to describe his feelings. He finally managed, "You look beautiful, Brenda."

"You sound surprised," she said in a flirtatious way.

"No not at all. You know what I mean." For whatever reason, he felt like he was sixteen and on his first real date. She had that effect on him.

For the next hour, they exchanged stories about what they had been doing since they last saw each other. She told Wade that she broke up with the publisher from Doubleday about a year ago and thought about calling him but just never did.

"I wish you had," Wade said.

She reached over and kissed him on the cheek and said, "So do I, but what has changed? You are in Las Vegas, and I am in New York. Since we last saw each other, I have moved up at Doubleday, and my father told me you are going to work at a casino in Las Vegas."

Wade sighed. She was right; what had changed?

His reminiscing was interrupted when his secretary knocked on his door to remind him that he had a meeting with Jeffery Wilson, the CEO, in an hour. Wade was not ready for the meeting; he had some more thinking to do.

He was about six months in the job at Moon Glow when he came across a strange transaction. There was an automatic payment of $50,000 being made every month to L&G Design Company in San Francisco. Wade knew that was Louie's company. He also knew that Louie and his partner were not doing anything for Moon Glow. When he called his friend to ask him about it, Louie told him to just forget about it.

"What do you mean forget about it? I'm the financial VP here. I need to know what this is for."

"Wade, there's some things you don't have to concern yourself with. This is one of them. Trust me."

"What the hell is going on, Louie?"

"Look, Wade, I'm going to be in Vegas next week, and I will explain what is going on. In the meantime, just sit tight, and don't say anything to Jeffery."

"Doesn't he know about this, Louie?"

"Wade, we'll talk about it when I get there."

He subsequently learned that the $50,000 being paid to Louie's company was somehow being transferred to Louie's father and Albert Kline. Louie told Wade that his father and Kline were responsible for Vegas Investment Associates, the brokerage firm Wade had been working for in Vegas, getting a piece of the casino.

"I don't get it. How did your father and Kline have anything to do with that? Are they involved in Moon Glow? I know AA Management LC, a company in the Bahamas, owns the biggest piece of the casino, but I don't know who the principals are. I'm not sure I even know who owns Vegas Investment Associates. It seems to me this whole ownership thing is very complicated. I never could understand how the Nevada Gaming Commission went along with that."

Louie told him he would explain it all later. For now, Wade just has to go along with the program. Wade knew if he went along with the program, he was stepping into unchartered waters.

As time went on, there were other financial transactions involving Louie's company, Louie's father and Kline, as well as Vegas Investment Associates that went unexplained. Wade had learned not to push for answers but was smart enough to figure them out on his own. Louie's father and these other guys were skimming the profits from the casino. Also, Jeffery Wilson was nothing more than a figure head. He wasn't sure who he reported to. In his mind, he was sure that the major portion of the casino owned by AA Management LC, the company in the Bahamas, was part of AA Financial, and that had something to do with the reason Kline wanted him to work in Vegas before joining him on Wall Street. He wasn't sure why, but he figured it had to tie in somehow. And as far as Vegas Associates was concerned, they were still the wild card, so to speak. Did they sucker him in on this whole deal? And who really did own Vegas Investment Associates? That was another one of these complicated ownership deals where one set of owners led to another set. And how about Louie, was he in on all this? Was he part of the scam?

Now three years later, Wade had been instructed to have their in-house accountants make changes in the financial statements of Moon Glow, which he knew were questionable, to say the least. And in about an hour from now, he was scheduled to meet with Jeffery Wilson to assure him that all of the "corrections," as Jeffery Wilson put it, had been made and that Moon Glow was now ready to go to the underwriters to discuss the final stages of taking the hotel-casino public. He didn't know who the underwriters were, but he had a pretty good guess. He found himself getting in deeper and deeper into something. Unfortunately, he didn't know what it was he was getting deeper into.

CHAPTER TWENTY-ONE

WHEN WADE WALKED into Jeffery Wilson's office, he couldn't believe his eyes. Albert Kline was sitting on the sofa with a drink in one hand and a cigarette in the other. He smiled and said, "Wade, it's good to see you." Then he put down his drink, got up from the sofa, and walked over to where Wade was standing. He put his arm on his shoulder and said, "Jeffery has been telling me good things about you." Then he pointed to a heavyset man with olive skin and jet black hair who appeared to be in his mid-fifties, sitting in a chair by the window smoking a cigar. "By the way, Wade, say hello to Sal Maggio. He is the owner of Vegas Investment Associates."

Wade was not the naïve young man that he was when he first met Albert Kline. The last three years at the Moon Glow and Vegas Investment Associates had changed that. He looked at Kline then at Jeffery Wilson who was sitting behind a large glass-top desk then at the ominous looking man with the jet black hair and cigar and very coldly said, "Will you guys please tell me what the fuck is going on?"

"Wade, nothing is going on," Kline said. "Sal and I are here to talk about the IPO for Moon Glow. Our two firms are going to be the underwriters. We know you have been working on getting things in order, and we just want to make sure we have all bases covered. That's it, nothing more."

Wade listened, but he knew what he heard was bullshit. He thought to himself, "*They may be here to talk about the IPO, but there is a hell of a lot more going on than just a normal public offering.*" He had made his decision. "You know Albert, I'm really not comfortable being part of the Moon Glow's IPO. There are some things regarding the ownership that give me a problem. I'm sure you know what I'm talking about." No reaction from Kline. "Anyway I think it would be best for me to hand in my resignation. I appreciate what you have done for me, but I think it's time for me to move on."

None of the other men in the room said anything. The man with the olive skin and cigar never changed expressions. Jeffery Wilson appeared to be waiting for instructions from Kline. Wade was waiting for someone to say something. After what seemed like an eternity, but was in fact only a couple of seconds, Kline asked Wade to sit down, then he walked over to the bar and took out a very pretty crystal decanter.

"Jeffery keeps this here for me," he said. "Do you know what it is, Wade?" Wade simply looked at him, understanding that it was a rhetorical question. "This is a bottle of fifty-year-old Dalmore Scotch. It was first distilled back in 1920, when they only made sixty bottles. Do you have any idea how much it cost?" Once again a rhetorical question. "It's $11,000, Wade. And do you know why I pay that much for a bottle of scotch, Wade? Because I can! Do you have any idea how much money I made last year? Of course, you don't. I made over twenty-five million, Wade, $25 million. Hard to believe, isn't it?"

Wade had no idea where this was going.

"Wade, in the early eighties, top traders, hedge fund managers, and private equity gurus were making millions, and they were rotten years. As the years got better, those same people were making hundreds of millions of dollars. I bet you had no idea anyone could make that much money in this cockamamie business. Wade, I own my own Learjet. I have a three-hundred-foot yacht docked in Fort Lauderdale with a captain, a cook, and a crew of three ready to take me anywhere in the world I want to go. All I have to do is call them. I own a house in Long Island, one in the Hamptons, and a condo in Palm Beach. Last year, I bought Brenda a small publishing company. I am sure you know that already.

"I guess you are wondering why I am telling you all this? You see, Wade, when Mr. Santino first suggested I hire you, it just wasn't out of the goodness of his heart, although he is a very generous man. No, in your case, he saw something special. He saw someone who someday could be my successor."

By the look on Wade's face, Kline could see he hit a nerve. "Surprised, huh?" Kline said. "Wade, the reason I am telling you all this, is because someday you can have all of the same things. However, everything comes with a price. Maybe the price is bending the rules a little bit, or possibly looking for some loopholes in the system. Who knows? The point I am making, Wade, is after we take the Moon Glow public, I want you to come to New York and work as my personal assistant. If things go as planned, I would like to retire in about five years and have you take over as CEO of AA Financial. I want you to take a day or so to think about what I have said. In the meantime, I would expect you to help us get ready for the IPO. However, if it is still your decision to leave now, I will respect that decision."

Wade sat there for a couple of seconds without saying a word then with a straight face, he said, "Can I have a drink of that $11,000 scotch?"

Kline smiled then poured Wade a drink and handed it to him. Wade drank it down in a single swallow. "Well what do you think?" Kline asked. Wade smiled and said, "Tastes like any other scotch to me."

Kline was no dummy. "Is that your way of telling me you are refusing my offer?"

Wade had regained his composure, "No not at all. What I am saying is just because something cost a lot of money doesn't necessarily make it better. For example, I am sure that tie you are wearing cost more than every piece of clothes I have on, but with all due respect, I think I look pretty good with what I'm wearing."

"I don't think I get your point, Wade," Kline said.

"I'm not really sure myself that I'm making one other than the fact I have to know exactly what is expected of me before I can commit. In other words, in the end, is it going to simply look better or is it really going to be better? Does that make any sense, Albert?"

"Perfectly, Wade. Why don't you and I have dinner in my suite tonight, and I will see if I can answer all of your questions. I am sure you have many."

Wade agreed and left. After he was gone, Sal Maggio asked Albert Kline what he thought.

"He is very bright, Sal, and I am sure he knows a lot more about what we are doing than he lets on. If I was a betting man, I would say 'he is all in.'"

"Are you sure we can trust him?" Sal asked.

"Sal, in our business, we measure trust with money, and we have more than enough of that."

CHAPTER TWENTY-TWO

SAL MAGGIO, THE son of an immigrant, came to this country when he was twelve years old. He was a tough kid and fit right in in the overcrowded tenement on the Lower East Side of New York. His father was a fish peddler, but Sal wanted no part of that. He hated both the taste and smell of fish. By the time he was thirteen years old, he was already part of a gang that stole from the local merchants and fenced what they stole to a supposedly "connected" guy. Sal was bold and brazen and refused to take any shit from anybody no matter how big or tough they were. One day, when the supposedly connected guy tried to cheat them, he got into a fight with him. The other gang members decided they didn't want him in their gang anymore. That was fine with him. This was penny-ante shit. He wanted to make some real money. He wanted to be with the real wise guys; that's where the money was. He knew that the only way he could do that was to do something to impress Gino Rosselli, the local mob-boss. So at the ripe old age of only sixteen, he managed to hijack a truckload of cigarettes. Then he went to the club where Rosselli held court every day and offered him the cigarettes. Rosselli was impressed.

"Whattayou want in return, kid?" Rosselli asked him.

"I wanna go to work for you."

Rosselli smacked him on the top of the head, laughed, and said, "You a-hired, kid!"

For the next couple of years, he did all sorts of work for Rosselli. He was part of a crew that hijacked cigarette and liquor trucks, and robbed warehouses and strong-armed local merchants for protection money. Then one day, Rosselli asked him if he ever killed anybody. Of course, he hadn't, but his answer to his boss was, "I'm not really sure."

"You-a-not-a-sure, whattayou mean?"

"Well I know I beat up some guys pretty bad, and they may have died. I'm not sure."

That was good enough for Rosselli. He told Sal there was a guy who owed him a lot of money. It was money the guy lost betting with Rosselli, and he was the kind of guy who would rather take a beating than pay back the money. Rosselli told Sal he couldn't let the son of a bitch live. "He go around tellin' all-da-people, he no hafta pay, that no good for my business, so I want you should whack him. You can do this?" Sal agreed to take the contract.

Sal took all the information from Rosselli, including a picture of the man he was going to kill. Once he knew the victim's schedule, he decided on a day and time. On the night he planned the hit, he was parked up the street from the man's house, waiting. After thirty minutes, the man came out of his house and got in his car. Sal got out of his car and ran up to the man and opened the car door.

"What the hell is it with you, you crazy?" the victim said.

Sal looked at him closely to make sure he had the right man. He did. He then fired three shots into the man's head, spit on him, and left. If anybody asked him in the future if he ever killed anybody, he wouldn't have to say, "I'm not sure."

When he told Rosselli, the old man said, "Gooda work, kid. I owe you."

Over the next ten years, Sal moved up in Rosselli's operation to the point where he was practically running everything. Then one day, Rosselli told him he was moving to Florida. He had made arrangements with one of the New York families to take over his entire operation with the exception of the sports betting book he ran out of a small lunch room just off Wall Street. A lot of the "suits" from Wall Street would come there for a quick lunch and at the same time make bets on ball games and horse races. He gave that to Sal. It was an easy job and provided Sal with a couple hundred grand a year. Sal would hang around all day, reading the racing form. Sometimes he would help out at lunchtime just to keep busy. He became friendly with a lot of the Wall Street suits, some of whom would occasionally take him to a ball game or to the fights at Madison Square Garden. It was an easy life and easy money.

One of the Wall Street suits that Sal became friendly with was Albert Kline. Every so often, Kline would stop at Sal's place for a quick lunch or some coffee. Kline knew that Sal was running a betting operation, and one day, more out of curiosity than anything else, he asked Angelo Santino if he knew him. Of course, being in Chicago, Angelo didn't know him, but after asking around, he got the full story on Sal. He told Albert what he learned and asked him why he wanted to know.

"You can never tell when you might need the services of someone like him," Albert said.

Angelo cautioned Albert about getting involved with him and told him if the situation ever arose when he needed someone like Sal, he was to call him. "You run the brokerage business. I will take care of the rest," he said. Although they had a good relationship, Albert did not like when Angelo gave him orders. After all, he was doing all the work, and all that Angelo did was put up the money. How quickly people forget!

One day, when Sal and Albert were casually talking about the stock market, Sal told him he never owned any stock. "That's where you can make big money, Sal," Albert told him.

"Yeah, well if you ever come across a hot tip, let me know. Maybe I'll try my luck."

Albert laughed. "You know better than that, Sal. Luck is for suckers. The house always wins. Nobody knows that better than you."

"Yeah, you're right. That's why I'll wait until you give me a hot tip."

It didn't take too long before Albert did have a hot tip for his new friend. Albert came across a company that in the world of wireless headsets had carved out a small but significant niche. The product was no big deal, but it was ripe for an IPO. AA Financial provided the company with inventory financing in the amount of $500,000 from a group of investors, which in effect, were nothing more than false names and a post office box in the Bahamas. For their early investment, Kline told the president of the wireless company that he had to give these people stock options at a dollar a share. When the wireless executive questioned it, Kline said, "Don't worry, you will end up making so much fucking money those stock options will look like chicken feed." Actually it was Albert Kline and Angelo Santino who were getting all of the options. AA Financial handled the IPO and brought out the stock at $5. Kline arranged for Sal to buy ten thousand shares at the offering price and told him to sell them when the stock reached $10. AA Financial had their broker's hard sell the stock, and within a week, the stock was $10.50. Sal sold his ten thousand shares for a profit of over $50,000. Albert executed the $1 option on the 1.5 million shares on behalf of the phony investors and sold them at $10.50. After deducting the $500,000 he gave the wireless company for inventory financing and the costs involved to take the company public, Kline and Santino made a cool $12 million. After sharply reducing their support of the stock, within a week, it dropped to $3 a share, and by the end of the month, the stock was trading at under a dollar. The company's capital-raising ability was in tatters. When the president of the wireless company questioned Kline as to what happened, his reply was simply, "That's the stock market for you!"

In the meantime, Sal told Kline that if he ever needed a favor, he owed him one.

Less than two months later, Kline went to Sal to collect.

CHAPTER TWENTY-THREE

AT ABOUT THREE o'clock in the afternoon of October 11, 1985, Sal Maggio appeared on the fourteenth floor of 196 Broadway, Manhattan. He walked into the offices of Empire Capital LP, a dealer in over-the-counter stocks. He was wearing a black leather jacket and had on a New York Yankees baseball cap. He also had a forty-five-caliber revolver in his belt.

Days later, the confidential police report of the incident (Complaint No. 165784, First Precinct) would read as follows:

"According to an unnamed witness, a man in a black leather jacket asked the victim what stock he was trading in. Then he slapped him in the head and stated again, "What the fuck are you trading in?" Then he slapped the victim in the head again, and according to the witness opened his jacket exposing the .45 caliber pistol in his belt.

Another witness recalls the man in the black leather jacket saying, "Don't fuck with our stock." The stock: Fashion Plate Inc. After the man in the black leather jacket left, Empire Capital stopped trading in Fashion Plate Inc."

To the New York Police Department, the incident at Empire Capital Inc. was about as serious as a scuffle over a parking space. Albert Kline knew that the assault, categorized as a low-grade misdemeanor at best, would not be investigated because the victim was not seriously hurt, and as a matter of fact, no gun was displayed—even though one was observed— and the perpetrator was unknown, and he was right. The case was closed without any further investigation.

This was the favor Sal owed Kline, to intimidate Empire Capital Inc., thereby eliminating a competing market maker and allowing only those brokers who were cooperating with him to bid on the stock. The result is kind of a rigged auction, with the prices where desired, and the spreads between bid and ask prices kept as wide as possible. In Wall Street terms, this is called "boxing."

The irony of the incident is that the trader at Empire Capital Inc. was suspected of "cracking the spread." According to market sources who were familiar with the trading in Fashion Plate that day, Empire Capital was blamed, in effect, for doing what a market maker is supposed to do—get the best possible price for its customers and keep the spreads as narrow as possible, which they did. However, they were blamed for that benign—to most people—market action.

In the weeks following Sal's visit to Empire Capital Inc., Fashion Plate Inc. shares were trading at the kind of spreads that can only happen when the market is tightly controlled. This allowed AA Financial to make a killing on the stock. Albert never told Angelo Santino about what he had Sal do. No need to. All is well that ends well.

In the weeks and months that followed, Sal and Albert Kline became very friendly, and Kline invited Sal in on several more IPOs where he was able to get in and get out with a quick profit. In January of 1986 Kline approached Sal with the idea of buying a small brokerage firm in Las Vegas.

"I know the guy who owns it," Kline said, "And he is a gambler and a drunk. The firm is slowly going broke. We can steal it. You're a smart guy. I can teach you how to run it, and we can hire a couple of experienced brokers and we're off and running. AA Financial will put up the money and take 50 percent ownership. I guarantee by the end of the first year you'll make ten times what you are making from that shitty betting operation you got."

Albert had not discussed this with Angelo Santino but felt confident he would go along with the idea. He was wrong. Angelo didn't want any part of it. However, Kline felt it was a good move, and he was going to do it with or without his partner. He went back to Sal and told him he decided not to involve AA Financial. Instead he was going to be his partner. Sal liked that better. On February 15, 1986, with a little convincing from Sal, the owner of Vegas Investment Associates sold his firm to Sal Maggio and Albert Kline. Sal went from being a mobster to being the president of an over-the-counter brokerage firm.

However, you might be able to take the man out of the mob, but it is difficult to take the mob out of the man.

He had been running the brokerage firm for several months when one day, while talking to Kline on the phone, he heard a commotion outside of his office. He ended the call and went to see what was going on. There was a big guy from the order department yelling at the janitor, an elderly black man, for spilling some water on the floor next to his desk. Sal approached him and said, "Hey, what's going on here? Why are you yelling so loud? You're in an office, not a bar." The big guy said, "Look at what that spook did," and he pointed to the water on the floor.

"And that's what you're yelling about. And where do you get off calling this old guy a spook, you asshole." The big guy was taken aback. He started to say something when Sal grabbed him by the jacket, smacked him across the mouth with an open hand, and then pushed him back, almost causing him to fall down.

"Look, asshole, I want you out of here before I rip off your nuts and shove them down your throat, you got that?" The big guy felt his knees grow weak. "I'm sorry, Mr. Maggio, I didn't mean it, I am sorry really." Sal pointed to the janitor and said, "Apologize to him, not to me."

"I'm sorry, Sam. You know I didn't mean anything."

The janitor, who had been taking shit from this guy even before Sal bought the firm, looked at Sal then back at the big guy and said to him, "Fuck you, Herman." Sal started to laugh, and the other people in the office clapped. Sal was the boss, and everyone knew he wouldn't stand for any shit. There was a new sheriff in town!

CHAPTER TWENTY-FOUR

BECAUSE OF THE mere fact that Vegas Investment Associates was in Las Vegas and not located on Wall Street and did not trade on either one of the major exchanges, Albert Kline decided to be more aggressive in the type of scams he was going to have Sal work. To provide some insulation for himself, he placed his share of the firm in a shell corporation in the Bahamas. Then he found a local attorney who, for a fee, transferred the shell corporation into a trust of which he was the trustee. It would be very difficult for anyone to track the ownership back to him. The way he devised receiving his share of the profits was even more complicated, but eventually he got his money. He told Sal they were going to specialize in selling IPOs.

"And how do you intend to do that?" Sal asked. "I thought you would never ask," Kline said with a smile.

"The first thing you need to do is find a business, any kind of business: A bagel maker, some sort of newfangled water purifier, a guy selling fancy sneakers out of his garage, almost any kind of business will do. What we need is not so much an actual business, but a business entity with a story, any kind of story, that we can convert into a company that we can sell to the public. And trust me, Sal, the public loves to buy dreams. Now here is how this works. The IPO stock will not really be sold to the public."

Sal said, "I don't get it!"

"You will. Just follow me, Sal. The IPO stock will actually be sold to Vegas Investment."

Sal asked, "Can we do that?"

Kline laughed. He was enjoying this. "No, we can't. We're only permitted to buy a small percentage. However, we can sell it to our close friends who will immediately sell it back to us for a small profit. Say we come out at $4.. Our friends would 'flip' it back to us for $4.25 a share. Not a bad deal for them without any risk. In the meantime, we train our guys to promote the IPO to their customers. Remember, Sal, suckers aren't born. They are trained. Smart guys can very easily be trained to become suckers. So let's take a hypothetical case. Our guys hype a hot IPO that is coming out at $4. They ask their suckers how much of the stock they want, telling them there is no guarantee they will get any. Tell that to a sucker, and he will ask for as much as he can afford, or in a lot of cases, more than he can afford. Once we know how many shares they have committed, we then know how many shares we want to issue. Before the IPO, our salesman get back to their customers and tell them the stock is so hot that they will only be able to get them a small amount at the IPO price of $4, and they need their approval to buy the rest at market. Some guys will balk, but trust me, most will go along. The bottom line is we end up selling our shares, which cost us $4.25, for anywhere from $4.75 to $5.75. Assuming we issue four million shares, after all of our expenses, we can easily clear over $3 million on one IPO. You do that three or four times a year, well you do the math, Sal."

Sal asked, "After all that, what happens to the business we took public?"

"Do you really care, Sal?"

CHAPTER TWENTY-FIVE

AFTER THE MEETING with Albert Kline, Wade returned to his office to call Brenda. Over the past three years, they saw each other a couple of times a year. He would visit her in New York when he went to the East, and she came to Vegas several times. Once when she was attending a publisher's convention in Los Angeles, Wade flew there, and they spent a long weekend together. He really thought they had something, but in reality, they were both holding back. There was no doubt they cared for one another, but the fact that they lived three thousand miles apart created an invisible barrier. Wade often thought about it. He really felt good when he was with her. They both enjoyed the sex, however infrequent, but that didn't change the fact that he lived in Las Vegas, and she lived in New York.

During the weekend they spent together in Los Angeles, Brenda asked him why he didn't leave the Moon Glow and come back to New York. She said he could easily get a job there. "I'm sure I can," he said, "but not for the money I make in Vegas." Afterward, he realized that if he really loved her enough, he would leave Vegas regardless of the money. But he chose to stay there. Now that Kline had offered him a job in New York, he wondered what would happen with him and Brenda?

It was seven o'clock in New York when he finally reached Brenda. As always, she was glad to hear from him. He wasn't sure if she knew that her father was in Las Vegas, or that he was offering him a job in New York.

"Tell me what's going on out there Wade, and then I have some great news to tell you."

"You first," he said.

"Well I have been working with this woman who has written a marvelous story, and I have agreed to publish it. The manuscript is one of the best I have ever read. I gave it to my old boss at Doubleday to get his opinion, and he said it is a real winner."

"That's fantastic," Wade said.

"Wait, that's only part of it. Did you ever hear of Arthur Cannon?"

"Are you talking about the guy who makes movies?"

"Yeah, well I met him at an award ceremony in New York a couple of months ago and happened to mention this manuscript I'm telling you about. Anyway he asked me to send him a copy. After he read it, he called me and said it would make a good movie. He was going away on location but promised to call me when he returned."

"And," Wade said, waiting for the other shoe to drop.

"And," she said, "He called me yesterday and said he wants to option the movie rights. He asked me to fly out to California next week to work out the details, and get this he wants me to be an associate director on the project. He said because I have been so close to the gal who wrote the story, I could add something to the film, can you believe that? Just think, we will be less than an hour away from one another. I was thinking maybe you could fly into LA next week, and we can spend a couple days together, what do you think?"

Wade couldn't believe what he was hearing. Was there some special kind of god whose only purpose in life was to keep them apart?

"Wade, are you there? You haven't said anything."

"No, I'm here. That is great news, Brenda. I am very excited for you. Let me know when you will be in LA, and I'll fly in." *"Now wait until you hear my news."*

Wade finished talking to her without mentioning the offer he had received from her father. He didn't know why, maybe he didn't want to rain on her parade. It was almost five o'clock in Las Vegas and he had a meeting before he was supposed to meet Kline for dinner. He used the shower in his office to freshen up and change clothes and then left to attend his five-forty-five meeting. He stopped thinking about Brenda and thought about his dinner meeting with Albert Kline. The man said he would answer all of his questions. The problem was, Wade was not sure what it was he wanted to ask him.

CHAPTER TWENTY-SIX

WHILE WADE WAS debating if he should continue working on taking the Moon Glow public, and whether or not he should accept Kline's offer to go to work for him in New York, and while Sal was busy scamming investors at his brokerage firm, and while Brenda was excited about going to California to work in the film industry, the F.B.I. was busy trying to develop a case against Sal Maggio and Vegas Investment Associates. Over the past two years, they had received complaints from investors who bought stock in IPOs underwritten by Vegas Investment Associates that turned out to be worthless; however, they were never able to get any evidence of wrongdoing on the part of Vegas Investments. Finally, they decided on another course of action.

Almost everything Sal Maggio said in his office over the past year—conversations he never assumed anyone would overhear—had been recorded by the F.B.I. The first bug they placed in his office was done with the help of a man named Johnny Esposito.

Before Sal hired him, he was a small-time bookie from New Jersey. When he came to Vegas, the first thing he did was contact Sal and asked him for a job. It was not unusual for Sal to hire someone like him. As a matter of fact, most of the so-called brokers who worked for Sal had no formal financial training, were not licensed by any agency to trade stocks or bonds, and were basically either con men or loan sharks.

There was one broker in Sal's firm, who when he applied for a job as a registered stockbroker, mentioned that his only previous experience was as a labor foreman. He neglected to say anything about his reputed association with one of Cleveland's largest crime families. However, he was glib and convincing, the kind of guy who could talk you out of your underwear, the kind of salesman Sal liked.

Unfortunately for Sal, Johnny Esposito wasn't satisfied with just working for him; he was also running a bookie and loan shark business on the side. Then one day, he got nabbed by the local cops who turned him over to the F.B.I. They knew they were looking for someone in Sal's operation that they could turn, and Johnny was their man.

The agreement that Johnny made with the F.B.I. was a good one, maybe one of the best ever negotiated by a cooperating witness. And since Johnny had no real allegiance to Sal, he had no regrets about what he was doing. The first thing the bureau did was put him on their payroll for $600 a week. They also agreed to allow him to continue his loan shark business. All he had to do was keep them informed as to what Sal was doing. For Esposito, there were no qualms about him being a "rat." However, he knew that if Sal ever found him out, he would probably kill him.

The problem the F.B.I. had was that even with what Esposito told them from time to time plus the taped conversations, there was still nothing concrete enough to take to a grand jury. They needed more two-way conversations. They needed corroborating statements. Finally, they told Esposito he had to place a bug in Sal's office phone, his home phone, and in his car. They also wanted him to wear a wire. Johnny said that's impossible. They told him either that or his ass goes to jail. He had to figure a way to get out of the corner he had backed himself into. When he originally got involved with the agency he allowed himself to forget one important thing: the only way to survive in the corrupt and treacherous world in which he lived was to be more corrupt and more treacherous than those you were dealing with, and he was not. He was out of his league with Sal Maggio. However, he knew that the day he strapped on a wire, his days were numbered.

The first time they asked him to wear the wire was at a cocktail party that Vegas Investment Associates was hosting at the Moon Glow. The F.B.I. knew that local politicians, the firm's salespeople, and of course, Sal himself would be attending the party. They thought that would be a good time to get corroborating statements. Esposito convinced the F.B.I. they would be better off videotaping the party. He could hide some cameras, and that would be better than a wire. They agreed. Johnny knew the tapes would have little or no value because there was too much noise, and the place was too crowded for individual conversations to be picked up in any coherent manner. And of course, he was right. Unfortunately for him he knew he couldn't bull-shit the Fed's forever, which meant sooner or later he was going to have to wear a wire.

CHAPTER TWENTY-SEVEN

WHEN WADE ARRIVED at Kline's suite for his dinner meeting, he was surprised to find Sal Maggio there. Kline saw the surprise in Wade's face and said, "There has been a change in plans, Wade. We have decided to delay the public offering for the hotel."

Wade looked at both men and smiled. "I don't know what kind of games you guys are playing, but you chose the wrong Jew to play with you! First you give me a whole line of bullshit about taking this place public and then coming to work for you in New York, and now you nonchalantly tell me you have decided to postpone the offering. I don't need this type of nonsense, Albert. I think I am out of here. This is not my idea—"

But before he could finish, Kline interrupted him. "Wade, please sit down. Let me explain."

Wade looked at the men, who both nodded as if to say, "Give us a chance to explain."

Albert said, "Wade, I am going to tell you some things that must never leave this room. I am telling you because I trust you and believe you are going to accept the offer I made to you this afternoon."

Wade simply nodded.

"We have a friend who works in City Hall here in Vegas. He is on our payroll. He gives us information that we would not otherwise have. Does something like that surprise you?"

"Not really."

Kline continued. "Shortly after our meeting this afternoon, our contact called Sal to tell him that about a year ago, the F.B.I. had turned one of Sal's people into an informant."

Wade said, "I don't understand. Why do they want one of Sal's people to be an informant? Be an informant for what? And you say this happened a year ago, but your friend just found out. What took him this long to tell you? Either you're not paying him enough money or he is not paying attention."

"No, that's not the case, Wade. Let me tell you how this all came about, and then I'll explain why the agency thinks they need an informant to spy on Sal. It seems the local police picked up this guy last year but never charged him with anything, so there was no record of his arrest. The Vegas police have been working with the F.B.I., looking for someone to plant in Vegas Investment, and this guy was perfect. He works for Sal. It was just dumb luck our friend found out. Yesterday, the F.B.I. asked our friend if the Las Vegas Police Department had a layout of Sal's house. When our friend asked why, the stupid F.B.I. guy was more than anxious to tell him about their mole and how he was going to bug Sal's house. When our friend asked who the mole was, again the F.B.I. had a big mouth and told him, Johnny Esposito, an old friend of Sal's and one of his brokers."

"***Holy shit***," Wade said, half under his breath.

"Yes, that's one way of putting it," Kline said as he poured himself a drink of scotch and then continued.

"Let me tell you something, Wade. Gamblers, bookmakers, and stockbrokers all have something in common. Gamblers only think about winning, and so they will take chances not weighing the consequences. On the other hand, bookmakers only think about how much they might lose so many times they will do things to give themselves an edge without weighing the consequences. And it has been my experience that stockbrokers constantly worry about both winning and losing, so once again they will do things without weighing the consequences. Johnny Esposito, is allthree: He is a gambler, a bookmaker and a stockbroker and has turned on his friend without weighing the consequences."

"You know, Albert, this stuff is really out of my league. I mean, I appreciate you confiding in me, but I have the feeling you are going to tell me things that I really don't want to know."

"Wade, you need to know this. If you are eventually going to take over AA Financial, you have to step into the real world. And the real world is not always black and white. There are a lot of gray areas. You asked why the F.B.I. wants an informant to spy on Sal. The reason is Vegas Investments operates in a lot of these gray areas. Is that illegal? We don't think so. For years, the F.B.I. and the SEC have been trying to get rid of the gray areas, close the loopholes if you will, and in so doing, they harass small brokerage firms like Sal's company in an effort to accomplish this."

"Okay, let's assume that's the case," Wade said. "I have two questions. First, why should any of that have an effect on taking Moon Glow public? And second, if Vegas Investments isn't doing anything illegal, why should you and Sal be concerned the F.B.I. is spying on you?"

"Once again, Wade, the gray areas can be interpreted by a court to be illegal. We don't want to have to defend that issue. And the reason we want to hold off with Moon Glow is we think it is wise for Vegas Investments to keep a low profile until this blows over, and trust me, it will."

"I have another question, Albert. You mentioned this guy Esposito didn't weigh the consequences when he went to work for the F.B.I. exactly what are the consequences?"

Before Albert could answer, Sal said, "You don't have to concern yourself with that, Wade. I will take care of that." Wade felt a chill go down his back. This was the first time the man with the jet black hair and olive skin had said more than two words.

Albert sensed Wade's reaction to what Sal said. He laughed and said, "This isn't a Godfather movie, Wade. It's not as ominous as it sounds."

Wade looked at Sal, whose eyes said, "Yes, it is!"

Albert jumped in with, "So that's the story, Wade. Things are back to square one."

Wade nodded. "Okay, so where does that leave me?"

"My offer is still open, and since the Moon Glow is not going public now, and we don't have a date for when we might do it, there is no reason for you to hang around Las Vegas. You might as well come to New York and play with the big boys. I spoke to Jeffery and asked him how long it would take him to free you up. He said two weeks. So if you are on board, wind up your affairs here, and be ready to come to New York in two weeks."

Wade thought about Brenda. She wasn't moving to Los Angeles forever. It was just to help on this one film, or was it? Then he thought about the job offer from Albert. It was a once in a lifetime opportunity. He walked over to Albert, shook his hand, and said, "We got a deal. I'll be in New York in two weeks." There was still one thing that bothered him, the man with the jet black hair and olive skin. Who was he really?

Albert Kline returned to New York the following day.

Three days later, while Sal was sitting ringside at the Caesar's Palace showroom with Jeffery Wilson, the Moon Glow's CEO, and two city councilmen, watching Tony Bennett perform, Johnny Esposito was having dinner at Dante's, a small nondescript neighborhood restaurant on the other side of town. He loved their clams and spaghetti in white sauce. Just after the waiter had served him his dinner, a man approached his table. He was wearing horn-rimmed glasses, and he had long blond hair and a moustache. He had on a UCLA sweatshirt and a Marlins baseball cap. He pulled a small handgun out of his belt, pointed it at Esposito, and shouted loudly enough so that everyone in the restaurant could hear him, "This will teach you to fuck around with my wife!"

Then he fired eight shots point-blank at Esposito's face and body. Everyone in the restaurant was in shock. Then quickly the man was gone.

The next day, a nice-looking, well-dressed man with short brown hair was on a plane from Las Vegas to New York. He had disposed of the blond wig, fake mustache, and horn-rimmed glasses. Before leaving Las Vegas, he stopped at a locker in the airport to retrieve an envelope containing $10,000. As always, he didn't know who ordered the hit.

That same day, there was an article on the third page of the Las Vegas Sun about a jealous husband shooting a stockbroker in an Italian restaurant in downtown Las Vegas.

When Wade read the article, he couldn't believe it. He knew the jealous husband story was bullshit, but how? Once again, he thought about the man with the jet black hair and olive skin. And he wondered what he was really getting himself into. Deep down, he knew damn well what he was getting into, and if he had any reservations about it, now was the time to get out. But he didn't.

Albert didn't learn about the Esposito shooting until after he was back in New York almost a week later. He had called Sal to ask him what he was planning to do about Esposito when Sal said, "We got lucky. A jealous husband shot the poor bastard while he was eating dinner how about that?" Not knowing if Sal's phone was bugged, Kline simply said, "Oh how sad."

After he hung up the phone, Kline thought for a couple of minutes and then called Angelo Santino in Chicago. He filled him in on what had happened with Esposito and said, "I recommend we get out of the Moon Glow in Vegas." Without hesitation, Santino agreed. He added, "I assume you will also sell your interest in Sal's brokerage firm as well?"

Sheepishly Kline said, "You know about that?"

Santino laughed. "Are you surprised?"

"No, I guess not. I hope that hasn't hurt our relationship."

"Just get us out of everything in Vegas, and we'll talk about it later. By the way, although I was not involved in Sal's firm, I would expect you to share the profits from the sale with me."

Although that had never entered his mind, Kline said, "Of course, Angelo. That goes without saying." He thought to himself, "*The Mafia is alive and well!*"

CHAPTER TWENTY-EIGHT

WADE WAS SITTING on the bed, watching Brenda as she walked from the bathroom to the balcony wearing just a towel. She had true, pure sex appeal. She was devoid of any of the sleaze associated with the word sex. Her svelte tall frame, her long legs, and her shapely torso would make any man wish he knew her. She knew he was watching her, so she dropped the towel just enough for him to get a peek at her smooth behind.

"Very nice," he said. "Why don't you bring that over here?"

She turned around and smiled. She had a great smile. Then she dropped the towel and walked over to the bed and sat down next to him. He took her hand and pulled her close. He stared deep into her eyes, suddenly seeing the future he really wanted. She gently touched his face and returned his gaze. Her eyes were moist. He leaned closer and kissed her. She gasped when he put his arms around her. She put her hands lightly around his neck, and whispered, "Do you love me?"

He could feel his heart starting to beat faster. In all the times they spent together over the last three years, this was the first time either of them spoke of love when they weren't making love. She once said to him, "You know there is a difference between saying 'I love you,' while eating a hot dog, as opposed to saying 'I love you,' when you are making love.

"You know I do," he said.

She got up and wrapped herself in the towel again then walked across the room and sat on the chair by the window. "Do I?" she asked.

They were spending the weekend together at the Beverly Hills Hotel. Wade decided to fly to California and see her before leaving for New York. It was Sunday, and he would be leaving for New York in the morning. They hadn't talked about it since he got there on Friday. When he told her that he had accepted the job with her father in New York, she was disappointed. She hoped that now that she was working on the film in Los Angeles, they could spend more time together, but evidently that was not to be. Nothing much had changed other than the fact their roles were reversed. Now he would be in New York, and she was here in Los Angeles, three thousand miles away.

He got up, slipped into a pair of denims over the shorts he was wearing then walked across the room and sat down next to her: "What's wrong, baby?"

She fluffed her hair back and said, "I am not your baby. You call everybody baby!"

"No, I don't. I call everybody babe. You're my only baby."

"Come on, Wade, get serious."

"About what . . . baby?"

They both laughed.

"About us, Wade what is going to happen with us? I feel like I'm in that movie with Alan Alda, *Same Time Next Year*."

"What movie is that?"

"It's about two people who meet while on vacation and fall in love, but they are each married to someone else. So they agree to meet once a year at the same place. That goes on for twenty-six years, and they never do end up being together. Is that what's going to happen with us?"

He knew she was being serious; however, he couldn't help laughing.

"Wade, don't laugh. That's not funny!"

"I'm sorry, Bren, I'm not laughing at you. It just sounded funny, that's all. First of all, we are not married to other people, and secondly, we see each other more than once a year. Really, Bren, I understand how you feel. I feel the same way. Look I would like to be with you all the time, you know that. But our careers keep getting in the way. That's the problem when you put two good-looking, smart people together."

"Bullcrap, Wade."

"Come on, baby, you can curse better than that."

She gave him a look that only she could give.

"Brenda, I understand how important it is for you to make this movie, and believe me, I am happy for you. It's a great opportunity. But by the same token, so is my job with your father. From what you told me, you should be finished with this movie in less than six months. That's not the end of the world. In the meantime, I can fly out here every so often, and then when you come back to New York . . ."

"When I come back to New York what?"

Wade thought to himself. *Was she looking for a commitment? Damn right, she was.*

“When you come back to New York, we can talk about making this thing permanent.”

“By this thing, you mean us?”

“Of course us Brenda. Look you know I love you. Do I want to spend the rest of my life with you? …I think I do.”

“You think!”

“Come on, Brenda.”

She leaned over and kissed him. “I’m sorry, Wade. I’m starting to sound like a nag. I don’t want to ruin this weekend.” She stood up, dropped the towel, and walked over to the bed. She turned her head, winked at him, and said, “Come make love to me . . . baby!”

CHAPTER TWENTY-NINE

ARCHITECTS MAKE A set of plans, and usually a building gets built. People make plans, and only God knows what will happen. It's a little profound, but it's pretty much what happens. More to the point, that's pretty much what happened with Wade and Brenda. Her plan was to stay in California and work on just one film. However, before the movie was halfway finished, Arthur Cannon, the film's producer and director, was so impressed with her work that he asked her to consider working on another film with him. And so instead of spending six months in California, Brenda had now been there off and on for almost two years. On one of her trips back to New York, she worked out an arrangement with the gal who was managing her publishing company to give her half of the company. This was a great deal for the woman since she didn't have to put up any money. She told Brenda that when she decided to come back to New York, she would still be the boss. When she told Wade, he couldn't believe it.

"This looks like you are settling in for the long haul in California. I thought you wanted us to be together," he said.

"I do, Wade, but . . ."

During the next two years, Wade's trips to California became less frequent, partly because he thought that would motivate Brenda to come back to New York sooner than later, and partly because he met Katrina. Katrina Soloff was a Russian concert pianist who lived in New York. Wade met her at a charity event shortly after Brenda told him she was staying in California to do another film with Arthur Cannon. Katrina was available, and he was vulnerable. She was also a couple of years older than him. As the cocktail party drew to a close, Wade asked her what she was planning to do about dinner. She looked at her watch and told him she had an early rehearsal in the morning and wanted to get to bed early. "That's no answer," he said, applying the Wade Simon charm. "Let me take you to dinner, after that I will take you straight home to bed."

She smiled and said in a charming Russian accent, "Is that one invitation or two?"

He took her by the hand and said, "Let's play it by ear."

They went to a small, expensive restaurant in the village where he was well-known, and the waiters made a fuss over him. It had antique Meissen candelabras and excellent Czech food.

"How intuitive," she said. "How did you know I liked Czech food?"

"Czech, Russian, is there any difference?"

She laughed and said: "Only if you are Czech or Russian."

They found talking to one another very easy. She told him about the summers in Russia, living on a farm, about the chickens and the fruit trees, and about her two brothers and three sisters. How she came to New York and studied at Juilliard and about her first concert at the Met. She listened while he talked about his days in college playing basketball, his time in Las Vegas, and his job on Wall Street. As promised, as soon as they finished dinner, he drove her back to her apartment building. When the doorman opened the car door, Wade leaned over and kissed her affectionately on the cheek and said, "I really enjoyed this evening. Sleep well."

Reluctantly she started to get out of the car, debating if she should ask him to come up for a night cap, realizing she didn't want the evening to end.

"Dobrou noc," she said. "Dekuji."

He smiled. "You're very welcome. I suggest you get out of the car now before I change my mind," he added softly as she sat with one foot out of the car. It was not conscience that was restraining him but experience. Tonight was not the night.

Katrina did not sleep much that night. Instead she replayed the evening over and over in her mind. She could not remember ever having enjoyed herself more. And it was nothing more than dinner. However, she found Wade to be interesting and exciting, not like any other man she had known before. She began to feel like a school girl who just went out with the captain of the football team. "*How foolish*," she thought. But she could not wait to see him again. The next morning, she got up eagerly, looking refreshed and full of energy. She got dressed, had her morning coffee, then climbed into her Fiat and drove to rehearsal. Unfortunately, things did not go well at the concert hall. There was a problem with technical matters; the lighting, the sound equipment, and the entire electrical system was out of whack. This caused her to forget Wade for a short time and put on hold those new and unexpected feelings she had when she awoke that morning. She tried to keep herself occupied while waiting to for the rehearsal to start. She read and chatted with members of the orchestra, but every so often, Wade popped back in her mind, and she felt strangely lonely.

During the past two years at AA Financial, Albert Kline continued to give Wade more control and insight as to what the company was really all about. There were a couple of times when he had second thoughts about continuing, but rationalization and money convinced him to stay. Several days before he met Katrina, Kline told him he wanted him to handle a bond issue for Monroe County in Florida. It was Angelo Santino who, through a friend, secured the account. Wade knew this meant no turning back. This was big-time stuff. The morning after his dinner date with Katrina, he had a full schedule of meetings, so he had little time to think about how much he enjoyed being with her. Nevertheless, he had already made up his mind. He wanted to see her again. However, that didn't happen until three days later when he showed up at the concert hall where she was rehearsing.

CHAPTER THIRTY

THE $100 MILLION Monroe County bond issue scam was as simple as it was convoluted. Unless you were in the municipal bond business or married to an anti-trust lawyer, you would never have heard of it. Or if you did, you probably wouldn't understand it.

Here is the way it worked. Monroe County needed to raise $100 million to build several new schools. The first step of the fraud is all perfectly legal and did not involve AA Financial. Monroe County goes to Wall Street, who issues a bond in their name and subsequently attracts cash from investors all over the globe. Once Wall Street raises all the money, it dumps it into a tax-free account, which Monroe County uses to build the schools. However, they don't spend all of that money right away. It could take years to finish building the schools. So Monroe County hires a middleman known as a broker, like AA Financial, to set up a public auction and invite banks to compete for their business. This allows them to collect interest on the money while waiting for the schools to be built. In most cases, the broker is legally required to invite a minimum of three banks to submit a bid.

Now here is the scam. Instead of the banks submitting competitive bids and letting the highest rate win, AA Financial rigs the auctions by making a deal with three banks. One bank would be allowed to "win" this bid; the second would be awarded another bid, maybe some county building a hospital, and the third bank would be awarded with a bid from some county that wants to build a sports stadium. What AA Financial does is tell each bank what the other bank's bid is, thereby allowing the bank of choice to win by giving Monroe County an interest rate just a fraction higher than the other bidding banks but lower than it would be if it were a legitimate auction. The winning bank then rewards AA Financial with kickbacks, totaling in the millions, disguised as fees for swap deals that they were never involved in. The banks, some of the biggest and most reputable in the country, were in on the scam.

The end result of this type of scam is that cities and towns all over the country systematically lose millions while the banks and the broker win big. By shaving tiny fractions of a percent off their winning bids, the banks pocket fantastic sums over the lifetime of these multimillion-dollar bond deals, as does the broker who wines and dines the banks and then accepts millions of dollars in return for their part in the scam. Lowering a bid by just a hundredth of a percent, called a basis point, could cheat someone like Monroe County out of tens of thousands of dollars it would have earned on its deposits.

What is interesting is that Albert Kline did not invent this scam. Organized crime has been involved in this type of bid rigging for decades. When most people hear about organized crime and bid rigging, they tend to think about the garbage collection business or the garment industry. However, the mob moved into Wall Street bid rigging because they found it a far more lucrative business model than leg breaking. They figured it's much more efficient to control a market and set the interest rate than it is to run a loan-sharking business on the street where many times you need a baseball bat to collect every week. This scam was so clever that the victims, cities, and towns all across America never knew that they were being cheated. No thumbs were broken, and nobody ended up in a landfill in New Jersey, but money disappeared, lots and lots of it, and its manner of disappearance had a familiar name: organized crime.

When Albert Kline first explained this bidding process to Wade, the first question he asked was, "Is it legal?" Albert Kline's answer was, "I don't believe it is illegal." Wade knew better. He remembered what someone once told him. "There is no right way to do the wrong thing." But once again, he was able to rationalize the reasons to continue, not least of which was the large sum of money he was beginning to earn.

CHAPTER THIRTY-ONE

WHEN WADE WALKED into the concert hall, Katrina was in the process of rehearsing with the orchestra. She didn't see him. He stood at the back of the room and listened. He had never heard anyone play the piano like she did. He watched in awe. Her face, her hair, her hands, they were all part of the sound coming from the Steinway. Her fingers moved back and forth across the black and white keys as if she were daring the piano not to respond.

As she practiced the Mozart, she sometimes slowed to replay passages, slightly altering their emphasis. She had played the score only twice before, but she was a fast learner. She paused over a phrase, creating her own sound. Her playing was impassioned and focused. She was playing Mozart's "Sonata in A Minor," as if she were lashing a carriage down the streets of Salzburg; Mozart employs all twelve tones of the scale, and Katrina touched on every one.

Conductors are the social glue of the concert world, but today the conductor seemed to follow Katrina as opposed to the other way around. Wade had no idea who the best pianist was, but he couldn't imagine anyone playing any better than Katrina.

When she finished, he could not help applauding. The conductor turned and yelled, "Who is that back there?" A little embarrassed Wade walked toward the stage. "I am sorry, maestro, I got carried away. I never heard anything so beautiful in my life."

Katrina got up from the piano and put her hands to her face. She could feel tears running down her cheeks. "Wade how nice of you to come." Then turning to the conductor, she told him Wade was a friend. He replied with a look of disapproval. She waved her hand as if to say, "Don't pay any attention to him." She motioned to Wade to come to the stage, and they walked back to her dressing room, neither one saying anything. Finally, she said, "Thank you. That was very sweet."

With his best flirting smile, he said, "Thank you."

"What are you doing here?" she asked, not sure what else to say.

"I wanted to see you again and ask you to have dinner with me tonight."

Now she was flirting. "You could have called."

"Ah but I would have missed that beautiful performance."

"That wasn't a performance. That was just a rehearsal."

"Wow, I can't imagine what the real thing is like."

"Well then you must come to my concert in two weeks, and as you say, hear the real thing."

"You got a date, but I am not a true concert enthusiast. Will I understand what you are playing?'

"I am sure you will. You must understand I see myself as a beta in the music world. The in-between role is one I have always liked. I want to be the link, the medium between the composer and the audience. Most people who come to my piano concerts consider me a soloist, an alpha, my rhythms written to set the orchestra on its path, and I can cuff it when it strays. Of course, there is another alpha, the conductor whose every gesture and expression command obedience. Among wolves, the alpha male and the alpha female lead a pack. In the orchestra, they play out what Leonard Bernstein once called the age-old question: In a concerto, who is the boss, the soloist or the conductor?"

Wade listened and then said, "My money is on you, sweetheart, now about dinner . . . ?"

That night, they had dinner at a little Italian restaurant on the Upper East Side. Once again, it was one of Wade's favorite places, and when they entered the restaurant, the owner greeted him with a warm welcome and said to the maître d', "Make sure you-take-a-good-care of my friend, Wade." Katrina smiled. As they followed the maître d' to the table, Wade could feel the eyes of both the men and the women on Katrina. She was wearing a short Chanel cocktail dress, perfectly cut, perfectly simple, appropriate for dining out in any restaurant anywhere. She had straight black hair. When she walked, she held her head up high and had a smile on her face. In his mind, Wade was comparing her to Brenda. They were both beautiful women, both confident and very sure of themselves, yet they were also very different.

Once they were seated, the maître d' took their drink order, placed the menus on the table, and left. Wade said, "Well here we are again. It seems all I do is keep buying you dinner." Katrina laughed. It was a deep, hearty, infectious laugh, not at all phony. Then Wade leaned across the table and said, "You know you are a very beautiful woman." She smiled and said, "So I have been told."

As they sampled the Brie twists and picked delicately at their salads, the conversation was similar to their first dinner together, except this time they both went into more detail. Then out of the blue she said, "Can I ask you something personal?"

"I thought that was what we were both doing."

She smiled. "Are you involved with anyone?"

"Hmm, now that is personal."

"I'm sorry. I shouldn't have . . ."

He interrupted her. "No, no, that's quite all right. Actually no," he said hesitantly.

"That was a very weak no," she said.

"Before I explain, can I ask you the same question?"

"Yes, you can," she said, cupping her chin in her hands, "but first I need some more wine."

She then went on to tell Wade about a man she was involved with for almost three years. They lived together over two years. He was twenty years older than her. He was a booking agent she met after her first concert at Carnegie Hall. He convinced her to make him her manager. He told her that he could get her bookings all over the world, and after she signed with him, that's exactly what he did. He was her mentor; she trusted him, and eventually they became lovers. She didn't have a business manager. She used a stockbroker to handle her money. He told her that was a mistake. She didn't remember whose idea it was, but he ended up becoming her business manager and handled all of her money. About a year later, rumors started to circulate that he was passing bad checks. When she approached him, he was furious.

"How can you believe such lies?" he said to her. Then one day, she got a letter from the store where she bought her clothes. They said she owed them $6,000. They had not been paid in over six months, and when they called her manager, he always had an excuse. They felt bad writing to her, but they needed their money. When she asked him about it, he told her the check must have gotten lost in the mail. After that, she began to receive other letters and phone calls from different merchants, claiming they had never been paid. Finally, after several unpleasant scenes, he admitted he had invested the money for her, but the investments did not work out. She knew he was lying.

Then one day, she came home early from rehearsal, and there he was in their bed with the housekeeper. She became hysterical and insisted he move out. She retained a lawyer and found out that he had embezzled over $200,000 from her, her life's savings. Plus she owed different merchants almost $90,000.

Wade said, "I hope you fired the housekeeper."

"Are you kidding me? It is not easy to find good help these days."

She did have a sense of humor.

He reached across the table and took her hand. "I'm sorry, really."

She smiled. "That's okay. All of that is in the past, Wade."

"When did all of this happen?" Wade asked her.

"He moved out about a year ago. I am just now getting my feet back on the ground. So tell me, what's your story, big guy?"

CHAPTER THIRTY-TWO

BRENDA HAD COME home from the Dorothy Chandler Pavilion the night of the Academy Awards without celebrating and gone right to bed. She tossed and turned for hours, but she couldn't sleep. Every muscle in her body felt taut. It was a strenuous night.

Finally, she got up and made herself a cup of coffee. She felt impatient. Never in her wildest dreams could she have ever imagined a night like last night. The first film she ever worked on had been nominated for three different Academy Awards, and when the picture won for best director, she couldn't believe it. Of course, the award went to Arthur Cannon, but he insisted she join him on the stage for the presentation. She wished she could have shared the excitement with Wade and couldn't wait to call him. Unfortunately, she wasn't able to reach him.

She walked outside and stood on the balcony of her bungalow that she was renting on the beach in Santa Monica, looking into the dark night sky, her heart still beating rapidly as she thought about the night at the Academy Awards. "Enough," she said to herself. She went back into the bungalow, got dressed in white shorts and tennis shoes, and decided to go out for a run. As the red sun began to show itself over the horizon, she started to run. She ran faster and faster along the beach, trying to stay on the wet sand, trying to follow the coastline as the cold water washed over her feet. She had to clear her head. She had to separate reality from fantasy.

She thought about the studio. She thought about Arthur Cannon. But most of all, she thought about Wade, and she wondered if he was thinking about her. By the time she reached the large black boulders that meant the north beach ended, she was completely out of breath. She sat, trying to slow her heart down. She looked up as she heard the caw of seagulls as they swept down and seemed to glide along the water. She swallowed the lump in her throat, and suddenly realized what it was she really wanted. It wasn't the glitter of Hollywood or making movies;

it was Wade. She wished he wasn't so far away. "Stop," she told herself. "Think. It's up to you. It's your life. Live it the way you want."

It was midmorning before she walked back her bungalow. As she walked with her head held high and her eyes staring straight ahead, she knew what she had to do.

CHAPTER THIRTY-THREE

"SO TELL ME, what's your story, big guy?" Katrina asked again. Wade heard her the first time. He was just trying to decide what story to tell her.

"It's really not much of a story," he said. "I have been seeing someone off and on for the past six years, but we can't seem to catch up to one another."

"I'm not sure I understand," she said.

"I met someone when I was still in college. I was working here in New York during the summer, and we sort of connected. However, I went back to Las Vegas, and she lived and worked in New York. When I moved to New York, she was offered a job in LA as an assistant producer. It's kind of a long story. She is in the publishing business. She agreed to publish some woman's novel, but before it was ever published, she sold the story to a Hollywood producer."

"Wow, that sounds exciting," Katrina said.

"Yeah, well anyway, she is in LA, and I'm here."

"And . . .," Katrina said.

"The 'and' is I am here with you."

"Were you, or should I say, are you in love with her?"

"Would you believe me if I said I don't know?"

"I believe you are being as honest with me as you can. Let's make a deal. No more stories about the past. I like you, Wade, and I enjoy being with you. I know this is only our second date, but I am attracted to you. So let us see what happens. Deal?"

"Deal."

That night, when he drove her home, instead of leaning over and kissing her on the cheek like he did the first time, he got out and went around to the passenger side and opened the door. The apartment doorman was asleep in the lobby. Wade helped her out of the car and escorted her into the lobby, past the sleeping doorman, and up to her apartment.

Back in California, Brenda had made her decision. After the filming of the movie that she was working on was finished, she was returning to

New York and to Wade . . . permanently. She didn't want to call Wade and tell him until she told Arthur Cannon. She decided she would wait until the film was finished to tell him, which should be in about six weeks. She had waited this long. What difference would another two months make?

CHAPTER THIRTY-FOUR

WHEN KATRINA WOKE up, Wade was gone. There was a note on the pillow. "What a wonderful dinner, especially the dessert." She held the note to her lips and laughed. She couldn't wait to get up, get dressed, and go to rehearsal. Not so that she could rehearse, but because she knew she would hear from Wade. When she came out of thc shower, her phone was ringing. It was the doorman. "Miss Soloff, there is a delivery here for you. Can I bring it up?"

"Give me about twenty minutes, John."

"Yes Miss Soloff."

Twenty minutes later, the doorman arrived with two dozen champagne-colored roses in an extravagant arrangement with a note that read, "Dinner is at eight. I will pick you up at seven-thirty. Wear something sexy. On second thought, you better not. We may not make dinner if you do." The note was not signed.

The pattern was repeated the next day and the next. Never in her life had Katrina felt such a sense of excitement and anticipation. She called her sister who lived in Boston because she thought she would explode if she didn't tell someone how she felt. "But you have only known this man a couple of weeks, Katrina," her sister said when Katrina told her how she felt about Wade.

"I know it is crazy, but that's how I feel."

Then one night, the doorbell rang, and when Katrina opened the door, there was Wade, exactly on time, his thick brown hair slightly ruffled by the wind, his eyes smiling, this time holding a bottle of Louis Roederer Cristal in his hand. She put her arms around his neck and kissed him.

"Thank you, kind sir. Won't you come in? We are having dinner here tonight."

"You mean the lady cooks too?"

"I make one hell of a beef stroganoff," she said, still with her arms around his neck.

"Wade cupped her face in his hands and said, "Can we make love first?"

She moved away and said, "Dessert is after dinner, sir."

What Wade and Katrina had was a unique type of affair. She craved the sort of intimacy her parents had had with each other and that she had with them. Wade, on the other hand, didn't think he was capable of that type of intimacy. He knew that Katrina was falling in love with him, and as much as he cared for her, he wasn't sure that he was in love with her. There was always that thought lingering in the back of his mind, "*What would I do if Brenda suddenly came back to New York?*" He didn't want to do anything to hurt Katrina, but at the same time, he didn't want to end their relationship. Maybe it was love that he felt for her; he wasn't sure. He remembered what Brenda said about telling someone you loved them while eating a hot dog. He laughed to himself and thought maybe he would try that one day. All of this plus the pressure of his job made him perpetually restless.

The Monroe County bond deal was taking longer than he anticipated, and the banks that he had lined up for the rigged auction were becoming impatient. When he discussed this with Kline, he was told that sometimes it takes a little longer for the underwriter to sell all of the bonds, but that he should not worry, they will sell them. Then about a week later, he received a call from his contact in Florida that the bonds had been sold, and the money was in a tax-free account at the brokerage house. It was time for him to go to work.

Kline had instructed Wade to use certain code words when talking to the banks. When Wade asked him why, he said, "Just in case someone has bugged our phones." If there was ever a time for Wade to get out, that was it. The bank of choice to win the Monroe County account was The First National Bank and Trust Company of Iowa. The other two banks were much larger, and because of this, Wade had to do a selling job on the person at Monroe County who made the final decision. Of course, part of the scam was not to involve Monroe County. They were, in effect, "the mark." The next two weeks were very hectic, and Wade explained to Katrina that he could not see her every night, which had been their routine for the past several months. Of course, she understood but was disappointed. On the nights he did see her, sometimes they went to a neighborhood restaurant and other nights either she cooked or they ordered takeout, but in either case never too tired for dessert, to make love. She made it very easy for him.

To get the bond deal started, the first thing Wade did was call the three banks involved in the rigged auction. Unless you knew what the code words were, his conversation sounded like gibberish. He said things like "pull a nickel out" and "get to the next level" and "guide me down," and so on and so on. Actually what he was doing was guiding the banks along in an attempt to come up with the interest rate he was going to submit to Monroe County. The rate had to be very close to what Monroe County could get if they went out on their own. During this entire process, Wade never lost sight of the fact that what he and the banks were doing was outside the box, so to speak. Was it illegal? Kline assured him it was not illegal.

Once everyone was in agreement, Wade flew down to Florida to meet with the decision makers at Monroe County. Listening to what he told them would make you think he had worked his balls off to get them the best rate, when actually he knew what the rate was going to be at the start. Was there anything wrong with that? Wade didn't think there was. The two banks that didn't get the business this time around knew their time would come. The most difficult thing for him to come to grips with was why the world's most powerful banks were fixing prices of almost every adjustable-rate vehicle on earth, from mortgages and credit cards to bid rigging.

After Monroe County transferred the $100 million to First National Bank and Trust Company of Iowa, the bank sent AA Financial a check in the amount of $3 million. It was supposedly being paid to them for the consulting work they did for the bank on interest rate swaps, which of course, they had nothing to do with. Wade questioned Kline about this. His answer was, "This is the way it is done, kid." In addition, to show their appreciation, they sent Wade a check for $250,000. Wade told Kline he didn't want to accept it. "Give it to charity then. You can't insult them by returning it." He didn't donate it to charity.

To complete the circle, AA Financial sent the heads of the bond department of the other two banks that didn't get the Monroe County business to Las Vegas for an all-expense paid weekend vacation, complete with $1,000 in chips to play with and prostitutes at their disposal. All that time, Monroe County was thinking they got a great deal. All that time, Wade was wondering how legal it really was.

Wade was relaxing in his office, replaying in his mind the events of the last two weeks. All he could think was, "*Fucking unbelievable!*"

He was not religious nor was he a great moralist; however, he was not entirely comfortable with what had gone down. Was this the way every one of these deals would work? He knew the answer was yes. Is this what he wanted to do the rest of his life? He didn't have an answer for that one.

He was just about to leave to pick up Katrina and take her to dinner when his phone rang. It was Brenda. She told him she was coming back to New York.

When Wade arrived at Katrina's apartment to take her to dinner, he was unusually quiet. She knew he had been working on the bond issue for Monroe County. He often talked to her about it, and she assumed he was probably just worn out. She suggested they order in, but he told her he would rather go out for dinner. They went to one of their favorite places, a small French restaurant on the Lower East Side. After they were seated, and the waiter took their drink order, Katrina asked Wade if everything was all right. He looked at her for a moment and then said, "Brenda called me earlier to tell me she is coming back to New York. She said she expects to wind up her affairs in California and be back here in about a week." Katrina simply looked at him and then said, "And?"

"And nothing," Wade said very unconvincingly.

"Wade, neither of us has had any illusions. The past couple of months have been the happiest time of my life, but down deep, I knew sooner or later Brenda would be coming back to New York. I was hoping it would be later. I know whatever you two had is still unresolved and until that happens, we can never move on."

"Katrina, please don't say that . . ."

But before he could finish, she interrupted. "Wade, I love you, you know that, and I was hoping you could love me the same way."

This was not what he was expecting. He reached across the table and took her hand. "Katrina, I do love you."

She smiled while at the same time he could see the tears rolling down her cheeks. "I know you love me, Wade, but you are not in love with me. There is a difference. Wade, you are the sweetest, kindest man I have ever known, and I wouldn't trade these past couple of months for anything, but I am a realist. Until you can be sure that somewhere in the back of your mind you are not waiting for Brenda, I don't see how we can have a relationship."

By this time, the waiter arrived with their order. Seeing he was interrupting them, he quickly placed the food on the table and left.

"Katrina, all that I said was that she was coming back to New York, and you are assuming that means . . . I don't know what you are assuming."

"I am assuming you still care about her."

"That doesn't mean she is coming back because of me."

"But you do still care about her, don't you, Wade?"

"Shit, why does life have to be so complicated?"

"Nobody said it would be easy, my love."

Suddenly Wade's eyes began to tear up. How could she be so calm? Was she right about Brenda? Was she coming back to New York because of him? And did he still care for her?

Finally, she said, "Wade, I really don't feel like eating. Can we leave?"

"Absolutely," he said, and with that, he signaled for the waiter to bring his bill. Rather than wait to process his credit card, Wade gave the waiter cash and they left. Neither of them said much on the way home. When they arrived at her apartment, she reached over and took his arm before he turned off the motor. She smiled and said, "Would you mind if we skipped dessert tonight?" He had never felt so sad in all his life.

"Katrina . . ."

She interrupted him. "Go home and get some sleep. Call me in the morning, and Wade, regardless of what happens, I will be fine, really." The doorman opened the car door, and she got out. He watched her walk into her apartment building and realized he was crying.

After getting out of the car, Katrina did not look back. She didn't want Wade to see her crying. When she got to her apartment, she quickly undressed, then for no reason whatsoever, she washed her hair, rinsing it with lemon to bring out its highlights, took a long, luxurious bubble bath, gave herself a facial, a manicure, and a pedicure. Then she wrapped herself in a large, soft, fluffy white towel and got into bed. She thought about what she had said to Wade. They were the words that she had been saying over and over in her head for weeks, knowing that eventually she would have to say them to him. It wasn't that she was just giving him up without a fight, no way! But this was the only way she would be able to keep him. She had to gamble that what they had these past several months meant more to him than Brenda. She hoped she wasn't sending Wade to her on a silver platter. She would know one way or the other soon enough.

CHAPTER THIRTY-FIVE

WADE HAD HARDLY slept. At five o'clock, he finally got out of bed, showered, got dressed, and went to the office. He sat in his car in the parking lot, thinking about last night. If Brenda had told him she was returning to New York before he met Katrina, he probably would have been thrilled. Now he wasn't sure of anything. The parking lot guard knocked on the window of his car.

"You okay, Mr. Simon?"

Wade got out of his car. "Yeah, Charlie, I'm fine. Just couldn't sleep last night."

"Want some coffee, Mr. Simon?"

"Yeah thanks Charlie that's the best offer I've had so far today."

Wade juggled the coffee Charlie had given to him while he opened the front door of AA Financial. He looked around the office. It was dark and deserted. It looked different without the brokers at their desk, sort of eerie in a way. He went upstairs to his office, took out some files, and made himself busy, every so often looking at his watch to see if it was still too early to call Katrina. Finally, at nine o'clock, he called her. When she answered, he apologized for calling so early.

"I've been up for a while," she said. "As a matter of fact, you caught me just as I was getting ready to walk out the door."

"Really, where are you going this early?"

"I am going to meet the concert tour director from the New York Met. I decided to go on tour with the orchestra next week. They asked me a couple of weeks ago, but well that was before our talk last night."

Wade didn't know what to say. Was he losing her? Was Brenda coming back into his life? He had enough shit going on in his life with AA Financial; he surely didn't need this.

"Are you there Wade?"

"Yeah, yeah, I'm here. It's just that I don't know what to say about us?"

"That's part of the reason I'm going on tour, Wade. This will give you time to decide if there is still anything between you and Brenda. I will be away about six weeks. When I come back we can decide then if there still is an 'us."

"Wow, six weeks, that's a long time. You really play hardball, don't you?"

"Not really, Wade."

"Where will the tour take you?"

"I know we go to London first and then to France. I'm not sure where we go after that. I will know better when I meet with the concert tour director and go over the itinerary."

"Will I get to see you before you leave?"

She hesitated. "I don't know, Wade. I have a lot to do before we leave."

"I really want to see you before you leave, Katrina."

"Okay, what do you say we have dinner at my apartment tomorrow night?"

He felt like a schoolboy asking a girl on his first date.

He really didn't get much work done that day or the next. He was thinking about his dinner date with Katrina. He was also thinking about what was going to happen when Brenda came back to New York.

When he arrived at Katrina's apartment the following day, he was much more relaxed. Maybe that was because he had downed three vodka martinis a couple of hours earlier. She greeted him at the door wearing a Dior sweat suit. On anybody else, it would have appeared she was preparing to go to the gym and work out, but on her, it looked sexy. It was in a rich deep blue that complemented her pale azure eyes, brought out the creamy texture of her skin and the highlights in her dark, straight hair. He put his arms around her and pulled her close. "I have missed you," he said. She couldn't resist as she laughingly said, "I know. I can feel how much you missed me."

He moved away just a bit, smiled and said, "So much for romance."

"Come in before the neighbors start to talk."

They went into the kitchen where he opened a bottle of wine while she finished making the salad. She told him about the tour. He could tell she was genuinely excited. She had made two previous world tours, so she knew the routine. She told him she would be rehearsing for the next five days all day long, getting ready for the trip. Between rehearsing, putting together her wardrobe, tidying up the details in her apartment for the time she would be away, she told Wade she would not be able to see him again before she left. He was, of course, disappointed.

When they finished dinner, they took their coffee and brandy into the den and sat on the couch.

He said, "What would you say if I asked you not to go on this tour?"

"Are you asking me not to go?"

He looked at her and smiled. "No, I guess not."

She looked at her watch and said, "Wade, I have to be up really early tomorrow, and I have a long day . . ." Before she could finish, he leaned over and kissed her. "You have a wonderful trip, and when you return, I will be here."

She returned his kiss and let it linger for several moments then moved away and took his hand as they both got up from the sofa and walked to the door. He took her in arms and kissed her again, this time both of them lingering a little longer. Finally, she moved away, opened the door, and said, "I hope you will be here when I return, Wade." He didn't answer. He simply put his fingers to his mouth and blew her a kiss, and then he was gone. After the door to the apartment had closed, she stood on the inside, leaning her head on the door, tears running softly down her face. On the other side of the door in the hallway, Wade stood staring at the door, wishing he could see through to the other side. Then he heard her put the night latch on the door, and he turned and walked to the elevator.

CHAPTER THIRTY-SIX

WHEN HE ARRIVED at his office the next morning, he had two messages from the previous day. One was from Joe Cantor, the stockbroker who had befriended him the first summer he went to work at AA Financial. It was through him that he had met Brenda. He wanted Wade to call him; he said it was important. Joe had left AA sometime between the time Wade first met him and the second summer he went to work at AA. The other message was from Louie Santino. His message simply read, "Call me when you have a chance." Wade recognized the telephone number as being in Louie's office in California. With the three-hour difference in time, it was too early to call him, so he called Joe Cantor. He answered on the first ring.

"Hey, Joe, it's Wade. How are you?"

"I'm good, Wade. Thanks for getting back so quick."

He sounded kind of strange. "Is everything okay, Joe? You sound kind of funny."

"Yeah, Wade, I'm fine. I'm just a little bit jammed up right now.

"Where are you? Where am I calling you?"

"Not important Wade. I'll explain it all to you later."

"You'll explain what, Joe? What the hell is going on?"

"Wade, I really need to see you. It's important, but it's something we can't talk about on the phone."

"Don't tell me you're pregnant?"

Joe loosened up a little. "Huh, that would be easy. I could get an abortion. Look, Wade, I know it's short notice, but I really need to see you. Any chance we can meet for dinner tonight?"

Wade hesitated for a second then agreed. "Where do you want to meet?"

"How about Sparks Steak House at five o'clock?'

"Okay, Joe, you got a date. I'll see you there."

Later that day at four forty-five, Wade crossed one the most famous pieces of sidewalk in Manhattan and entered the bar of Sparks Steak House, a restaurant known the world over for the gangster who'd died where Wade had just tread. He was well aware of the history of Sparks and thought to himself that Joe had a weird sense of humor to pick it for dinner. Nearly fifteen years earlier, around Christmas 1985, the then-boss of the Gambino crime family, Paul Castellano, had a dinner reservation at Sparks. He didn't quite make it. On the sidewalk in front, four men wearing long coats and black Russian hats shot down Big Paulie and his driver while shoppers with bags of Christmas gifts in hand ran for cover. There lay Big Paulie on the cold ground in his expensive winter coat, blood oozing, his reign finished, and Sparks's reputation sealed. Guides on tourist buses pointed it out. Effete restaurant guides described it as a macho bastion with too much testosterone, but it just happened to be one of Joe Cantor's favorite restaurants. It was real New York, not Soho or Tribeca or any of those other precious neighborhoods where a lot of phonies hung out. This was a place where real men ate red meat and drank red wine and reveled in whatever little success they had achieved on their own, not because somebody gave it to them.

When Wade walked into Sparks, he didn't see Joe, so he sat down at the bar and ordered an Absolut on the rocks with a lot of olives. This was early in the evening on a Thursday in August, and Manhattan wasn't its usual bustling self, still the bar was unusually crowded. Wade chatted with the bartender and checked his cell phone voice mail. There was a message from his office that Joe had called and said he was running a few minutes late. By the time he finished his drink, he felt a hand on his shoulder.

"Wade good to see you. Sorry I'm late."

Wade turned around and greeted his old friend. "You haven't changed a bit." Then they exchanged hugs. The bartender leaned over and with a smile said. "Can I get you two ladies something to drink?" This was Sparks!

Wade ordered another Absolut, and Joe had a draft beer. After a few minutes of small talk, Joe suggested they move to a table so that they could talk in private. He signaled for the hostess who showed them to a booth in the back part of the restaurant. Joe nodded his approval, and after she left, he leaned over the table and said, "Wade, what I'm about to tell you is very confidential. You can't tell a living soul. If you ever do tell anyone, I will deny we ever spoke."

"Jesus Christ, Joe, what the hell is the matter with you? You know you can trust me. I don't know what the fuck it is you are going to tell me, but it sounds like something maybe I don't want to hear."

"Trust me, Wade. You want to hear it."

"Okay, go ahead. Shoot!"

"All right here it is." Joe took his wallet out of his pocket, opened it, and laid it on the table. In the middle of his wallet was a gold badge. Wade looked at the badge and then back at Louie. "So you got a Dick Tracey badge. Good for you."

"It's not a Dick Tracey badge, Wade. It's an F.B.I. badge. I work for the bureau. F.B.I. I work in the F.B.I. corporate fraud department. I started working for them as a clerk on the midnight shift while still in college. After graduation, I applied for a full-time position. I was lucky enough to qualify for their federal law enforcement training program, which included attaining several securities industry licenses. It wasn't long after that I was asked to work undercover on Wall Street to investigate the infiltration of organized crime. When we first met at AA Financial, I was working there undercover, trying to gather evidence of stock fraud. The agency had received a number of complaints from people who claimed they were duped by AA Financial into buying worthless securities. As it turned out, I wasn't able to come up with anything, so the department dropped the investigation. However, the reason I'm talking to you now is because we're looking at AA again, this time with some pretty incriminating stuff. I don't know how much you really know about what goes on there, but believe me when I tell you this guy Albert Kline is a bad guy."

Wade just stared at his friend then finally said, "This is a practical joke. Right, Joe?"

"It is no joke, Wade."

CHAPTER THIRTY-SEVEN

BY THE TIME Wade got home, it was almost ten o'clock. The phone was ringing as he walked in. It was Louie. "Hey, buddy, called you yesterday. Did you get my message?"

"Yeah, Louie, I did. Sorry I didn't get back to you. I was kind of tied up all day."

"No sweat. What's going on in the big city?"

"Oh a little bit of this and a little bit of that, you know, the same old shit."

"Yeah the same here however I do have some good news for you." After his dinner meeting with Joe, Wade thought he could use some good news.

"I'm moving to New York."

"You're kidding me," Wade said.

"Nope, I should be there sometime next week."

"So soon I mean, it's great you will be here, but what about your business and Gary?"

"Well it's kind of a long story, but the short version is Gary and I split up about two months ago."

"Oh I'm sorry to hear that, Louie. I thought you guys were good together."

"Yeah, we were, but sometimes things have a way of changing. Don't misunderstand me. We're still friends. It's just that we're not lovers anymore. Can you handle that boychick?"

Wade laughed, "Your Jewish is pretty good."

"Look who taught me."

"One word what can I tell you? What about the business, Louie? What's going to happen?"

"That was part of the reason for the breakup. We had artistic differences, so I decided to get out. Gary agreed to buy me out. He will do fine without me. When I told my father, he suggested I call you and see about coming to work at AA Financial. What do you think?" Wade didn't know why, but he didn't like that. However, he told his old friend that it would be great.

"So tell me, Wade, how is your love life?"

"Funny you should ask."

"Oh that doesn't sound good."

"No, on the contrary, Louie, it's a good thing. Brenda called to tell me she is moving back to New York."

"Wow that does sound like good news. Now I will finally get to meet her."

"Yeah, but that's only part of the good news. I met someone else a couple of months ago, and now I'm not so sure how I feel about Brenda or the fact she is coming back to New York."

"That sounds complicated. What's the deal with your new squeeze?"

Wade laughed. "That's a little bit complicated too. She is a concert pianist, and she is going to Europe on tour for about six weeks. She wants to give me time to be sure I'm over Brenda."

"Jesus, your team sure has funny rules. You should join my team. I think you and I would get along great."

"Yeah, I've been thinking about that. It might take all the pressure off." They both laughed.

"So tell me, when I come to New York, do I have a job? I'm a quick learner."

"Absolutely, pal, I'm looking forward to it."

"Okay, then I'll keep you posted and, Wade, all I can tell you about your love life is that your heart will tell you which girl is the right one."

"From your mouth to god's ears Louie."

After he hung up the phone, Wade sat back in the chair and replayed in his mind what Joe Cantor had told him earlier in the evening.

Joe told him that his department was working with the Manhattan district attorney's office and the New York attorney general's office, investigating one of the large New York banks. The investigation started almost three years ago when an executive of the bank went to the district attorney's office with the story that the bank was involved in collusion with other banks in fixing interest rates. He told them it was his job to determine the interest rates that the bank would pay to municipalities when they invested their funds with the bank. This was money the municipality had raised by issuing bonds to build either schools or some other public endeavor. However, after he developed the rate he thought the bank should pay, his boss would tell him they had to wait until they found out what the competing banks were offering. He didn't understand. That's when his superior told him the banks had an agreement to divide the business, so to speak. His bank would get the business from one municipality then a competing bank would get another, and so on. He asked about the legality, and he was told, "This is done all the time."

When the attorney general's office asked him how he could substantiate this, he told them all of the bank's telephone calls were recorded. At that point, the district attorney became involved and subsequently he called in our people to help with the investigation. The question we all had was, "Would anyone be stupid enough to commit a crime by phone when there was a big sticker on the phones that said all calls were being recorded?" The answer was they probably thought their conversations on the tapes could hardly suggest a secret conspiracy, since all the banks were doing it.

After we subpoenaed the tapes from the bank that is when we discovered AA Financial was in on the interest rate fix. They were supposed to be getting the best possible rate for the municipality when all the time they were in bed with the banks, getting a kickback for awarding the business to a particular bank. Wade couldn't understand why in all this time the F.B.I. or the state attorney general's office hadn't done something about this. Joe explained it was a very complicated and complex matter, and before they brought any charges, they wanted to have an airtight case. And when there are three different agencies involved, the red tape takes over. Then Joe dropped the real bomb. He told Wade what they really needed was someone on the inside at AA Financial, someone who could corroborate the phone tapes. Wade sat for a minute thinking about all that Joe had just told him and then said, "Are you asking me to become an informant for the F.B.I.?" Joe simply said, "That is entirely up to you."

Of course, Wade never told Joe that he had just put together a deal with a bank in Iowa and Monroe County, doing exactly what he said they were investigating. He wondered if Joe knew that, probably not. The tapes Joe had were from an earlier deal and a different bank.

CHAPTER THIRTY-EIGHT

THE FIELD OFFICE of the F.B.I. sits a block west of Foley Square, where Roman- and Greek-inspired courthouses with four-story colonnades loom over a city of judicial institutions in which the biggest of America's financial crimes are prosecuted. Seated in conference room 26, Joe Cantor and his immediate superior, Chief Agent Herman Carroll, sat talking with David Grimm from the attorney general's office and Willie Holland, an assistant prosecuting attorney from the district attorney's office.

Herman Carroll: "So tell me, Joe, what have we got? Did your friend agree to work with us?"

Joe: "Not really, Herman. I told him what was happening, but he wouldn't commit."

David Grimm: "Did you actually ask him, Joe?"

Joe: "I have to be honest with you. I didn't."

Herman Carroll: "What do you mean you didn't ask him? Wasn't that the purpose of the meeting? Unless we get somebody inside of AA, we don't have a case."

Joe: "I know, but the way things went, I didn't think that I could come right out and ask him. However, I am sure he understood that is what we want him to do."

David Grimm: "Joe, let me ask you something, when you were undercover at AA a couple years ago, do you think you ever slipped, and maybe this guy Wade Simon doesn't trust you?"

Herman Carroll: "C'mon, David, that's out of line."

David Grimm: "I'm just asking. Maybe that is the reason he won't commit."

Joe didn't like David. He was snotty and officious. "I'm a professional, David. In all the years I've worked undercover, I have never, as you put it, slipped."

David Grimm: "No offense, Joe, just asking."

Herman Carroll: "Joe was the first and only agent to successfully infiltrate Wall Street. You know as well as me, David, Joe has been responsible for obtaining evidence against more than thirty individuals committing frauds on Wall Street, spanning the spectrum from stock manipulation and currency scams to money laundering."

Joe wanted to ask David how many cases his office brought to trial and got convictions. He knew the answer: damn few!

David Grimm: "I know that, and that's the reason I think we should concentrate on having him work undercover on the kind of cases where we have a good chance of prosecuting. Look, guys, we have enough other shit going on that we don't need to spend all of our time and manpower on something that we may not be able to prove anyhow. I think we should put our efforts into nailing someone like Paul Samertina. Here is a guy who is running a scam operation right under our nose and racking in hundreds of millions of dollars a month. I say we set up a sting and bust this bastard. Between you and me, I think this shit with the banks is small potatoes compared to Samertina's operation."

Joe stood up, red-faced. "Are you kidding me, David? The banks are stealing millions, and AA Financial is taking a piece of that. How can you say that is small potatoes?"

Herman Carroll: "Relax, Joe. David is right. We should concentrate our efforts on Paul Samertina. Who knows? He may lead us to some other organized crime figures, and AA Financial will be there when we're ready. Tell you what, in the meantime, why don't you rekindle your relationship with this Wade Simon, and if you happen to come up with something, well we can take another look at it. What do you say?"

Joe shook his head. "Okay, if that's your decision, but now that he knows I am F.B.I., I don't know how close I can get."

The meeting was over.

Joe returned to his office, disappointed that the investigation of AA Financial had been put on hold once again. Unlike the time he worked there undercover, this time around, the agency had a lot of good stuff. He couldn't understand why David Grimm didn't want to pursue it. It didn't make sense. Then suddenly it hit him like a bolt of lightning. Grimm was in Albert Kline's pocket! He had to be! Why else would he not want to move ahead? It was bullshit to say, "We don't have enough evidence to get an indictment!" He sat and thought about it some more. What was Grimm's job? He was an assistant to the director of the organized crime unit. Not the top dog, but high enough to do Kline and his gang some good. If this actually was the case, did Wade know?

He didn't think so. "I'll be a son of a bitch," he said in a whisper. Should he bring this to his boss, Herman Carroll? How could he? He had no proof; it was just his gut. Just then his phone rang. It was David Grimm.

"Joe, you got a couple minutes? I want to talk to you before I go back to Albany."

"Sure David. Where are you?"

"I'm still in the conference room. I'll come over to your office. See you in a minute."

Joe didn't have time to think about what he wanted to say to him because it really only took David Grimm a minute to walk to his office from conference room 26.

"What's up, David?"

"I just wanted to talk to you again about the AA Financial investigation."

"Sure, what's on your mind?'

"Well I didn't want you to think that I was condoning what the banks were doing. It's just we have so many other irons in the fire that we have to set our priorities." Joe thought this guy said "the banks," he didn't say anything about AA Financial.

"I understand that, David, and I can appreciate your focus is on organized crime's invasion of Wall Street, but I honestly believe AA Financial is into a lot more illegal stuff than just what we heard on the bank tapes."

"We don't know that for a fact, do we, Joe?"

"No, but when I worked there undercover, there were things going on that were kept from the brokers, things that normally the broker should know about."

"Joe, it is possible that was their style of management, nothing more."

"Yeah, that is possible, but I don't think so. You do know, of course, that one of the major stockholders in AA is a guy by the name of Angelo Santino? You know who he is?'

"Absolutely, and we have looked into his involvement in the past and have never been able to come up with anything."

Wade thought to himself, "*This bastard has an answer for everything when it comes to AA.*"

"In any event, Joe, I just wanted you to know my job is to clean up Wall Street, and if we find it makes sense to reopen the investigation against AA Financial, you can be sure we will do just that. One more thing, if you do come up with anything, I would appreciate if you keep me in the loop."

Joe thought, "*How smart is this guy? In his own slick way, he has said the investigation against AA was closed, finished. Get on with your life. But at the same time, "keep me posted!" I'll be a son of a bitch!*"

"Well I certainly appreciate your taking the time to talk about this, David, and if I hear anything that I think you should know, I will call you."

"That's great, Joe. I knew you would understand."

After David Grimm left the office, Joe went to his computer. He wanted to see how many open cases the attorney general's office was working on. There were more open cases than there were convictions. There was also a pattern. Whenever Grimm was directly involved, the investigation seemed to get derailed. Then he cross-checked the files and looked at the past investigation of Angelo Santino. "*What a joke,*" Joe thought. Then he pulled up the Paul Samertina file. The file showed that the investigation has been ongoing for almost three years, and there was a note in the file from Grimm stating that there was not sufficient documentation to bring formal charges. "*Is this guy kidding or what?*" Joe sat looking at the computer screen, then after several minutes, he picked up the telephone and called Wade. He had made his decision.

CHAPTER THIRTY-NINE

WHEN WADE RECEIVED Joe's telephone call, he told him there was nothing for them to talk about. Joe insisted. He said that things had changed, and it was important they meet. "That is what you said the first time you called me."

"I know," Joe said, "but this is different. Please believe me."

Wade was up to his ass in work, and besides, Brenda was due in New York the next day, and he sure as hell was not going to put off seeing her so that he could meet with Joe. There was also another problem. Wade hadn't told Albert Kline about his meeting with Joe. Not telling him was almost the same as agreeing to help Joe. Finally, after his third request, Wade agreed to meet him the day after tomorrow. He had never asked Joe if he was still seeing the same girl that he was with the night he met Brenda. He wasn't.

That night, he had difficulty sleeping, which was becoming a habit. He was up, showered, shaved, and dressed before seven o'clock. He planned to go to the office for a couple of hours and then pick up Brenda at the airport at noon. He had the use of Albert Kline's limo and driver while he was in Paris with his wife. He wasn't due back in New York for several weeks, which would give Wade time to talk to Joe again and then decide what he wanted to tell Kline. Things were becoming very complicated.

To add to the mix, Louie was due to arrive in New York within the next couple of weeks, and Wade didn't think that was a coincidence. He remembered Louie's involvement with the skimming of the casino in Vegas. "How involved was Louie in all of this? And why didn't Louie's father simply call Kline and tell him he wanted him to give his kid a job? What was the charade with Louie asking him? Did Kline even know that Louie was coming to work at AA? Wade knew there was a lot going on at AA that he knew nothing about. And exactally what was Louie's father's involvement in this whole thing? And more to the point, how involved was he in this whole thing? Wade thought to himself, "*What whole thing? I don't even know what this whole thing is.*" He looked at his watch. It was time to leave for the airport. He would have to put all of these things on hold.

Whoever said that money doesn't have privileges didn't have money. When Wade arrived at the American Airlines Terminal at Kennedy Airport, there was an American Airline representative waiting to greet him and escort him personally to the American Airlines VIP lounge. Once there, he was shown to a private suite within the VIP lounge where he waited for Brenda. About half an hour later, Brenda was escorted into the private suite by a very pretty American Airlines stewardess. Wade thought to himself, "*This is the only way to fly!*"

For a short moment, he thought he was hallucinating. She looked so beautiful. She was wearing a white two-piece Calvin Kline pantsuit. In her ears, there was a pair of sapphire and diamond earrings. On the label of her jacket was a diamond leopard pin with sapphire spots and ruby eyes. The only word to describe her was radiant. She smiled at him with her beautiful eyes and said, "I missed you."

"Back at you," he said, standing there holding a bottle of Veuve Clicquot in one hand and a bouquet of pink roses in the other. She came closer and put her arms around him, and he returned her embrace, still holding the bottle of Veuve and the roses.

"Put those damn things down and hold me tight," she said laughingly.

He put the bottle and the roses on a table and obeyed her command. Wrapped in each other's arms, they kissed, each waiting for the other to say something. Finally, the stewardess who had escorted Brenda to the VIP suite very meekly said, "Is there anything I can get you?" Wade released Brenda, smiled at the pretty young stewardess, and said, "You can pour some cold water on us if you like."

By the time they got to the limo, Brenda's luggage was already in the car, courtesy of American Airlines' VIP service. When they got in the limo, the driver had a Barbara Streisand tape playing. Somehow he knew that was one of Brenda's favorites. She snuggled up close to Wade and whispered, "Do you think we can make love here in the backseat, or is that not included in the VIP service?" He leaned over and kissed her. He wasn't thinking about Katrina, or for that matter, anything else except the moment. She looked at him and smiled. Wade said, "You look great. California was good to you."

When they arrived at her apartment building and the driver opened the limo door, the two of them had their arms around each other in a bear hug. The driver wasn't sure what to do when Wade said laughing, "We'll be finished in a minute. Just hang on there." Brenda started to laugh and pushed him away. She had arranged for someone to come in and clean her apartment, stock the refrigerator and pantry with food, make sure there was a bucket of ice on the bar and plenty of booze. When they walked into the apartment, Wade said, "It looks like you never were away."

"That's the way it should be," she said as she took his hand and led him into the bedroom. It was at that point that he thought about Katrina and felt guilty. She saw the strange look on his face and asked if he was okay.

"Yeah, baby, it's just that I think we need to talk about something first."

"Is it that you want to tell me about the woman you have been seeing?"

He looked at her with a blank stare. She held his hand and walked with him to the bed. "Sit," she said. "When I told my father that I was coming back to New York for good, he mentioned to me that you were seeing someone. Is that what you want to talk about?"

Wade got up from the bed and walked to the window, then turned around and said, "With all due respect, Brenda, I don't understand why he thought it was necessary to tell you that."

"Wade, come on. After all, he is my father. He thought that if I was coming back to New York because of you, I should know."

"Did you come back to New York because of me?"

She walked over to the window, put her hands on his cheeks, kissed him gently on the mouth, and whispered, "Yes."

Wade had waited a long time for her to say that, and now that she did, he wasn't sure if that is what he wanted to hear. He looked at her. She was so charming and so lovable. "*Damn*," he thought, "*is it possible to love two women at the same time?*" He supposed a lot of men did, but he had trouble committing to one. Yet he had two women who he thought loved him unconditionally. They were both sensual worldly, and successful in their chosen field. What more could he ask for? Why couldn't he decide? Maybe it was because he was perpetually restless. Whatever deal or coup he pulled off at work didn't seem to satisfy him.

He always wanted more. In the back of his mind, he felt that life was out to shortchange him. Maybe that was because of his father. Maybe he was driven by the ambition to be better than his father. Who knows? And now, since speaking with Joe, he couldn't help wondering who Albert Kline really was. Surely not the man he thought he was when he first met him. And how would that affect any long-term relationship with Brenda? What confused him was that when he was with Katrina, he didn't think about any of this. Of course, she had no ties with his job or Albert Kline. Wow, was he fucked up? Here he was in the bedroom with a beautiful woman who couldn't wait for him to make love to her, and all he was doing was trying to psychoanalyze himself. Brenda was waiting for him to say something. He was waiting himself to say something, then finally, he did. "Let's talk, babe."

Brenda knew there was a lot more going on in Wade's head than just wanting to talk about someone he was dating while she was in California. After all, she didn't sit home every night either when she was there. Had she made a mistake coming back to New York, thinking Wade was waiting for her with open arms? She looked at him, and he looked sad. She never saw that look on him before. It made her sad too. She took him by the hand and walked back into the living room. "Tell you what, Wade, why don't we take a time-out? I could use a hot bath and a short nap after the long trip. You go and do what you do during the day and then come back here around eight. I will call Le Cirque and have them deliver dinner, then after dinner, we can talk. How does that sound?"

"Does that include dessert?" *Shit*, he thought to himself. "*That's the same line I used on Katrina!*"

"We'll see how dinner and the talk go," she said with a smile then kissed him gently and held him tight for several seconds. When he left the apartment, she leaned against the door and wondered if she had lost him. She would know one way or the other soon enough.

Sitting in the limo, Wade began to think again about all that was going on and came to the conclusion that there was some pretty serious shit at stake. First off, the F.B.I. was involved. If what AA and he were doing was, as a matter of fact, illegal, that could mean jail time. And Louie's father, he was Mafia, not make-believe Mafia, but the real thing. And who was behind the skimming in the casino in Las Vegas? And where did Sal Maggio fit in? How involved was he in all of that? It was then he knew he had to have answers to all of these questions before deciding who he wanted to spend the rest of his life with. He wasn't sure how he got to this point in his life, but he knew damn well that before he went any further, he had to know what was at stake, and more importantly, who all the players were. He reached for the phone in the limo and called Brenda. Hopefully he could reach her before she took her bath. She answered on the second ring.

"You caught me without any clothes on. What good timing," she said.

Normally Wade would have had a smart comeback, but there were too many other things swirling around in his head. He explained to Brenda that he had a lot of work to do tonight before an important meeting in the morning and hoped they could postpone their reunion until tomorrow night. She was disappointed but said okay. Wade had decided he needed to meet with Joe before talking to Brenda. There were too many unanswered questions.

When he got back to his office, he decided to look at the files from some of the most recent interest auctions that AA was involved in. There definitely was a pattern. It was evident the business was awarded to different banks almost systematically. And just about every large bank was on the list. Was it possible America's leading financial institutions were in on the scam? According to what Wade saw, the answer had to be yes. He left his office and went downstairs where the salesmen were on the phone looking for new accounts. They called themselves brokers. Most of them had no idea what a broker really was. These were either ambitious preppies who thought they were hot shit or young guys from the boroughs or close suburbs some who had gone to community college or no college at all. Most of them spoke with heavy New York accents, which they didn't try to hide when selling on the phone. They were riding the end of an era, the penny-stock era. Who did he think he was kidding? AA Financial was nothing more than a fancy chop shop. Most of the guys working for AA could be selling pools or roof siding for all they cared. No place else could these guys make the kind of money they were making here. Wade walked around the room and listened, and for the first time, he really heard the bullshit these guys were telling innocent, hardworking people in an effort to separate them from their life savings. Each salesman had a dark blue three-ring binder that was their client list. AA continually updated these books with leads. The better the salesman, the better the lead. Wade thought to himself, "*What a shitty way to make money, lots and lots of money!*"

CHAPTER FORTY

JOE TOLD WADE that he would meet him for lunch at a restaurant on Henry Street in Brooklyn. He wanted to go someplace where nobody knew either one of them and didn't want to take the chance they would be seen by anyone they knew. He was very secretive about the whole thing. Wade arrived a little after noon. Joe was already there, seated in a booth at the rear of the restaurant. It was early, plus they didn't do a large lunch business, so there were not many people in the restaurant. Wade sat down. The waitress came over with a coffeepot, and Wade nodded. She poured the coffee and left. After she was out of earshot, Joe leaned over the table and said, "I'm leaving the bureau, Wade. I handed in my resignation this morning."

Wade sipped some of his coffee and stared at his friend for a couple of seconds then in a monotone, said, "Okay, so what's the punch line?"

"No punch line, Wade. I'm out. I've been with the bureau almost nine years, Wade. Do you know how much I earn?" It was a rhetorical question. "I make $89,987.60 a year. I bet you make more than that in a month."

Wade couldn't resist. "Not quite but close."

"Yeah, that's what I mean. Wade, I drive a five-year-old Volva. I have never owned a new car in my life. I buy my clothes at Feline's Basement. I still have about two years left on my student loan from college, and I can't remember the last time I had a real vacation. When I work undercover, I get extra pay, but by the time they take out taxes, it doesn't amount to shit. I'm thirty-one years old, and I got all of $110,000 saved in my IRA, big fucking deal.

"Nothing personal, but there are punks in your business who earn four or five times a year what I earn, drive BMWs and would sell out their mother if it meant they made a commission."

"Don't you think that's exaggerating a little bit, Joe? There are a lot of good hardworking people in the business."

"Maybe, Wade, but I have seen these guys. Most of the ones I have met are hustlers and con men. Think about it. You don't need an MBA to be successful selling penny stocks or screaming out orders on the exchange floor. What you need is a certain inborn characteristic that comes from being a street guy. If you have the ability to be a smooth talker, if you are able to persuade someone to buy what you are selling, well that's all you really need to be in this business.

"Wade, I have always been a company man, never once have I said no when they asked me to do something, and I have never once taken a pay-off, and trust me when I tell you I have had plenty of opportunities. But that's all over. I bust my ass trying to do the right thing while some asshole in the attorney general's office is sitting up in Albany on the pad for who knows how many guys, including your guy at AA Financial."

"What are you talking about, Joe?"

"They pulled the investigation of your company, said there wasn't enough evidence to stay on it."

"So?"

"So that's bullshit. We have tapes that prove your guy was involved in rigging the bids from the bank. But this asshole from Albany said to drop it. I am sure Albert Kline has gotten to him."

"Look, Joe, I don't want to know who you're talking about, or for that matter, I really don't want to listen to any of this. I agreed to meet with you because there are some questions that need answers. Now I don't know where you are going with all this, but . . . well to be honest with you . . . I mean, how do I know what you're telling me is the truth? How do I know you're not trying to con me in . . . ?"

"Wade, I wouldn't do that. You know better. When I spoke to you the last time, I was up front. I don't play any other way. And after I tell you why I really asked you to meet me, I'll try to answer whatever questions you have, okay?"

"Okay, so all that you're saying is true. Why are you telling it to me?"

"I'll tell you why in a minute, but I want you to know the main reason I made the decision to resign is because of this guy in the attorney general's office. I want to nail his ass. It's not the money. Sure I wouldn't mind a piece of the pie along the way, but that's not the main reason I resigned. " Wade had the feeling the main reason . . . was the money.

"You lost me, Joe. I don't have a fucking clue what you are talking about."

"Okay, listen. The F.B.I. has more than fifteen thousand confidential human sources, people who feed them information for a fee. The Drug

Enforcement Administration has its own tipsters that they pay, as do the Secret Service, the Bureau of Alcohol, the Tobacco and Firearms Department, and the Department of Explosives. Over all, the Justice Department pays informants over a hundred million dollars a year. A hundred million dollars a year, Wade, and most of that money is being paid to convicted felons, ex-mob guys and the like. And I earn less than a hundred grand a year. Something is wrong with that picture. Once my resignation is officially accepted, I'm going to offer my services to the SEC and the bureau as an independent informer. They know that I know where all the bodies are buried. They can hire me as an independent informer to do things their own people can't do or are ordered not to do. I am sure the SEC would jump at the chance to put somebody inside one of the mob-owned firms or set up a sting to bust some of the bad guys."

"Jesus Christ, Joe, you're beginning to sound a little bit paranoid."

"I know this might sound like something out of the Godfather or James Bond and be difficult for you to believe, but trust me, Wade, you have no idea the millions, I should say billions of dollars, that is made illegally on Wall Street."

"Joe, you're right. I can't believe that. You may be right about a lot of guys pushing the envelope or taking advantage of the loopholes, but the way you're talking, everything that happens on Wall Street is a scam. You know better than that, Joe. For Christ's sake, Joe, when you went undercover at our place, you said you couldn't find anything illegal, and with all due respect, I agree we may push the envelope a little."

"Wade, I'm not saying everything. I'm saying a lot. And what I said about your joint was that I couldn't come up with anything that warranted a further investigation. That doesn't mean I think your place is squeaky clean."

"All right, I'll play along. So there are a bunch of crooks on Wall Street, and you are going to put on a cape and go fight crime. But tell me, what is the bit about you taking a piece of the pie?"

Joe looked annoyed at Wade's snide remark. "The six months that I worked at your place undercover, I earned over $50,000 in commissions, and I was mostly pitching legit stuff. Just imagine how much I could have earned selling some of those phony IPOs."

"What do mean mostly legit? And you know damn well we don't sell phony IPOs, and the reason you didn't get any is because they're not given to new salesmen. And be honest, Joe, while you were undercover, did you find anybody pitching illicit securities? I don't think so."

"Tell me about the bid rigging Wade do you think that's legal?"

"I don't know what you're talking about, Joe."

"C'mon, Wade, this is me. And what about the bonus stock everybody got from that phony IPO the first summer you were there? Give me a break, Wade."

"Maybe there are some things that are questionable, but by the same token, did you ever stop to think that maybe that is the way Wall Street operates? That is possible, you know."

"You are dreaming, Wade, but that's not important right now. What I'm saying is I didn't get to keep any of that money. I had to turn it over to the bureau. If I was operating as an independent, I get to keep whatever I earn whether I'm working undercover or setting up a sting."

"I can't believe that, Joe."

"Trust me. What I'm telling you is true. How do you say it in Jewish? It's the emus (the truth).

"Okay, Joe, so you are going to help the government bust some of the bad guys, and along the way you're going to get rich. I still don't understand what all of that has to do with me."

"Nothing directly really, Wade, but bear with me. I found out that during the last three years, the Justice Department and the SEC's Fraud Division have secretly been building a case against two of the largest Wall Street brokerage houses and seven of the country's largest banks. Included in the investigation is one Louie Malpeso, a reputed member of the Colombo crime family. If this case is successful, it will be a major strike against organized crime on Wall Street. They have some pretty strong evidence that Malpeso has infiltrated one of Wall Street's largest brokerage firms and has been manipulating the price of penny stocks. And trust me when I tell you he is only one of many. The mob is all over Wall Street. In some cases, the brokerage firm doesn't even know, but in most cases they do. The mob has become so powerful on the Street that they now have their own firms; they don't need to bust into one of the established houses. These investigations are like peeling the skin off an onion. You peel off one layer and you find another. In this case, they peeled off one layer and who did they find, none other than Angelo Santino? The more layers they peel, the more names are going to pop up. This investigation is so secret, Wade, that not even regular F.B.I. agents have been clued in."

When Wade heard Santino's name, his stomach growled. He took a deep breath.

"If it's so secret, how do you know? And what has all of this got to do with me and you leaving the Bureau?"

"In answer to your first question, Wade, I know people who know people who know people. That's how I know."

"Okay, so go on. What has that got to do with you leaving?"

"That in itself, nothing, but with this kind of an investigation going on, there is going to be a ripple effect. Like Santino's name coming up, other names are going to surface, and the SEC is going to need help. I am sure they will eventually go to local law enforcement agencies as well as the bureau for help. In the past, one of the most successful ways of getting the goods on the bad guys is to set up a sting operation. I've done that before. It's my plan to convince the bureau to let me set up one of the sting operations for them as an independent. I am sure I can convince them that I will be able to help them bust some pretty important players. However, I also want to get the goods on this prick in Albany."

"You really don't like that guy, do you, Joe? What's your beef with him?"

"No, I don't like him even a little bit. And my beef is he's too fucking lazy to be a real thief, he sits up in Albany and takes pay-offs. He's scum."

"You know that for a fact."

"Wade, I've been doing this kind of work long enough to know things like that. Trust me, he's a thief."

"Okay, we got off the track. So you're going to set up a sting, nail the guy in Albany, and oh yeah, take a piece of the pie along the way, so once again, please tell me, what does all that have to do with me?"

"First off, I wanted you to know that Santino was being investigated, and secondly, I may need your help in nailing this bastard in the attorney general's office."

"Joe, I appreciate you telling me about Santino. I really do, but like I said before, Joe, I don't want any part of being an informant or a spy. That's not my thing."

"This is different, Wade. It's not being either one of those things. What happens if the SEC investigation gets something on Santino? You know they will be all over AA Financial. What happens then? Believe me, those guys don't care who they bust. I don't understand why you are so adamant about not trying to help yourself. I'm giving you a chance to change horses, ride with the good guys."

"Helping myself is one thing spying on Kline is something else. And as far as I am concerned, I am riding with the good guys."

"Wade, I am not asking you to be a spy. And what's the deal with Kline? Are you guys that close?"

"It's not that. I'm still involved with his daughter Brenda."

"You're not!" Joe said, sounding very surprised. "I thought when she went to California it was all over between you two."

"It's kind of a long story, Joe, but she is back now . . . and well I'm not really sure what's going to happen, but I can't get involved with any of this shit with you and her father."

"It's not me and her father, Wade. It's the Justice Department and the SEC Fraud Department and her father, and it can become very messy."

"Joe, I'm still not sure what it is you want me to do."

"All I want you to do, Wade, is to keep your eyes and ears open and let me know if you hear anything about David Grimm. He is the guy who works in the attorney general's office. He is the guy I want to bust. That's all you have to do. Keep your eyes and ears open. I'll do the rest."

"Joe, we are right back to square one. If I learn there is something going on with Kline and this Grimm character, well like I said, I don't think I can get involved, sorry."

"Okay, Wade, if that's your final decision . . . but I think you're making a mistake staying at AA. Sooner or later, that whole operation is going to blow up, and I would hate to see you get blown up with it. By the way, you are not an officer of the company, are you?"

"Not really. My title is executive director. I don't remember signing anything that officially made me an officer of the company."

"Good. That could help if this thing really busts wide open, although the fact that you are in charge of the operation really doesn't give you much insulation."

"Man, you really cheered me up today, Joe. Thanks."

"Sorry, pal, but that's the way it is."

"Joe, before we go, I have a favor to ask of you."

"Shoot."

"Can you find out if either the F.B.I. or the SEC is looking at a company in Las Vegas by the name of Vegas Investment Associates?"

"Yeah, I still have access to the computers. Any particular reason?"

"I worked for them for a short while, and I'm just curious."

"Okay, I don't believe that's the reason, but I'll check into it. What else?"

"I would like to know if Angelo Santino's son Louie is involved with any of his father's business."

"That sounds like a little more than idle curiosity."

"Yeah, well he was my roommate in college. After college, he went into business in California with another guy. But when I worked at the Moon Glow Casino in Vegas, some things came up that made me wonder about him. I would rather not say anymore. Anyhow he called me the other day to tell me he is moving to New York and wants to go to work for me. Maybe I'm just becoming paranoid, but it seems there are too many loose pieces."

"Man, you should go to work for the bureau. That's the way those guys think. Let me ask you something. Suppose I do find out Santino's kid is in the family business, what am I supposed to do then?"

"Good question."

"Did you stop to think that the old man wants him here to look after his interests?"

"If he wanted to do that, then why didn't he just send him out and put him in charge?"

"Because if he feels Kline is not cutting the pie down the middle, this is a better way to have the kid look around."

"Jesus Christ, Joe, do you think that's the reason he's coming to New York?"

"Who knows, Wade? We'll have to wait and see. In the meantime, I'll check into all this stuff for you and let you know what I come up with. I'll also let you know how I make out with the bureau about setting up a sting."

"I'm not sure I want to know that, Joe."

"Sure you do, Wade. And Wade, think about what I told you."

It was almost three o'clock when they left the restaurant. The waiters were already setting up the tables for dinner. Driving back to his apartment, Wade thought about everything Joe had said. He came to one conclusion. What Joe was doing had very little to do about busting David Grimm's balls and more to do about making money. He was sure about that. What he wasn't sure about was how involved he was in everything that Joe told him. Then he thought about what he said about Louie coming to New York to be his father's watchdog. Could that really be the reason? He looked at his watch. He had enough time to stop at the office, then go home, shower, change clothes, and meet Brenda for dinner. Nobody said life was easy!

CHAPTER FORTY-ONE

WADE SUGGESTED TO Brenda they have dinner out as opposed to having Le Cirque deliver dinner to her apartment. "How about we eat at that French restaurant in the village where we used to go when we were both poor?"

Brenda laughingly replied, "I was never poor."

She was waiting for him at the entrance to her apartment building. When she got into the car, he told her how beautiful she looked.

"I'll bet you tell that to all your dates," Brenda said.

"Oh my, that sounds very catty."

"It was meant to be," she said and kissed him on the cheek.

As they entered the restaurant, Brenda asked him how his meeting went.

"Let's order something to drink first, and then I will tell you."

"Oh-my that sounds serious," Brenda said.

After they were seated, the owner came over to say hello and take their order. He briefly mentioned the specials he had prepared that day and then left. Wade looked at Brenda, wondering if he should tell her about his meeting with Joe. She could tell he had something on his mind.

"Okay, fellow, spill it. You got something on your mind. Am I the loser?"

He realized she was talking about Katrina. He reached across the table and held her hand. "No, of course you are not the loser, but you are right I do have something on my mind, but it's not that."

"Okay, so what is it?"

"Brenda, how much do you know about your father's business?"

"Probably not as much as you do. After all, you have been working for him off and on for almost five years. Why do you ask?"

He decided to jump in with both feet. "Do you remember Joe Cantor?"

"I'm not sure. The name is familiar."

"He worked for your father that first summer when I was there. He was the guy who brought me to your friend's party. That's where we first met."

"Oh yes, of course, now I remember."

"Well it seems that when he was working for your father, he was actually working undercover for the F.B.I."

Brenda looked shocked. "What are you saying?"

"I know that sounds crazy, but it's true. Anyhow, that's who I met with today. First off, you should know that while he was working at your father's firm, he didn't find anything wrong. He was very vague when I asked him why the bureau F.B.I. had an interest in the firm back then. As I said, he really didn't tell me anything other than they had reason to believe the firm was engaged in some improper activities. Then he proceeds to tell me that the F.B.I. is looking into your father's company again and he asked me if I would help his investigation. I told him he must be crazy to ask me something like that. He wouldn't tell me what they were looking for he just said he wanted me to find out things about the firm, and more particular, about your father."

She pulled her hand back and stared at him. "Is this some sort of sick joke, Wade?"

"No baby its no joke."

"This is insane, Wade. What happened? What did you tell him?"

"I told him I had no interest in being a spy, and I was sure there was nothing going on at our firm that would interest the F.B.I."

"Did you tell my father?"

"Not yet. I wanted to wait until he got back from vacation."

"Why are you telling me this, Wade? And if you don't think there is anything illegal going on at AA, what was your reason for asking me what I know about the firm's business? What's going on here, Wade? What haven't you told me?"

"There is nothing more than what I told you, Brenda. I simply thought you should know that's all. And I apologize. There was no reason for me to ask you what you knew about the business."

"Wade, this is crazy. I can't believe this is actually happening. Do you mean to tell me that when Joe brought you to the party, he was working for the F.B.I.? Jesus Christ, Wade, I think I'm going to be sick."

Wade handed her a glass of water. She took a sip and looked at him in disbelief. She leaned back in her chair and shook her head. "Wow, is there anything else going on that I should know about, Wade? Let's see . . . I know you are involved with another woman. I know you have been approached by the F.B.I. to spy on my father. Other than that it's been a pretty quiet day at the office. Tell me, have I missed anything?"

"Brenda!"

"Wade, I really don't feel like eating right now. Can we go back to my apartment?"

"Of course Brenda I'm sorry . . ."

"Wade, not now. Let's go back to my apartment. We can talk there."

On the ride from the restaurant to her apartment, Brenda asked Wade to tell her again exactly what Joe said and what he said in return. It was like she was analyzing every word. Wade was wondering if he made a mistake by telling her about Joe's visit. He really hadn't told her everything. He did enough damage by just telling her what he did. What would she say if she knew that he actually had some doubts about her father? He knew damn well what she would say. When they arrived at her apartment, she got out of the car without saying a word. Wade told the doorman to park the car and then followed her into the building. He had no idea what he was going to say once they were in her apartment.

While in the elevator, she turned to him and asked, "Do you think my father is doing something illegal, Wade?" Without hesitation, he put his arms around her and said, "Of course not." He knew he was lying.

When they entered her apartment, she took Wade by the hand and led him into the bedroom. He stood and looked at her. She was all woman. "I think this is about as far as we got last night," she said. He finally put his arms around her and drew her close. His mouth covered hers, and he touched her ever so gently, his hands finding their way under her thin layer of clothing, caressing her skin.

"Oh, Wade, I have missed you so," she said between kisses.

"I know baby and I missed you."

She wrapped her arms around him and ground herself into him, wanting to be closer as close as it was possible to be. When they both finally came up for air, he cupped her face in his hands and said, "You wanted to talk."

"I did? When was that?"

He kissed her again, took her by the hand, and led her to the bed. "I want to make love to you," he said very softly as he began to remove her clothes.

She returned his kisses and whispered back, "I thought you would never ask."

They made love several times before falling asleep in each other's arms, never once mentioning her father or the F.B.I. He woke up to the smell of fresh coffee. He slipped on his pants and went into the kitchen. Brenda was standing by the kitchen window, which gave her a view of Central Park West. He came up behind her put his arms around her and kissed her on the back of the neck. "Good morning," she said without turning around. "And who might you be?"

They spent the rest of the morning talking about Joe Cantor's visit. Wade had expected her to be angry, but instead she was more curious. Why was the F.B.I. interested in her father and his company? Wade told her he had no idea. Again he was not telling her the truth. She assured him that all of this had no effect on their relationship. After all, he couldn't be held responsible for what the F.B.I. does. She believed him when he said he would not help Joe. They talked about how her father would react to hearing that Joe was an F.B.I. agent. Wade thought to himself, "*He probably already knows that.*"

He didn't tell her what Joe said about Louie. Was he coming there to spy on her father? Was her father really stealing from Santino? Did the old man intend to force her father out? There were still a lot of unanswered questions. Wow, the issue with Santino could be more serious than the F.B.I., at least the bureau had rules, or at least he thought they did, he knew Santino made up his own rules as he went along. There was a lot he didn't tell her. "*No need to,*" he thought. She was smart; he was sure she had to have some doubts about her father after listening to what he told her, but who knows? When he left her apartment, he felt relieved that he had told her about Joe Cantor. However, there was still something troubling him. Something that was unresolved. Driving home, he realized what it was. Katrina!

CHAPTER FORTY-TWO

OVER THE NEXT two days, both Wade and Brenda found themselves very busy, and as a result, they had dinner together on only one night. Brenda did not bring up the subject of her father or Joe or the F.B.I., and neither did Wade. AA Financial was in the midst of preparing an IPO for a company in New Jersey that made a special kind of knee brace for football players. They barely had any sales. They were losing money, but they had a great P.R. company and a CEO who presented a business plan that showed the company could make millions if they had capital, hence an IPO. In view of his conversations with Joe, Wade insisted his people didn't miss a thing during the due diligence period. However, there were two brokers in the firm who told him to ease up on the due diligence. "Look Wade don't be such a hard ass," one of them said, "Kline wants these deals to work." Wade told him he wanted an accounting firm other than the one the knee brace company was using to do an audit. The broker argued that was not necessary.

This wasn't the first time he had a difference of opinion with this broker. Although Wade was in charge at AA, these two men seemed to be able to work on their own, and when he brought this to Kline's attention, Kline told him he would handle it. The knee brace IPO was being handled by the broker who refused to have the company audited by another accounting firm, and he made it clear to Wade that he wanted the IPO to happen. That morning, when Wade told his people what he expected during the due diligence, the broker told Wade that if anything came up that might delay the IPO he wanted to know about it right away. "We're going to make this happen," he told Wade in no uncertain terms. Had this happened before he spoke to Joe, maybe Wade would not have given it as much thought as he was now. In his heart, he knew Joe was right. Kline was not Mr. Clean!

Meanwhile, Brenda was busy with her partner in the publishing company. Like a lot of people, her partner had a short memory. Brenda had given her half of the company for nothing, and now she was doing her best to freeze Brenda out. She was messing with the wrong lady. Her father had bought Brenda the company, which included the building.

The lawyers put the building in Brenda's name and then leased it to her publishing company. She sent her partner a registered letter notifying her she was canceling the lease. If she wanted to sue her, fine. She could afford the best lawyers in town. Then she went to the bank and changed the signatures, taking her partner off the account. Since her father was one of the bank's largest accounts, they obliged without asking any questions. Then she sent registered letters to all of the authors they did business with and told them she had made a deal with a Hollywood studio to supply them with at least four manuscripts a year. If they wanted their work to be included, they had to sign an agreement stating that they would submit all of their work only to her. Now the ball was in her partner's court. Brenda knew the broad was no match for her.

Wade looked at his watch. It was almost seven o'clock. He had told Brenda that if he finished early enough, they would have dinner. He was just about to call her when his private phone rang.

"Wade, this is Louie. How are you?"

"Great, buddy. What's happening?"

"Well I'm in New York, got in two days ago. I wanted to get settled before I called you."

"Hey that's great. I didn't expect you here so soon. When will I see you?"

"How about dinner tonight I got a lot of things to talk about?"

"*I bet you do,*" Wade thought. He was going to tell him he promised Brenda dinner, but the truth of the matter was he was anxious to see Louie and find out what was really going on. "Okay sounds like a plan, where do you want to eat?"

"This is your town."

"Okay. There is a great little Italian restaurant about three blocks from here. The tourists don't know about it yet. I know the owner. They don't have a menu. The waiter just asks if you like fish, pasta, or meat, and then he brings dinner family style. You'll like it."

"Sounds like a good place to eat, give me the address. I'm uptown, so it should take me about thirty to forty minutes."

The Italian Kitchen was one of Wade's favorite places to eat. It was not fancy, and very few people outside of the Wall Street crowd knew about it. Bebe Mantonia, the owner, was a former chef at the Four Seasons Hotel. When the hotel changed management, he decided to leave and open up the kind of restaurant that he wanted to run, hence

The Italian Kitchen. Wade was already there when Louie arrived. He was sitting at a table, talking to Bebe. Louie came over to the table, and Wade introduced him to the owner. Bebe instructed the waiter to bring a bottle of wine to the table for his friends and then left to cook dinner.

Wade could not get over the way Louie looked. He had shaved his head and grown a thin mustache and a very neatly close trimmed beard. He was dressed in a very expensive suit and a white open-collar silk shirt. Louie smiled and asked, "You like the new look?"

"Yeah you really look very nice."

"Is it too much California?"

"No not at all. In fact, it is very much New York."

"I missed you, pal," Louie said.

"Me to so tell me where do you intend to live?"

"My father bought me a condo at 94th and Park. I had a decorator furnish it, and I moved in. All you need is money, Wade."

"Good for you, Louie. You deserve it."

"You're full of shit, Wade."

"What are talking about?"

"Deserve it, deserve what? You know my father has always taken care of me. I've never had to worry about making a living. Not like you, Wade. That's what I admire about you. You did it on your own."

"Yeah, like the Beatles say, 'with a little bit of help from my friends.'"

"That's okay everybody can use a little help. It's what they do with it once they get it."

"Could be, but the truth of the matter is I owe a lot to your father. After all, he was the one who introduced me to Albert Kline."

"Yeah, I know," Louie said with a strange tone.

"What's up, Louie? Is there something I should know about?"

"Wade, would you like to know why I really came to New York?"

"You told me. You and Gary split."

"Well that's only part of it."

"Oh!"

"I've been spending a lot of time in Vegas."

"And . . . ?"

"And I lost a lot of money at the tables."

"What are you talking about? You're not a gambler."

"You mean I didn't used to be a gambler."

"Louie, what's going on?"

"I owed the casinos around town almost a half mil."

"You did what?"

The waiter brought the wine, opened the bottle, poured some in Wade's glass, and offered him to taste it. Wade waved him away. "Louie, are you out of your fucking mind? How could you lose that kind of money?"

"Very easy . . . you bet that kind of money." Then Louie poured himself a glass of wine, touched his glass to Wade's glass, and said very calmly, "Salute!" Then he began to explain what had happened.

Last year, a very rich Arab asked him and his partner to decorate the penthouse apartment he purchased in the new Trump Tower in Las Vegas. Money was no object. During the first month, Louie made no less than fifteen trips back and forth to Vegas. The Arab was unhappy with this arrangement since Louie was not always there when he needed him. So the Arab rented Louie an apartment in an upscale building in Vegas. This way, he could spend his full time in Vegas and be available at the rich Arab's beckoncall. The two became very good friends, and Louie started to accompany the Arab to the casinos where the Arab was an exceptionally high roller.

At first, Louie simply watched his friend play, but then after a while, he began to play himself. It was easy for him to get credit at the different casinos. After all, he was with the rich Arab, and it didn't take long for the casinos to learn who Louie's father was. It is interesting how having money buys off your guilt. Sure he knew he was doing something wrong, but it was only money. It wasn't like he was killing somebody. He forgot what his father taught him about gambling and what the priests taught him when he was growing up. All of that was bullshit now. He was having fun. However, it didn't take long before Louie's gambling was no longer recreation; it was a compulsion. His game was blackjack. He'd sometimes play a little craps, but he stayed mainly with blackjack. He heard about people who were card counters, but that took the fun out of the game. You had to remember too many things. However, when he saw a lot of tens or picture cards being dealt, he thought he had an edge and would do crazy things, Like doubling down on twelve, which was unheard of. He was betting $1,000 a hand. People used to watch because the dealer had to announce, "Doubling on twelve!" It was insane. Sure there were times he pulled an eight or nine and beat the dealer, and he loved when the crowd cheered him on, but more times than not, he lost. When he beat the dealer, he would turn to the crowd and shout, "I'm the man!" Louie had become a different person. When he couldn't take any more markers from one casino, he would go to a different casino and start all over again, until one day he ran out of credit, and the casinos began to put pressure on him. That is when one of the casino bosses contacted Louie's father to let him know what was happening.

By the time he finished telling his story, Wade was aghast. He couldn't believe this was the same Louie he roomed with for four years at UNLV.

"Do you want to hear the rest of the story?" Louie said after refilling his wine glass.

"There's more?" Wade asked, leaning back in his chair, almost afraid to hear the rest of the story.

"Yeah, pal, there's more. I'll give you the short version."

"When my father found out what happened in Vegas, he sent out one of his guys to settle up all of my markers. Then he insisted I come to Chicago, so I did. Believe me, Wade, that was not easy. I love the man, but he is tough. He has a way of asking you to do something but in such a way what he is really doing is telling you to do it. Playtime was over. I was going to have to deal with the real world, but on his terms."

"Louie, since this is confession time, let me ask you a question."

"The answer is yes," Louie said.

"I haven't asked the question. What do you mean the answer is yes?"

"You want to ask me if I was in on the skimming at the Moon Glow Casino."

Wade simply looked at his friend and shook his head. "How did you know that was what I was going to ask?"

"I knew."

"Louie, I can remember back in college when you told me you didn't know anything about your father's business, and now you tell me you were helping him skim the Moon Glow."

"Wade, back then when I said "I didn't know" I was being honest, I didn't. But things change. When my father asked me to help him, I couldn't say no. It's that simple. I guess that's what they mean when they say, 'Honor thy father!'"

"Wow," Wade said as he poured them both some more wine.

"Yeah, wow! Okay, pal, are you ready for the final chapter of my story?"

"At this point, Louie, there is nothing that you can tell me that would shock me."

"Don't be too sure, my friend."

"Wade, my father controls a multimillion dollar empire, and he has no one else to leave it to but me. My mother has two sisters, so I am sure he will take care of them, but other than my two aunts, I am his only heir. Unfortunately, I will not give him any grandchildren, and so I am the end of the line of the Santino family. My father suggested that I move to New York, get settled, and think about adopting a little boy. In that way, the Santino name lives on."

Wade was wrong. Louie did tell him something that shocked him.

"What do you mean adopt a child? That's not like buying a car. Who would raise the kid? First of all, I don't think a single man can adopt, especially a single man like you."

"You mean a gay man like me?"

"Yeah, that's exactly what I mean."

Louie laughed. "You worry too much about details, pal. Money, that's the answer. With money, you can do just about anything you want, even adopt and raise a kid. Believe me when I tell you my father has those types of contacts. I don't think there is anything that he can't do."

"You're crazy, Louie."

"Wait, you haven't heard the whole story. There is more. He wants me to learn the business of Wall Street, and there is no better teacher than you. He also wants me to get my broker's license, and then with your help turn AA Financial into a first class clean operation. In order to do this, he has to get rid of Albert Kline, and then he would transfer ownership to me."

"Louie . . ."

"Hold up, Wade, let me finish before you say anything. To begin with, my father knows you have been approached by the F.B.I. to help them get something on AA. He also knows you turned them down. He respects you for that. He said you are a stand-up guy."

"Tell me, Louie, how does he know about the F.B.I.?"

"I am not going to bullshit you, Wade. He has a guy in the attorney general's office in Albany on his payroll. Surprised?"

"Jesus Christ!"

"What's the matter?"

"Joe Cantor . . . he is the guy from the F.B.I. who tried to talk me into helping him, told me he was at a meeting when a guy from the attorney general's office voted to squash the investigation at AA. He felt for sure Kline had him on the payroll. The guy's name is David Grimm. Is that the same guy your father has on the payroll?"

"I shouldn't be telling you, Wade, but yes, that's him."

"Wow, Joe was right about one thing. The guy is a crook. He just had him working for the wrong man. Let me ask you something, Louie. Does Kline know about the F.B.I.?"

"I don't think so. No, I'm sure he doesn't."

"Let me ask you something else. Is your father aware of the fact that Joe Cantor was working undercover at AA when I first started?"

"Get out of here!"

"Oh you mean I told you something you guys didn't know."

"If I had to guess, I would say that was before my father was tapped in."

"Tapped in?"

"Yeah, before he had this guy in Albany on the take."

"Is that Mafia lingo, Louie?"

"Very funny, Wade. Now let me ask you something. Do you think the F.B.I. has any idea this guy in Albany is on the take, or do you think that's all Joe Cantor?"

"If I had to make a bet, I would say it's all Joe Cantor. The way he talked, it didn't sound like the F.B.I. had any idea."

"What do you mean the way he talked?"

"Come on, Louie. Give it up. I said enough."

"Wade, I need your help. I don't know why you are holding back."

"Louie, I appreciate the confidence your father has in me, but this stuff is out of my league. First of all, I have no idea how you are going to force Kline out of AA. Christ, he makes millions of dollar a year. He's not going to walk away from that. I'm going to tell you like I told the F.B.I. I don't have any beef with him, besides which I am still involved with his daughter."

"Yeah, you did mention his daughter. That can be a problem."

"Maybe it's a problem for you, Louie, not for me."

"Would you feel any differently about it if I told you Kline was stealing from my father? He has proof that Kline has been shortchanging him for years. You would think with all the fucking money they make that he would at least give my old man an honest count. And that's only the half of it. He's stealing from the stockbrokers who work for you."

"How does he know all of that, Louie?"

"He has ways, Wade."

Wade remembered what Joe Cantor said, *"Maybe old man Santino is sending his son here to watch Kline. Maybe Kline is not giving the old man his fair share?"*

"Louie, listen to me. What's happening between Kline and your father is really not my business. You say he is stealing from your old man. Come on, Louie, do you really know this or is that what someone told you? Am I concerned that he might be shortchanging our salespeople? Sure I am, and I will look into that. Both you and the F.B.I. have reasons to nail Kline. Fine, that's up to you guys, but I don't want to be part of that. I got my own problems. To tell you the truth, Louie, after these past couple weeks, I have been seriously thinking about leaving AA Financial. I don't need all of this shit. I can go anywhere on the Street and replace my income. Why should I stay there and subject myself to . . . I don't know what?"

"Maybe, Wade, but think about this. If we are successful in getting Kline, and there are ways we can do this, my father wants to make you a full partner in the firm. You and I will own AA, and my father wants you to run it. This is my inheritance, Wade, and you are going to share it with me. You will become an instant millionaire, Wade . . . Think about that for a minute."

By the time Wade got home, it was eleven o'clock. He checked his voice mail, and there was a message from Katrina.

"Hi, Wade, so sorry you're not home. Hope you are well. I really miss you. Our tour is going great. Right now I am in London. We were invited here to do a command performance for the queen. How exciting is that? When we leave here, we are headed to Vienna and Budapest. We are going to perform at Esterhazy Palace and then a master class with a local professional pianist, and finally, a concert at the Bela Bartok Conservatory. This is all so wonderful. We have visited some of the places where the great pianist-composers lived, performed, and wrote their music. Unfortunately, the tour has been extended an additional two weeks. I hope you are missing me as much as I miss you. I love you, Wade, and hope we will be together when I return."

Wade looked at his watch. It was 5:00 a.m. in London, too early to call. He thought about what she said. "The tour has been extended two weeks." Maybe by that time he will know what he is going to do with his life. Was it really possible to love two women at the same time? He had asked that same question many times since meeting Katrina. Then he recalled something he read about that. "If you think you are in love with two women, then choose the second, because if your love was strong enough for the first woman, you would not have fallen in love with the second." *That's a lot of help*, he thought. He tried to remember where he read that and suddenly began to laugh. He remembered he read it in a fortune cookie so much for that good advice.

CHAPTER FORTY-THREE

WADE WAS SITTING in his office the day after his dinner meeting with Louie, thinking about what he had told him, thinking about all that Joe said, thinking about Albert Kline and Louie's father and about Katrina and Brenda. The phone rang. It was his father calling from Las Vegas. "Jesus Christ," he mumbled to himself. What now? Actually there was nothing wrong. His father simply wanted to talk to him. He had changed jobs several times and was now working as a security guard in one of the shopping malls away from the strip. He remarried a couple of years ago, and it seems his new wife was keeping him on the straight and narrow. Good for him. Shortly after starting to work at AA Financial, Wade began sending him a check every month. At first, his father said that it wasn't necessary to send him money. "I am not your responsibility," he said. However, after the first couple of checks, neither of them mentioned it again. That was fine with Wade. The fact that his father wasn't gambling, or at least not enough to cause a problem, makes sending a check every month okay.

When he finished speaking to his father, he thought about his mother. She and her husband had moved to a retirement community in Fort Lauderdale, and Wade had not seen her in almost a year, much too long. He decided he would fly down to Florida, visit with his mother, and maybe clear his head. He needed a break anyhow. The phone rang again. It was Albert Kline. He had returned from his vacation in Europe. One of the first things he said was that Angelo told him about Louie moving to New York and coming to work at AA. Wade was not sure how he was going to take that, but to his surprise, he told him that was good. He always liked Louie. Was Kline conning him? Did he know the real reason Louie was there? Wade wondered if he should call Joe to tell him it was Angelo who had the guy in Albany on his payroll, not Kline. Maybe he should. He had a reason to call him anyway. Joe never got back to him about Sal Maggio. Wade already had his answer about Louie: he was involved in his father's business, maybe even more than he had admitted to.

Then he began to wonder how old man Santino knew Kline was stealing. There was only one way he could know that: Alan Goldman. Alan Goldman was the comptroller at AA, and he reported directly to Kline, as he should. However, when Wade needed something that was not normal office information, Alan Goldman told him he had to clear it with Kline. If Kline was stealing from Santino, and the old man did know, that meant he had gotten to Alan Goldman. Jesus H. Christ, this was becoming more and more involved! More reasons for him to take a little time away to sort things out.

When he called Brenda to tell her he was going to Florida to visit his mother, she offered to go with him. "We could use some time away, just the two of us," she said. He needed to be alone for a couple of days, he told her. She didn't argue. She told him to have a safe trip and hurry home. "Will I see you before you leave?" she asked him. "I'm going to catch the red-eye tonight. I just about have enough time to run home, pack a few things, and get to the airport. I'll call you tomorrow."

Brenda sighed and said, "I love you."

He hesitated then said, "I'll talk to you tomorrow."

There was no "I love you too" back.

CHAPTER FORTY-FOUR

WHILE WADE WAS relaxing at the Bay Harbor Hotel in Fort Lauderdale, his friend Joe Cantor, the former F.B.I. agent, was busy setting up a sting operation authorized by the bureau. Although the not very fancy office he occupied in a small strip shopping plaza on Third Avenue didn't look like a setting for a hedge-fund manager, should he have any visitors, he had no doubt he could convince them there was good reason to be there. His pitch was very simple: He was a hedge fund manager with a $3 billion New York firm and did not want to be on Wall Street with all of the expense and the prying eyes of his competitors. He took the name John Brown, a nice, plain, unassuming name. Dressed in a gray suit and a pale blue button-down collared shirt and maroon tie, he looked as legit as any phony Wall Street con artist.

The office, his embossed business cards, the website and professional looking logo were all props in an investment fraud sting sponsored by the F.B.I.. He was running a scam and looking for willing conspirators. The target was the murky world of penny stocks, a historical haven for con men and hustlers. Penny stocks or microcaps, as they are sometimes called, are typically very small companies with share prices of a penny or less. They don't trade the same as stocks on the major exchanges, and because they often trade at a record pace, it is difficult for investors to really know how much they are paying when they buy the stock. Even though these are small companies, scams involving them can run into tens of millions of dollars.

Here is how Joe's F.B.I. scam worked. The phony hedge fund manager running the scam finds a middleman who helps him find an executive of a small down and out penny stock company in desperate need of cash, willing to pay a kickback in return for an investment of, say, $5 million by a hedge fund. And there are more of these types of companies than you could imagine.

Once the middleman finds his "pigeon," he arranges for him to meet the hedge fund manager. In some cases, it means flying the executive across the country. This alone impresses the poor sucker. Finally, the executive is introduced to the fraudulent hedge fund manager who explains to him that he can arrange for his fund to invest $5 million in his firm, irrespective of its prospects, in exchange for secretly being handed back half of the money as his fee. He then tells him he can do whatever he wants with the remaining $2.5 million. The executive is happy to pay the $2.5 million fee since he knows there is no other place he can go to raise capital, plus he is already thinking how he can keep part of the $2.5 million for himself. The hedge fund manager tells the executive there is no reason to tell his CEO about the backroom deal they are making, which effectively involves stealing millions of dollars from investors of the company. "My hedge fund doesn't need to know either," he tells the executive.

Once the executive is reeled in, the hedge fund manager tells him he also wants a substantial block of the company's stock. The executive agrees. Greed will win every time! At this point, the executive has committed to taking $2.5 million from his company for an illegal payoff, in addition to giving away some of the companies treasury stock. Then things start to move so quickly that the executive loses sight of what is happening. All he can see is the $2.5 million he thinks he is getting. The hedge fund manager tells the executive that to show good faith, he needs to pay him the $2.5 million in cash and issue him the treasury stock before he can wire the $5 million. Sometimes the executive may be hesitant because the company doesn't have that much cash available, but the hedge fund manager finds a way for him to raise the money. Hock the receivablesthen make a short-term bank loan . . . he finds a way. To convince him that there is no risk, he shows the executive a list of companies he has helped, including thank-you letters, all of which are false. There is no reason to doubt the integrity of the man.

Almost immediately after the fraudulent hedge fund manager receives the stock from the executive, he begins to manipulate the stock of the company until it reaches a point where he dumps his shares and makes a huge profit. Immediately thereafter, the stock drops to nothing. The $5 million that the executive of the penny stock company was supposed to get is never transferred to him, but in the meantime, he has already paid the scam hedge fund manager the $2.5 million. Because the transaction is illegal, he can't call the cops, and now he has to find a way to cover up what he did in order not to lose his job, or worse, go to jail. The fraudulent hedge fund manager is smart enough not to leave a paper trail, plus he has sent the executive fake invoices in the amount of $2.5 million for "consulting fees." This is only one variation of the way small companies and investors are cheated out of millions of dollars every year.

Joe Cantor had studied all of the F.B.I. files involving this type of scam and was ready. But because the F.B.I. had limited funds, and because they had to actually invest the money with the coconspirator (the executive of the penny stock company) in order to prove their case, they told Joe he should only find firms looking for small amounts of money, maximum of $50,000. Their goal was to find and convict as many of the executives of the penny-stock companies they could who were participating in a corrupt payoff scheme. And they were sure that as soon as these executives knew they might be facing jail time, they would give up some of the bad guys who were operating on Wall Street to save their own ass. The F.B.I. was counting on the fact that most of these executives were involved with either mob-related con men or other fraudulent brokers. In almost all cases, these were the only people who would deal with them. Although at the start it was never Joe's intention to profit from this sting other than what the F.B.I. was paying him as a consultant, he would soon change his thinking.

And while Wade was in Florida and while Joe Cantor was setting up his sting operation, Louie Santino was making arrangements to get his broker's license. His father had spoken to Albert Kline and told him that his son was going to request some building alterations be made at AA in order for him to set up his office. Kline did not like that. He didn't see why Louie couldn't work within the framework of the existing offices, but the old man insisted, and so Kline reluctantly agreed. In the short time that Wade was away, a lot was happening.

CHAPTER FORTY-FIVE

AFTER FIVE DAYS of lying in the sun, taking his mother and her husband to three different early bird special dinners, and watching late night TV, Wade was ready to return to New York. However, while he was in Florida, he was able to make up his mind about Brenda and Katrina. Which one did he miss the most? When he realized who it was, he knew he had to make a choice. He loved them both, but he was in love with only one of them. He also decided not to call Joe Cantor. There was no reason to. He realized that finding out about Sal Maggio and Vegas International was nothing more than idle curiosity, and he already had his answer about his friend Louie. He was involved in his father's business.

And as far as telling Joe that it wasn't Kline who had the guy from Albany on his payroll, that it was Angelo Santino, he didn't want to get involved. If the opportunity presented itself, he would tell him, but for now he wanted to stay out of it. The big decision he had to make was if he wanted to throw in with Louie to help oust Kline from AA Financial. To begin with, he had no idea how Louie planned to do that. If he did, and they were successful, it meant a big payday for him. He would own 50 percent of AA Financial. That's not chicken feed! Of course, the fly in the ointment was Brenda. Albert Kline is her father. Whether or not they stayed together, he didn't want to do anything to hurt her. How would she feel knowing he helped to force her father out of the firm he started? Not good, he was sure.

On the day he planned to leave Florida, he called her. She had just returned from her lawyer's office. She told him she resolved the issue with her partner. She bought her out for $10,000.

"If I wanted to keep it going, I probably could have forced her out with nothing, but to tell you the truth, Wade, I felt sorry for her."

"You're a good person, Brenda," Wade said.

"So when are you coming home?"

"That's why I called you. I have a noon flight to Newark, which means I should be home in time to take you to dinner."

"That's the best offer I had all day," she said.

"Great. I'll call you as soon as I get to my apartment."

"I can't wait. I miss you, Wade."

"Yeah, I know. Talk to you soon." He didn't say, "I miss you too!"

On the plane ride back to New York, Wade thought about a lot of things, but one thing he had put in the back of his mind and tried not to think about was what Louie said about him owning 50 percent of AA Financial. Things like that don't happen to people like him . . . or do they? He wished he had asked Louie exactly how he planned to oust Albert Kline. The truth of the matter was that he didn't want to know. What would it be like to be a multimillionaire? He was making a lot of money now and was able to buy whatever he wanted. When you are a multimillionaire, do you automatically want more? He fell asleep and dreamed he was on his private yacht, cruising off the coast of the South of France. There was a beautiful woman sunbathing on the deck. As much as he tried, he couldn't tell if it was Brenda or Katrina.

CHAPTER FORTY-SIX

WADE CALLED BRENDA as soon as he got to his apartment. She told him that she ordered dinner from a French restaurant near her apartment. They had eaten there often, and she knew Wade liked the food. "I would rather we eat here tonight," she said. "Do you mind?"

"No, that's fine. What time?"

He sounded so formal. "Whenever you get here is fine," she said.

"Okay, got to make a couple of calls then grab a quick shower and change. I should be there no later than seven."

Not that he planned to be so prompt, but he arrived at Brenda's apartment at exactly seven o'clock. When she opened the door, she was wearing a tight-fitting white sheath that showed off her great figure. He was willing to bet money she didn't have a stich of clothes on under the dress. She saw the pleased look in Wade's eyes. "He likes?" she said flirtatiously.

"He likes," he said then leaned over and kissed her. Not the kiss she was hoping for.

She took his hand and led him to the sofa then she poured them each a glass of wine and slid into the seat next to him. He felt like there was an apple stuck in his throat, and his pulse was beating so hard across his chest that he imagined she could actually hear it.

"Are you okay?" she asked, aware that something was wrong. "Are you sick?" she said, almost in a panic. "No, no nothing like that, Brenda . . . I'm fine."

"You sure as hell don't look fine."

He managed to cool himself down. He never in his entire life ever had a panic attack, but he thought to himself maybe he was having one now. Then as quickly as it came on, it went away, and he felt better.

"You're not on drugs, are you, Wade?" she said, half-kidding and half-serious.

"Drugs . . . No, baby, you know I don't do drugs. I think I got a little woozy because I really haven't eaten anything today, and the flight home, well maybe it just got to me." He knew he was full of shit. It had nothing to do with any of that. It had to do with what he wanted to tell her. This was not going to be easy. He felt her sitting next to him and could remember the times they both lay naked on a hot bed with a cool breeze blowing all the way in from Santa Monica through the open window in a hotel on the beach. He reached over and took her hand and just looked at her. She smiled, but there were tears in her eyes. Suddenly she knew what was wrong. She let go of his hand and got up from the sofa.

"I need something stronger than wine," she said as she walked to the bar and poured herself a glass of scotch. Then she turned to Wade, smiled, and said, "You were about to tell me something, Mr. Simon."

It was almost ten o'clock when he left the apartment. They never did eat dinner; however, they did finish almost a half a bottle of scotch between the two of them. And there were a lot of tears, what ifs, "are you sure," "maybe if we gave it more time," from Brenda and "I'm so sorry," "I wish things could be different," from Wade. He had never really broken up with anybody before, at least nobody who he cared for as much as he cared about Brenda.

When he walked into his apartment, the phone was ringing. It was Louie. Wade had called him earlier but was unable to reach him.

"Welcome home, pal. Have a good vacation?"

"Yeah, yeah, Louie, it was nice, but I'm glad to be back. What's been going on?"

"Not a hell of a lot. Getting my offices set up. That's kind of exciting."

"Good for you. How are you doing with your broker's license? Have you signed up for the course?"

"What do you mean signed up for the course? I already have my license."

"What the hell are you talking about?"

"I got my license."

"Louie!"

"Wade, if you have enough money in this business, you can get anything you want. I can see how they make it so easy for guys to steal and swindle on Wall Street. You want a broker licenseit costs you three grand. You need some sales leads? There are people who will steal them for you from one of the large brokerage houses, two grand. This whole goddamn business is a scam, it's a disgrace."

"Are you telling me you bought a broker license for three grand?"

"That's what I'm telling you, partner."

"Jesus Christ, Louie . . ."

"Wade, tell me you don't know that half the brokers who work for us didn't do the same thing."

"I don't know that, Louie."

"Wade, I've only been here a couple of days, and I can give you the names of three different guys who can get you a license or will steal as many leads as you need. And I'm gonna level with you. I wouldn't put it past Kline. That's the way he gets his leads."

Wade didn't want to get into this type of discussion now that he was still recuperating from his ordeal with Brenda. He told Louie he would meet him for breakfast in the morning, and they could talk more about it. When he hung up the phone, he thought about calling Brenda. He wanted to make sure she was okay, but he decided that was not a good idea. What he really wanted to do was call Katrina. He looked at his watch and realized that just about wherever she \was in Europe, it was much too early to call her. She had given him the name and telephone number of the New York–based tour director in case he ever needed or wanted to call her. He decided he would call her the first thing in the morning and find out where she was. Better yet, he would fly there. That was his plan. Now that he had made up his mind that she was the one, he didn't want to waste any more time. He wanted to see her face when he told her. He called Louie back to tell him he couldn't meet him for breakfast.

"How come got a better offer?"

"Something like that. I'll tell you all about it later. In the meantime, try to stay out of trouble for a couple days."

"Are you going somewhere?"

"Yeah."

"Where?"

"Not quite sure."

"Wade, what's going on?"

"I'm going to find out where Katrina's tour is in Europe and fly over to see her."

"What about Brenda?"

"What about her?"

"What about her? Didn't she come back to New York because of you?"

"Look, pal, I have a lot to tell you but not now. Just stay cool for a little while, and Louie, do me a favor, stay away from those guys who sell broker's licenses and sales leads."

"Wade, you need to get with the program if someday we are going to be partners. You know what I mean?"

"Yeah, I know, but I can't think about that right now, Louie, okay?"

"Okay, buddy, don't worry. Go do what you have to, and we'll talk about it when you come back. Have a safe trip."

"Thanks. Talk to you later."

After talking to Louie, Wade knew that sooner rather than later, he would have to make up his mind about helping him take over AA Financial. After tonight, he couldn't use Brenda as an excuse for not helping him. The problem was he really didn't know what it was he wanted him to do. He thought about calling Joe Cantor, but he wasn't sure why. And if he didn't agree to help Louie, would Kline be forced out anyhow?

Just then the phone rang. It was Brenda. She was very calm, and for some reason, that made him feel guilty. She wanted him to know she would always have a place in her heart for him, but she wished him happiness with Katrina. Now he really felt guilty. She said the real reason for calling was to let him know she decided to move back to California. She said that she really enjoyed the movie business and felt sure she could make a name for herself in either producing or directing. He agreed. She was going to put her apartment up for sale and contact a business broker to have him sell her publishing company. "It's probably not worth that much, but whatever," she said.

By the end of the conversation, he felt much less guilty. Brenda was a smart woman, and he knew she would eventually find someone who would appreciate those qualities. He thought to himself that whoever that person is would be a very lucky man.

Before going to bed, he checked the different flights leaving from New York to Paris, London, and Zurich, not sure where Katrina was, but at least he had some idea as to what was available. He didn't sleep much that night, and by seven o'clock, he was already up, shaved and showered, and waiting to call the New York tour director of Katrina's company. He reached her at nine o'clock. She told him the group was in Paris. They arrived there yesterday and would be there for three days. They were staying at the Hotel des Champs-Elysees, and they had a concert scheduled tomorrow at the Paris Opera House. She also told him that they would probably be rehearsing there in the afternoon. As soon as Wade finished talking to her, he called American Airlines and booked an 11:00 a.m. flight to Paris from the Newark Airport. He had already packed what he needed, found his passport, and ordered a car to drive him to the airport. At 11:35 a.m., the jumbo jet took off from Newark bound non-stop to Paris, with Wade sitting in a first-class seat, anxious as a schoolboy on his first date.

He arrived in Paris at midnight, too late to call Katrina. He had made reservations at the La Tremoille Hotel, which was near the Paris Opera House. By the time he had checked in, unpacked, and took a shower, it was almost 2:00 a.m. He decided to try to get some sleep. He had a big day coming up. However, as much as he tried, he had difficulty falling asleep. He finally dosed off at 4:00 a.m. but was up and wide awake at 8:00 a.m. He called room service, ordered some coffee and then looked at the notes he made when he spoke to the New York tour director. He called the Paris Opera House, and after finally getting past the language barrier, he learned that Katrina and her group were scheduled to arrive for rehearsal at 11:00 a.m. It was now nine-thirty. He had an hour and a half to decide how he was going to surprise her. He decided to take a walk. In less than fifteen minutes, he found himself standing in front of the Paris Opera House. It was breathtaking. The design of the building turned out to be exactly what Emperor Napoleon III had in mind when he ordered it to be built back in 1862. Wade couldn't resist taking a peek inside the magnificent structure. The inside of the opera house was opulently decorated with marble friezes, columns, and statuary, many of which were used to portray Greek mythology. He closed his eyes and imagined Katrina performing before a sold-out audience sitting under a gigantic crystal chandelier. The thought made him feel good. He looked at his watch; it was almost ten o'clock. He walked back outside and stood on the marble steps of the opera house, thinking about what he would say to Katrina, when suddenly he looked across the street and saw it. It was perfect absolutely unbelievable It couldn't be better if he had planned it. He smiled and looked at his watch again. It was only ten o'clock.

Someone once said, "Love is horrible. It makes you vulnerable. It opens up your heart and allows a perfect stranger to enter. All your life you build up these defenses, a whole suit of armor so that nothing can ever hurt you, and then suddenly, bang! The armor is no longer there. How can one person, no different from any other person do that to you? One minute it makes you feel good, and the next minute you are not sure how you feel. It makes you do stupid things." Wade was in love.

Since the weather was nice, he decided to hang out around the opera house rather than go back to the hotel. Every so often, a tour bus would stop, and he could see the tourists looking out of the windows of the bus, admiring the Paris Opera House. Finally, at 10:45 a.m., a small version of a tour bus pulled up in front of the opera house, and the people on board got out. And then he spotted her. He watched as she talked and mingled with the other people from the bus. As the bus pulled away and Katrina and her group were walking up the marble steps to the entrance of the opera house, he shouted her name from across the street. Several people heard him and turned around to look. Katrina evidently didn't hear him and continued walking up the steps. He called her name again, this time much louder. She stopped walking and looked across the street. It took her a couple of moments before she realized that it was Wade standing there yelling her name. She put both of her hands to her face and screamed. The people standing next to her had no idea what was happening. Then before anyone had a chance to say or do anything, she ran down the steps, across the street, and into Wade's arms.

"Oh my god," she screamed between tears and laughter. "Oh my god what are you doing here? How did you know I was here? Oh my god . . ."

He cupped her face in his hands and said, "Well to tell you the truth, I got up this morning and had nothing to do, so I thought I would fly to Paris and have a hot dog." And then he pointed to the hot dog vendor next to him. "Would you like one?"

She had no idea what was going on.

He casually turned to the vendor selling the hot dogs and held up two fingers. "Oui, monsieur," the vendor replied. Wade took the two hot dogs from the Frenchman, handed one to Katrina and said, "Somebody once told me it is easy to tell someone you love them when you are making love to them, but true love is when you can tell someone, in the middle of the afternoon, while you are eating a hot dog, that you love them." He took a bite of his hot dog and between munching said, "I love you, Katrina, more than anything else in this world. I love you."

Wade and Katrina stayed in Paris for a week after her concert tour was finished. They were like two kids in love. They went sightseeing, attended several concerts, ate in romantic places, and made love. Wade called Albert Kline to tell him about Katrina and that he would be back in New York in about a week. He was perfectly fine with that. Brenda had already told him she was returning to California and that she and Wade were no longer seeing one another. Kline, however, did tell him that he was not happy with Louie. "He has been here only a couple of weeks, and he thinks he is running the place. When you come back, we need to talk about this." Wade was not in the mood to talk about Louie, or for that matter, anything to do with AA Financial. He was in Paris with the woman he loved. That was enough for now. He simply told Kline they would talk about it when he got back to New York.

CHAPTER FORTY-SEVEN

ALBERT KLINE DIDN'T get to be as rich as he was by being either stupid or intimidated. During the years he was associated with Angelo Santino, he learned how to deal with all kinds of adversity. He had crossed the line so many times that in his mind that was the only way to do things. He had kept other members of organized crime from infiltrating his business, avoided investigations by the SEC and other regulatory bodies, and kept Angelo Santino from interfering. He was smart enough to call on Angelo when he needed him, and at the same time kept him on a need-to-know basis as far as AA Financial was concerned. Now he had to deal with Angelo's son.

Kline was no dummy. He knew why Angelo sent his kid to New York. It had nothing to do with his gambling problem in Las Vegas. Angelo could have handled that with him in a hundred different ways. He wanted his kid there to watch him, and then who knows what. What Kline wasn't sure of was whose side Wade was on. Had Angelo and Louie convinced Wade to help them unseat him? How could they do that? This is my company. No smart-ass kid is going to come in and try to take it away from me. Then he thought, did Angelo know that he wasn't giving him an honest count? "*Shit, Angelo is making a fortune just sitting on his ass in Chicago while I'm doing all the work. I'm entitled to a larger share of the profits! Fuck him and the horse he rode in on.*"

By the time that Wade returned from Paris, Albert Kline had decided he needed to find out real quick whose team he was on. Was he the guy he could depend on, and then maybe, just maybe be the one to succeed him in operating AA, or was he in cahoots with the Santinos? Wade's breaking up with his daughter did not matter to Kline. Business was business; personal relationships did not affect his business decisions.

Before leaving Paris, Wade told Katrina that he wanted her to move in with him. Neither of them talked about marriage, but Katrina felt in her heart that they were destined to be together, and it didn't matter to her if they got married or not. Just being with him was good enough for her. Although Wade sometimes talked to her about his business, he never really told her all that much about the way AA operated.

What was he going to say? "We do things a little differently than other brokerage firms? What is different? Well we tell a few lies, we cheat a little, you know, things like that." Right he could imagine her reaction to that!

On his first day back in the office, Albert Kline told Wade to arrange for a meeting with him and Louie. Wade knew this was coming, and he was glad it was sooner than later. He had spoken to Louie the night before, and nothing had changed. Louie was hell-bent on finding a way to force Kline out of the business. Wade called Joe Cantor and was surprised to learn that he no longer had any interest in either Kline or the guy in the attorney general's office. When Wade asked him why, he said, "Got a lot on my plate now a lot more important stuff." Wade didn't tell him about Louie. He figured since he wasn't interested in AA Financial anymore, there was no need to. Wade thought to himself, "*How nice if all this shit would go away and I could just do my job,*" but he knew that wasn't going to happen. He didn't know what it was that was going to happen, but he knew it wasn't just going to go away!

Wade and Louie met with Albert Kline in his office after the market closed at four o'clock. Kline didn't waste any time with small talk. He asked Louie straight up what his plans were with respect to AA Financial.

"I'm not sure what you mean," Louie said, trying to think of an answer.

"Well it's obvious you don't want to have a menial job here at AA. You're too bright for that, and besides which I am sure your father wants more for you."

Wade looked at Louie and then at Kline. Kline was winning the battle of wits.

"Actually, Albert, my father has nothing to do with what I want."

"Come on, Louie, you know that's not the case. Every father wants the best for his child, and I am sure your father is no different. And if he can help further your career, well then he should."

Louie didn't know what to say. Kline turned to Wade. "What do you think, Wade?"

"About what?"

"About Louie's future here at AA do we have a place for him?"

"I am sure we have a place for him. Where he goes from there is really up to you and him."

"Don't be so modest, Wade. You know I am grooming you to take over some day. How would you feel about being Louie's boss, knowing that his father owns half the firm?" Kline was really busting their balls.

Wade knew what was happening, and he had no intention of walking into Kline's trap.

"Look, Albert, you know I appreciate what both you and Louie's father have done for me, but I really don't think it's my place to discuss Louie's future. That's between you and Louie, and I guess, his father."

Kline smiled. He liked Wade; he hoped that he could trust him, and only time would tell. Then he turned to Louie. "You never answered my question, Louie. What do you want to be doing here at AA two, three, four years from now?"

Louie had regained his composure. "Like Wade said, that's up to you, Albert. I know Wade is the heir apparent, and I'm fine with that. AA is a profitable firm, and I am sure there is room for me, if not at the top, somewhere close." Kline couldn't help smiling.

"Tell you what, guys, why don't we table this for now and concentrate on making money. You are right, Louie, AA is profitable and can be even more so with the right kind of business. I'm going to depend on you two to help grow our firm to be one of the top firms on the street. Can I can count on your support?"

Both Louie and Wade agreed. This is not what Wade expected. Nothing had changed. After they left his office, Wade and Louie stopped for a drink before going home. "Well what happens now?" Wade asked his friend. Louie smiled. "Not really sure, paisano, but I am sure I will think of something."

CHAPTER FORTY-EIGHT

ALMOST SIX MONTHS had gone by since Wade and Louie met with Albert Kline to discuss Louie's future with AA Financial. During that time, Brenda had subleased her apartment and decided to just close up her publishing company since she could not find a buyer. Before she was ready to move back to California, she had lunch with Wade. After all, they had known each other a long time, and she wanted to see him one more time. They wished each other good luck and knew their paths would probably never cross again.

Wade and Louie were both busy growing the business at AA, which gave Louie little time to work on a plan to unseat Kline. Not that he had abandoned the idea to oust Kline from his firm the fact of the matter was he was simply to busy doing his job. To Wade's surprise, Louie had taken to the business very quickly and within a very short time had developed some good clients. He also brought a deal to the firm, an IPO for a relatively small medical supply company. He told Wade one of his clients had a friend that owned a company that wanted to go public, so he contacted the man and convinced him to let AA handle the offering. Had he really thought more about it, Wade might have realized the deal was not kosher nevertheless, he was happy to see that Louie was doing well and not talking about pushing Kline out. He wasn't anxious to help him with some cockamamie plan to force Kline out of his own company. However, the problem for Wade was the fact that the business at AA Financial had not changed significantly even though Kline indicated it would.

After their meeting, Kline told Wade, "I want to clean up our act here at AA. There is plenty of good business around. Let's focus on that." But Wade knew Kline had spent too many years doing things his way to change now. He thought, *"How much fucking money does that guy need?"* The answer was, *"As much as he could get!"*

By 1997, the lives of the chophouse kids were becoming worth less and less, and brokerage firms like AA Financial were being scrutinized more closely by the SEC. First, the regulators, the guys in the polyester suits with their pain-in-the-ass restrictions cutting into deals and making investors wary, and now the press was calling for more controls and investigations. In the past, the financial press had been very passive. They were docile, uninformed, and blind as to what was happening on Wall Street. But now the publicity had begun.

In July of 1997, Fortune published a full-length dissection of the decline and fall of a major Wall Street firm, which contained numerous unflattering references to firms like AA Financial. Kline brushed them off, saying, "If they had proof we were doing something illegal, they would do more than just make inferences."

His arrogance and greed were beginning to cloud his good judgment. The money was too good for him to stop doing what he had been doing for so many years. Even with deals a little more difficult to pull off, AA Financial was still a cash cow. Wade knew that sooner or later AA Financial was going to be in real trouble with the SEC. He began to think that maybe it was time he left and find a position with a different firm. The problem was that he had become accustomed to making big money at AA, and he knew he couldn't replace that, at least not right away. Once again, the two things that drive Wall Street, greed and fear, were at work. Then several things happened that changed his thinking.

On August 1, 1997, the lead story in the *Wall Street Journal* read:

> Joseph Cantor, a former F.B.I. agent, has been accused of conspiring with members of a major New York organized crime family to manipulate stock prices, defraud an insurance company, and coerce a number of different stockbrokers to give them inside information on pending IPOs. Cantor, who still had access to confidential F.B.I. information about ongoing investigations, also supplied this information to members of organized crime. In the thirty-three-page indictment, among other things, the complaint against Cantor states that he was paid to provide members of organized crime families information obtained from confidential government databases about criminal histories and continuing investigations of small publicly traded companies. Organized crime members then used this information to bribe and otherwise coerce the executives of these companies. Organized crime

> members also used that information to sell the stock of those companies under investigation, short, borrowed and then immediately sold shares in anticipation of buying them back at a lower price for a profit. Cantor would publish the pending investigations of these small publicly traded companies on a Web site he operated, hoping the price would plummet further. Federal prosecutors also charge that Mr. Cantor and his associates engaged in extortion, telling a number of small companies they would disclose bad news about them if they did not give them heavily discounted, and sometimes free, stocks. Mr. Cantor's lawyers have called the charges ludicrous. His lawyer also contends that his client is a victim of the Justice Department, the F.B.I., and Wall Street venom for the detective work that he was doing undercover for the SEC and the F.B.I.. He went on to say they are looking forward to getting into a courtroom and responding.

After reading the article in the *Wall Street Journal*, Wade tried to call Joe but was only able to get his voice mail, which said that the message box was full, please try again. "Shit," he mumbled. He wanted to know more about the charges against Joe. He wondered if this could have any effect on AA Financial. "*Suppose Joe cuts a deal with the federal prosecutor to give him information he has about some of the firms on Wall Street including AA? And does Joe really have anything on AA? Shit!*" He had plans to meet Katrina for lunch that afternoon. He decided it was time she knew more about the company he worked for.

Louie also read the article in the *Wall Street Journal*, but unlike Wade, he didn't have much interest in Joe Cantor. His concern was the fact that the SEC and other regulatory bodies were beginning to crack down on illegal trading and organized crime on Wall Street. What Wade and Louie's father didn't know was that shortly after moving to New York, Louie started making regular trips to the casinos in Atlantic City, and his luck there was no better there than it was in Las Vegas. It wasn't long before he was in debt not only to several of the casinos, but he also owed money to Mickey Esposito, a loan shark who worked for Andy Costilano, a self- proclaimed crime boss in South Philly. His biggest fear was that his father would find out about his gambling. He wasn't sure if Mickey knew who his father was. He only hoped that he didn't.

Then one day, Mickey told Louie there was a way he could wipe off what he owed him plus put a couple hundred grand in his pocket.

"How can I do that?" Louie asked him.

"I got a good friend of mine in the medical supply business. From what he tells me, it's a pretty good business. He has a deal with a bunch of retirement homes in Philly and New Jersey to sell them all their medical supplies. He has maybe, I dunno, six to seven locations, and he wants to open more, you know, expand into upstate Pennsylvania and New Jersey. He tells me he does a lot of business with Medicare. I don't know much about that, but he tells me you can bill them whatever the hell you want. Do you believe that? Some fucking government we got. Unfortunately, he can't get bank financing, and he is running short of cash. He tells me in order for him to expand he needs about a mil, maybe more."

Louie said, "What has that got to do with me?"

"Well here's the scoop. My friend knows some guys who have taken their companies public and made a lot of money. So I told him about you. I told him you're in that business and could probably help him. So that's the deal. Here's a chance we can all make a lot of money. I figure you can put a deal together for my friend, and we all walk away happy. And you got a clean slate. You don't owe me, and you can pay off the casinos. How sweet is that?"

"Mickey, you must be kidding. You don't just put a deal together like you say. First of all, the company has to be making money and have something special to offer the public. Just selling medical supplies is no big deal. "

"Look, Louie, I hear what you're saying. I ain't stupid. I know all about that crap. I also know a lot of guys who had shit companies, took them public, and made a lot of money. The guy I work for would be very appreciative if you did this. Another thing, this guy Kline you work for is no saint. I know you can convince him to do this deal."

"What the hell are you talking about? What makes you say something like that?"

"Because I know, that's why. And if you don't know, then you're not as smart as I thought you were."

"Well I don't know, and if you are so sure then why don't you just go to Kline yourself?"

Mickey was getting angry. He knew who Louie's father was, and he was sure Louie didn't want his old man to know about his gambling. He didn't want to have to negotiate with Louie. He just wanted him to take the deal to Kline and do it.

"Look, Louie, don't get smart with me. You know damn well I can't just walk into Kline's office and tell him to do the deal, but you can."

"What makes you think that?" Louie said, knowing he was in trouble.

"Because Kline is a crook, that's why, and he loves money. I know some guys he has dealt with in the past. I also know who your father is, and I am sure he would not like to know that you owe over a hundred grand around town. Be smart, Louie. Make this deal happen, and you are debt free plus you got money in your pocket to play with. Don't be a pussy about this."

And so Louie took the deal to Kline. Although the medical company was only slightly profitable, Kline knew how to put together a prospectus that would look good. Increase the receivables, show more inventory than Sovereign really had, and decrease the accounts payable. Then show a business plan that will increase sales and develop new locations. An added twist was to show in the business plan that Sovereign intended to sell franchises in other states. Nobody in their right mind would buy a franchise in that company. He really didn't give a shit what happened to the company, or for that matter, the investors, after he made his money on the offering. This type of deal wasn't new to him. He had done this many times before. More important, this put Louie in his pocket, so to speak. If Louie was involved in this, then he couldn't very well be a spy for his old man at the same time. Kline also found out about Louie's gambling habit, and that was another trump card for him. So with very little thought, Kline told Louie he would do the deal. Louie couldn't believe how easy this was. *"Maybe Kline wasn't such a bad guy after all?"* Once again, greed and fear had taken over.

CHAPTER FORTY-NINE

IT TOOK ALMOST nine months for Kline to put the medical company deal together. On May 4, 1998, Sovereign Medical Supply Company was ready to go public. However, Kline had decided that the first thing he was going to do was commence a private placement of Sovereign Medical shares. That is a conventional and usually a perfectly respectable way of raising capital and a technique used by thousands of companies. It is like an IPO but without all the "dumb" SEC paperwork. In a private placement, wealthy investors—they have to have a lot of money by law—invest money in a company that is not yet public, often with the expectation that it will go public somewhere down the road.

One of the reasons Kline decided to commence a private placement was due diligence. Due diligence is enshrined in the securities laws. When a company is preparing to sell its stock to the public, it has to do so through an underwriter. An underwriter is a fancy name for an investment bank, which is a fancy name for a brokerage house that raises money for companies who want to sell their stocks to the public. Since the SEC would not be involved in the private placement, Kline decided he could skip the due diligence exercise. It would have been meaningless in any event, since he would only see what he wanted to see.

When a private placement works out well, the investors can walk away with a lot of money. If it goes wrong, they can lose every penny. A lot of things can happen. The business doesn't work out as planned or the business model changes. In some cases where the mob had infiltrated a Wall Street firm, they had a private placement for a company that didn't even exist. This was not the case with Sovereign. They were a real company. However, Kline knew in his heart that this business would never be a winner, plus the fact the owner of Sovereign would not be able to operate a large business. If he had to make a bet, he would bet the company would go bust in a year, but that had nothing to do with him offering the private placement. His philosophy was, "Fuck 'em. Let the buyer beware!" And the good thing about this deal was the SEC was not involved at least not at this point.

Kline's plan was very simple. The private placement would raise money for Sovereign and lay the groundwork for taking the company public, assuming that he decided to do that. With the way he was structuring the private placement, everybody would make a lot of money: Sovereign, Louie, the Costilano Family, some of his brokers, and more importantly . . . himself!

Kline told Louie and Wade and a few selective brokers in the firm to sell units in the private placement to their clients, each of then costing $50,000. Actually the units were in the form of a loan at 10 percent, with some stock thrown in as a sweetener, if and when the company went public. This wasn't an easy sell since Sovereign was not really a sexy company, but Kline knew they would be able to sell all of the units offered, for 10 percent was a good return, and greed was always a driving factor on Wall Street.

Wade never questioned Kline about the private placement. As far as he could determine, it was a legitimate deal. When he asked Louie about the company, Louie told him he had met with the owner and visited some of their locations. "This is a good solid company and has great potential." He was full of shit. He never visited the company and didn't have a clue as to how successful the company might be. His only interest was getting out of debt with the casinos in Atlantic City, paying off Mickey Esposito, and having more money to gamble with. And he hoped his father would not find out about any of this.

In the meantime, Wade told Katrina about his mixed feelings regarding AA Financial.

"I'm making a ton of money," he said, "more than I ever dreamed of. But there are days when I think to myself that this is not the way I want to earn my living."

"Is what you do illegal?" Katrina asked.

Wade thought a minute then said, "I don't know if it is illegal, but I know it's not right. When I talked to Kline about this, his answer was, 'this is the way firms do business on Wall Street.'" I don't believe that. I think there are firms on the Street that are much more ethical than AA Financial."

"Then why don't you leave AA and go to work for one of those other firms?"

Wade leaned over, kissed her, and then said, "I'm making well over a million dollars a year, baby. It would be very difficult for me to replace that, at least not at the start."

She put her hands on his face and said, "Wade, I love you, and it doesn't matter to me how much money you make. I just want you to be happy. I want you to know that whatever you decide, I will support your decision."

He told her that before he decided, he wanted to talk to Joe Cantor. She really wasn't sure what that had to do with his making a decision to change jobs, but she respected his judgment and did not question it. As it turned out, he was never able to get in touch with Joe, and before he knew it, the months sped by, and he had not made any decision. About a month after he had discussed it with Katrina, she asked him if he decided what to do. He simply said he was still thinking about it. She didn't ask him again.

In June of 1998, Wade read an article in the *Wall Street Journal* stating the judge handling Joe Cantor's case was going to set a trial date. The *Wall Street Journal* reporter speculated that whatever the date the judge set, Cantor's lawyers would appeal and claim they could not be ready. In his opinion, the trial would not happen for at least a year. The reporter also stated that if and when a trial date was set, he estimated the trial itself would take about six to eight weeks. Wade decided he would try to contact Joe again. He wasn't sure why, but he had the feeling he needed to talk to him before he made any decision about changing jobs.

Shortly after the Sovereign Medical Company private placement came out, Wade was able to reach Joe Cantor and set up a lunch date. They agreed to meet at Sam's Place, an Italian restaurant in the village.

CHAPTER FIFTY

AFTER THE SOVEREIGN private placement offering was completed, Louie walked away with almost $300,000. He thought he had died and gone to heaven. As agreed, Mickey wiped the slate clean, so Louie didn't owe him any money. Then after paying off the casinos, he still had close to $200,000. However, he wasn't street-smart enough to realize that he was a low man on the totem pole. Everybody, including Mickey, came out of the deal with a lot more money than he did, but he was as happy as a pig in shit. There was something else that he never thought about, and that was Mickey and his pals had no intention of this being a one-shot deal. As far as they were concerned, Louie was now their guy on the inside, and they expected to do more deals. Mickey was an old-time con artist he knew how to play a guy without the mark knowing he was being set up. He made it very clear to Louie from the start that he was going to be more than just a friend. "I want to be one of your clients," he told Louie. At first, Louie was hesitant, but once again, the greed factor took over. In his mind, Louie saw Mickey investing a lot of money, which meant large commissions for him. That was not going to happen.

One day, Mickey showed up at AA Financial and told Louie he wanted to open an account with $10,000. Louie was a little bit disappointed since $10,000 was not a lot of money. Mickey sensed Louie's disappointment and told him he wanted to start small, get his feet wet, so to speak, before he invested big money. That made sense. Now all he had to do was find a good investment for Mickey so that he would invest more money. AA was promoting a new stock in a company called American Gold Holding. Louie had no idea the stock was one of Kline's scams. He told Mickey he was going to make a bundle—at least $25,000 in a very short time. But of course, things didn't go as planned. The stock began to drop, and within less than a month, it was trading for fifty cents a share. It was one of those chop and swap deals that Kline had done so often. Louie couldn't figure it out. He went to Wade. "I'm in trouble," he said. "I got this new client, a guy who is connected, and shit, Wade, I put him in American Gold Holding, and he lost ten grand. What the fuck am I going to do?"

"A guy who is connected what the hell are you talking about?"

"It's kind of a long story, but that's not important. What is important is this guy lost ten grand."

"Look, Louie, I don't know what you got yourself into, but just tell the guy the truth. Investing in the market is risky. Sometimes you win, and sometimes you lose. By the way, didn't you know about American Gold?"

"Didn't I know what?"

"This was one of Kline's deals. It smelled bad right from the start. I told Kline I didn't like it and was not going to offer it to any of my clients."

"What did Kline say?" Louie said in a panic.

"Not much he just gave me one of his sweet smiles and said 'we'll talk later.'"

"Why didn't I know this?" Louie said.

Wade just shrugged his shoulders.

When Louie told Mickey what happened, Mickey simply said, "So what are you going to do about it?"

"What do you mean, Mickey, what can I do about it?"

Mickey stared at Louie with a look that scared the shit out of him. "What you can do is get me my money."

"Mickey, you don't understand. There is no money left in your account. I feel bad, but you know that's the stock market."

"Louie, it's you who don't understand. I want my $35,000."

"What are you talking about, Mickey? You only lost ten grand."

"You told me I was going to make $25,000 on my ten grand, Louie, and that's what I want. End of story."

Louie looked at Mickey and knew he wasn't kidding. He knew he had to come up with the $35,000. He didn't like it, but he still had over $100,000 left from the Sovereign deal, so he did have the money. He thought about trying to offer Mickey half the amount but knew that he would not take that offer; he wanted the whole $35,000 and not a penny less.

After Louie had finally agreed to pay Mickey the $35,000, the con man and bookie said to him, "Okay, Louie, now we can start over. I like the stock market. I'm going to give you another ten grand to invest, and I expect the same return."

"Jesus, Mickey, I don't know . . ."

Mickey interrupted him. "Louie, like I said, I'm going to give you ten grand, and I expect the same return, so you better go to work and find the right investment. And by the way, I have a couple of friends who want to get in on the bandwagon I'm going to have them call you."

Louie couldn't talk. He just sat there, thinking his life was over.

Although Louie's father Angelo Santino had been out of the rackets for years, he still had friends involved in organized crime who he spoke to from time to time. It was one of these friends who told him how his son had gotten himself involved with the Costilano crime family. "I hate to tell you this, Angelo, but your kid . . . he gotta himself tied up with a bad a guy, Andy Costilano. He's one a them young punks from South Philly. Not a like the old guys, this *piscione* (pisser) he-gotta-no respect. He is a real *figli-un-cane!* (son-of-a-bitch)"

"Does he know Louie is my son?"

"I'm a sure he does. What I heard was that Louie owed one of Andy's bag men in Atlantic City a real *chooch* (ass) named Mickey Esposito a lot of money. This Esposito wanted your kid to pull some sort of scam where he worked. I'm not a so sure what that was. Anyhow he threatened your kid if he didn't play along, he would make sure you found out that he was gambling at the casinos in Atlantic City and owed them a lot of money. "*Merde* (shit). Why didn't he call you, Angelo?"

"Ah who knows, my friend? Tell me again all you know about the trouble my son is in."

Like any other business, organized crime has a line of inside information. It didn't take very long before word spread on the street about Louie. After Angelo's friend explained to him all he knew about Louie's problem, Angelo called another old friend of his who lived in Philadelphia. This was a man who had at one time been an important member of the Nicky Scarfo crime family in Philadelphia. Although he too was out of the business, so to speak, he still commanded respect from most of the older connected guys in Philly. They were old but not feeble. When Angelo told him about Louie, he said he had already heard and as a matter of fact was planning to call him.

"What-can-we-ado?" Angelo asked his old friend in Philadelphia.

"Well, if this-a-was the old days, we would kill the son of a bitch."

This brought a chuckle from Angelo. "Yes, I know, but this is not the old days."

"Too bad," his friend said. "By the way, does Louie's momma know about his trouble?"

"No, no reason to tell her. I just gotta fix it and quick."

"Okay, my friend, I understand. Can I ask you a question, Angelo?"

"Anything at all."

"The Jew who was in on the scam that Castilano and his guy pulled, how-can-I-say-it, is he your partner?"

"My friend, you seem to know an awful lot about my business."

"Angelo, I-a-am-a-sorry . . ."

"No need to be, my good friend. Yes, he is my partner, and like you say, if it was in the old days, how did we say it? 'He would be swimming with the fishes by now!'"

"I understand. If you want, he still could be doing that, my friend."

"No, no, I will take care of him in my own way. But this Castilano and Mickey Esposito, they need to be taught a lesson. They can't go around recruiting my son without having to pay the consequences."

"I no gotta the people do take care of this myself, Angelo, but I'm a gonna make some calls, Angelo, and get back to you as soon as possible. One more a thing, does Louie have any idea that you know he is in trouble?"

"I don't think so. Any reason you ask?"

"No, I just think it is better he doesn't know. Angelo, there is bad blood in Philly between some of the more traditional men and that asshole Castilano. He has made a lot of enemies. The man I am going to call is one of his enemies. I know he will take care of your problem, but in his own way. Do I have your permission to talk to him?"

"We have known each other a lot of years. I trust you. I want the problem with my son to go away. However you do that is not my business. Just tell me how much it costs."

"I understand, good friend. I will call you soon. Don't worry we will find a way."

"*Grazie.*"

CHAPTER FIFTY-ONE

BY THE EARLY seventies, the Sicilian American Mafia was regarded to have become obsolete in Philadelphia, culturally and philosophically. The old Mafia had practiced certain principles to defend honor and operate within a code, but the new generation of Mafioso disregarded these traditions. However, there were still some of the older dons who kept up the tradition, one being Mario Testa. Over the years the remnants of the Philadelphia Sicilian American Mafia was able to be sustained through neighborhood interactions. Although among other things they dealt in illegal cigarette stamps, sold protection to the shopkeepers, and organized labor unions, they also lent money to the immigrant Italian families, made sure the Catholic Church had what they needed, and gave to the local charities. And as a result, the people in the neighborhood both feared and respected them.

The new breed of Mafia families were much less concerned about the needs of the neighborhood and more concerned about how much money they could make. It didn't make any difference to them if their money came from dealing drugs, prostitution, extortion, or loan sharking. Andy Castilano was one of these men. Actually he was not really a Mafia don. He was more like the leader of a gang, but he considered himself to be a made man. The Mafia's definition of a made man is a man who has committed murder on behalf of a Mafia family. Although Castilano alluded to the fact that he had fulfilled that requirement, nobody was ever able to confirm it.

Over the years, Mario Testa and Andy Castilano had many disputes. On one occasion, Castilano attempted to muscle in on Testa's protection racket in South Philly; however, Testa made it clear to the young Turk that he would retaliate in such a manner that he would be sorry he ever tried it. Then there was the time he started taking football bets in a neighborhood that Testa had controlled for years. When Testa told him to stop, he so much as told him to go fuck himself. Testa was reluctant to spill blood, so he went to the commission and complained. Castilano told the commission the same thing. He didn't give the real Mafia any respect. The commission wasn't sure if he really understood what the

Sicilian American Mafia in Philadelphia was because no matter how many times they warned him, he did whatever he wanted. He was both a nuisance and an embarrassment to the organization.

Testa knew that eventually Castilano was going to cause either him or members of his family real harm, so when Angelo's friend called and told him what Castilano and his man Mickey did to the son of a respected true Mafia don, he made up his mind to deal with him once and for all.

Three days after Angelo's friend spoke to Testa, Andy Castilano was in a barber shop on the corner of Seventh and Bainbridge Street. "Make me look good, Tony. I got a wedding to go to tonight," he said to the barber as he relaxed in the barber's chair and read an Esquire magazine. When the barber finished, Andy gave him a $5 tip then took a quick look in the mirror. Satisfied with what he saw, he walked out of the shop. As soon as he did, the barber locked the door, pulled down the shade, and crawled under one of his barber chairs. Just as Castilano reached the curb and was about to get into his car, a black sedan with a New York license plate sped around the corner and stopped in front of the barber shop. Four young men all wearing masks got out of the sedan and began shooting at him. The assassins were gone even before Castilano crumpled to the sidewalk, so certain were they of having hit their target. Less than five minutes after the police arrived on the scene, they called the mortuary wagon.

Hardly anyone heard the crackle of exploding bullets on that deserted corner of South Philly when the air was rent for an instant with the unnerving bark of gunfire.

The police homicide report wrote that when he was taken to Pennsylvania Hospital, he had "two gunshots to the head, three in his left side, one in his chest, two in his face, and one in his left shoulder. He was DOA."

The following day, when Mickey Esposito opened his front door, there was a copy of the Atlantic City Press newspaper on his front step. The paper was opened to the third page where the following story was underlined with a red magic marker:

> Local Philadelphia mobster killed Mafia-style outside of a barber shop in South Philadelphia. The victim's name is Andy Castilano. There were no

> witnesses to the shooting. Police believe the murder was in retaliation from one of the other Philadelphia crime families. When the police questioned the barber, he said he didn't see anything. Castilano was his last customer, and he closed the shop after he left. The homicide police report stated that Castilano had been shot at least nine times in different parts of his body. When questioned, the police commissioner was not optimistic about finding the shooter or shooters. The commissioner, an old Irish cop who used to walk the beat in South Philly told this reporter, "Let those Mafia bastards kill off each other. It will make my job that much easier."

Under the story, also written in a red magic marker, was a very short and direct message.

"Leave the Santino kid alone."

Later that day, Mickey Esposito drove to New York and showed up at AA Financial, looking for Louie. When Louie saw him, his stomach began to growl. He couldn't imagine what he wanted, but he didn't think it could be anything good. Mickey asked him if they could go and have a cup of coffee. "I need to talk to you in private," he said. They went to a coffee shop around the corner from AA's office. They sat in a booth in the back of the coffee shop and after the waitress served them coffee Mickey took an envelope out of his pocket and handed it to Louie.

"What's this?" Louie said, looking at the envelope.

"Open it," Mickey said.

Louie opened it and took out a check for $35,000 made out to him.

"I would have given you the cash, Louie, but I didn't want to wait. I hope a check is okay."

Louie stared at him for a minute while holding the check. "What the hell is this, some kind of sick joke?"

"No joke, Louie, this is the $35,000 you gave me last week. I realized I was being a real asshole expecting you to give me back my money plus another $25,000. I know investing in the market is risky. I hope there are no hard feelings."

Louie was in shock. He had no idea what was going on. He continued to stare at Mickey then at the check and then at Mickey.

"Mickey, what the hell is this all about? Last week, you were busting my balls, and now you're sitting here giving me back the $35,000 and apologizing. I don't get it."

"Louie, please just take the money. Look, I'm just a bookie. I don't want to get involved in all that Mafia shit."

"All what Mafia shit? I don't have a clue what the hell you're talking about, Mickey. Are you taking something?"

"No, no Louie, I'm perfectly sober. Look all I want you to do is to tell your old man that I'm sorry. It was not my idea. It was all Castilano's idea."

"Castilano, who the hell is Castilano? And what has my father got to do with this?"

"Louie, I don't blame you for bustin' my chops, but I just want to forget about this whole thing. Take the money, and I swear I will never bother you again. I swear on my mother."

Louie was totally confused. "Look, Mickey, I'm not busting your chops. Believe me I don't have any fucking idea what it is you are trying to tell me. Now, please start from the beginning, and tell me what this is all about."

Mickey finally realized that maybe Louie really didn't know what he was talking about. Was he mistaken thinking that it was Louie's father who ordered the hit on Castilano? That is impossible. How about the note in the Atlantic City Press? "Leave the Santino kid alone!" Maybe the kid's old man did this on his own without Louie knowing about it? Shit!

"Mickey, for the last time, will you please tell me what this is all about?"

When Mickey finished explaining to Louie who Castilano was and then showed him the Atlantic City Press with the message about leaving him alone, Louie simply sat there without saying a word.

"You really didn't know about this, did you, Louie?"

Louie shook his head.

"Jesus Christ," Mickey said. "What happens now?"

"I don't have the faintest idea," Louie said.

Mickey thought for a minute and then said, "Nothing changes, Louie. You got your money back, and you have my word that I am out of your life. Matter of fact, I'm thinking seriously of moving to Florida."

Louie simply nodded.

Then Mickey asked again, "Will you explain this to your old man, Louie?"

Louie put the envelope with the check for $35,000 in his pocket, looked at Mickey without saying a word then got up and left the coffee shop. Mickey started to call after him but decided against it. He just sat in the booth, staring at the blank wall. When the waitress came over and asked him if he wanted anything, he smiled and said, "Yeah, a new life."

Earlier that same day, Angelo received a telephone call from his old friend in Philadelphia.

"Angelo, I just learned that our friend in Philly has had a terrible accident."

"Is that so?"

"Yes, I was told he was shot and killed coming out of the barber shop."

"How terrible," Angelo said. "Do you think we should send flowers to his funeral?"

"No, I don't think that is necessary, but it is very thoughtful."

"And our other friend, the *chooch* in Atlantic City, what is he doing?"

"From-a-what-I-a-hear, he is going out of the bookie business in Atlantic City and thinking about moving to Florida."

"Do we need to be concerned about him?"

"I'm-a-sure we don't. You don't have a problem no more."

"I can't thank you enough for telling me this. Now tell me, how much do I owe your friend for this information?"

"Not a penny. He was a happy to help. He knows of your reputation and said it was his honor to help."

"That is very kind. Please tell him that I am in his debt. If I can ever help him in any way, all he has to do is call me."

"I am sure he knows that, but I will tell him. Now what about that Jew Louie works for in New York? Your partner! That piece of shit!"

"That is my problem. I will handle it."

"And Louie what are you going to do about him?"

"I am sending someone to New York to help him wind up his affairs and escort him back to Chicago."

"Good luck, my old friend."

"The same to you, and once again *grazie*."

William Pascalle was a suave, dapper figure with none of the coarseness that characterized the majority of the Italians who toiled for the various organized crime families. He was descended from an aristocratic family in Milan. His father was a professor of languages at the University of Milan. His mother had blood ties with Massimo d'Azeglio, who had been prime minister of Italy during the nineteenth century. He received his law degree from Harvard. His clients were some of the more well-known members of organized crime. He had only represented Angelo once before in a tax matter, but when Angelo called and explained to him what he needed, the sixty-five-year-old lawyer told him he would be more than happy to take care of it personally. He charted a plane and flew from Chicago to New York, where he instructed the pilot to wait for his call; he expected to be in New York no longer than a couple of days.

When Louie arrived in his apartment after meeting with Mickey Esposito, William Pascalle was waiting for him in the lobby of his apartment building. The lawyer approached him, introduced himself, and then told Louie that his father had requested he come to New York to help him wind up his affairs, put the condo up for sale, and return with him to Chicago. He told him he had a private plane waiting for them at JFK, so he wanted to get started as soon as possible. He suggested that the first thing that Louie should do, if he had not already done so, was to call his father. Although Pascalle spoke in a soft voice, it was very definite. He wasn't asking Louie; he was telling him, and not for one minute did Louie have any doubts that he was going to do exactly what he said. Louie had dipped his toe, so to speak, in the world of organized crime but realized very quickly he was not suited for that type of life. He didn't have the balls or the smarts. In a way, he was relieved when William Pascalle laid out for him what he was going to do, and even though he still had to deal with his father when he returned to Chicago, it could be no worse than dealing with the likes of Mickey Esposito.

CHAPTER FIFTY-TWO

WHEN WADE ARRIVED at Sam's Place, the Italian restaurant in the village where they had agreed to meet, Joe was already there sitting at the bar, talking to Angie Falcone, the owner. At first, Wade almost didn't recognize him. He had lost weight and was dressed not like an F.B.I. informant but more like an investment banker. Even his persona was different. Joe saw him and waved him over.

"You know Angie, don't you?" Joe asked Wade.

Wade didn't know the owner but introduced himself, shook hands, and took a seat.

"What are you drinking?" Joe asked, at the same time waving to the bartender.

"Nothing, thanks," Wade said, "too early for me."

The owner told them to enjoy their lunch, motioned for one of the waiters to show them to a table, and left.

"You look great, Joe. It's been a while. You okay?"

"You mean because of the shit with the charges against me? Yeah, I'm fine. You only know what you read in the papers. The government only gives the press the stuff they want people to see. Believe me, Wade, when this is all over, a lot of heads are gonna roll. They're fucking with the wrong guy when they decided to trap me."

Wade had not expected this. He thought Joe would be despondent, apologetic, anything but not this arrogant.

"You look surprised, Wade."

"Well to be honest, Joe, you are right. I do only know what I read in the papers, and well . . . they make it sound like you're the bad guy. What do you mean they trapped you?"

Joe smiled, finished his drink, and signaled to the waiter for another. "You sure you won't have one?" he asked Wade. Wade shook his head.

"Wade, the entire bureau, the SEC, and the Justice Department are all pissed at me because I found out what they were doing."

"I don't understand. I thought you were working for them undercover."

"That's the thing. I was. But in doing so, I found out things they didn't want anybody to know about. I really can't talk too much about it, Wade, because of the trial, but I'll tell you this: Wall Street has become so lucrative for the mob that it's probably now the major source of income for several high-level members of organized crime. When that happens, it doesn't take long before guys in the bureau and the SEC find themselves on the pad. And worse than that, they lose sight of what the hell they started out to do in the first place. Those guys are really fucked up. I found out where federal investigators who were supposed to be probing mob-linked short-sellers had actually invested government funds into some of the mob's phony deals unknowingly. When I asked a guy at the NASD about it, he said he had no knowledge of that and refused to discuss it."

"I hear what you're saying, Joe, but what about the charges against you?"

"Wade, the stuff I was doing was on behalf of either the SEC or the Justice Department, now those bastards are denying that and claiming I was doing it on my own. They figure if they throw enough shit at me, some of it will stick, and in the meantime, the heat is off of them. When this is all over, they will regret the day they ever started this."

Wade heard what his friend was telling him but was not sure he really believed him.

"Wade, let me tell you something. People think because guys go to Harvard, buy their suits at Brooks Brothers, and belong to a private club that they are the pillars of the community. That is a lot of bullshit. I don't trust that image anymore. In a lot of cases, that's all it is . . . an image. The presentation and everything now has become so polished that you can't see what is really behind all that. Believe me when I tell you that today Wall Street has a problem that the industry and the regulators are reluctant to face, or for that matter, even acknowledge. It's called organized crime, the Mafia, wise guys, call it whatever you want. It's easier for them to jump on guys like me rather than bust the real criminals."

Wade thought to himself that his old friend had really crossed the line. Joe really believed what he was saying. Didn't he understand he had become one of those guys he was talking about?

Before they left the restaurant, Wade asked Joe if he heard any more about the SEC or the F.B.I. investigating AA Financial. Joe told him he hadn't heard anything. The last thing he remembered was the conversation he had with his people about the tapes they had that implicated Kline and one of the nation's largest banks illegally fixing the rate of interest on a large deposit.

"And as far as you know, nothing more ever happened with that?"

"Not to my knowledge, Wade."

"Let me ask you something, Joe. If you were me, would you stay at AA?"

Joe laughed. "What kind of a question is that?"

"What's so funny? I was just wondering what you would do."

"Wade, if you're asking me if I think that sooner or later AA Financial is going to get their pipes cleaned, my answer would be yes. I can't imagine they can keep doing what they are doing and not get caught. So if your decision is based on that, then my advice would be for you to get the hell out of there before the house caves in on you."

"Joe, I'm a little confused. On one hand, you say the authorities don't know what the hell they are doing, and then on the other hand, you tell me AA will eventually be brought down."

"I didn't mean to imply that they wouldn't nail some of the guys on Wall Street. Trust me, they will. What I was saying is there is so much graft and corruption on the Street that a lot of the smart connected guys are going to last a little longer. You're never going to get rid of white-collar crime in this country, and where better could it happen but on Wall Street. Wade, between me and you, I don't think you're cut out for all that shit."

"Yeah, you could be right."

"There is one thing that I heard about AA. Well not really about the firm, about Santino's kid."

"Louie?"

"Yeah, I heard he has made friends with some not so nice guys. If you're his friend, I would suggest you warn him to be careful who he does business with."

"Is that all? I mean, you don't think he is involved in anything illegal, do you?"

"I don't really know, Wade. All that I can tell you is what I heard on the street."

"Okay, Joe, thanks. I appreciate that. And I wish you luck with what's going on with the SEC and all."

"Thanks Wade."

"Joe . . . do you need anything? I mean, like, are you okay for money? I'm sure your legal bills must be killing you. Not to get too personal, but what are you doing for money . . . you're not working, are you?"

"Hey, Wade, that's sweet of you to ask. I'm okay for now. No, I'm not working, but I had put aside a fair amount of money while I was. And I have a good friend who made a lot of money with me, and he is helping me with some of the legal bills." Then laughingly he said, "If I run out of money and things don't look good, well I have plan B."

Wade looked at him, smiled, and said, "Joe, I am sure you will come out of this on top. I have confidence in you."

Leaving the restaurant, Wade replayed in his mind the conversation with Joe. He had no doubt that his old friend had changed sides. He was no longer that honest, hardworking F.B.I. agent trying to clean up Wall Street. Now he was part of what he used to try to clean up. Money will do that to some people. As he got into his car, his cell phone rang. It was Katrina. She knew he was having lunch with Joe, and she was anxious to know how the meeting went. Wade told her it went fine. He didn't go into any detail. He simply told her that Joe said he was innocent of the charges against him. She didn't understand.

"You told me he was working undercover for the F.B.I.," she said. "Why then are they accusing him of all those things in the paper?"

"I really don't know, baby. It gets a little complicated. I guess it's like they say, there is his side, their side, and the truth!"

"That's a shame."

"Yeah, I guess."

What Katrina really wanted to know was if Wade had made any decision about leaving AA. She didn't ask, but Wade knew that was what she was calling about. He decided he would talk to her later about that. Right now, he was still trying to sort out all that Joe had told him.

CHAPTER FIFTY-THREE

WHEN LOUIE CAME to work after the Andy Castilano incident he was accompanied by William Pascalle. Louie introduced him to Wade and Kline as a friend of the family. He then proceeded to tell them he had decided to leave the brokerage business and go back to Chicago. Kline knew immediately that the dapper-looking Mr. Pascalle was more than a friend of the family. He definitely had something to do with Louie's returning to Chicago. Of course, Wade remembered Louie telling him he was in trouble with a connected guy, so the fact that he was leaving the brokerage business and returning to Chicago did not surprise him. Of course he didn't know anything about the murder of Andy Castilano, why would he? Castilano was a small-time Philadelphia hood who was shot in South Philly. That didn't make any headlines in the New York papers.

Kline had no desire to continue this get-together any longer. He wished Louie good luck and told him he would forward any monies due him and left. "I have an important meeting in Manhattan," he said to Wade. "Would you mind helping Louie wind up his affairs here?" Wade said he would. Then Kline left, hardly acknowledging Pascalle. He thought about calling Angelo to find out what was really going on but decided against it. He figured if the old don wanted him to know, he would have called him. He was beginning to think that maybe he should try to find a way to buy out the old man, but there was no way he could come up with that much money. If he only knew that Santino was thinking the same thing. But that was only part of his plan.

After Kline left, Louie told Pascalle he wanted to talk to Wade alone. Pascalle said that it was not a problem; he would wait for him in his office. He said he had several phone calls he needed to make. Louie told him to make himself at home. Then Wade and Louie went to Wade's office. Louie closed the door and said to his friend, "Wade, I owe you an explanation."

Wade held up his hand as if to say stop. "You don't owe me a thing," he said. "You are doing what you have to do, and that is all I need to know."

"No, you need to know everything. We have known each other a long time, and we have always been there for one another." Wade simply nodded.

"When I left Las Vegas and came back to Chicago, I thought my life was over. I was ashamed of what I had done. Of course, my mother was very sympathetic, but my father was not in the mood for sympathy. We spent a lot of time together those first couple of weeks, and he convinced me that I could follow in his footsteps. Or maybe I should say I convinced myself. Anyhow I told him I was ready to carry on the Santino tradition. 'Just tell me what it is you want me to do,' I told him. So after discussing it for a couple of days, he decided to send me to New York. Of course, you know that part of the story. Trust me, Wade, when I tell you I truly believed I could pull it off. But I was kidding myself. I am not cut out for this life. Sure when I first got here, I put on a great act. I met some guys, bought myself a broker's license, and talked a tough game, but to tell you the truth, I was scared shitless. Then one thing led to another, and before I knew it, I was in Atlantic City, gambling again."

This totally surprised Wade. "You are kidding. When did you have a chance to go to Atlantic City?"

"I found the time that's not important. What is important is that I ended up losing my ass, and I owed the casinos a lot of money. Somehow I got tied up with a loan shark from Philly, and well you know how that goes."

Wade was beyond surprised. "Holy shit!" he said.

"Yeah, you could say that. Now here is the topper. This loan shark is the guy who had me put the Sovereign Medical Deal together. They must have been laughing at me all the way to the bank. That company had no more business being an IPO then, I don't know what. And what makes matters worse, I am sure Kline knew that, but he saw a way to make a fast buck."

"Why did you do it?" Wade asked.

"That was the only way I could pay off the casinos and the loan shark. I am sure I didn't make anything close to what those guys did."

"Where does this guy Pascalle fit in to all of this?"

"I'm coming to that. He showed up at my apartment house last night and told me my father sent him to New York to escort me back to Chicago. He also filled in a lot of the blanks. He told me a friend of my father called to tell him I was being threatened by some bad guys from Philly. You don't know my father that well, but let me tell you something, you don't fuck with anything that belongs to Angelo Santino, and that includes his son."

Wade was speechless.

"You remember when I told you about the connected guy who lost the ten grand with me?"

Wade nodded.

"Well that was this loan shark. By the way, when I told him about his loss, he didn't want to hear that. I had told him his ten grand had a good chance to become thirty-five grand, and that is what he wanted."

Wade said, "You didn't."

"I did, and that's what he wanted. Anyhow he threatened to call my old man and tell him about my gambling, so like a putz, I gave him thirty-five grand. Now before you say anything, hear this. Yesterday this guy calls and tells me he has to see me. When we meet, he starts apologizing all over the place and begging me to call my father and tell him he was just following orders. None of what he forced me to do was his idea. Then he gives me back the thirty-five grand and tells me he is going to Florida. When I left him, I didn't have a clue as to what was going on." Then Louie took out a folded up page from the Philadelphia Inquirer and handed it to Wade and said, "Last night, Pascalle gave me this." Wade read the article about Castilano being murdered.

"I don't understand. What has this got to do with what you're telling me?"

"The loan shark worked for this guy Castilano."

"Jesus Christ, Louie . . . you're not telling me . . ."

"I'm not telling you anything, Wade. You figure it out."

"Jesus," Wade said again.

"So you see what I mean when I tell you I am not cut out for this shit."

"Louie, I don't know what to say."

"There is nothing you have to say. I just wanted you to know the reason I am leaving. And one other thing, be careful."

Wade wasn't sure why Louie said that, but he had already decided that on his own. He most definitely was going to be careful.

It only took Louie a couple of hours to wind up his affairs at AA. He gave all of his client files to Wade and briefed the cashier on some pending issues. Then he packed up the few personal belongings he had, said his good-byes to the people in the office, and left. He told Wade he would probably be leaving for Chicago the next day. He told him that Pascalle was taking care of closing up the apartment, arranging for his personal items to be shipped to Chicago and then listing it with a real estate agent to sell it. Louie was indeed a lame duck. At this point, he simply did what Pascall told him. Wade really felt sorry for him. He wondered what would happen to him when he got back to Chicago.

Wade left the office early that day. He had a lot to think about, and he couldn't do it there. When he arrived home, Katrina was there with her tour director, who had arranged her tour to Europe, and a man he didn't know. Katrina quickly introduced him, "Wade, this is Carl Smyth. He is in charge of putting together the show at Madison Square Garden for the Millennium, and he has asked me to appear, isn't that exciting?" Under normal circumstances that would be very exciting, but Wade's head was so full of other shit that he didn't give Katrina the kind of response she was expecting. The other two men in the room got the same impression. Katrina was smart enough not to pursue it anymore at this time. She told the tour director and Carl Smyth she would consider their offer and get back to them in a couple of days. They knew their meeting was finished. They said their good-byes and left.

Wade made himself a drink and then looked at Katrina. "I'm sorry, baby . . ." She didn't let him finish. "You have nothing to be sorry for, Wade. I know you have a lot on your mind. We can talk about the Millennium show later."

"No, baby, it has nothing to do with that. I think you doing the show would be great. It's Louie."

"What happened?"

"He started gambling again in Atlantic City."

"Oh no," she said.

"Yeah, and he lost a lot of money and got involved with a loan shark down there. It seems the loan shark worked for a guy in Philly who was connected. You know what that means don't you?"

"I think so."

"Well one thing led to another, and these guys convinced him to bring a deal to AA that we never should have touched. It's difficult to explain, but then some things happened after that. Well to make a long story short, he is going back to Chicago."

"I don't understand, Wade. That doesn't make sense. Why did he do it? The whole thing sounds crazy. It really does."

Wade put his drink down on the bar and walked over to her and put his arms around her. "I know, sweetheart, this whole goddamn business doesn't make sense."

She looked at him and could see the stress in his face. She wanted to say, "Get out of that business or at least leave Kline and go somewhere else," but she didn't.

"You know something, Katrina I don't think I could get through all of this without you. You are the only thing that makes sense anymore."

She looked at him with tears in her eyes. She loved him very much. "So what are you going to do?" she asked between kissing him.

He smiled, "What am I going to do? Do you mean before or after I make love to you?"

She took him by the hand and led him into the bedroom. He held her so close that he could hear her heart beating as if it were in his own chest. Within minutes, they were naked, still holding one another, kissing and whispering their love for one another. There was no Louie; there was no Albert Kline; there was no AA Financial. There was only the two of them. When they finished making love, and before falling asleep, he cupped her face in his hands and whispered, "I love you very much . . . marry me." She kissed him tenderly and said, "We'll see how you feel in the morning."

CHAPTER FIFTY-FOUR

WHILE WAITING FOR his son to come home, Angelo Santino was trying to think of a way he could get even with his partner Albert Kline for allowing Louie to get sucked in with those *momolukes* in South Philly. He should have warned him; instead he saw a way to make a fast buck with no regard for what might happen to his son. The fact that he was his partner made it more difficult. Anything he did to cause financial harm to AA would hurt him as well. However, had he known the trouble that Kline had brought upon himself, he could have stopped worrying about what to do.

For years, Albert Kline had had a mistress, several, as a matter of fact. The most recent, Carolyn Thomas was a financial secretary at Bank of America. They met two years ago while Kline was doing a bond deal with the bank. First it was a casual dinner date, then Kline invited her to go to Bermuda with him for a weekend, and two months later, he rented her an apartment on Park Avenue. She was in her late twenties, very pretty, and very smart. Kline bought her expensive gifts, took her on trips, and introduced her to the good life. However, he made it very clear to her from the start that he would never leave his wife. As smart as she was, she believed she could change his mind. That was a big mistake. At just about the same time Louie told him he was returning to Chicago, Carolyn told him she was two months pregnant. "How can that be?" he screamed. "Aren't you on the pill?"

"Of course," she said. "But sometimes this happens."

"Bullshit. You let it happen. If you think you being pregnant will make me leave my wife, you have another think coming. One thing I don't need in my life at this point is another fucking kid. You find out where you can get an abortion and get it done. I mean now, not later."

Carolyn started to cry. "No, I want this baby. With you or without you, I want to keep this baby."

Kline slapped her hard across the face. "Are you out of your fucking mind? You're getting an abortion."

"No, I'm not," she said, afraid he would hit her again.

"You bitch. By the way, how do I know this is my baby? I don't know that I can make a baby at my age."

"You know damn well it's yours. I don't sleep around. You are the only man I have been with since we started dating over two years ago."

"Well if that's the case, then I think I have as much say in the matter as you and I say you get rid of it, end of story."

The following day, Kline called his old friend Sal Maggio in Las Vegas. Sal was no longer in the brokerage business. The State of Nevada had closed him down almost a year earlier. He pleaded no contest to a number of charges from the SEC and as a result paid a fine of $25,000, which was just chicken feed for him. He was put on probation for a year, banned from the brokerage business forever, and did sixty days of community service. He was back in the bookie and shylock business in Las Vegas; once a crook always a crook.

Kline told him he needed a favor. There was a woman in New York who was pregnant, and he didn't want her to have the baby. He wanted someone to scare the shit out of her and convince her to have an abortion.

"How rough do you want to get?" Sal asked.

"Do whatever it takes," Kline said. "I don't have a problem if she gets roughed up enough that she loses the fucking baby."

"Man, you really don't like her, do you?"

"It's not a case of liking or disliking her. It's simply a case that there was a deal, and she didn't stick to her end of the bargain."

"It's none of my business, Albert, but are you the father?"

"You're right, Sal. It isn't any of your business."

"Hey I'm sorry, I didn't mean to get personal."

"That's okay, Sal, we have known each other a long time. I wouldn't admit this to anyone else, but as a matter of fact, she claims it is my baby. To tell you the truth, I am not sure. But she is making all kind of threats, and I don't need this kind of aggravation in my life. This bitch has lost her mind. Not only does she want to keep the baby but she wants the kid to have my name. 'I want this baby to have a good life. You can afford it,' she says to me. Do you fucking believe her? I have been very good to her, Sal, and now she is busting my balls. Enough is enough. It's time for me to change dancing partners."

"How soon you want this taken care of?"

"Like now."

"Okay, I'll take care of it. I still know some guys in New York."

"That's great, Sal. I knew I could depend on you. Just let me know how much it costs. And by the way, there is an extra $25,000 for you. I heard that's how much your fine was with the SEC."

"That's very nice of you, my friend. You got a deal."

CHAPTER FIFTY-FIVE

THE LAST CLEAR thing that Carolyn remembered was pushing the remote in her car to open the gate to the garage at her condo. She had difficulty remembering what happened next. She vaguely recalled a man knocking on her window as she pulled into the garage. Now she found herself waking up in the trunk of a moving car, her hands bound behind her back.

Panic overcame her. Was this a bad dream? Was this really happening to her? She could feel the bile build up in her throat. Afraid that she was going to throw up, she swallowed it. Would all of this hurt her baby? She tried to move, but it was impossible. She could feel the ropes cutting into her wrists. She wanted to cry but couldn't. Then suddenly she felt the car shaking, and she couldn't stop from rolling back and forth in the trunk.

"What if she dies?" Joey, the taller of the two men asked. "This is a pretty bumpy street."

The other man in the front of the car was Tommy Benito, a friend of Sal Maggio. He was a real thug. He would do almost anything for money. Correction, he would do anything for money. Sal asked him to grab Carolyn and slap her around a little, then tell her that unless she got an abortion, this was only a preview of what was going to happen to her. He made sure to add that if along the way she lost the baby, there would be an additional $1,000 in it for him.

"How many times I gotta tell you?" Benito answered with a scowl, "we just putting a scare into the bitch so she gets an abortion. She ain't gonna die."

"What we gonna do with her? We can't just ride around all night? How long does it take to lose a baby?"

"What, do I look like a pediatrician?"

"Like a what?"

Benito was getting pissed off at his friend Joey Amato. He had brought him along to help, but now he was sorry. He could have taken care of Carolyn by himself. He turned to him and said, "Will you quit with the fucking questions already. I told you we are gonna ride around a while then drop her off somewhere, and let her find her own way home. That should be enough to scare the shit out of her. And if we get lucky, she will lose the kid, and we make an additional thousand bucks." As soon as the words came out of his mouth, he was sorry. He had promised to pay Joey $500, and no matter what happened, that was all he was going to get.

"What do mean $1,000 more? What does that mean?"

"Nothing I just wanted to get your attention so I could tell you to shut you up, that's all."

"I don't know why you're always getting mad at me, Tommy."

"I'm not always mad at you. It's just that you ask too many damn questions."

Joey had to ask another question. "Do you think anybody saw us, Tommy?"

"Jesus Christ, Joey, I should have put you in the trunk with her."

"You're just kiddin', right, Tommy?"

Carolyn felt the bile rise in her throat again, and this time she almost choked swallowing it. She tried to calm herself down. Why was someone doing this to her? Was it a sex maniac? Was it robbery? If they wanted to rob her, they could have just done that and left her. Then she remembered. Albert Kline was coming to the condo so that they could talk about the baby again. He was still adamant about her getting an abortion, but he agreed to come over and discuss it with her. She tried to think ahead. "*He will come to the apartment, and I won't be there. He will see my car in the garage when he arrives. He will have to wonder what happened to me. Unless . . . no, impossible . . . he can't have anything to do with this . . . stop thinking crazy things, Carolyn.*" Tears filled her eyes and began sliding slowly down her cheeks. Then she felt the car shaking again, and she rolled over and hit her head on the spare wheel.

They had been driving around for almost two hours. During that time, Joey must have asked a dozen times, "So what are we gonna do with her?" Then finally, "I'm hungry, Tommy. Let's get something to eat."

Tommy just stared at him. He had been given a job to do, and he was going to do it, but he didn't know when enough was enough. How long before she loses the baby? Had he scared the bitch in the trunk enough that she was going to get an abortion? And Sal never told him who the father was. "He is somebody important and very rich, that's all I can tell you," that's what Sal said. Tommy thought to himself, *five grand*, that's not much if the guy who knocked up this bitch is really rich. He wondered how much the guy was paying Sal. Then Joey nudged him. "Tommy, I gotta take a piss, and I'm hungry. Let's pull over, open the trunk, and see if she is still alive. I don't want to be involved in no murder rap."

"Jesus H. Christ, Joey, you are really getting to be a pain in the ass."

"Come on, Tommy . . ."

"Okay, okay, I'm getting a little hungry myself. I'll pull over, and you can open the trunk and take a look at her. If she is okay, then we'll go get something to eat."

"Why I gotta do it? Why I gotta look at her?"

"Because I said so, that's why."

"What am I looking for?" Joey asked.

"First make sure she is still breathing then look between her legs to see if she is bleedin'."

"Look between her legs? I ain't doin' that."

"Joey, remind me never to take you with me again, ever."

"Come on, Tommy . . ."

Tommy pulled off on a side street, took a flashlight out of the glove department, and walked around to the back of the car and popped open the trunk. He shone the flashlight on Carolyn. She was lying there, motionless, which scared the crap out of him. He could see she had blood on the side of her face. His first thought was, *"the* puta *is dead."* He slammed the trunk closed.

"Is she okay?" Joey yelled from the car.

"I dunno," he said as he got back in the car. "Anybody home at your place, Joey?"

"Nah who would be there you know I live alone."

"Yeah, but sometime your asshole cousin shows up with his coked-out friends . . . never the matter, we're gonna take her to your place."

"Why does it have to be my place?"

"Because I fuckin' said so, and if you say one more word, or if you even moan or grunt or even cough, I'm gonna blow your fuckin' head off, do you hear what I'm sayin'?"

Joey leaned his head back and under his breath said, "Jeeze!"

Tommy took his gun out of his waistband and pointed it at Joey's head. "I fuckin' dare you, say one more word . . . one word . . . any fuckin' word . . . come on, say something."

Joey pushed the gun away from his head, crossed his arms, and didn't say another word until they arrived at his house. Getting out of the car, Joey said, "Can I talk now?"

Joey lived in a dump of a house that belonged to one of his cousins who was a drug dealer. Tommy parked the car among the rotting garbage in the alley at the back of the house. Then with a complaining Joey, he managed to drag Carolyn into the house, drop her on the ratty smelly couch in the living room, and untie her hands. The good news was that she was still breathing. The bad news was that there was no blood between her legs. Tommy didn't know much about what was supposed to happen when a woman loses a baby, but he knew enough to know that there had to be some bleeding. Then he dragged her into the bedroom and threw her onto the bed. He pulled her hands up over her head and tied them to the bed frame, making sure she wasn't going anywhere then went back into the living room and slumped into a chair where Joey was watching TV. His gut told him this was not a healthy scene. What if this bitch dies? He sure as hell wasn't going to take a murder rap for $5,000. Who the hell was the father? That's what he had to find out. One thing he knew for sure was that he had to come up with a plan, and soon.

Gaining consciousness, Carolyn realized she must have passed out after she hit her head on the spare wheel. She looked around the dark room and tried to move her arms, but she couldn't. She was lying on a narrow, sagging bed in a dark room with her hands tied over her head to the bed frame. She could hear voices. She didn't know if someone was in the room with her or if the sound was coming from another room. Slowly as her eyes became accustomed to the darkness, she realized that she was alone. The voices were coming from another room. Waves of fear overcame her, and she was desperate to go to the bathroom. Her stomach ached, and the strain of her arms being tied over her head became increasingly more painful. The room was cold and damp, and the smell of cigarette smoke was making her nauseated. She tried to remain rational to figure out why she was here. She wasn't rich or famous, so why would someone want to kidnap her? Then the voices from the other room became clearer, and she understood what was happening.

"Look, Tommy, why don't you call your friend? We get the money and just leave."

"And what do we do with her?" Tommy asked pointing to the bedroom. "Nah, Joey, I need to come up with a better plan." He wanted to call Sal, but he didn't want Joey to listen in. "Do me a favor, Joey, go down to the 7-Eleven and get us some hot coffee and donuts. Here take this twenty and keep the change." As soon as he left, Tommy called Sal.

"Hey Sal its Tommy what's up?"

"You tell me. Did you get the broad?"

"Yeah, that went good, matter of fact she is in the other room. I don't think she lost the kid, but I am sure she's gonna agree to getting an abortion."

"What do mean she is in the other room? Why didn't you just drop her off somewhere?"

"Well here is the thing, Sal, she don't look so good. You know, rollin' around in the trunk and all, I mean what I want to ask you is . . . suppose this bitch dies . . . what then?"

"What the fuck are you talking about? Who said anything about killing her?"

"Nah, I understand we never said that, but she was in the trunk a long time, and I don't know, Sal, for $5,000, well I think there should be a little more in it for me."

"You son of a bitch are you trying to blackmail me?"

"No, Sal, you know I wouldn't do that, but you said the guy who knocked up this broad was very rich, well I thought you could go back to him and we both get some more money, you know what I mean?"

"Listen to me, Tommy. You better make sure that bitch doesn't die because if she does, your life ain't worth a shit. I don't know where you are, and I don't want to know, but wherever it is, get her out of there and dump her somewhere where she will be found, and make sure she understands about the abortion. Do I make myself clear?"

"Yeah yeah Sal you make yourself clear. Don't worry I'll take care of it."

"And the next time you call me, it better be to tell me the job is done, *capisce*?"

Carolyn closed her eyes and thought about what she had just heard. She had to will herself to live so that she could make sure Albert Kline was punished for this horrible thing he had done to her. And then suddenly she got a warm wet feeling between her legs and terrible pains in her stomach, and she knew immediately what was happening.

The two vice squad detectives staking out Joey's cousin's house had a tip that a drug deal was set to take place there. They had been running around for weeks with nothing to show for it, and their captain was on their ass to make something happen.

"For Christ's sake, can't you guys make a simple drug bust? You're the only guys in the squad with no busts this month."

The captain worked on quantity, not quality. Sure the two detectives had a line on a couple of small-timers dealing drugs to delinquent school kids, but the local uniforms usually took care of that. But now they had this hot tip, and they were going to sit it out and wait.

Detective Harvey West was slumped in the backseat of the unmarked car parked across the street from Joey's house, drinking coffee. He was disgusted; he hated his job. With his thinning hair, pinched nose, receding chin, and steel-rimmed glasses, he looked like somebody's uncle Harvey rather than a vice squad detective. His partner, Andy Macon, who definitely looked like a cop, was sitting in the front of the car, his eyes peeled on Joey's cousin's house. It was his turn to watch. When Tommy parked in the alley behind the house, detective Macon got out of the car so that he could see who was going into the house. He didn't recognize either Tommy or Joey or the woman they were helping into the house who he assumed was drunk or stoned. Dumb cop!

Finally, Detective Macon saw Joey's cousin pull up in front of the house in a shiny new Buick with brass spoke wheels, a car any respectable drug dealer would be proud to own. Then he saw Joey coming down the street carrying something, probably drugs, he thought. Wrong, dummy, it was coffee and donuts. He saw Joey and his cousin greet each other and enter the house. He turned to his partner in the backseat and said, "Let's go. It's about to go down!" With guns drawn, they got out of the car, ran across the street, and broke down the front door of Joey's cousin's house.

"Freeze, all you motherfuckers, and get down on the floor!"

CHAPTER FIFTY-SIX

CAROLYN FORCED HERSELF to stay awake. She knew that unless she was able to escape her life was not worth a plug nickel. She heard the front door open and close and gathered from the conversation that the man who had gone out for coffee had returned. She also heard the voice of a third man. "What the hell is Tommy doin' here?" he said. She assumed that Tommy was the man she heard on the phone. All of this time, she kept struggling trying to get her wrists free. Each time she tried, she rubbed more skin off her wrists, and she could feel the blood trickling down her arms. Finally, she was able to free one of her arms. Quickly she freed the other arm and gathered up enough strength to get out of bed and make her way to the window. As quietly as she could, she opened the window and crawled out. Just as she did, she heard someone break down the front door and scream, "Freeze, all you motherfuckers, and get down on the floor!"

It had just started to rain. By the time Carolyn climbed through the window and ran out of the alley and reached the street, she was soaked to the skin. Her wrists and arms were covered with blood as was the front of her dress and legs. As she ran past Tommy's car parked in the alley, she made a mental note of the license plate. Having been a legal secretary, her mind was trained to remember things, and something inside of her told her that remembering the license plate on the car would be important.

Looking up and down the deserted street, she realized she was in a bad part of the city, probably somewhere way uptown, more than likely a crime-ridden area. "Stay strong," she whispered to herself, "you're going to make it." There was no one around. Most of the streetlights were broken, and the only two places that were open were an all night 7-Eleven and a seedy-looking bar. The bar was the closest. She half-walked and half-ran toward it. If she could only get to a phone . . . that's all she needed to be safe. One call to 911, and they would come and get her. It had to be quick before those men found out she had escaped. She knew they would come looking for her.

When she tried to push open the door to the bar, a large black man stood in the doorway, blocking her way. "Get the hell out of here, you goddamn tramp. How many times I tell ya filthy vagrants that ya all ain't gotta come here? Now get you're raggity ass outta here!"

"But I've . . ."

He wasn't having it. He grabbed her around the waist and propelled her outside shoving her so hard she fell in the gutter.

"And don't ya all come back, ya hear?"

This was impossible. She'd escaped a devastating kidnapping, more than likely lost her baby, and was now being treated like a piece of garbage. Just when she was about to lose all hope, a middle-aged black woman appeared in the doorway and said, "What the hell is goin' on here?"

The large black man pointed to Carolyn lying in the gutter and said, "This here piece of trash was tryin' to come in and get something for free."

The woman looked at Carolyn, who by this time was sobbing uncontrollably.

She turned to the man, who was her husband, and yelled, "What is wrong with you, Herman? Can't you see this poor baby is in trouble? She ain't from around here. Look at her dress, and that ring and that watch. That ain't stuff a vagrant wears. And can't you see she has been hurt? What's wrong with you man this poor girl been beat up or something. Look at the blood all over her."

Herman still wasn't having any of it. "Shit," he said.

Carolyn heard what the woman had said. She knew this was her last hope. She gathered up all of her strength and managed to get to her knees, wiped away her tears, and said, "Thank you, thank you. Please help me. My name is Carolyn Thomas, and two men kidnapped me and held me prisoner. They tied me up and put me in the trunk of a car. I . . . I think I had a miscarriage," and she pointed to the blood on her dress and legs. "I just escaped, but I know they will come looking for me . . . oh dear God . . . please help me." She had nothing left. After that, she simply passed out and lay face down in the gutter.

"Herman, get that lady out of the street and in here before I smack you on your dumb head. I'm going to call 911, and you hear me, you fool, anything bad happens to this poor baby you gonna have to deal with me, you stupid ass."

CHAPTER FIFTY-SEVEN

ALMOST A MONTH had gone by since Albert Kline asked Sal to convince Carolyn to have an abortion. The more he thought about it, the more he realized that it was a bad idea. Now that he hadn't heard from him, he began to worry. He called him several times but each time got his voice mail. That alone wouldn't concern him, but the fact that he had not seen or spoken to Carolyn in almost a month did concern him. He hadn't been able to reach her by phone, and when he called the doorman at the condo, he told Kline that he hadn't seen her in a while. Kline thought about going to her apartment but decided against it.

It was just about that same time that Wade received a call from Joe Cantor. He told him that things were not going well. They had moved his trial date up, and the prosecuting attorney told his lawyer that they had a witness willing to turn state's evidence. They claimed he was unimpeachable.

"I thought you told me you could prove what you were doing was undercover work," Wade said.

Joe laughed. "Yeah, I know, but it's not that simple, Wade."

"I don't understand, Joe. Either you were or you weren't."

Joe laughed again, "You know, Wade sometimes you get so involved in something that the colors get blurred. It's not always black and white. Some of the guys I was working with were pretty tough dudes, and they made it very attractive for me to . . . well let's just say if they got somebody who was on the inside willing to testify, then I have real problems, you know what I mean?"

"I guess I do. So what are you going to do?"

"I like you, Wade. You are one of the few really honest people in this shitty business."

"Thanks, but you didn't answer my question."

"Meet me at Sparks Steak House for dinner. I'll tell you then."

So that night, Wade once again crossed the most famous piece of sidewalk in the city and entered Sparks Steak House, known the world over for the gangster who'd died where Wade had just walked. Joe was at the bar. When he saw Wade, he motioned for him to join him. Wade ordered a drink, and then the two men followed the maître d' to a booth at the back of the restaurant.

Joe repeated what he told Wade on the phone, this time in more detail. Then he added that there was something else he needed to tell him.

"What's that?" Wade asked.

"It's not about me."

"So what is it about, Joe?"

"You're not going to believe what I'm about to tell you. It was difficult for me to believe."

"What the hell are you talking about, Joe?"

"I still have this friend at the bureau who told me your boss is in some real trouble."

"Oh I think I have heard that tune before."

"This has nothing to do with the brokerage business. This is a different kind of trouble."

"Joe, let's have it. What's going on?"

"My friend told me the bureau is investigating a case of kidnapping and that Kline's name has come up. They have been working on this thing for over a month."

"What . . . Are you crazy, Joe?"

"I'm not bullshittin' you, Wade. My friend is reliable."

"What the hell are you talking about? Kidnapping who? This is insane, Joe."

"Wade, I know how crazy it sounds, but trust me, this gal knows what she is talking about."

Wade sat and looked at his friend. He couldn't believe what he just told him.

"Wade, I know this is hard to believe, but it's true.

They both sat looking at one another for what seemed like an eternity. Finally, Wade said, "Joe, can you imagine how crazy this sounds? I mean, it doesn't make sense. I know Kline is a manipulator and all that, but a kidnapper . . . Jesus Christ, Joe, give me a break."

"Wade, I wish I had more details, but all I can tell you is that the bureau was called in by the local cops after they busted a couple of guys for a drug deal. Somehow it became a kidnapping case, and then Kline's name came up."

"Joe, I never heard anything so crazy in my life. Did she tell you who was supposedly kidnapped? My god, it sounds crazy to even ask a question like that."

"She didn't have a name, but she knows it's a woman."

"Where is the woman now?"

"I don't know, Wade."

"Man, this is really unbelievable."

"Yeah, I know, Wade, but I thought I owed it to you to tell you."

"Joe, I hear what you are saying, and I don't doubt your friend at the agency is reliable, but think about what you're saying. A man like Albert Kline doesn't go around kidnapping people."

"I didn't say he was the one who actually kidnapped somebody. I said his name came up in the investigation."

"That's the same thing, Joe. For what purpose would he be involved in something like that?"

"I don't know, Wade. I can only tell you what my friend told me."

"Do you think Kline knows about the investigation?"

"I doubt it very much unless he has somebody on the inside at the agency, which is highly unlikely."

"How long before they do something?"

"That's hard to say, pal. It depends on how strong of a case they have. They usually wait until they feel they are solid before they act."

"If you had to guess what would you say?"

"Don't know, Wade, really."

"How do you think this will affect me, Joe? I mean, what happens if all of this is true? What happens at AA?"

"You would know that better than anybody, Wade."

Wade finished his drink and signaled to the waiter for another; Joe did the same.

"So what happens now, Joe?"

"As far as your boss is concerned, I'm not sure. Depending what kind of a case the agency puts together, he could be charged."

"Charged with what?"

"Who knows? Depending what they come up with, could be any number of things. I will try to find out."

"Wow, this is really a shocker, but the funny thing is, Joe, I have noticed that he seems a little jumpy lately. I don't know. Maybe it's because you're telling me this, I am reading something into something that isn't there."

"That's very possible Wade, I don't know."

"Oh boy."

"Yeah, anyway I have some other news.

"Why is it I have the feeling it's not good news."

"I'm leaving the country."

Wade shook his head. "I don't believe you, Joe. First, you tell me Kline is a kidnapper, now you tell me you are leaving the country. Holy shit, what is next?"

"I know, Wade . . ."

"Joe, how can you leave the country with your trial pending? You can't do that."

"Yes, I can. I haven't been arrested. I've only been charged. I still have my passport, so I can go wherever I want."

"What happens when the trial starts?" Wade asked, knowing the answer.

"I guess that's when I'm in trouble, pal."

"Joe, you know they will find you and bring you back."

"Wade, there is no way I am going to jail. I would rather kill myself first."

"Joe, don't talk that way. First of all, you don't know that you would go to jail. And your case could drag on for months, maybe years. And suppose you do lose? Maybe you end up with paying a fine and probation. Look, this is your game. You know how to play it. I am sure you will find a way out."

"I wish I could believe that, pal. But trust me when I tell you these guys are out to get me."

"Just promise me you won't do anything drastic, Joe."

"Depends what you call drastic."

When Wade got home, Katrina was sleeping. He wanted to wake her and tell her what Joe had told him, but she looked so content that he couldn't do it. He had to talk to someone, someone he could trust, someone who could help him make some decisions about AA. Should he stay? Was this actually an opportunity for him? Suppose it was true about Kline? Suppose Kline went to jail? Who would run AA? The whole thing was crazy. He sat looking out of the window at the dark sky, and then it hit him. There was one person he could talk to who he could trust and help him decide what he should do. He would call Louie in the morning and ask him to arrange for him to see his father. After all, it was Angelo Santino who first introduced him to Albert Kline, and he did own half of AA Financial. He owed it to him to tell him what Joe had told him. He also owed it to himself. He thought back to when he first came to Wall Street; that was an exciting time. He wondered, "*Was it the bad guys who corrupted Wall Street or was it Wall Street who ended up creating the bad guys?*" No matter, Wall Street was not for the faint of heart. That notwithstanding he decided right there and then that he was going to stay in the game. What he needed to do was make sure he had all of the right cards.

CHAPTER FIFTY-EIGHT

SOMETIMES EVEN TWO not-so-smart detectives stumble upon an important case in the course of their careers. Such was the case with detectives Harvey West and Andy Macon. When they broke into Joey's cousin's house, thinking they were going to make a drug bust, they had no way of knowing they would find two kidnappers.

After entering the house and ordering the three men who were in the living room to lie on the floor, they realized that all that the men were doing was drinking coffee.

"What the fuck?" Joey's cousin said, recognizing the two detectives. He had been busted by them once before. "What you guys want? What's goin' on?"

"That's what we want to know," Detective Macon answered.

"Nothin' man. Now can we please get up off the floor?"

"Not yet," Macon said, then looking around, he asked, "Where is the girl?"

"What girl?"

Joey, who by this time had wet his pants, said, "He must mean the girl in the bedroom."

Tommy turned and looked at Joey in disgust.

"Go look in the bedroom," Macon said to his partner.

Macon slowly opened the bedroom door, turned on the light switch, and yelled out, "You better come and look at this, Andy."

During the next hour, Joey went over in detail what had taken place that night. His cousin was just as surprised as were the two detectives. By that time, both Macon and West were convinced that Joey's cousin had nothing to do with what had gone down that night. It took a while before they all figured out how Carolyn had escaped, after which Detective West went out in the alley to see if there was any trace of her. He walked out to the street, which was deserted. By this time, Herman and his wife had taken Carolyn into the bar and called 911. Joey even told the detectives about Sal. The detectives believed Joey and Tommy when they said they didn't know who the rich guy was who ordered the kidnapping.

After seeing all of the blood on the empty bed, Tommy was afraid that maybe Carolyn didn't make it. Maybe she died on the street, and somebody took her to a hospital. He decided he wasn't going to take a murder rap for Sal, so he told the detectives he wanted to make a deal. Joey said the same thing. Joey's cousin said they were two assholes and deserved whatever would happen to them.

Detectives Macon and West handcuffed Joey and Tommy and placed them under arrest. They decided to let Joey's cousin go. "Thanks for nothing," he said as he left the house. No good deed goes unpunished.

CHAPTER FIFTY-NINE

WHEN WADE ARRIVED in Chicago, Louie picked him up at the O'Hare Airport. Wade thought Louie looked much better than he did the last time he saw him in New York. He told Wade that his father really went easy on him for what happened in Atlantic City. He also told Wade that he decided to stay in Chicago. "I feel better being close to home," he said.

"So what do you intend doing?"

"I plan on opening an interior decorating business. My mother has a lot of friends who have indicated they would love to have me help them redecorate their homes. I'm not like you, Wade. I need the security of my family. I really envy you being on your own. I guess I just wasn't cut out for the world of finance."

Wade thought to himself that if he had a rich father, he too might like the security of being close to home, but that really wasn't true. Wade was competitive. He was that way in college when he played basketball and that way when he started on Wall Street. And he loved a challenge. It would be easy for him to walk away from AA Financial, or for that matter, leave Wall Street altogether, but in his mind, that would be giving up.

Louie had arranged for him to meet with his father the next day. When they arrived back at the house, it was after ten o'clock at night, and Louie's parents had already retired for the evening. The two young men sat and talked for several hours. Louie never asked Wade the reason he wanted to see his father, and Wade elected not to discuss it. They talked about old times at school, and Wade talked a lot about Katrina. It was after midnight when Wade went to the guest room and got ready for bed. He had gone over in his mind several times what he wanted to say to Louie's father. He was ready.

At 8:00 a.m., Louie, Wade, and Louie's parents were having breakfast in the dining room. When they finished eating, Louie told Wade that he and his mother were going downtown to look at some properties that were for sale that would serve as a showroom and office for his new business venture. After they left, Angelo suggested to Wade that they go into his study. The last time Wade was there was when Angelo first told him about AA Financial. How ironic.

CHAPTER SIXTY

"ANY IDENTIFICATION ON her?" Detective Lennon asked the female doctor.

"No sir but the couple that called 911 said she told them her name was Carolyn Thomas."

"Tell me again how they came to be the ones who called 911." The female doctor related once again the story that Herman and his wife told the 911 people when they arrived at the bar. Herman's wife asked if she could go with Carolyn to the hospital, but the officer-in-charge wouldn't allow it. Carolyn had gone into a semi-coma after passing out on the street in front of Herman's bar. The female doctor explained to the detective that she was in shock but that all of her vital signs were good, and she expected her to recover. She also told him about the miscarriage.

Detective Lennon commented to the nurse about the street violence in the neighborhood where the 911 people picked up Carolyn. "Do you think she was really kidnapped?" he asked the pretty lady doctor.

"I can't say, Detective. That's your job."

"Poor kid," he said, and handed the doctor his card. "Do me a favor and have someone call me when she starts talking."

"Absolutely are you going to try and locate any of her family?"

"We have someone checking into that now. They are looking at all the Carolyn Thomases in New York and checking all of the missing persons report. I would sure like to find the son-of-a-bitches who were responsible for this."

"I hope you do," the lady doctor said.

When Detective Lennon returned to his precinct, his captain called him into his office. "I think we got a break on this Carolyn Thomas case you are working."

"Oh."

"Yeah, when we put out a wire checking all the missing persons report, we got a call from a Detective Macon at the 43rd precinct. He said they picked up a couple of guys last night who admitted to kidnapping her."

"Are you shittin' me?"

"No, really it seems these are two small-time punks who were doing a job for some guy in Vegas. They were just supposed to scare her into getting an abortion."

"I don't fucking believe that."

"I know what you mean. Anyhow I spoke to Macon's captain, and we both agreed we should call the F.B.I. since this is technically a kidnapping case now."

"Hey c'mon, Captain, I would like to handle this here."

"No can do, Lennon. You know the protocol."

"Jesus Christ."

"Tell you what I can do. I'll suggest to the bureau that you act as the liaison so you can remain in the loop. How is that?"

Detective Lennon agreed.

Later that same day, he received a call from the pretty doctor who was taking care of Carolyn. She was awake and alert but very frightened. He told her he was on his way. After listening to Carolyn's entire account of what happened, including her statement that she was sure it was Albert Kline who was responsible, he decided she should not return to her apartment. He suggested she remain in protective custody until they had apprehended everyone involved. She agreed but wanted to call her sister who lived in New Jersey. That was not a problem.

Once the F.B.I. became involved, it wasn't long before they located Sal Maggio in Las Vegas. When they picked him up for questioning, he denied everything, and then they showed him a video of both Joey Amato and Tommy Benito implicating him.

"How do I know you didn't doctor the video?" Sal said.

The agent ignored the question and told him between the trouble he had with the SEC and the fact he was a three-time loser, that unless he cooperated and gave up Kline, he would spend the rest of his life behind bars.

Initially the idea of cooperating was moot because Sal didn't believe the bullshit the bureau was giving him. He had been arrested before, and he had done time before. Going to jail was an annoyance. And he also beat some raps in the past. Who the hell did they think they were dealing with, an amateur? Maybe he could pay these guys off nah, these are the feds, these tight-ass bastards with their wing-tip shoes. Shit.

"How old are you, Sal?" The agent asked him very much aware he was thinking about cooperating but needed some convincing.

"What the hell that got to do with anything?"

"I was trying to figure how many weekends you have left and how it would feel spending every last one of them in the joint. You know, in the state of New York, the judge can give you up to ninety-nine years in jail for kidnapping or conspiring to kidnap. That's a lot of weekends, Sal."

"You guys are really a bunch of pricks, you know that?"

"Flattery will get you nowhere, Sal."

"What kind of a deal can I make?" he asked the agent.

"Don't know Sal, up to the federal prosecutor and the judge. What I can tell you is whatever it ends up being will be a hell of a lot better deal than spending your dying days in prison up to you."

And so he gave up Albert Kline.

CHAPTER SIXTY-ONE

ON HIS FLIGHT home from Chicago, Wade thought about his conversation with Angelo Santino. He was quite a man. First of all, he appreciated the fact he thought it was important enough for him to fly to Chicago and tell him face-to-face what his friend Joe Cantor had told him about Kline. To Wade's surprise, the old man was not shocked by the news. He said, "When you have so much money, many times, you lose sight of things. There is no right or wrong, only what it is you want to do. I would hope, of course, our friend didn't do what Mr. Cantor said, but if it is true, I am sure he will deal with it, as we will. He was very up-front, very matter of fact, and to the point. And when Wade asked him what he thought he should do, once again, the old man's answer was simple.

"Absolutely nothing you have a good job and a good future. Regardless of what happens to our friend, you will always have me as your ally. My suggestion to you is that you go back to New York and do your job."

Wade wanted to ask, "And that's it?"

But the old man answered that question before Wade asked it.

"There is one more thing Wade, and I know I can depend on your confidence."

Wade simply nodded.

"I am negotiating with a bank in Rome for them to buy AA Financial. I am very optimistic we will be successful. When that is completed, Wade, you will take over running the firm. That is part of the deal." The old man smiled. "I hope you will like being a millionaire."

The old guy sure had a way with words.

Katrina was glad when Wade called her from the airport. He told her to meet him for dinner at Le Cirque.

"I assume your meeting with the Mafia went well," she said.

"That's very funny my lady."

"I thought so. What time should I meet you?"

"How about we meet in about an hour?"

"See you there, my love. By the way, I have been thinking about that question you asked me a couple of weeks ago."

"What question is that?"

"You know damn well what question. Anyway I was thinking I may take you up on that."

"I don't have the faintest idea what you are talking about," he said, trying not to laugh.

"Good-bye, Wade. See you in an hour."

It took Wade longer than he anticipated to drive from the airport into the city, and when he finally arrived at the restaurant, Katrina was sitting at the bar, talking to a very distinguished-looking man. When he walked over, she kissed him on the cheek and said, "Wade, this is Martin Hanover. He is the CEO and founder of Mahan Electronics."

"It's very nice to meet you Mr. Hanover I'm not sure I know Mahan Electronics."

"We are a relatively new company, only a couple of years old. I was an engineer at Yahoo!, and when they took the company public, I took my $10 million and started my own company. And please call me Martin."

"Well good for you, Martin."

Katrina chimed in. "Tell him the good part, Martin," Katrina turned to Wade and said, "We have only been sitting here talking for about twenty minutes and . . . well you tell him, Martin."

Wade had no idea what was going on

Martin Hanover then proceeded to tell Wade that he was in New York to meet with Smith Barney to discuss taking his company public. He had already had meetings with two other New York brokerage firms and had agreed to meet with Smith Barney before he made a final decision.

"Well your lovely lady here suggested that I talk to you before I decide. She said you manage AA Financial, and although it is not the size of some of the others, your success rate with IPOs is very high."

Wade almost fell off his chair. He didn't know that Katrina even knew what an IPO was.

"Do you think we can get together sometime tomorrow, Wade?"

"Absolutely Martin, by the way are you dining alone?"

"As a matter of fact, I am."

"Well then why don't you join us?" he said, looking to Katrina for her approval. Katrina took Martin Hanover by the arm and said, "I was just going to suggest that."

As they walked away from the bar, Katrina turned and winked at Wade and said, "Remember that question yet, big guy?"

During dinner, Martin Hanover told Wade that he had invented a device that would allow you to record all of your vital signs, blood pressure, heart rate, pulse, etc. while you were running, exercising, or even swimming, and transmit it electronically to your computer, or direct to your doctor, if that is what you wanted it to do. Although this same type of electronic device was on the drawing board of Apple and Microsoft as well as an Israeli computer manufacturer, Hanover claimed his was ready to go to market. That was the reason he wanted to take his company public. Wade asked him why he just didn't sell his company to one of the Internet giants. Hanover said he could do that, but he wanted to create his own Internet giant. Something didn't seem right to Wade. First off, it was too easy. This guy meets Katrina at a bar, and a half hour later, he is willing to talk to her boyfriend about taking his company public. It didn't make sense. In any event, Wade set up a meeting with Hanover for the next day. He told him he would like Albert Kline to sit in on the meeting.

On the way home from dinner, Katrina was more than excited. "I can't believe I put you together with Martin. What a charming man."

Wade thought, "*Yeah, a little too charming*".

The first thing Wade did when he arrived at the office the following morning was to have someone run a check on Hanover and his company. They came up with very little. There was a company called Mahan Electronics, but neither Dun nor Bradstreet or any of the other financial services had any information on the company. Wade had one of his people check with Yahoo! to see what they could find out. The only thing they came up with was there had been a Herman Hanover who used to work in their engineering department, but he left shortly after Yahoo! went public. There was no Martin. There was no record of a Martin Hanover receiving any shares or payout when they went public. Wade used his contacts to check with several different banks but came up empty. Hanover said his company was based in Akron, Ohio, so Wade tried contacting the banks there . . . Nothing. His meeting was set for two o'clock. He planned to meet with Kline first but really had nothing to talk about. Plus the fact he was uncomfortable having to sit and talk to Kline after what Joe Cantor had told him. This was no fun.

Kline showed up at the office shortly before ten. Wade decided to get together with him early before he got tied up in other things. He was anxious to get it over with.

"Good morning, Albert. How is everything?"

"Hello, Wade . . . Fine . . . Well actually not so fine . . . I haven't been feeling well."

"Oh I'm sorry to hear that is there anything I can do?"

"No . . . Thanks . . . Just have a lot on my mind right now. How is everything here?"

"We're good, Albert."

"I've been thinking about taking a trip, Wade. I need to get away for a while."

Wade could not help thinking about what Joe had told him. Did Kline know? If he did, how could he go away?

"Sure, Albert, no problem I have things under control here. There is one thing I want to run by you though. It's kind of strange actually. I met a guy last night at Le Cirque. He was at the bar talking to Katrina when I got there. Well before you know it, he was talking to me about us taking his company public. I mean, we talked all of fifteen minutes before we were asshole buddies."

"What's his name?"

"Martin Hanover. His company is Mahan Electronics. As a matter of fact, he is due in here this afternoon."

"Are you kidding me?"

"Do you know him?"

"Wade, he is one of John Gotti's associates!"

"Thee John Gotti?"

"The one and the only."

"Jesus Christ."

"How did you meet him?"

"Like I said, he was at the bar talking to Katrina."

"Wade, this guy makes his living by being Martin Hanover, the same way John Gotti makes his living by being John Gotti."

"You lost me, Albert."

"This guy is a smooth-talking con artist. He works with Gotti to set up blind pools, companies set up for the sole purpose of making investments and buying other companies with investors' money, money they never see again. They form shell corporations and then look for a firm like ours to take the company public. My guess is this Mahan Electronics company doesn't even have a product."

Wade didn't bother to tell Kline the story Hanover told him about his "invention."

"They have more different scams going than you could imagine. If you check out this Hanover character, you will find him in a bunch of SEC files, not because he is under surveillance or anything like that. He is in their files because of SEC filings he made. He was the CEO of different companies, and he went by the book as far as the SEC was concerned, but his deals were all scams. He always seemed to fly under the radar. He and Gotti are the perfect team. Gotti is flashy and loudmouthed and uses his scare tactics to get into firms like ours. This guy is low-key, educated, and very smooth but just as dangerous. He is a very smart guy and knows all of the ins and outs of our business. Once the two of them get a small brokerage house like ours in their grip, forget about it, you belong to them. Before he teamed up with Gotti, this guy worked for the Gambino family. He is bad news."

"How do you know so much about him?"

"This is Wall Street, Wade. You have to know what goes on here, or they will eat you alive."

"I understand what you're saying, Albert, but how did he know I would be in the restaurant last night?"

"I am sure he didn't. It was probably a coincidence. He met Katrina at the bar. You showed up, and he saw a chance to make a score."

"Man, do I feel stupid or what?"

"No need, fortunately, we didn't get involved with him."

Wade thought to himself, "*Yeah, we got enough illegal shit going on without his help!*"

"Wade, do you know how to get in touch with him?"

"Yeah, he gave me a telephone number to call in case there was any change in the time we were to meet. He said he would get the message and then return my call."

"It's probably an answering service. I want you to call him and cancel the meeting, use any excuse you want. He will catch on. I don't want him coming to our place."

"I'll do that right away, Albert."

In the late nineties, the NASD was under very competent leadership, run by an ambitious former broker executive and government official by the name of Frank Zarb. Arthur Levitt, a publicity-conscious former chairman of the American Stock Exchange was the man in charge at the SEC. They both were good solid men. They were honest, hardworking professionals.

Overall, the good of the system outweighed the bad. There were the hardworking stockbrokers who went to work every day and did their job as best they could. However, all of that didn't mean a thing to the thousands of tattooed, Armani-clad, unregistered kids who operated the chophouses and people like John Gotti and Martin Hanover. To them, it was business as usual on Wall Street, let the buyer beware.

When Wade called Martin Hanover and left a message with the person who answered the phone telling her he wanted to cancel his meeting, he never received a return phone call. Kline was right. Hanover got the message. There was no need to call back. Wade was angry, thinking that he almost allowed himself to get suckered into a deal with Hanover. That evening, when he told Katrina, she was more than angry. She was hurt and felt she had been violated.

"That lousy son of a bitch," she said, and she rarely—if ever—cursed.

Wade understood. But one thing was for sure, something like that would not happen again. It also became much clearer to him now that even crooks had their standards. Kline had no problem doing the things he did at AA so long as they were of his doing. He just didn't want to share. Wade no longer had any illusions about Wall Street. It was what it was. The bottom line was: did he want to be part of that?

CHAPTER SIXTY-TWO

RANDY CLAYMORE WAS known to the other agents in the bureau as unfailingly professional. He was honest, hardworking, and beyond reproach. He had worked his way up in the agency, and he was now the lead prosecutor in the New York office of the bureau. Everyone knew that when he decided to prosecute a case, he did so bent on winning. He was a fierce competitor.

He was a tall, lean man, with a handlebar mustache and a head full of thick black hair. And he was always nattily dressed. He was very likable. He was the person in charge of the investigation into the alleged kidnapping of Carolyn Thomas. He was holding a meeting with Detectives West and Thomas, the two buffoons who broke into Joey's cousin's house; Detective Lennon, the liaison between the bureau and the NYPD; his assistant, a young attorney by the name of Harold Cohen, one of the few Jewish men in the Bureau; and Curley Jones, his investigator. The room wasn't large enough to accommodate any more people.

He started the meeting off by going around the room, asking each person how they felt about the chances of getting convictions on each of the accused in the case: Albert Kline, Sal Maggio, Joey Amato, and Tommy Benito. After almost an hour of listening to varying opinions, personal accusations, and not-so-clear evidence, he made his decision.

"Gentlemen, I want to thank you all for the time and effort you have put into this investigation. Detective Lennon, I especially want to thank you for making sure that Ms. Thomas has remained safe during this past month. By the way, how is she doing?"

"She is doing exceptionally well. However, she would like to go back to her apartment and get on with her life."

"I am sure she would, and we will see how quickly we can make that happen.

"Now let's take a look at what we have here. First off, I want to review the criteria for what actually constitutes a kidnapping. Number one, has the victim been taken from one place to another against his or her will? Secondly, are they being held in a place where they are not likely to be found? Was there force used in taking this person, as an example, were their bruises on the person's arm? Then of course, there is the question of a ransom. Was the victim threatened? Did they fear for their life? These are all the types of questions a defense attorney will ask in defense of the accused.

"Based on what Ms. Thomas and Sal Maggio have said, the purpose of this meeting here today is to determine if we have enough evidence to charge Albert Kline with kidnapping. So with that in mind, let's do a little role playing. First, I will play the part of Joey Amato, and my assistant Harold Cohen will play the part of the defense attorney. Okay, let's start.

"Mr. Amato, had you ever heard the name Albert Kline before you were arrested?"

"No, I don't think so."

"Who told you to kidnap Carolyn Thomas?"

"Kidnap her? We didn't kidnap her. My friend Tommy asked me to help him scare her, that's all."

"Not a very good witness for the prosecution," Claymore said. "Okay, let's try Tommy Benito."

"Mr. Benito, did you ever hear the name Albert Kline before you were arrested?"

"No sir."

"Who told you to kidnap Carolyn Thomas?"

"Nobody told me to kidnap her. Sal Maggio told me a friend of his wanted me to scare her so she would have an abortion."

"Did he tell you his friend's name?"

"No sir."

"Did he ever mention the name Albert Kline?"

"No sir he never did."

"Another not such a good witness," Claymore said. "I think you get my point. The only person who has implicated Albert Kline is Sal Maggio, and he is not the most credible witness. I am sure a good defense lawyer will point out that Mr. Maggio gave up Albert Kline in order to make a deal for himself, plus the fact Kline never actually instructed him to kidnap Ms. Thomas.

"Now let's take a look at Ms. Thomas's statement. She has been Albert Kline's mistress for about two years. She admitted to that voluntarily. She stated he never abused her or threatened her. As a matter of fact, she made a point to tell us how generous he was. She also stated that he made it very clear at the beginning of their relationship that he would never leave his wife, and he surely did not want to have children with her. She said it was when she told him she wanted the baby to have his name that he 'went crazy,' to quote her. That doesn't mean he would want to have her kidnapped. Did he ask her to have an abortion? Absolutely. Did he ask somebody to kidnap her? I don't think so.

"In the state of New York, it is necessary for a person to use force to commit a kidnapping. You can't charge somebody with kidnapping based on a hearsay telephone call, especially from a person who is less than credible. Now Kline may be guilty of aggravated harassment, but even in that case, as a first-time offender, I don't foresee him doing any jail time. There is something else, gentlemen. Transportation from one borough to another might not stand up as kidnapping. And in some cases, the courts have taken into consideration both the motive and the length of time the victim has been missing or held. I have to be honest with you. I don't think there is enough evidence to charge Kline with kidnapping."

Detective Lennon was becoming very agitated. "Don't tell me we're going to let that son of a bitch get away with this."

Randy Claymore held up his hand. "Easy, Detective, we're here today to decide if we have enough evidence to charge this guy Kline. It's not up to us to decide if he is guilty or not. That's up to the court."

Detective Lennon was not happy. The bureau prosecutor continued.

"Gentlemen, if we did charge him, and we ended up in court, you can be sure Kline would have the best defense lawyer money can buy. The fact Kline is a well-known philanthropist and a respected member of the community would make our case even more difficult. Why in the world would he ever ask somebody to kidnap his girlfriend? I am sure his lawyer will argue that he has enough money to buy her off. Can we prove he asked this Sal Maggio piece of shit to scare her probably, but that is not kidnapping.

"There is one other thing I might as well mention. I am sure Kline's attorney would also argue that there is no proof the baby was his. Even though that has nothing to do with the alleged kidnapping, and the judge might ask to strike it, the jury will have heard it, and trust me, they will think about it. Ms. Thomas, of course, will testify that she didn't have sex with anyone else during the time of her relationship with

Kline, but that would be her word against his, and you never know how a jury looks at something like that.

"Gentlemen, I don't think we have a case we can win. I am not even sure the judge would allow this to go to trial since most of the testimony is hearsay." Then he addressed his next remarks to Detective Lennon. "Detective, my suggestion to you is that you decide what you want to do with Amato and Benito. My guess is you could probably charge them with assault and battery, but that's up to you. As far as Sal Maggio . . . he is in Nevada, and I don't think we have reason to try and extradite him. I will send the Nevada authorities his file, and they can do whatever they want. With respect to Kline, I think you would be wasting your time trying to charge him with anything more serious than aggravated harassment. You might be able to get a restraining order against him, that is, if Ms. Thomas wants one, but it is my guess now that there is no 'baby issue,' she may decide she wants to kiss and make up with this guy."

Detective Lennon did not like that last remark.

"With all due respect, Mr. Claymore, I think that is out of line. You make it sound like this was a simple lovers' quarrel. This poor girl was kidnapped, plain and simple."

Claymore realized right away that the detective had more than just a professional interest in Carolyn Thomas. "I apologize, Detective. It was not my intention to minimize what happened to Ms. Thomas."

Lennon simply nodded.

Harold Cohen spoke up. "Pardon me, sir, but is there any way we can use some of the things in the bureau's file on Albert Kline?"

Detective Lennon perked up and said, "You guys have a file on this guy!"

CHAPTER SIXTY-THREE

WHEN DETECTIVE LENNON drove Carolyn Thomas home, he told her he would feel better if he waited until she was safely inside her apartment before he left.

"You don't think they planted a bomb in my apartment, do you, Detective?"

"I sure hope not. That would really ruin the day. And by the way, my first name is Fred."

"I know that. I saw it on your name tag when I was in the hospital."

"Oh."

"Look . . . Fred, I know you did your best with the bureau to have them charge Albert with kidnapping, but believe me . . . I understand."

He simply nodded. What else could he say?

When they entered her apartment building, Charles the doorman told her that Albert Kline had called several times, asking about her.

"What did you tell him, Charles?"

"I told him I hadn't seen you in a while. Hope that was okay, Ms. Thomas."

"Of course thank you Charles."

Then looking at Detective Lennon, and noticing his badge clipped to his belt, he very politely asked, "Are you okay, Ms. Thomas?"

"Yes, I am fine, Charles I was away on some family business. Oh by the way," she added, pointing to Detective Lennon, "This is Mr. Lennon, an old friend."

"How do you do, sir?"

"Just fine, Charles It's nice to meet you."

When they got to her apartment, Carolyn asked the detective if he wanted to come in for a while. "I just don't feel like being alone right now."

He didn't need a second invitation.

Carolyn offered him some wine, after which they went into the living room.

Getting comfortable on the couch with her legs tucked under her, she said, "I think I can understand why the F.B.I. can't charge him, but

I hate to see him get away with this scot-free. I think he should pay for what he did to me."

Detective Lennon thought for a minute and then said, "When you say he should pay . . . did you mean pay like in money pay?"

She looked at him for several seconds, thinking about what he said.

"I'm sorry," he said. "I didn't mean to . . ."

She interrupted him. "No, no, that's okay. Actually that is not what I meant, but now that you mention it, yes . . . I would like him to pay . . . like in money pay. How do you suggest I go about doing that?"

"I'm not sure."

He was sitting in a chair opposite her; she patted the sofa and suggested he sit next to her and said, "Well put on your thinking cap, Detective. We need to come up with a plan."

He put down his empty wine glass and accepted her invitation to sit next to her.

"We?" he said.

"Yes we I can't do something like that alone."

He thought for a minute then asked, "What is the deal on this apartment? Is it in your name or what?"

"No, that is, I'm not sure. I know he pays the rent from his firm, and I'm the tenant, but I'm not really sure how the lease reads."

"I assume he leases it from the owner."

"Yes, all of the rest are occupied by the owners. I know some of the people in the building who are the owners."

"Well I think the first thing you want to do is have him buy this apartment for you, in your name, free and clear."

"Can I make him do that? Suppose the people who own it don't want to sell it?"

"Yes, you can make him do it, and in a minute, I will tell you how you can. And if the owners of this apartment won't sell, then tell him to find you something else. Tell him you want an apartment like this one."

"I like the way you think, Detective. What else?"

He laughed. "You want more?"

She patted his cheek. "We're on a roll. Let's not stop now."

"Okay, then here is the capper. You tell him you also want . . . let me think . . . how does $500,000 sound to you?"

"It sounds pretty damn good to me."

"Okay, then that's our plan."

"One thing, Detective, what kind of a drug do you plan on giving him that will convince him to go along with this plan?'

He got up, went into the kitchen, and refilled their wine glasses then returned and handed her one.

"I know this is all going to sound out of character for a cop, but here's the deal. First off, I have to believe he has no idea what happened to you. I am sure Sal Maggio hasn't called him, no reason. And the two guys who put you in the car and took you to their apartment for sure haven't talked to him. All he knows at this point is that you were missing for six weeks. That has to worry him, not knowing what happened to you or where you were."

"Didn't someone from your office get in touch with him?"

"No. That's the thing. Nobody has. I would be the one locally, and up to this point, I was waiting to hear what we were going to do. So right now, we have that edge. He doesn't have the slightest idea what is going on."

"Okay so far. Now let me hear the out-of-character-for-a-cop part."

"I want you to call him, and tell him you want to see him. When he asks you where you've been the last six weeks, simply tell him you will explain it all when you see him."

"Do you think he will see me?"

"Are you kidding me? He will jump at the chance. He has to find out what happened. Sal Maggio claims he hasn't spoken to him since he asked him to convince you to have an abortion. Then you go missing for six weeks. Trust me, he will meet with you."

"Okay, so where do I meet with him?"

"Here at the apartment."

"Is that a good idea to meet here?"

"Yeah, I'll tell you why later."

"Okay, then what?"

"Then you tell him what happened. Two men grabbed you, put you in the trunk of a car, and eventually took you to some rundown house up town. Make it sound dramatic, go into detail. Explain how you escaped and how the lady at the bar helped you. Then tell him when 911 took you to the hospital, you were in shock for a couple of weeks and didn't remember who you were. Oh don't forget to tell him about how you lost the baby."

"Wow. Can I remember all of this?"

"Just keep thinking about the apartment and the $500,000. You'll remember."

"Okay, go on."

"He will probably ask you why you didn't call him sooner. Make up any excuse you want. You didn't know if you wanted to go to the police or what. You were very confused. But now you know what you want. That's when you tell him about the apartment and the money."

"Gulp!" she said.

"Yeah, I know. He will probably tell you that you're crazy. There is no way he is going to pay you that kind of money. That's when you drop the bomb. You tell him that's your price for not going to the police or telling his wife. I am sure he will call your bluff and tell you that you don't have any proof he had anything to do with what happened. That's when you tell him that you heard the two men who kidnapped you talking on the phone to a man named Sal Maggio. Tell him that before you escaped, the two men bragged to you how they were going to be paid a lot of money to force you to have an abortion. And when you asked them who would do that they told you 'your boyfriend, Albert Kline, the big-shot stockbroker.' And to make sure he knows you are serious, tell him that you have given a detailed account of everything that happened to you to a criminal lawyer. It includes the names of the two men, plus Sal Maggio's name, and most important, his name. You also have the address of the house where the two men kept you prisoner. Tell him if he doesn't agree to your demands within the next thirty days and guarantee that no harm will come to you, the lawyer will go to the police and to the newspapers. And you will call his wife."

She almost choked on her wine. "Are you serious? Isn't that blackmail?"

"You said you wanted him to pay. What he did to you was criminal, and if you let him, he is simply going to walk away unscathed. He is a multimillionaire. He will think he is getting off cheap."

"Okay, I hear everything you are saying, and I like it. However, I know this man. He is not just going to lie down and roll over. Suppose he thinks I'm bluffing and he tells me to go ahead with my threats. What then?"

"Don't worry. I have an ace in the hole. I haven't been a cop in this stinking city for over twenty years without learning some dirty tricks of my own."

"My, oh my, will you listen to you."

"Do you have a problem with that?"

"Absolutely not but I have just one question, what do you get out of this?" she asked in a flirtatious manner.

"I get to see that justice has been served," he said with a straight face.

It was almost ten o'clock by the time they finished going over what she would say. He had her role play with him until he was satisfied she had it all down pat. "You will do great," he said. When he was getting ready to leave, she said, "I would really feel better if you could stay until I fall asleep. Do you mind?"

"I'll do better than that. Give me a pillow and a blanket, and I'll bunk out here on the couch."

She got up from the couch, took him by the hand, and said, "No need for that. I have a big double bed, and I would feel a lot safer if I knew you were lying there beside me."

CHAPTER SIXTY-FOUR

THE FOLLOWING MORNING, Carolyn called Albert Kline on his private line.

"My god where have you been I have been worried sick about you."

"I bet," she thought.

"Don't you know?"

"How would I know?"

"It's a long story, Albert. I have a lot to tell you."

"Are you all right?"

"I'm fine . . . That is, I am fine now."

"What does that mean? I don't understand."

"I don't want to discuss it on the phone. Can you come over?"

"Well I have a couple things to do, say I get there about eleven."

"That's fine, Albert."

"Are you sure you are okay, Carolyn?"

"I am fine, Albert. I'll see you at eleven."

As it was, he got to her apartment at about ten-thirty. He had his own key and let himself in. Carolyn was sitting in the living room, drinking coffee, and watching TV. He thought to himself she looked very pretty. *"Maybe if we can get over this having a baby shit, we can go back to where we were. There was no doubt about it. She was a great piece of ass."*

She got up as he walked over to her, and when he leaned over to kiss her, she turned her head.

"Let's talk first, Albert."

He was no fool. He could see things were not the same. He didn't know what had happened, but whatever it was had changed her. "Okay, Carolyn. Let's have it. What's on your mind? If it's about you getting an abortion, I think we have talked that to death."

He was making it easy for her. She really hated him now. "You don't give up, Albert, do you?"

He just shrugged his shoulders.

She said, "It's not about getting an abortion, Albert. Please sit down here." And she pointed to a chair opposite the TV. "We need to talk."

He sat down, crossed his legs then pointed to her as if to say, "Go ahead. This is your show."

At first, she was a little bit nervous, but once she got started, the words just flowed out of her mouth. For the most part, he listened without making the comments that Detective Lennon thought he would. Finally, she finished and held her breath, waiting for him to say something.

He smiled and looked at her for a couple of minutes as if he were trying to digest all that she had said.

"Carolyn, are you on drugs?"

"What do you mean am I on drugs? What is that supposed to mean?"

"Because if you're not on drugs then you must be out of your fucking mind to concoct a story like that."

"I didn't concoct a story. You know it is all true, Albert."

"You know, I underestimated you, Carolyn. I have to give you an A for effort, but it's no sale. And do you know why?"

She didn't answer.

"Because there is no way you could ever prove any of that. First of all, I never told Sal Maggio to hire two guys to kidnap you. Do you think I am that foolish?"

"But you did tell him to scare me into having an abortion, didn't you?"

"What if I did? If you would have agreed to an abortion when I first asked you, I wouldn't have had to call him. Jesus Christ, Carolyn. Do you think I would ask somebody to throw you in the trunk of a car? I don't know who those guys were, but that part was Sal's doing, not mine."

"Albert, none of this would have happened if you hadn't called that monster in Las Vegas."

"Carolyn, you are right. I never should have called him. I'm sorry, but be reasonable, it's over. You are okay, and believe me, its better that you lost the baby."

"You son of a bitch how can you say that?"

"Carolyn . . . come on, stop crying, it's over. Look we had a good ride, think of all the nice places you went during the last two years, and all the clothes and jewelry . . ."

"Albert, stop it . . . stop it!"

"Okay, okay, let's wind this up. First of all, there is no way I am going to buy you this apartment and give you $500,000. And as far as you going to my wife, that would be the biggest mistake you ever made in your life. You don't even want to think what would happen to you. Trust me, when I got finished with you, your own sister wouldn't recognize you. The same goes if you decide to go to the police. You are in over your head, Carolyn. I eat people like you for lunch. But I am going to be a nice guy. I will give you thirty days to gather up all of your stuff and move out of this apartment. And I'm even going to let you keep all the presents I bought you. And . . . I'm going to give you $5,000 to help you get started on a new life, preferably somewhere else . . . not in New York."

Then he got up and said, "Now if you will excuse me, I have more important things to do. Oh and one more thing, don't ever call me again on my private line. Remember thirty days."

As he started to leave, Detective Lennon walked out of the bedroom, holding a video tape.

"Wait just a second Mr. Kline I have something I want to show you."

Kline looked at the detective and then back at Carolyn. "Who the fuck is this guy?" he said, looking at the badge the detective was wearing in full view. "What's going on, Carolyn? I'm leaving . . ."

Detective Lennon opened his jacket so that Kline could see his service revolver. "You're not going anywhere, Mr. Kline, until you watch this tape."

Albert Kline knew he was in trouble.

CHAPTER SIXTY-FIVE

THAT WAS DETECTIVE Lennon's ace in the hole. He had a friend of his hook up a video camera to the TV in the living room with a remote in the bedroom. As soon as Kline came in and sat down, Detective Lennon started recording. The decision he had to make was if he should risk revealing himself to Kline. After thinking it through, he decided to go ahead with the plan.

After Kline watched the tape, Detective Lennon said, "With a little bit of editing, we take out the part where Carolyn asks you for the apartment and the money. What we end up with is a pretty nice confession to conspiracy to abduct, sexual harassment, assault and battery, and at the end, a threat to cause severe physical harm and maybe even murder. Now I'm not a lawyer, but I think a good prosecuting attorney can get a conviction on some of these charges, if not all. And by the time the newspapers and TV are finished with you, your reputation on Wall Street will be shit. Oh I almost forgot to mention, you probably will need a damn good divorce lawyer by the time your wife is through with you."

Kline was no pushover. After Lennon finished, he said, "Fuck you, you think the two of you can blackmail me? Do you know who my partner is? You son of a bitch dirty cop, I will make you sorry you ever started with me." Then he turned to Carolyn and said, "And you bitch, how many times did you have to fuck this guy for him to agree to risk his badge?"

Lennon had heard enough. He grabbed Kline by the lapels and pulled him close and then punched him so hard in the stomach that his feet almost left the ground. He let out a shriek and fell to the floor.

Carolyn started to cry. "Oh my god, Fred, what have we done?"

He put his arms around her. "It's okay Carolyn relax everything will be okay"

She nodded. "I'm okay."

Lennon bent over Kline and said, "Listen to me, you asshole. This is my business. I deal with jerks like you every day. Maybe they don't have as much money as you, but you are all the same. Now I want you to apologize to Carolyn for what you just said."

Kline was still gasping for breath. "I'm . . . I'm sorry," was all he could get out.

Lennon sat him up and put his face close to his and said, "The way I see it, I didn't risk my badge. Carolyn called the police, and we decided this was the best way to get a confession. For your information, the F.B.I. was called into this investigation, and they are waiting for my report to decide if they want to charge you." A little white lie, but it scared the shit out of Kline.

"Now what do you say, does Ms. Thomas here get what she asked for, or do I test you to see how many more punches you can take then handcuff you and throw your ass in jail? By the time you call your lawyers to get you out, you will be lucky if some drunk doesn't try to cornhole you. You're playing by my rules now, Mr. Kline, and I must warn you, I don't play fair."

Albert Kline held up his hand and said, "No more please, we have a deal."

CHAPTER SIXTY-SIX

TIME HAS A way of making people change. Sometimes they try to change their personality, hoping other people will like them more. At other times, they change jobs in an effort to make their life better, and sometimes, well sometimes they simply want to change for the sake of change. Not sure what all of this has to do with Wade Simon, but here it was a week before the great millennium, and not much had changed over the past year and a half. Kline was still at the helm of AA Financial. Wade was still making a ton of money but remained unhappy about the way AA Financial was run. Joe Cantor had left the country, as he said he would, and Wade had no idea what was happening with his pending trial.

Finally, the millennium was here, the start of a new century. Billions of people around the world were preparing to welcome in the new millennium with some of the most spectacular celebrations ever seen. The first people to witness the dawn of the new era would be the Pacific Islanders – among the last were people like Wade and Katrina—the Americans.

Although Wade was excited about Katrina's performing at the millennium celebration at Madison Square Garden, his excitement was jaded by his fears that the dreaded millennium bug would cause a computer meltdown around the world, a fear that was dispelled when the world welcomed the year 2000 without any problems, to the relief of Wall Street and the millions of investors around the world.

The unique global experience of the new millennium, which will never again be witnessed by any person alive at the time, was marked by all denominations and all classes and creeds of people across the planet. Here it was two thousand years after Christ's obscure birth in a dusty town in Judea, when the world's people—most of them non-Christian and many of them preoccupied with terrorism, computers, diets, bank accounts, politics, the mob on Wall Street, and the perils of the future—were riding the turning blue planet across the invisible line of today, and by common consent, looking into the dawn of the new millennium.

Outside Madison Square Garden where Katrina had just finished her concert and was receiving a standing ovation, over two million people packed Times Square and much of Midtown Manhattan for the biggest public event ever held in the city, a twenty-six-hour, $7 million marathon of music, fireworks, confetti, and deafening voices as a 1,070-pound crystal ball descended at midnight, and the crowds roared berserkly while the police sweated out an enormous potential for trouble. Trouble that fortunately never materialized.

More than two million people lined the banks of the River Thames to watch a fireworks display. Amongst them was Carolyn Thomas. After Kline made good on his promise to buy her the apartment and give her the $500,000, she and Detective Lennon developed a very close relationship. However, after about six months, it began to cool. The fact that Carolyn had all of that money made Lennon uncomfortable. Carolyn wanted to share some of the money with him, but he would not hear of it. In addition, during the two years she spent as Kline's mistress, Carolyn had become accustomed to a lifestyle that was much different than Lennon was used to. And neither one of them could adjust to the other's lifestyle. So that was the end of the romance. Not too long after that, Carolyn met Jeffery Abbott, a very rich and successful owner of a chain of supermarkets. And he was not married; he was a widower. He was only fifty-two years old when his wife died three years earlier. Carolyn had gone back to work at a law firm as a private secretary, and Jeffery was one of their clients. It was love at first sight. They were in Paris on their honeymoon watching the Parisians celebrate the millennium. Sometimes nice things do happen to nice people.

In Edinburg, to celebrate the millennium, five tons of fireworks were set off in a period of four minutes. Joe Cantor watched from a small house he had rented when he first arrived. To his surprise, his trial date had been postponed indefinitely. He spoke to one of his previously 'connected' business associates who told him he had some good friends who were doing their best to help him. This was in repayment for Joe being a stand-up guy and not ratting out any of the guys he did business with. He decided that regardless of what happened, he was in no hurry to return to the States.

In Chicago, Angelo Santino was watching the pre-millennium celebration on television. Although this was a universal event that had captured the attention of almost everybody on the planet, Angelo was preoccupied with other things. He was still trying to think of a way to get even with Albert Kline. He was not a man to let someone cheat him without taking revenge. Before he could think of an answer, and before the new century began, Angelo had fallen asleep.

It was the year 2000. There had been an avalanche of millennial overkill leading up to this moment. There was talk of 'the last game,' 'the last meal,' 'the last baby,' and even 'the last sunset.' World leaders in government, religion, science, and other fields even spoke of the millennium's meaning in very scary terms. However, nothing bad happened. Computers didn't crash; Wall Street was still around; there were still an equal amount of good guys and bad guys, and the clock in the London Tower was still keeping time. For all practical purposes, it was simply the start of a new year.

CHAPTER SIXTY-SEVEN

KATRINA FINGERED THE Cartier leopard pin on the lapel of her suit. Wade had given it to her as he had given her so many things in the past year and a half since they had become lovers: flowers, clothes, jewelry, and—most important of all—his love, the sort of love she never could have imagined. His love was total, equal, supportive, the sort of love that allowed for differences of opinion, that bowed to greater need, that understood all and forgave all, the sort of love she believed could only happen once in a person's lifetime.

She had gone to great lengths to protect that love, nurturing it, and not allowing her career to interfere with it. She made sure her concert tours were within the greater New York area and never more than a couple of nights away from home. She never told Wade that the New York Metropolitan Opera House wanted her to join a group touring Europe. There was no way she could bear being separated from him for that length of time. She knew that she wanted to spend the rest of her life with him but would not allow herself to push him into getting married. He had asked her that one night after they made love, and she foolishly said, "We'll see how you feel about it in the morning." "*How stupid was that?*"

She had just finished getting dressed and was waiting for him to call. He had a meeting and was running late. They were having dinner at Le Cirque with Albert Kline and his wife. In all the years that Wade worked for him, this was only the third time he had dinner with him and his wife. Katrina had met her once at a charity event they all attended shortly after she moved in with Wade. Albert and his wife had just recently returned from a three-week vacation in California where they welcomed the new millennium. Katrina was looking forward to hearing how California welcomed the new century.

When Wade and Katrina walked into the restaurant, Wade couldn't help comparing Katrina to all of the other women there. They were mostly high maintenance, overdressed woman dripping in jewelry accompanied for the most part by fat men in suits and ties. Katrina, on the other hand, was classy-looking. She was wearing a black suit with a white turtle neck and looked better than all of the other women there combined. The restaurant itself was an explosion of lights and color, and it always took Wade a couple of minutes for his eyes to focus. The maître d' greeted them and ushered them to an 'A' table where Albert Kline and his wife were already seated.

Albert's wife, Esther, was a very elegant-looking woman. It wasn't just the specially-designed clothes or the expensive jewelry that made her look elegant; it was her whole self. The way she carried herself, the way she spoke, and to top it off, she was exceptionally attractive. She and Albert had been married for over forty years.

They met when they both attended Boston College. Albert was a finance major, and Esther was an English major. Her plans were to become an educator of some kind, not necessarily simply a school teacher, something more challenging. However, when she graduated, the only job available was teaching at a grade school in Boston, her hometown. Her father was the sales manager at a large wholesale meat packing firm in Boston and she was brought up not wanting for anything. They liked having her close by and convinced her to continue living at home after she graduated college.

Albert lived in New Brunswick, and when he graduated, he decided to try his luck on Wall Street. He was raised by a single mom—his father had passed away before his bar mitzvah. His mother worked as a health care assistant in a retirement home in Elizabeth, New Jersey. With the money she earned, she was only able to pay part of Albert's tuition and living costs. The rest he paid by working his way through college. He made up his mind at a very early age that he was going to have money, and he succeeded. He worked his way up at the brokerage firm until he eventually became the executive vice president.

They continued to date after college, and about six months after graduation, Albert convinced Esther to move from Boston and live with him in New York. He had a small apartment in Soho. Her parents were furious. They didn't want her living with a man, especially in New York. However, she did what she wanted, and that was to move in with Albert. They married about a year later. She found a teaching job at a small private school in the village, and between their two salaries, they were able to move to a nicer apartment on the Upper East Side.

As soon as Esther became pregnant with Brenda, she stopped working. By that time, Albert was earning enough for them to buy an old brownstone on Madison Avenue, which over the years they continued to remodel until they moved to a luxury condo when Brenda was about ten years old.

Now all these years later, they were sitting in Le Cirque, waiting to have dinner with Wade and Katrina.

"Esther, Albert, you remember Katrina?" Wade said as the maître d' made sure they were comfortably seated.

"Of course," Albert said, extending his hand first to Katrina and then to Wade.

"Wade, nice to see you again," Esther said to Wade and then to Katrina, "You look stunning, darling."

"Thank you, Mrs. Kline."

"Please, dear, Esther."

"Thank you, Esther."

"Okay, now that we got that settled, how about we order some wine?"

Everyone nodded as Albert signaled to the captain.

"Does anyone have any suggestions?" Albert asked.

"You are the connoisseur, Albert. Why don't you decide?"

Wade couldn't get over how congenial Albert was. Not that he was an unpleasant person, but he seemed to be going out of his way tonight to be extra nice. Wade thought about what Joe told him before he left the country, ***"Your boss is in trouble with the SEC and the F.B.I.. I would not be surprised to see him charged."*** And what the hell was all this about Albert being involved in some sort of kidnapping? All of that was months ago, and nothing ever happened. Wade wondered if Kline knew about it. If he did; he never showed any concern. However, he did recall last year when Kline was really distressed for a period of time, and then he seemed to snap out of it. Of course, Wade had no way of knowing about Carolyn Thomas and Detective Lennon. Nor did Wade have any idea that his boss was never without a mistress. Albert Kline first started cheating on his wife when Brenda was only two years old. Amazingly, he is married to a beautiful, smart, classy lady, and he still needs something on the side.

After Kline ordered the wine and did the whole tasting and swirling in the mouth bit, he told the captain to fill their glasses and said, "I want to make a toast." Everyone raised their glasses and waited.

"This is to Wade, the new CEO of AA Financial."

Esther smiled and reached over to touch her glass to both Wade's and Katrina's glasses and said, "Congratulations, darling. Nobody is more deserving."

Wade was stunned.

Katrina was 'double' stunned.

Kline simply sat and smiled as if he had just pulled off the coup of the year.

"I don't know what to say, Albert . . . I mean . . ." And then he laughingly said, "I'll drink to that."

Katrina was baffled. She had no idea what was going on. She turned to Wade and asked, "Did you know about this?"

"Are you kidding me? I am as surprised as you."

Albert Kline was enjoying this. Finally, Esther said, "All right, Albert, now tell them how this all came about."

Wade added, "Yes, Albert, please do."

"Well it's kind of a long story. About a year ago Angelo called to let me know a bank, which is owned by the Vatican, was interested in buying a brokerage firm in this country. Angelo did business with them in the past and knew the president of the bank personally. Although Angelo had an interest in selling, at that time, I didn't. Nevertheless, Angelo asked me if I would go to Rome with him to meet some of the people from the bank and at least talk about it. I did. You may remember I flew to Rome last year a couple of times for some meetings. They were with the bank.

"It's not like any bank in this country. Their whole style of doing business is different. Anyhow they were very cordial and made a very attractive offer. They said, 'You will be a very rich man if you accept our offer.' I had to laugh. I told them I already was a rich man. On the flight back from Rome, Angelo asked me if there was anything that would change my mind about selling. I told him there wasn't. Then about three months ago, he called and asked me to meet him in California. When I asked why, he said it was important I meet him, and he would explain when I saw him. It is not often he makes that kind of request, so I flew out to California. He met me at the San Francisco Airport. The limo driver proceeded to drive us out to Sonoma Valley, part of California's wine country, which was about forty miles north of San Francisco. When I asked him why we were going there, he simply said, "You wait. It's a surprise."

"The bottom line is, Angelo told me the bank in Rome held the mortgage on one of the most beautiful vineyards you have ever seen in Sonoma Valley. And it included a house fit for a king. It was magnificent. He said the owner had passed away, and the estate didn't have enough money to pay the back taxes, so the bank foreclosed. Angelo knows I am a wine lover, so after we pulled into the main gate of the winery, he said, 'How you would you like to own this?'

"He told me that he had spoken to the president of the bank, and he agreed to structure the purchase of our firm to include the vineyard, which would go to me. Angelo knew my passion for wine and thought that would be enough of an incentive for me to want to sell."

Wade looked at Esther. She didn't seem to share Albert's enthusiasm about the vineyard.

"I have always wanted to own a winery but was never able to convince Esther to move out of New York." Wade looked at her again. She still didn't look like she was convinced.

Albert continued. "We spent all day there, most of the time going through the winery itself. There were acres and acres of fields where they grew the grapes. There were also a couple of old buildings on the far end of the property where a group of Mexicans did some kind of farming. Angelo said the ground there wasn't good to grow grapes. Part of the deal was to allow the Mexicans to continue to stay there, Angelo said. In exchange for letting them farm there, they took care of all of the landscaping and stuff like that, so it was best to keep them there."

"I told Angelo I was prepared to reconsider selling my share of AA. However, it hinged on how Esther felt about it." Esther gave a polite smile.

Albert then went on to explain that because Brenda now lives in California, it made it a little more attractive for Esther to move from New York, but there were conditions. First of all, she insisted they keep their condo in New York, the one in Palm Beach, and in addition, buy one in San Francisco. Esther added, "I want to know that if I decide to get away for a while, I still have my own place to go to." No one knew that there was another reason Esther was agreeable to them owning the vineyard. She knew about his mistress and hoped that if they left New York, he would end his affair. With all of his shortcomings, she did love him, and of course, enjoyed the lifestyle they led. She never even thought about a divorce. She knew a lot of divorced New York socialites, and their life was not all that it was cracked up to be. She enjoyed being Mrs. Albert Kline.

After a lot of negotiations, a deal was finally reached. The Roman National Bank was buying AA Financial from Albert Kline and Angelo Santino. As part of the deal, Albert would own the vineyard located just north of San Francisco. Angelo also negotiated, on Wade's behalf, that he be appointed CEO at a salary of $5,000,000 a year, plus a percentage of the profits. The bank had no problem with this, considering how much money Albert now took out of the business. Wade would have a potential of earning over $9,000,000 a year. Not too shabby for a Jewish kid from Strawberry Mansion in Philly.

CHAPTER SIXTY-EIGHT

OVER $50 BILLION in securities, gold reserves that exceed those of industrialized nations, real estate holdings that equal the total area of many countries, opulent palaces containing the world's greatest art treasures, these are only some of the riches of the Roman Catholic Church, more specifically the Vatican. And of course, banks. There are those who claim the riches of the Vatican are partly due to what is called the "Vatican Mafia."

It has been almost impossible to prove that the Vatican and her hierarchs have been the origin of the Mafias or clandestine criminal organizations. The Catholic Church with her canons and laws is the best organized secret society in the whole world. However, the archives of agencies that investigate crime: Interpol, the F.B.I., and the CIA have shown how the Vatican's apostolic nuncios, cardinals, and delegates have been involved in unlawful activities over the years together with the New York Mafia.

It is documented that in 1929, the Vatican was destitute. Pope Pius XI was living in a damaged, leaky, pigeon-infested Lateran Palace, and he worried how he would pay for such basic repairs as fixing the leaky roof or unclogging the overburdened sewer lines. Yet with the stroke of a pen on February 11, 1929, the fascist leader Benito Mussolini and the Vatican signed the Lateran Treaty, and the Vatican's financial problems were solved. Mussolini gained the support of the staunchly Catholic populace, and in return, the Church received, among other benefits, a payment of $90 million, sovereign status for the Vatican, tax-free property rights, and guaranteed salaries for all priests throughout the country. However, it is believed that by signing this treaty, the pope put the Vatican, a great religious institution, in league with the bad guys.

Many religious scholars, some former priests, and some Vatican finance ministers are critical of the way in which the Vatican—which some of them refer to as the Vatican Mafia—enriches itself, and the business of canonizations, with millions from the nation's coffers, which should be distributed to mitigate the hunger and unemployment of the poor, or to increase health and education, instead of ending up in the Vatican coffers. And then the money is used for questionable purposes.

There are numerous credible publications that set out to prove that Mafia proceeds from Sicily, whose origin is Rome, and have been dependent on the Vatican. They claim the Vatican "cleans" the money for the Mafia for a fee, which amounts to hundreds of millions of dollars every year.

None of this is to imply that the pope, the Vatican itself, or for that matter, the Catholic religion as a whole are anything like the monstrous Mafioso that we all know who deal in drugs, prostitution, murder, and other unspeakable crimes absolutely not. What we are talking about here has to do with one thing and one thing only . . . money! That is the one thing that organized crime and organized religion have in common, money, and it is not restricted to Catholicism.

Giovanni DeLuca, the president of the Roman National Bank, is the son of Carmen DeLuca, a former Mafia chieftain in Sicily. When the Vatican bought the bank from a group of Italian businessmen in 1965, Giovanni was a young man working for his father as an accountant in his oil importing business. Because it was Carmen DeLuca who convinced the group of businessmen to sell the bank, the Vatican owed him a favor. The payment for the favor was the appointment of his son Giovanni as the president of the bank. Back then, Angelo Santino was doing business with Carmen. Carmen introduced Angelo to his son and told him that now that his son was the president of the bank, the bank was available should he need it. It didn't take long for Angelo to use the bank to "clean" money for him. When other New York Mafia families learned of this, they too took advantage of the bank's services. Before long, the Roman National Bank was doing business with Mafia families in New York, Chicago, and Miami. Did the Vatican know about this? That is questionable.

Several years ago, Giovanni decided he wanted to get involved in Wall Street. Some of the families he was doing business with told him of the easy money to be made there. However, he was never able to really get a foothold in the American financial district, so when Angelo approached him with the idea of buying AA Financial, he jumped at the opportunity. His question to Angelo was, "Who can I put in charge that I can both trust and depend on?"

"There is already someone there," Angelo told him. Of course, that someone was Wade. Angelo felt sure that when Wade learned how much money he was going to earn, he would be very cooperative.

CHAPTER SIXTY-NINE

IT TOOK ALMOST six months for the deal to be finalized, but on September 1, 2000, the Roman National Bank took ownership of AA Financial, and the *Wall Street Journal* ran an article profiling Wade. Katrina was not quite sure how she felt about the whole thing. On one hand, she was happy for Wade. He could now run AA the way he wanted to . . . or could he? Of course, she had no idea who the Roman National Bank was other than the fact it was owned by the Vatican. How bad could that be?

Two weeks after the bank took ownership Angelo called Wade and asked him if he could come to Chicago. He told him that the president of the bank, Giovanni DeLuca, was an old friend of his and asked him to set up a meeting so that he could meet him. Angelo suggested they meet at his home in Chicago. In the meantime, Albert agreed to stay on for as long as Wade needed him to help with the transition. Although Albert reviewed a number of things with Wade, there were certain transactions that he never spoke about, and as a matter of fact, he took the folders relating to those transactions out of the office and kept them at home.

On the same day that Wade flew to Chicago to meet the new owner of AA Financial, there was a high-level meeting taking place in Washington. Tom Franklin, the chief of the organized crime section at the F.B.I. headquarters in Washington was meeting with a senate sub-committee about organized crime on Wall Street.

He wanted to explain the F bureau's role in investigating organized crime's involvement in the financial and securities markets. He emphasized the fact that organized crime groups have become much more active on Wall Street. He said, "The reason for this is very simple. It's much like when they asked Willie Sutton why he robbed banks. He said, 'Because that's where the money is.' That is the reason organized crime has infiltrated Wall Street because that's where the money is. Mob-related activities on Wall Street are definitely a priority with both our office and the office of the Manhattan District Attorney

Robert Morgenthau, and we continue to work together investigating all complaints."

He went on to explain that historically organized crime's role in the financial and securities markets was limited to shaking down and extorting stockbrokers who had found themselves indebted to the mob for any number of reasons and attempted to work off their debts through stock manipulation. However, now with new technologies, the mob has found it just as easy to actually take over a small brokerage firm and work their own schemes rather than depend on a broker who owes them money. This allows them to reach a much broader pool of potential victims and operate with a certain measure of anonymity. He added that organized crime groups involved in the financial and securities markets tend to use offshore bank accounts, which make it more difficult for the authorities to follow the money.

This brought him to the primary reason he was meeting with them. He said, "We have learned that a bank owned by the Vatican has just concluded a deal to purchase AA Financial, a medium-size brokerage firm located in the New York financial district. The firm was previously owned by Albert Kline and Angelo Santino. Mr. Santino is a known member of organized crime."

Before he could continue, a member of the senate sub-committee asked how that was possible.

"You mean to tell me that you knew this Santino person was part of the mob, yet he was allowed to own a Wall Street brokerage firm? How is that possible?"

Tom Franklin explained that although the bureau knew who Angelo was, he was not doing anything illegal. He was simply an investor in the firm. He didn't have a broker's license and had nothing to do with the running of the firm. And it was not up to the F.B.I. to prevent him from being an investor. That was the job of the SEC. That didn't satisfy the senator.

"That is not good enough, Mr. Franklin. There must be laws that prevent someone like him from being an investor."

Since Angelo was no longer involved in AA Financial, Tom Franklin decided not to get into a debate with the senator. He simply said that both the bureau and the SEC will be more diligent in the future.

"First of all, I think you should know both the SEC and the bureau have investigated AA Financial in the past. However, there were never any charges for wrongdoing."

One of the senators asked why they had investigated them.

Franklin explained that there had been some complaints from disgruntled investors, but the investigation proved negative.

The same senator who complained about Angelo being an investor in AA said, "Franklin, where there is smoke, there is usually fire. Don't you think it strange that you receive complaints about a firm that is partly owned by a reputed mob figure, and yet your people can't come up with anything?"

Franklin didn't like the insinuation. "What are you implying, Senator?"

"Not a thing, I'm simply asking a question."

"I'm sorry Senator, but I don't have an answer. What I can tell you is both the SEC and the bureau periodically receive complaints both from investors as well as stockbrokers who feel they have been deceived, and all of these complaints are investigated. Over the last three years, between the bureau and various state securities regulators there have been an average of three hundred criminal convictions a year for securities fraud. The problem is security cases are complex, costly, and time-consuming. The truth is some prosecutors shy away from them because the subject is so complicated and difficult to understand. But I want you to know this, from my perspective as chief of the organized crime section, whether it's a white-collar criminal or a mob figure makes no difference. If they commit any type of security fraud, they deserve to do prison time just like any other thief.

"However, one of the problems we have is both state and federal agencies need to change their collective mindset about white-collar crime. Make no mistake they are as bad as organized crime figures. Securities fraud is not a victimless crime. It destroys lives just as surely as street crime does. Think about this, Senator, someone steals your car . . . they go to prison. A con artist steals the money you worked all your life for so that someday you can retire . . . and in many cases, he receives a fine. That's not right. The law needs to be changed so the bad guys pay the price for being a bad guy."

One of the senators said, "Mr. Franklin, believe me, there is no doubt in our minds that you and your people are doing a good job, and we are well aware of some of the deficiencies in our laws, but somehow we need to get more convictions, many more. That said, I would like to acknowledge the cooperative efforts of the U.S. Attorney's Office and the Manhattan District Attorney's Office in working with the states securities agencies, the Securities and Exchange Commission (SEC), the NASD Regulation, and your people in committing the resources to build cases against white-collar security criminals, the mob on Wall Street, and corrupt microcap stock firms. I truly believe your willingness to pursue these cases, which as you say has resulted in over three hundred convictions a year for the past three years, has sent a message and had an impact in reducing some of the securities fraud on Wall Street."

"Thank you, Senator, and I agree with you wholeheartedly. We need more convictions. Now if I may, I would like to get back to the sale of AA Financial to the Roman National Bank. I think the reason the bank has purchased AA is obvious. Keeping in mind the bank is owned by the Vatican, and who would dare question their integrity? For one, I would. That notwithstanding, I believe the bank has a plan to provide money laundering, participate in microcap stock fraud as well as foreign currency trading schemes. They may even try some pump and dump schemes. This type of securities fraud is one of the mob's favorites, and the reason it works so well is that it plays on the two things that drive the market, greed and fear.

"I have begun to put together a task force to concentrate solely on AA Financial and the Roman National Bank's dealings in this country. I realize this is a very sensitive issue because of the fact the bank is owned by the Vatican. However, if we ignore the matter, we will be negligent in our commitment to stop the growth of security fraud by organized crime."

One of the senators spoke up. "Mr. Franklin, I am a devoted Catholic. My wife's sister is a nun. I have had an audience with the pope, and I support numerous Catholic charities, and I want you to know that you have my full support in this investigation. I have just one request. Before you make any public statements regarding the Vatican, I would appreciate it if you clear it with this committee. Keep in mind that the Vatican is a sovereign state and has diplomatic immunity. The fact that they own the Roman National Bank does not necessarily guarantee they are aware of what you believe the bank plans to do. Is that a problem?"

"Absolutely not, Senator, and I appreciate your support."

After the meeting, that same senator returned to his office, told his secretary he did not want to be disturbed, and placed a call to Corrine "Lindy" Boggs. In 1997, President Bill Clinton nominated her to be the fifth U.S. Ambassador to the Holy See. At the age of eighty-two, she brought with her to Rome a lifetime of informal diplomatic experience. She had served nine terms in the U.S. House of Representatives, having succeeded her husband who died in a plane crash in 1972.

She had no known enemies and unending scores of admirers from every end of the political spectrum. These attributes proved to be essential as she strove to represent the Clinton administration to the Holy Father. With genial dexterity, she raised awareness at the Holy See of this country's efforts to help stamp out the threat of drugs and the criminal elements, and promote religious freedom. She became an outspoken leader in the worldwide fight against trafficking in human beings, a cause the U.S. Embassy supported wholeheartedly. The senator felt she should be made aware of Tom Franklin's mission. He was not asking her to do anything; he just thought it important that she knew.

She thanked him and asked if he would keep her posted.

He sat at his desk and looked at the picture he had taken with the Pope when he visited the Vatican several years ago. It was inconceivable for him to believe the Holy Father had any knowledge of what the Roman National Bank was up to, if as a matter of fact they were up to anything at all.

CHAPTER SEVENTY

WADE CONVINCED KATRINA to go with him to Chicago. "I don't expect to be tied up with Angelo and my new boss for more than half a day. After that, we can spend a couple days there and celebrate my new job. I'll call Louie and see if he can meet us for dinner one night. It'll be fun." Katrina agreed.

When Wade called Louie, he insisted that he pick them up at the airport. "Are you staying at the house?" he asked. Wade told him they were staying at the Ambassador Hotel downtown. Angelo invited him to stay at the house, but because Katrina was with him, he preferred to stay at a hotel. Louie told him that Giovanni DeLuca was planning on staying at the house.

Louie picked them up at O'Hare Airport on Wednesday night at about six o'clock. Wade told him his meeting with his father and Giovanni was for ten o'clock the following morning. Louie offered to pick him up at the hotel and drive him to the house, but Wade told him his father was sending a car for him. He suggested it would be nice if he picked up Katrina and showed her a little bit of Chicago. He said he would catch up with them later, and they could all have dinner together. That was the plan.

On the following morning, Wade arrived at Angelo's house a little before ten. Although Angelo made it a point to tell him he could dress casual, Wade chose to wear a suit and a tie. When he walked into Angelo's study and looked at his new boss, he knew he made the right decision.

"Good morning, Wade, it's good to see you again. I hope all is well with you," Angelo said, greeting him with a warm handshake. "I would like you to meet Giovanni DeLuca, president of the Roman National Bank, the new owner of AA Financial."

Giovanni DeLuca was a man in his early sixties. He was over six feet tall and looked like he was in excellent shape. He was wearing a dark blue suit with a white silk shirt. He had on a paisley tie with a matching pocket handkerchief. With his longish jet black hair, intense black-as-night eyes, Greek nose, and strong jawline, he looked like a model for

Esquire magazine. He possessed great style, not at all what Wade had expected. It wasn't the fact that the man was incredibly good-looking, or the fact that he was probably very rich it was just a certain something.

"Wade, how nice it is to finally meet you. I have heard a lot about you."

"Mr. DeLuca, it is my pleasure."

"Please, Wade . . . Giovanni."

Wade simply nodded.

"You know, Wade, I am a fan of yours."

Wade didn't understand.

Giovanni smiled. "I went to college here in the States. I went to Duke. You do know Duke, don't you, Wade? They have a very good basketball team!"

Now it was Wade's turn to smile. "So I have heard."

"I attended the final game of the championship series back in 1990 when your school, UNLV, blew my alma mater away."

"I am sorry about that, Mr. DeLuca . . . Giovanni," Wade said with a smile.

The Italian banker went on to tell Wade that he was attending an international banking conference in Denver, and when he heard the final game of the championship was being played there, he made arrangements to attend. Wade liked the man; he exuded charm. He was looking forward to working for him.

"We got lucky that year," Wade said.

"You are too modest, Wade. It was not luck. It was sheer talent."

"Thank you. That's nice of you to say that."

"Do you still play any ball?" Giovanni asked.

"Once in a while, I will play in a pickup game at the gym, but to tell you the truth, between working and trying to keep my girlfriend happy, well I am sure you know how that goes."

"Yes, I do. However, I have always enjoyed basketball. I was never good enough to play at school, but believe it or not, I still play once in a while with some friends. Of course, at my age, once in a while is more than enough."

"I hope you don't mind me asking, Giovanni. Are you married?"

"Yes, I am, and I have two wonderful children. As a matter of fact my oldest, Mario, is attending UCLA. He is in his final year. When he graduates, I hope he will join me in the bank."

"That is great. I am sure you are looking forward to that."

"So Wade, let's talk about AA Financial."

By noon, they were both talked out. Wade told his new boss how he thought they could grow the business, and Giovanni indicated his full support. Occasionally Angelo would interject something, but for the most part it was the 'Wade and Giovanni' show. Just before Angelo's housekeeper served them lunch, Giovanni matter-of-factly told Wade he wanted to send one of his people to New York to work with him. He said the bank had several clients in this country who could be potential clients of AA Financial, and the man he was sending was the person at the bank who handled their accounts. "You will like him, Wade. He too is a basketball fan."

CHAPTER SEVENTY-ONE

TOM FRANKLIN WAS holding the first meeting of his newly formed task force. As the chief of the organized crime section of the F.B.I., he had a lot of atomicity, and it was his intention to use it to wage his fight against organized crime's invasion of Wall Street. The task force consisted of eleven people: eight men and three women. Each one had been with the bureau for at least five years. There were two former stockbrokers, three former undercover police officers, a former lawyer, a former insurance broker, and four agents who came to the bureau directly out of college. However, now they were all F.B.I. people handpicked by Franklin for this assignment. They all had six weeks of schooling on how Wall Street operates. Now they were ready to go after the bad guys.

When Franklin stood up in the front of the room, a slight murmur passed through the group in anticipation of what he was going to say. He looked around at each person in the room and said, "Going forward, any evidence acquired through honest error or misunderstanding will no longer be considered illegal and inadmissible." The former lawyer, now an F.B.I. agent, leaned forward in his chair as if to say, 'Are you kidding me?'

"It will not poison the well. In other words, if you happen to have the wrong date on a court order to search the premises of a broker's office, a defense attorney won't be able to cry foul and get any evidence you might have gathered thrown out of court."

"What's he saying?" the former insurance broker asked.

One of the former cops said, "He's telling us, if we catch some smart-ass broker trying to con some poor schmuck, and we got no evidence, then all we got to do is lock the bastard up for speeding."

"What?" the former insurance agent said.

Franklin laughed. "What he means is we will have a lot more leeway now than we had in the past. If for some reason you conduct a search and seizure at a wrong location and happen to find incriminating evidence, then you will use these."

"What are they?" the youngest of the direct out of college F.B.I. agents asked.

One of the other agents answered for Franklin. "They are blank warrants. We fill them in later."

"Holy shit," said one of the female agents.

Tom Franklin ran his hand through his head of thick brown hair and ducked his head as if he were about to ask a girl to dance. He looked up at his team.

"Listen up everybody the people we are after are thieves. They may dress up in coats and ties, but they are thieves. Some are regular guys, brokers who have become greedy and crossed the line. They should not present any problem when it comes to confronting them. Others are mob guys who think they are smart enough to get away with the shit they are doing, but the bottom line is they are all scum as far as I am concerned."

"I am not asking you to do anything illegal or anything that will put you in harm's way. Some of you will probably work undercover, others may be doing surveillance, and some of you will be assigned to internal investigations which will involve a lot of research, but everybody's job is equally important. I know you're all a little bit nervous today, not sure how far we can go in our investigation. Like I told you last week, one of our targets is a brokerage firm owned by an Italian bank that is owned by the Vatican. Now if any of you feel that is a conflict of interest, I want you to speak up now."

Bernie Cohen spoke up. "I don't know, Chief that may be against my religion."

Franklin looked at him. "Cohen . . . you are Jewish!"

"Oh now you tell me." Everyone in the room laughed, including Agent Cohen.

"Okay, let's get serious," Franklin said. "We're about to embark on matters of great importance. The financial industry, Wall Street in particular, is confronting a major problem. We know for a fact that substantial elements of the small-cap market have been turned into a veritable mob franchise. We also know that white-collar crime in this country has become more rampant than any other type of crime. That is totally unacceptable."

"We're going to give the criminal element that has invaded Wall Street the word that we are mad, and we are not going to take it anymore. I want arrests, and I want convictions. You have to go and do what you have to do in order to gather evidence and build cases that'll result in arrests, prosecutions, and convictions."

Then looking at the Jewish agent he said, "No place is sacred, Agent Cohen, not the church and definitely not even the synagogue!" A lot of laughter ensued.

Franklin continued. "We will not allow any broker, any chop shop, or any bank to get us tangled up in paperwork in an effort to kill our investigation. That doesn't mean you can grossly abuse anyone's rights. But if you can prove to me your actions were well-meant, then you won't have any problem with me. You do your job within the guidelines I've just given you, and I personally will be your shield against any accusation of improper or illegal conduct."

One of the agents said, "With all due respect, Chief, I didn't hear any guidelines."

Franklin said, "You attend to the spirit of the law, and I will attend to the letter. Are there any questions?"

There were none.

CHAPTER SEVENTY-TWO

WHAT TOM FRANKLIN was intending to do was nothing new. Almost twenty years earlier, Rudolph Giuliani, then the United States attorney in charge of New York's Southern District, the largest and most important branch of the Justice Department was on a similar crusade to rid Wall Street of financial criminals. His most spectacular bust, other than the Mafia characters he went after, was that of Dennis B. Levine, the former investment banker who pleaded guilty and implicated a bigger target, arbitrager Ivan F. Boesky. The prosecutor discovered, with the help of the Securities and Exchange Commission, an insider trading scandal of historic significance. Although some of his cases fell through when indictments were dismissed, Giuliani went right back to the drawing board and began mapping a new assault on the financial district's crooks.

Some of Giuliani's other major cases were Marc Rich, a major commodities trader who pleaded guilty and paid $200 million in fines from two of his companies; Don King, the promoter who staged the Mike Tyson–Michael Spinks fight; and a man by the name of Charles Atkins who had created more than $350 million in fraudulent tax shelter schemes.

Tom Franklin studied all of the cases that Giuliani was involved in and soon realized there was no significant difference between today's mob and yesterday's. Some of today's financial criminals attempted to put on a front of respectability, but in Franklin's mind, "a crook is a crook is a crook."

One of the things that Franklin found very interesting was, back in the day when the mobster Dutch Schultz wanted to kill racket buster Thomas Dewey, the mob told him they thought murdering a federal prosecutor would put too much heat on them. Giuliani was asked whether he had thoughts that the mob might target him one day. He responded with a laugh, saying, "I probably agree with them when they said it's a mistake to kill a prosecutor. The whole world would fall in on them." Franklin hoped that today's mob leaders felt the same way!

CHAPTER SEVENTY-THREE

ON THE FLIGHT home from Chicago, Wade was exceptionally quiet.

"Is everything okay?" Katrina asked, snuggling up as close as she could.

"Yeah, I guess . . . it's just . . . well I've been thinking about what DeLuca said about sending one of his people to New York . . . I don't know why, but for some reason, that doesn't sit right with me."

"Why is that? Didn't you say the man he is sending handles some of the bank's clients in New York?"

"Yeah, he did, and that's probably the reason, but the fact that he and Angelo are so friendly, well that makes me wonder."

"Wade, I am sure it will be fine. You said he liked your ideas about what you wanted to do to increase the business."

Wade smiled, kissed her on the cheek, and said, "I guess so. We'll see."

Actually if Wade knew the real reason that Giovanni DeLuca was sending Gerardo "Jerry" Costello to New York, he would probably hand in his resignation the minute he got off the plane. Carmen Vizzini, the head of one of New York's largest Mafia families, was both a close friend and a business associate of DeLuca. Among other things, DeLuca's bank was presently laundering money for him, and when DeLuca informed him he had purchased AA Financial, Vizzini couldn't wait to use his brokerage firm for some of their security scams. It was going to be Costello's job to make sure things went smoothly. DeLuca hoped that Wade would be part of his team, but he was sending Costello to New York for insurance.

In terms of whether Costello was characteristic of the old Sicilian Mafia, he displayed only a few of the traits of the classic Mafioso, which he inherited from his father, who as a matter of fact was old Sicilian Mafia. He was forty years old and had worked for Giovanni DeLuca for ten years in several different capacities, none of which really had to do with banking.

His thick curly black hair had strands of gray along the side. He was almost six feet tall and very muscular. He had a photographic memory that astounded anyone who tested him. He read avidly in English although he retained his accent that made some English vowels sound unintelligible. Depending on whom he spoke to, it might be in English or Italian or a little bit of both.

Although his father was a true old Mafioso, Costello did not believe in the old world live-and-die traditions that his father lived by. He was more inclined to be Americanized. However, when needed, he could be as ruthless and as dangerous as any of his contemporaries. That said, what he had retained was the Mafia heritage of respect and honor. He once told a friend, "I was born this way . . . no matter who asks me for a favor, I'll do him the favor because I believe that is what my nature prescribes to me." This was the man Wade was going to have to deal with.

CHAPTER SEVENTY-FOUR

WADE HAD BEEN back in New York almost a month before he heard from Giovanni DeLuca informing him that Jerry Costello was due to arrive in New York in two days.

"We have arranged for him to stay at the Plaza Hotel until he finds an apartment. If you don't mind, I would like you to set up a meeting for him with a real estate agent one day next week."

"Absolutely Giovanni tell me is there anything I need to know to help Mr. Costello?"

"No, I don't believe so, Wade. He will fill you in when he gets there, and by the way, I am sure he will want you to call him Jerry."

On schedule, Jerry Costello arrived in New York two days after Wade spoke to DeLuca. Wade had expected him to call to arrange for transportation from the airport, but Costello was very self-sufficient. He didn't call Wade until he was already checked in at the Plaza Hotel.

"Why don't I meet you at the hotel for breakfast?" Wade suggested when he called.

In his broken English, he told Wade that he would meet him at the Garden Restaurant at nine o'clock.

At nine o'clock sharp the next morning, Wade arrived at the restaurant, and from the description Jerry had given of himself, Wade had no difficulty spotting him. He was sitting by the window, reading the *Wall Street Journal.* Wade walked over, introduced himself, and sat down. Not sure where to start, Wade told him he had made an appointment for him with a real estate agent for next week. Then he told him he had set up an office for him next to his. Jerry thanked him and suggested they order breakfast. Over breakfast, Jerry admitted to Wade that he knew very little about how to run a brokerage business; that was going to be left up to him. His job was to bring in the bank's New York customers. Little did Wade know there was only one customer, and that was DeLuca's business partner, mob boss Carmen Vizzini. Jerry spoke to him before leaving Rome, and Vizzini told him he already had a plan in place. "We ready to go," he told him.

"What kind of business are these people in?" Wade asked.

Jerry told him they were all investors, some in the market, some in real estate, wherever they could make money.

"I'm not quite sure what it is you plan to offer them," Wade said. "Are we going to try to sell them securities, or do you have something else in mind?"

Jerry was very vague in telling Wade that he would know more when he met with them. He said there was one customer in particular who DeLuca wanted him to concentrate on.

Wade had the feeling that Jerry was not telling him everything, and he was right. What was the big secret? Were these people potential investors or what? He decided not to push. Then Jerry told him one of the men had recently formed a new company and wanted to take it public. "We-cana- do-that-no?"

Wade smiled and said to Jerry, "It's not that easy to just take a company public. There are all kinds of rules and regulations, and of course, it has to be the kind of business that will appeal to the public."

"Yeah, I think I understand, but Mr. DeLuca, he-atell-a-me you guys do this in the past with . . . how I-a-say . . . not so sexy-a-company."

Wade thought to himself, "*This guy is not as dumb about the market as he pretends to be.*" "Yes, that's partly true, Jerry."

Jerry grinned and said, "We see . . . we see!"

CHAPTER SEVENTY-FIVE

THE FIRST MONTH that Jerry Costello was there, nothing much changed. He spent most of his time shadowing Wade, talking to the other brokers in the office, and reading just about everything that came through the office. Then one day, he walked into Wade's office and asked,

"How a come we don't sell more of them low-priced stocks where we can make a lotta more commissions? I been-a-readin' about them."

Wade explained to him that AA was not a chophouse.

"I read-about-that-a-too. I'm not-a-sure I understand."

"The chophouse brokers live in their own world, Jerry. In many cases, they are ex-storm window or house siding salesmen. They are really separate from the rest of the street, both by education as well as class. They don't care about the blue-chip or high-tech stocks, and they don't know the difference between a municipal bond and a urinal."

"Yeah, but from what Ia-read, those guys make a lotta money, so the brokerage house, they must–a-make a lotta money too, eh?"

"You're right. They do make a lot of money, but they move around like cockroaches. Trust me, Jerry that is not the kind of business you want to be in."

"But some of your guys here, I see they sell those kind of stocks . . . what you call . . . small-cap I think you call them."

"Right, but that's only a small part of our business, and to tell you the truth, I intend to weed that group of brokers out in the near future."

Jerry didn't like to hear that. "You think that's a good-a-idea?" he asked.

"Yes, I do."

"You talk to Mr. DeLuca about that, Wade?"

"Not in detail, but it was part of my overall plan that I discussed with him. Why do you ask?"

"I'm a-just-a-curious."

"I see. If you would like, I can show you my long-range plans for how I want to operate our sales force."

The Italian smiled. "That's okay, Wade, not-a-now . . . I dunno, maybe later, Wade . . . we see . . . we see."

Not knowing about the market or stocks or money markets put Jerry at a disadvantage, but that is not what he was sent there for. His job was to make sure the Vizzini family was able to infiltrate their scams through AA Financial, thereby allowing Giovanni to make more money. That was the only interest the Italian banker had . . . to make as much money as he could. The way he made it didn't matter. Notwithstanding all of that, Jerry decided to tell Giovanni about the chop shop operations.

"What do we have to do to get into that business?" Giovanni asked.

Jerry explained that AA already was selling some small-cap stocks; however, most of the brokers were into more traditional blue chip stocks, and of course, AA did a big job in municipal bonds. From his vantage point, he thought all that AA had to do was hire more of the right kind of salesman in order to cash in on the chop house business. Then he went on to tell the banker that Wade had mentioned he wanted to weed out the brokers who were doing this now. He didn't think that was a good idea. "I think the Vizzini family would like this business . . . maybe they already do this someplace else," he said.

Giovanni told him to talk to Vizzini and let him decide. "And keep your eye on Wade," he said as an afterthought.

Strip joints and chophouses served very similar functions. Chophouses took money from people to satisfy their fantasies of greed—fantasies that were almost never realized. Strip joints took money from the public as well as from a lot of chophouse brokers to satisfy their fantasies of sex—fantasies that were also not realized very often. The little bit that Jerry had found out about the chop shop business allowed him to fantasize about the riches it could provide. And some of those riches might end up in his pocket. Whether that fantasy would ever be realized was yet to be determined.

Two weeks after Jerry and Wade had the conversation about chophouse brokers, Jerry brought a large, heavyset man named Bobby Kane to the office. The man was six feet tall and weighed all of maybe three hundred pounds. Jerry asked Wade to meet with them in his office. When Wade walked into Jerry's office, Bobby Kane was slouched in a chair alongside Jerry's desk. Jerry said, "Wade, this is Bobby Kane. We gonna make a lotta money with him."

Wade knew immediately this was not going to be a good day.

Bobby Kane sat in Jerry's office with comfort, regally, because he was at home. He was always at home in a brokerage office no matter where it was located—New York, New Jersey, wherever. He was working with stocks and stockbrokers as far back as the late seventies. In 1981, he was convicted by the feds for his role in a stock swindle involving several oil-drilling companies. He and his crew got oil company stock that was nearly worthless and gave brokers cash under the table to sell the stock to the public at high prices.

By 1989, he was back in the stock business, only this time, he was much more careful and didn't get caught. In 1992, he went to work for the Vizzini crime family, pushing phony stocks, promoting IPOs in nonexistent companies, and any other financial scam the family needed him to handle.

Wade waited patiently for Jerry to tell him how the big, fat, very cocky-looking man was going to help them make a lot of money.

Finally, Bobby Kane spoke up. For a big man, his voice was soft. That's probably what helped make him a good con artist.

"Tell me, Wade, do you know what a 'rip' is?"

"Of course it's another word for a commission."

"Yeah, you can call it that, but a 'rip' is where the money is. Like I told Jerry here, your brokers can earn big money with the right system in play. I mean, what do your guys earn in commissions on the blue chip stocks they sell? Boobkas! Now on the stocks that I can bring in, both AA Financial and your guys will make a lot of money. Get my drift?"

"You mean chop stocks?"

"Yeah, there's nothing wrong with them."

"That's a matter of opinion, Mr. Kane."

"Hey why so formal, Wade? We're gonna be partners."

"Oh that's news to me," Wade said.

Wade looked at Jerry, who simply smiled.

Nobody really knew where the term "rips" originated. Nobody cared.

Rips were the huge sums of money chophouse brokers received for pushing stocks that had the appeal of a fart in an elevator. They stunk!

Here is how it works: A chophouse finds a stock listed on the pink sheets for say $8. That is the price the public sees. Often the stock is obtained by the brokers from corporate insiders or offshore accounts at a fraction of the price listed on the quote terminals. It is usually a stock that has a legend, which means it is restricted and can't be sold to the public until a certain date. That is why the chophouse can buy it at a cut rate. The chophouse puts it on their books for say $5 and splits the $3 profit evenly with the broker. A difference between a rip and a markup is very subtle. A $3 markup on a $100 stock wouldn't be so bad; that's only 3 percent. But $3 on an $8 stock ends up looking like 60 percent.

So the brokers are paid vast sums of money, and the regulators, who are looking for excessive markups, don't take notice.

The brokerage firms might add on a few cents of commission, making the customer think he is only paying three cents a share commission, which is very reasonable.

Basically that's what chop stocks were all about—paper, moving paper from one place to another. The chop stock brokers moved paper, stocks that were often barely worth the paper they were written on, if they were actually even written on paper—and in many cases, they weren't because by this time the actual stock certificates were being phased out. So the poor bastard, the investor, didn't even have a nice-looking stock certificate to use as wallpaper in his bathroom.

Ask most regulators and they will tell you that it's fraud of the most fundamental kind. The public doesn't know that they are buying stocks that are worth nothing more than pennies shelled out by their brokers.

However, to many other regulators, this is a small—if troublesome—fringe of the securities industry. Mob infiltration is their biggest concern, and the U.S. attorney recently maintained that they will continue to spend their resources in weeding out the criminal elements in Wall Street. So is any of this legal? I guess it depends on who you ask.

The fact remains that behind all the charges, there is a simple thing that has received little attention. Vast, interlocking networks of brokers are managing to obtain shares in hundreds of companies at dirt-cheap prices and are unloading them on the public. Among the people who make their living this way are rouge brokers like Bobby Kane and the Vizzini crime family.

After Bobby Kane left the office, Wade told Jerry that they needed to talk.

"I had no idea this was the direction that Giovanni wanted to go," Wade said.

"Why, Wade? Money is money."

"I hear what you're saying, Jerry, but I don't know that I can run that type of firm."

"Hey you mean to tell me you never sell a stock that sinks?"

"No, that's not what I'm saying. What I'm saying is the stocks we sell now are legitimate investments. We hope the investor is going to make money."

"Hey, Wade . . . you a listen. It's a more important we make money, don't you think?"

Driving home that night, Wade couldn't stop thinking about what had happened at the meeting with Jerry and his friend Bobby Kane. Nobody said it, but he knew damn well what was happening. Giovanni was allowing the mob to come into the firm. This guy Bobby Kane was no ordinary stockbroker. He was a front for the mob; he had to be. All that shit about just selling chop stocks . . . who did he think he was kidding? And this guy Jerry, what was his real job? He began to think he was getting in over his head. Sure he was going to make a ton of money and have the title of CEO, but would he really be running the firm?

Then he thought about Angelo. Had he set him up? Did Angelo know what Giovanni was planning to do? "*Would he do such a thing? Let Giovanni make me the front man for a mob-run firm?*" He couldn't believe he would do such a thing. He decided he would call Angelo; he had to find out the truth.

CHAPTER SEVENTY SIX

SITTING IN THE den in his home in Chicago, Angelo Santino had just finished speaking with Agent Carl Montrose, head of a federal task force working in California to stop the flow of drugs there. The agent flew to Chicago to meet with Angelo after he was told by a mutual friend that Angelo had information vital to his investigation into the drug trade between Mexico and California.

When Angelo was negotiating with the Roman National Bank to sell them AA Financial, his biggest challenge was getting Albert Kline to agree to sell his share of the firm. Angelo wanted out and knew that unless Kline agreed to sell, he would have difficulty just selling his share of the firm. Combined with wanting to end his partnership with Kline, he also wanted revenge. Revenge because he knew that Kline had cheated him. An easy way to take his revenge would be to simply kill him, but that would be too easy. Kline wouldn't know he was being punished; he would be dead. The old Sicilian Mafia theory was the victim had to know he was being punished for what he did. Angelo wanted to take revenge in such a way that Kline would remember for the rest of his life that what had happened to him was because he had betrayed his friend. Then one day, he found out the bank in Rome owned a winery in California. That was kind of strange. Why would they want to own a winery in this country when they could do the same thing in Italy or France? Then he found out the reason.

The original owner, an Italian immigrant, was an old friend of Giovanni DeLuca's father, and when he bought the winery, Giovanni's bank lent him the money to do the deal. The old immigrant had died about a year ago, owing the bank a lot of money. Giovanni sent someone from Italy to run the winery until they could sell it. About two months after Giovanni's man was here, he called the banker to tell him that there were a group of Mexicans growing marijuana on part of the winery's property. Giovanni was into a lot of illegal things, but he didn't want anything to do with drugs. That is when he called Angelo and asked for his help.

"What do you think I should do?" he asked Angelo.

Angelo told him he would think about it and get back to him. That was when he knew he had found a way to take revenge against Kline. He didn't care how long it would take, how much money it would cost, or how convoluted the plan was. The important thing was Kline would know he was being punished for betraying his friend.

He told Giovanni that his partner was a wine lover. He said if he could make the winery part of the deal that might convince Kline to sell.

"What about the Mexicans growing the marijuana?"

"We gonna take care of that too," Angelo said.

The banker liked the idea.

"Everybody wins," Angelo said. "You get AA Financial and at the same a time get out of the marijuana business, and my good a friend, he own a winery."

"How about you, Angelo what do you get besides a lot of money?"

Angelo laughed, "Donna you a worry about me, paisano, I'm a-gonna do just fine."

When Kline took over the vineyard, he paid little or no attention to the small group of Mexicans who lived and worked on the far edge of his property. The view of the fields that they worked in was mostly blocked by the old shacks there, and the road leading in and out to that part of the vineyard was separate from the main entrance to the vineyard. As a matter of fact, the grapes that the vineyard used to make their wine stopped about sixty feet from where the old shacks were, so it was almost like they didn't exist.

About the only time anybody from the winery saw them was when they were doing gardening around the house or fixing something. And since Kline spent very little time at the vineyard, he practically forgot they were even there. After Kline took over the vineyard, Esther decided there was no way she could live there full-time, so Kline purchased a luxury condo in San Francisco, and when they weren't traveling or at the vineyard, that is where they lived.

Kline hired a man to run the winery, and things were going very smoothly. They were producing a variety of wines including a cabernet, a chardonnay, and a sauvignon. Since his reason for wanting to own a vineyard had nothing to do with it being a profitable business, it didn't bother him that it was a losing proposition. He was enjoying the best of all worlds. He was able to see a bottle of wine with his name on it and have the pleasure of drinking his own wine.

Due to the divergent array of soils and the success he was having in the acreage he was using to grow his grapes, the man running the winery for Albert Kline never even thought about looking into the possibility of using the ground adjacent to the ground occupied by the Mexicans. He often wondered why they had stopped planting the grapes so far from the end of the property, but he had enough to do to keep him busy without worrying about that.

However, he began to notice a lot more activity there in recent months. One day, when he saw one of the Mexicans cutting the grass in front of the house, he questioned him about it. In his broken English, the Mexican gardener told him they were growing more fruit and sending it to San Francisco to sell. He hoped they weren't disturbing him. Kline's man said, "Absolutely not," and wished him luck.

The real reason for the increased activity was due to the increase in the amount of marijuana the Mexicans were growing and selling. Angelo found a way to get word to one of the drug lords in Mexico that there was a marijuana farm a little north of San Francisco just waiting for the right people to help them sell their product. It didn't take long for the Mexican drug lord to contact the Mexicans on Kline's property and set up a pipeline for distribution. He also made a deal with them to recruit mules to take some of his product out of Mexico to their location and then package it and ship it to drug dealers around the country. Within a relatively short time, without Kline being aware of it, there was a fairly significant drug operation going on right under his nose on his property.

When Agent Carl Montrose left Angelo's house, he had enough information to justify a raid on Kline's vineyard, close down the marijuana farm the Mexicans were operating, arrest all of the Mexicans there at the time, and issue an arrest warrant for Albert Kline.

The deal that Angelo made with Agent Montrose was very simple. First of all, no one could ever know that he was the one giving him this information. No problem, the agent agreed.

Secondly, the agent had to promise they would prosecute Kline to the fullest extent of the law. Angelo was able to give the agent documented information showing that some of the marijuana the Mexicans were growing on Kline's vineyard was ending up being sold to schoolchildren. Angelo may have been out of the "business" for a long time, but he still maintained a lot of important contacts, plus when he retired he was owed a lot of favors. Now he was collecting on them.

And the final nail in Kline's coffin was when one of Angelo's friends promised one of the Mexicans who was involved in the growing of the marijuana on Kline's property $10,000 in cash and a house for his family if he would testify that Kline knew what was going on and that he accepted an envelope full of cash from him every week. They told the Mexican that not only would he have all of that money and a house, but he would be able to make a deal with the authorities for cooperating because they weren't really interested in him, they wanted the main guy . . . Albert Kline!

This was Angelo's revenge.

CHAPTER SEVENTY-SEVEN

THE BUST WAS conducted by multiple agents, including the Sonoma County sheriff's office, the California Fish and Wildlife Department, the California Highway Patrol, and the Federal Drug Enforcement Agency. The paramilitary operation involved three different teams with up to twenty-five officers. Accompanying the raiding party were six tractor trailers driven by employees of the United States Forest Service. These would be used to transport the marijuana that was confiscated. This was going to be a major drug bust.

When the drug raid on Kline's vineyard was reported in the news, they claimed that $2.5 million worth of pot, illegal guns, and several hundred thousand dollars in cash had been seized. The guns and the cash were found in the shacks near the field where the Mexicans were growing the marijuana.

The Sonoma County Police Chief said that this was the largest drug bust in the history of the county. The California Wine Growers Association president also issued a statement blasting Kline for using the vineyard as a front for an illegal drug operation.

"He has damaged the reputation of all of the honest, hardworking wine growers in Sonoma Valley." He said that Kline should never be allowed to drink another glass of wine. Pretty severe!

During the raid, the agents discovered crates of wine tightly packaged around bags of pot in the vineyard's own marked crates, addressed to different locations out of state. This would make any statement that Kline might make that he didn't know about the marijuana very difficult for the authorities to believe.

When Angelo read this, he had to laugh. He had nothing to with that. He assumed the Mexicans must have stolen the wine and the packing material from the winery at night and then packaged the wine with the pot and used either the U.S. Post Office or UPS unknowingly as their shipping agent. Pretty clever guys!

When the authorities questioned Kline's man who was running the winery for him, he told them that Kline specifically told him not to bother the Mexicans on that part of the vineyard. "They are growing fruit, besides which the ground there is not conducive to grow grapes," Kline said. Ironically when the California Wine Growers Association was called in to test that ground, they said their findings proved the ground there was no different from the rest of the vineyard. This was another strike against Kline.

On one of the nightly newscasts, the news anchor said, "You can tell by the quantity of marijuana they had on site that this was a major operation." And by the time he got to report the value of the pot that the authorities seized, it had grown to over $10 million. It was also reported that three of the Mexicans arrested were members of a known Los Angeles drug gang who were wanted by the Orange County sheriff's office on multiple counts.

The mayor of San Francisco said, "We believe that the raid on the vineyard owned by Albert Kline, a retired New York Wall Street stockbroker, will have a crippling effect on the Mexican Mafia criminal operation in California."

As he had promised, Agent Carl Montrose called Angelo after Albert was arrested at his condo in San Francisco to inform him of the charges that were going to be filed against him.

"He will be charged with conspiracy to manufacture and possess marijuana, mail fraud, harboring a known felon and maintaining a place to store drugs. I have been told some other drug-related charges are going be filed by the California attorney general's office. There will be a bail hearing in the morning. I can't imagine the judge not setting bail for him. It will probably be very high, and I would not be surprised if the judge asks him to surrender his passport. I want to thank you again, Mr. Santino, for your help."

Angelo was pleased with what he accomplished. He had no regrets, no remorse. In his world, there was no gray: things were either black or white. Kline had no reason to cheat him. He had all the money he could ever spend, so why did he do it? Angelo thought to himself that Kline would have a lot of time behind bars to answer that question.

CHAPTER SEVENTY-EIGHT

IN THE CAR on his way to work, Wade heard the news on the radio that Albert Kline had been arrested and charged with growing and distributing marijuana and using his winery as a front. He couldn't believe it. As soon as he arrived at the office, the receptionist handed him a copy of the *Wall Street Journal* and said, "Wade, did you hear about Mr. Kline? Is it true?"

It made front page headlines in the *Wall Street Journal.*

"Respected CEO of a Wall Street Brokerage Firm Arrested in Drug Raid!"

He wanted to call Brenda, but he didn't know what to say. His next thought was to call Angelo. He had planned to call him anyhow about what was happening at AA. Could what just happened to his former boss have anything to do with what was going on at AA? "Impossible, that would be crazy, but . . ."

When Jerry came to work, Wade was on the phone, talking to Katrina. She had just heard the news about Kline on TV and called him.

"Is it true, Wade? Did Albert do what they said he did?"

"I don't know, baby . . . I don't know."

"Oh my god I feel so bad for Esther."

"Yeah, I know. Look let me call you back. Jerry just came in, and I want to talk to him."

"Okay, by the way, are you still planning to go and see Angelo?"

"I'm not sure. At this point, I can't tell the good guys from the bad guys."

"I love you."

"I love you too, baby. Talk to you later."

When Wade went into Jerry's office, he was on the phone with Bobby Kane. From his end of the conversation, he could tell they were talking about what happened with Albert Kline. When he hung up the phone, he looked at Wade as if to say, "I don't know anything about this."

Wade asked him if he had spoken to Giovanni.

"You mean about Kline?"

"Well yeah, that . . . and also about what Bobby Kane wants to do."

"No, I dunno talk to him yet."

Wade knew he was lying.

"I didn't know this Kline fellow . . . is all this stuff true?" Jerry asked as if he were really concerned. Wade thought to himself, "*This guy couldn't care less.*"

"I don't know, Jerry. I've known the man a long time, and we have had our differences, but it is hard for me to believe he would get involved in something like this. First of all, he has enough money to last him five lifetimes. Why would he get into this kind of shit?"

Jerry simply shrugged his shoulders. "Who knows?"

Wade knew that Kline got the vineyard from Giovanni as part of the deal when he sold AA Financial. Was the marijuana farm there when he took over? He didn't own the place long enough to set up the type of drug operation the papers were reporting. The whole thing smelled of bad fish.

Jerry changed the subject.

"I just speak to-a Bobby. He-wanna move ahead with what-we-a-talk about the other day."

"Yeah, I bet he does. Look, Jerry, I would like to talk to Giovanni about this before we do anything."

"Sure you can do that. In the meantime, Bobby he is talking to some a-guys he wanna bring in to sell the . . . whatta you call them . . . chop stocks."

"Jerry, first of all, we don't have room here to bring in a crew of cold-callers, plus we need someone to manage them."

"I think about that, Wade . . . we can fix up the top floor . . . get rid of the apartment. Nobody use that. And Bobby, he-amanage that part of the business . . . it-a-be like-a separate business upstairs—we can-a-put in some phones . . . it work a-very good."

"Sounds like you have been giving this a lot of thought, Jerry."

"That's - my job, Wade . . . to help you."

"Yeah, and I appreciate that, but I still want to call Giovanni before we do anything."

"Sure, sure you do that, Wade."

It took Wade a couple of days before he was able to catch up with the Italian banker. In the meantime, he checked out Bobby Kane with some people on the Street. What he learned was enough to assure him that he was right about Kane. He really was a bad guy.

When Giovanni returned Wade's call, he was as cordial as can be. Before Wade could ask him about Bobby Kane, Giovanni told him he heard about Albert Kline, and he felt terrible. Wade wanted to ask him if the marijuana farm was there when he owned it but decided it was not his place to ask. When he began to talk about Jerry and Bobby Kane, Giovanni interrupted him. "Wade, why don't you fly to Rome for a couple of days? I don't think it is a good idea to talk about these things on the phone. Tell you what why don't you bring your lady friend, and the two of you stay at our house, we have plenty of room. That way, you and I can spend some time together and talk about all of the things on your mind, and at the same time, you can have a little vacation."

Wade was not sure that is what he wanted to do, but he needed to talk to him, so he agreed. When he told Katrina, she was very excited. "I love Rome, Wade. It is so romantic. Have you ever been there?"

"No, but I once went to Wildwood."

"Very cute," she said.

Two days later, they were on their way to Rome. Giovanni made arrangements to have a car pick them up at the airport, a Rolls Royce limousine, no less!

It was about a fifteen-minute drive from the airport to Giovanni's villa. The villa was in the seaside town of Positano on the Amalfi Coast. The entire property was gated with a uniformed guard at the entrance. When the guard saw the limo approach, he opened the gate and waved to the driver.

Giovanni and his wife greeted Wade and Katrina when they arrived at their villa. Giovanni gave Katrina a warm hug and did the same to Wade. Then he introduced his wife. She looked to be a little younger than Giovanni. She was very pretty and looked like "money." She was definitely high maintenance.

The villa had spectacular views of both the coast and Rome. Behind the villa, there was a private lake surrounded by a beautifully manicured landscape. The villa itself was built on two floors, and Giovanni said that after they bought it about ten years ago, they completely remodeled the inside to provide all the modern conveniences but at the same time retained the charm and splendor of the hundred-year-old dwelling.

When they entered the villa, they passed through a large marble foyer with a crystal chandelier overhead. It looked more like a museum than a house. The inside of the villa itself was breathtaking. The walls were covered with original works of art from the masters. There was a sunken living room that looked out over an Olympic-sized pool. On the opposite side of the pool was the guest house, which was as nice as any house you might want to live in. Giovanni didn't spare anything in furnishing the villa either. Most of the furnishings were custom-designed. Off to the side of the living room was a music room with a grand piano. Giovanni noticed Katrina's eyes light up when she saw the piano. "Do you play?" he asked her. She smiled and said, "A little."

After a tour of the house, Giovanni took them out to the guesthouse. One of the housemaids had already unpacked their suitcases and put everything away. On the bed were bathing suits and robes in case they wanted to take a swim in the heated pool before dinner. There was no doubt about it; Giovanni DeLuca went first class.

After Giovanni left, Katrina plopped down on the king-size bed and motioned for Wade to come lie down beside her. "Come and make love to me in Rome," she said with a giggle.

Wade looked at her; she was beautiful. "I can't," he said. "I feel like I'm in church."

"Wade!"

"Look at this place, baby, how do you expect me to make love here? I bet there are more statues here than in the Louvre. And all this marble, the floors, the bathroom, I've never seen so much damn marble in my life."

She got up from the bed, walked over to him, and put her arms around him and kissed him on the neck, then on the cheek and then on his lips and said, "I love you very, very much. Will you marry me?"

Still holding her close, he moved his head so he could look at her. "Are you proposing in the middle of all this marble?"

"I guess I am," she said.

"Wow, I never had anyone propose to me before. Shouldn't you get down on one knee or something?" he said, trying not to laugh.

"Wade!"

"I'm kidding, and the answer is yes."

She moved back a step. "Are you kidding?"

"Were you kidding when you asked me?"

"No of course not."
"Me either."
"Oh, Wade, I do love you."
He pulled her close and kissed her gently on the lips then said, "Is that offer still open?"
Coyly she said, "And what offer might that be?"

CHAPTER SEVENTY-NINE

DINNER WAS SERVED in a large formal dining room. Giovanni had his own full-time chef who prepared a special Roman-style dinner for them. After dinner, Giovanni invited Katrina to play the piano; she was delighted to accept. After she started to play, Giovanni and his wife looked at one another in amazement. "Do you play often?" Giovanni asked Katrina.

She stopped playing and turned around and smiled. "I'm sorry. I should have told you, I'm a concert pianist."

Again Giovanni and his wife looked at one another, again with amazement. Finally, Giovanni clapped his hands and said, "Bravo, bravo." His wife did the same. After Katrina played several pieces for them, Giovanni could not say enough about how well she played. "I would love to arrange for you to perform here in Rome one day. Would you consider that?"

Katrina was flattered and said she would definitely think about it. Wade was very proud of her. She had a certain way about her that put her in a class of her own.

Giovanni suggested they have their coffee and dessert on the patio that overlooked part of the formal gardens. Katrina looked out over the garden and said, "I have never seen such a beautiful place in my life. You two must love living here."

Giovanni's wife thanked her and said no matter where they go, she can't wait to get back home. "I don't blame you one bit," Katrina said.

Giovanni asked the women if they would excuse him and Wade; they had some business to discuss. His wife suggested to Katrina they take a walk in the garden since it was such a nice night. "We'll leave you two men to solve the world's problems," she said as she took Katrina by the hand and led her to the garden.

Giovanni ushered Wade into his study and offered him a cigar, which he chose not to accept, and then poured them each a glass of brandy.

"So, Wade, how is everything in New York? Jerry tells me you two are working on a new brand."

"Well that's not actually true. It's Jerry that is working on a new brand, as you call it. Giovanni, do you know a man by the name of Bobby Kane?"

"Only from what Jerry has told me."

"Has Jerry told you that he is a convicted felon, that he is selling securities without a license? Has he told you that his reputation on the street is so bad no legitimate house will hire him?"

"And because of this, you don't think we should bring him into the firm and consider his plan to sell low-priced stocks." Evidently Jerry had discussed Bobby's plan to sell chop stocks at AA. Wade thought for a moment before answering.

"To be perfectly honest, Giovanni, no, I don't."

"Wade, before I bought AA, I did some fairly extensive due diligence." Giovanni saw the surprised look on Wade's face. "You were not aware of this, I am sure. Angelo helped me do it without anyone knowing, not even Albert." Wade wanted to ask him how he did it without anyone knowing but was sure he wouldn't get an answer. He thought it had to be the AA comptroller who Louie told him was his father's eyes and ears at AA. Wow.

"Anyhow, Wade, I am fully aware of the municipal bond deals that AA continues to do with certain banks. I am sure you know what I am talking about."

Wade simply nodded.

"That is one of the reasons I bought AA. Those deals generate big profits. However, in the minds of some people, they are considered to be unethical. Is that any worse, or maybe I should say any different than what Bobby Kane wants to do?"

"That's difficult for me to answer. However, I think what is more important here is Bobby Kane himself. With all due respect, Giovanni, he is a bad guy."

"So what you're saying is you are not opposed to AA selling small-cap stocks, you just don't want this Bobby Kane fellow doing it for us."

This guy was smooth and smart, and he was his boss. Wade knew he was not there to argue or debate the subject with him: he was there simply to tell him how he felt about what was going on. AA Financial was his company. He could do whatever he wanted with it. He could hire or fire anybody he wanted. The decision Wade had to make was whether he wanted to go along with him.

"Wade, let me tell you something. When I was about ten years old, I found an envelope on the floor in a bakery. There was fifty thousand lira in the envelope, which was equivalent to about $40 American money. To a ten-year-old kid, that was a small fortune back then. I picked up the envelope and gave it the shopkeeper. I saw him take the money out of the envelope, throw the envelope away, and put the money in his pocket. When I told my father what I had done, he smacked me on the back of the head and called me stupid. 'You don't give money back,' he said. 'Do you think the shopkeeper is going to look for the *momaluke* who lost the envelope? No.' He said, 'Giving back money someone else had lost makes no sense.'

"My point is, people who invest in a stock and lose money, well that's not your responsibility. Would you give them back their money? Of course not, that would be stupid, like me giving the fifty thousand lira to the shopkeeper. And as far as Bobby Kane being a bad guy, the difference between you and me and him is simple. We are smarter than him . . . we have never been caught. Surprised? Don't be. This is a cruel world Wade nobody gives you anything for nothing.

"When I was a kid, I played marbles with some of the older kids in the neighborhood. Because my father was let's just say because he "knew people," sometimes they would let me win. I didn't like that. I wanted to win on my own. One day, I told this to my father. He laughed and said, 'It don't make no difference how you win. The important thing is you win.' I always remembered that and applied it to the way I built my fortune. There was a football coach in your country who once said, 'Winning isn't everything—it's the only thing.' I am sure that is how you felt when you played basketball. Always keep that in mind, Wade, and you won't go wrong.

"Wade, I am Catholic, and I go to church. As you know, the Vatican owns the bank, and I respect the priests and the pope, but I only believe in what I can see and what I know. I know how to make money. Does that make me evil? I don't think so.Trust me there is no Santa Claus or Easter Bunny. And did Jesus really walk on water? Good trick if he did. And did a snake tell Eve not to eat the apple. I don't think so. I don't know anything about the soul and afterlife, I only know about this life. And then there's the myth about the Ten Commandments. Sure somebody sat down one day and wrote them. But people want to believe that Moses came down some mountain carrying them like two bags of groceries from Super Fresh. And heaven and hell—where are they?

"Now if some people want to believe all of that stuff, more power to them. They are probably the same people who believe they can get rich overnight from buying a cheap stock and watch it soar through the roof. Are we supposed to feel sorry for those people when they lose all of their money? We don't hold a gun to their head, and we don't scare the shit out of them like the church does. The priest tells them believe or they will go to hell. We simply ask them to buy a stock with the possibility of making some money. We don't threaten them with heaven or hell if they don't buy the stock. It's their choice. The bottom line is the money we make does not come from God. It comes from hard work on the part of our salesman.

"Now what you need to think about is . . . Do you have the balls to handle Bobby Kane? Then you need to decide if you want to play on my team."

Wade said, "I can handle Bobby Kane, and I can handle Jerry Costello. That's not my problem. My problem is I need to be sure what we are doing is legal."

"Unfortunately, Wade, you can't go to a lawyer for a legal opinion on this. What I can tell you is the sale of microcap stocks in your country run in the billions of dollars every year. That's billions with a B. Wade we are not going to be doing anything different than what most of Wall Street does."

Wade knew in his heart that it was not true. One thing was true, and that was Giovanni had only one god, and that was the almighty dollar.

CHAPTER EIGHTY

ON THE FLIGHT home, Wade was just as quiet as he was going to Rome.

"It seems that when you fly, you can't talk," Katrina said as she nudged closer to him. He smiled and reached over to hold her hand.

He had told her about his talk with Giovanni, and when she asked him what he planned on doing, he said, "I'm not sure!"

The morning after he had spoken to Giovanni, Wade was up before dawn. When Katrina woke up, he was already in the pool. She put on her robe and watched him glide back and forth in the pool from the window. Finally, she walked out to the pool and sat on the steps with her feet in the pool. When he saw her, he swam over to her, reached up, and kissed her.

"You're getting me all wet," she said.

"Okay, no more kisses."

"I didn't say stop. I just said that you're getting me wet."

Still in the pool, he laid his wet head on her lap. She ruffled his wet hair then bent over and kissed him and whispered, "You know I love you very much."

Without picking up his head, he said, "Yeah, I kinda got that feeling last night."

She gently patted him on the head and said, "You are a mess." Then as she began to stand up, he said, "You wanna know what I decided about AA?"

"Can I guess?"

"Okay, shoot."

"You decided to stay around for a while and see what happens."

He climbed out of the pool, picked up a towel, wiped off his face, and gave her a big smile and said, "You think you are so damn smart!"

She stuck out her tongue at him and started to walk back into the guesthouse with Wade trailing closely behind her.

As the American Airlines flight soared through the clouds on the way to New York, Wade fell asleep while still holding Katrina's hand. Before falling asleep, he replayed in his mind the conversation he had with Giovanni and the question the Italian banker had asked him, "Do you want to play on my team?"

Wade hoped he had made the right decision.

CHAPTER EIGHTY-ONE

WILLIAM J. GOLDENBERG was one of the finest criminal attorneys in the country and probably the most expensive. His specialty was handling drug-related cases. He had recently achieved a non-guilty verdict for John Sabella, head of one of New York's major crime families. Sabella was one of those quiet Mafioso often termed a "sleeper" —someone in the mob who was active enough to be respected and known but passive enough not to draw attention. When he was arrested and charged in one of the nation's most publicized drug cases, the media had him tried, convicted, and put away for life. They claimed that with the evidence the government had against him and the statements from the undercover drug agent who had infiltrated the Sabella family, he didn't have a chance.

However, after almost two years of motions to dismiss, motions to disallow certain jurors, flaws in the evidence collected by the undercover agent, a change of venue, a mistrial and witnesses being discredited, William Goldenberg was able to have him acquitted. Newsweek magazine did an article on Goldenberg after the trial, citing him as the best criminal defense lawyer of our time. He was the lawyer Albert Kline hired to handle his defense.

Only hours after Albert Kline was arrested in San Francisco, he contacted his attorney in New York who immediately got in touch with one of William Goldenberg's associates. He explained the importance and the severity of the situation and said he needed someone to attend the bail hearing the following morning in San Francisco. By this time, it was already midnight in New York. Goldenberg's associate told Kline's lawyer that Goldenberg was out of the country, but expected him to return in two days. In the meantime, he said he would contact someone in San Francisco who would attend the bail hearing in the morning and ask the judge to allow him to post bail but hold off a formal reading of the charges until Goldenberg could get to California.

He anticipated a high bail and was sure the court would ask for Kline's passport. Kline's lawyer said he would arrange to wire the bail money as soon as he told him the amount, and he was sure Kline had his passport with him. Goldenberg's associate said he could not get away right now and suggested to him that he go to California and stay with Kline until Goldenberg got there. He agreed and said he would take the first flight out to California in the morning.

Goldenberg's associate told him that if all went well, by the time he got there, Mr. Kline should be home. "I am going to suggest he wait there until you arrive. When you speak to him, instruct him not to say anything to anyone until you meet with him. Hopefully Mr. Goldenberg will be there in a couple of days, and he will take charge."

CHAPTER EIGHTY-TWO

RELUCTANTLY JUDGE LENORE Madison agreed to Albert Kline's lawyer's request to allow them to post bond and wait until William Goldenberg was available before formally charging him, at which time he would enter a plea. Judge Madison was a middle-aged African American who had been on the bench for almost fifteen years. She had seen her share of drug-related cases and had no sympathy for drug dealers, be they from the ghetto or Wall Street. Her sixteen-year-old niece died of an overdose shortly after she became a judge, and she vowed then to show no mercy to any convicted drug dealer. Several times defendants attempted to have her removed from a case because of the incident with her niece, but they were unsuccessful.

She set the bond for Kline at $1 million. Kline's lawyer objected vigorously, claiming the evidence against him was weak, and he did not pose any threat to society. Judge Madison said, "If you want, I can read the formal charges against Mr. Kline now. Then you can enter your plea, after which I might reconsider. However, if you want me to wait until Mr. Goldenberg is available, that will cost you a million dollars. This is a one-time sale, Counselor, take it or leave it." Three hours later, Kline's bank had wired the million dollars to the court.

Now it was three days later. Albert Kline, his New York lawyer, and William Goldenberg, and two members of his defense team were in Kline's condo in San Francisco. Esther was not there. She told her husband she couldn't sit through a meeting with the lawyers and all of their bullshit. She just wanted all of this to go away.

Goldenberg was fifty-three years old. His father was a dentist, and his mother was an English teacher. He was born and raised in Boston, where he went to college and then on to law school. He was a little over six feet tall and carried himself with the confidence of a winner, which he was. He was always suntanned, which complimented his brown hair. He was married for five years before getting divorced. He didn't have any children. He lived in New York in the penthouse in the Trump Towers, and he flew his own private jet.

Before the meeting, Goldenberg's associate spoke to Kline's attorney about the fee. He let him know that depending on how the trial progressed, assuming there would be a trial, the legal fees could exceed $2 million. He also told him they required a retainer of $500,000. After discussing it with Kline, Kline's attorney advised Goldenberg's associate that Kline agreed and would arrange to wire the $500,000 that same day.

Goldenberg was explaining to Albert Kline and his lawyer the consequences of the charges he faced.

"Drug-related charges run the gamut from minor possession, which usually results in a court referral to a drug diversion program, to the very serious charges of manufacturing and or growing and distributing, which carry the potential for a long prison sentence."

This made Kline shiver. Goldenberg saw this and told him to relax. "I just want you to understand what you are faced with, but trust me nobody is going to prison so fast."

That didn't make Albert Kline feel much better. Goldenberg continued.

"The charge of manufacturing is very technical, and sometimes a prosecuting attorney will attempt to lump manufacturing and growing into the same charge. I will make sure that doesn't happen here. Now amongst other things, you have been charged with drug sales and drug possession for sale under the Health and Safety Code sections 11351 and 11352.

"I know you don't want to hear this, but you need to know. Conviction under section 11351 is a felony punishable by imprisonment for up to four years. Conviction under section 11352 carries a sentence of up to five years. However, the sentence in both cases is greater, could be up to nine years, if the transportation of drugs crossed two county lines here in California."

Albert Kline turned pale. "Jesus Christ," he said in a whisper.

"Mr. Kline, I am telling you all of this so you will understand how important it is that you tell me everything that happened that put you in this situation. I am your lawyer, and whatever you tell me is confidential."

Kline simply nodded. Goldenberg continued.

"When a person is found to possess an illegal drug in an amount considered to be more than an amount for personal use, which is the case here, and in addition to the drug itself, various other items are found such as scales, packing materials, shipping labels, and the like, the prosecution will always press for jail time.

"The drug enforcement people in California will almost always go for the juggler when they find a person is not only growing the weed but packaging it and selling it. The way you have been charged allows the prosecution to determine which code section should be enforced. Believe or not, there are no less than fifteen different sections they can use, all of which are considered to be a felony. I intend to file a deferred entry of judgment, which if successful, would result in a dismissal of the charges."

This gave Kline a ray of hope, which was soon extinguished when Goldenberg added, "But I don't think the court will agree."

"As I said, the prosecution is going to go for the juggler in this case. Their claim will be: 'Here we have a successful Wall Street executive with ties to the Mexican Drug Cartel.' That will make great headlines, but we won't allow them to build on that.

"What is important for you to remember is, it is not up to us to prove you are innocent . . . it is up to the prosecution to prove you are guilty, and we are not going to allow that to happen."

Albert Kline finally managed a small smile and said, "From your mouth to God's ears."

"As you know, we have entered a plea of not guilty, and that is the verdict I expect from the jury, assuming we go to trial."

Albert asked if there was a real possibility the case would not go to trial. Goldenberg told him, "Absolutely." He explained to Kline how complex the law was in these cases. How did they find out about the Mexicans? Was there a deal made? If so, who with? Plus the fact it was his intention to file motion after motion to delay the case, and who knows what can happen in the meantime. Then there is always the possibility of a plea bargain. Goldenberg said he was not in favor of that. When the prosecution offered a plea bargain, it showed weakness. This made Kline feel just a little bit better. Goldenberg continued.

"Now, Mr. Kline, I want you to start from the very beginning. When did you buy the vineyard and why did you buy it? Who did you buy it from? Did you have any idea what the Mexicans were doing on that part of your land? No detail is too small, Mr. Kline. Something that may seem incidental to you could be very important in our defense."

Goldenberg then gave some instructions to the two young men on his defense team. It had to do with them filing different types of motions: change of venue, cause for dismissal, entrapment, and asking for a different judge were just a few.

"As you know, Mr. Kline, you can't leave the state without permission from the court. I plan on filing a motion to have that restriction lifted. I know this is a traumatic time for you, but believe me when I tell you that we are going to give you the best defense possible, and I feel confident that in the end, you will be vindicated."

Kline said, "I'm not used to not being in control, Mr. Goldenberg, but I trust you."

"Okay, that sounds fair. Now first thing, let's get rid of this mister business. After all, we are going to be spending a lot of time together from now on."

Kline smiled, "Deal. Is it William or Bill?"

"It's Bill, Albert."

CHAPTER EIGHTY-THREE

WHEN WADE RETURNED to New York from his visit with Giovanni in Rome, he knew that things would be different at AA. They were now going to be in the business of selling chop stocks. He thought to himself, *"Is making money all that important?"* Evidently it was.

The first day he was back in the office, he met with Jerry.

"So, my friend, how did you like a Rome?"

"It's beautiful. You must have hated leaving."

"I go back some day."

"Yeah, that would be nice."

"So you-tell-a-me, how you make out with Mr. DeLuca?"

Wade looked at Jerry and said, "How about you stop fucking around and say what you mean."

Jerry was caught off guard. Wade never talked to him like that before.

"Whatta-you-a-sayin, Wade? Whatta you mean?"

"What I mean, Jerry, is I know damn well you already spoke to Mr. DeLuca, and I am sure he told you that I agreed to go along with you and your buddy Bobby Kane. We're going into the chop stock business."

"Hey Wade that's-a-great when do-we-a-start?"

Wade was not going to let him off the hook so fast.

"You don't fucking quit, do you? Why can't you just tell me you spoke to Giovanni? And then we can move on. If we're going to be working together, you can't be fucking around behind my back all the time, and that goes for your good buddy Kane. I'm still running this place, Jerry, and until Mr. DeLuca says otherwise, I call the shots, not you, and sure as hell not Bobby Kane."

Jerry saw a different Wade. "Hey, Wade . . . you sound-alike-a-tough guy. I like that. You know I'm a pretty tough guy too."

"Okay, Jerry, so we're both tough guys. What do you want to do? Go outside and see who is tougher?"

Wade was surprised at himself for the way he was acting, but he decided it had to be his was or he was out of there. Yes, he had agreed to sell chop stocks and basically change the way AA had done business in the past, but he was still the CEO, and as long as DeLuca left him in charge, he wasn't going to take shit from Jerry or this Bobby Kane.

Jerry laughed and put his arms on Wade's shoulders. "You okay, Wade. I-likea-you. I first think you a pussy, but you got balls to talk to me that way. Bravo. You right, you the boss, and I will give you that respect—no more as-you-a-say fucking around-behind-you-a back. Deal?"

Wade shook his hand and said, "Deal."

"Just-awanna-thing-boss, you don't-awanna go outside with me to see who is tougher. But if you need-a-me to take-a-somebody else outside for you . . . aha that's-a-whata-I do for you *Capish?*"

Wade realized he had just made a good friend in Jerry. He guessed it had something to do with that Italian macho shit.

"Okay, Jerry, now that we got that out of the way, what's the first step?"

Jerry smiled. "The firsta step is we bring in that son of a bitch Bobby Kane . . . and we watch him like a fuckin' hawk. He is gonna help us make a lot of lira," he said with a laugh, "But I work for you, boss. You got my loyalty. *Capish?*"

Wade thought to himself, "*What the hell am I getting myself into?*"

What Wade was getting into was doing business with Giovanni's partners, the Vizzini crime family. Sure Jerry pledged his loyalty to Wade and gave him the impression that Bobby Kane was the bad guy here, but the bottom line was Jerry was sent to New York to make sure things went smoothly between AA Financial and the Vizzini family. And Bobby Kane worked for them.

Once Wade laid out the ground rules for how he wanted the sale of the chop stocks to work, he hired a contractor to change the top floor of the AA building into a makeshift boiler room. It became a room where a group of cold callers and canvassers could work the phones, selling worthless stocks to unsuspecting customers. Like he said to himself once before: "What a shitty way to make a living! A very good living!"

It took several weeks before the boiler room was set up with the desks, the phones, the poster boards that would show everyone who was selling the most stock, and the computers. Jerry hired Bobby to run the operation. He was to be paid a draw against commissions. Bobby never questioned how much he would earn. Why should he? He was also being paid by the Vizzini family.

Wade decided to keep the separate entrance to what used to be the firm's apartment. He didn't want the guys who were selling the chop stocks hanging around in the main office. He thought back to his college days when he first started at AA and lived in the apartment that he just turned into a boiler room. It sure looked different now. Finally, they were ready to get started. Bobby Kane began to bring in his crew of cold callers. Wade refused to call them brokers or salesmen. They were the bottom of the barrel parasites feeding off poor innocent people who thought they were making a good investment. But that was being a hypocrite. He was part of it.

CHAPTER EIGHTY-FOUR

BOBBY KANE'S CREW was a bunch of psychos from Brooklyn and the Bronx. They were street kids, some real thugs, cheats, guys who were always looking for a quick buck. None had ever graduated college, and only a few had even started. They were wild. They came to work in jeans or in shorts, in sweatshirts and sneakers, and in most cases, needing a shave and a haircut. They carried Styrofoam coffee cups and milkshakes from McDonalds.

After work, they would either party at a local bar, find some sort of crazy game to play, like wrestling on the floor in the office, or bring in a prostitute after hours and pass her around. They were really scum.

Only half of them had passed the Series 7 test. That's the test administered by the National Association of Securities Dealers, or NASD, that gives brokers the solemn right to sell stocks to the public. As long as they were producing, selling the chop stocks, they pretty much came and went as they pleased.

Bobby Kane started every day with the soundtrack from the Blues Brothers movie. The kids would bang their desks and yell and scream in rhythm with the music. This was Kane's way of motivating his crew. Actually the only motivation they needed was . . . money. The real Wall Street didn't know they existed, and the financial publications ignored them.

You could say what you want about Bobby Kane, but he knew the chop stock business, and he knew how to train his crew to sell them. Those that had experience in the business were turned loose to make sales calls. The new kids started out by making cold calls. It was called qualifying leads, which meant they had to find out if there was any point in calling the prospect back. Actually it was pretty easy once you knew the pitch. You would tell the person you are calling right off that you are not selling anything. You didn't want them to hang up on you. The cold caller would say something like, "This is Joe Blow from AA Investments. I would like to send you some information. It's free, and you're under no obligation. I would just like to find out what kind of investor you are. Our stocks aren't for everybody." It's human nature. Nobody wants to think they are not good enough!

Most of the kids used phony names, which in itself was illegal. When their prospect was Jewish, they would use a nice Jewish name like Henry Cohen. When the prospect was Irish, the name might be Bill Sullivan, and if by chance they called a Polish prospect, which was very rare, the name was something like Fred Wysenski. Bobby Kane sat in the front of the room and between making calls himself, he listened to the various pitches his crew made. When he overheard something he didn't like, he would be all over the kid and tell him he wasn't going to get any more good leads until he sold a certain number of shares to a new prospect. Good leads were the kid's bread and butter.

Nobody could match Bobby when it came to closing. One day, when Wade was there, he heard Bobby trying to sell a chop stock to a retired schoolteacher in Kansas. Evidently the schoolteacher wasn't buying. Then Bobby said, "You know something, Robert, I must be a real asshole. Here I am wasting my time trying to sell you an investment opportunity of a lifetime when I got guys waiting in line to buy. With all due respect, Robert, I really need to end this conversation. This stock isn't for you. You're better off keeping your money under your mattress where it will be safe. It won't grow, and as a matter of fact, with inflation, it will shrink, but that's okay, at least you can take it out and look at it every so often. I have to go, Robert, nice talking to you . . . What's that? You want me to go over it one more time? Nah, Robert, this isn't for you." Then silence, as Bobby laughingly held the phone up in the air while the retired teacher was practically begging him to give him another chance.

"Okay, okay, Robert, maybe I can get you a thousand shares, but I'm not promising you anything. Hold on while I check with one of our vice presidents." Then Bobby put the phone between his legs as if he were masturbating. It was disgusting.

Finally, he got back on the phone and said, "I'm sorry, Robert, the stock is all gone. Wait a minute, Robert, you're in luck. Our vice president just handed me a note telling me he will give you half of what he had put aside for himself. How many shares is that? Let's see . . . three thousand shares, Robert, that's the best I can do. Okay, let me put my secretary on the phone so she can write the order."

There was no denying it. Bobby Kane was the best at this scam.

CHAPTER EIGHTY-FIVE

THE VERY FIRST change that Giovanni made was to send his own accountant from Rome to replace the comptroller who had been with AA for years. Giovanni told Wade that the financial end of the business would be handled by his people and controlled from Rome. Although he agreed to maintain an account at the Bank of America branch on Wall Street for the office payroll, salesmen's commissions, and day-to-day expenses, all of the 'big' money was set up to be wired to Rome every day. Both Wade's and Jerry Costello's checks were paid to them from the bank in Rome, and of course, that is how the Vizzini crime family received their money. Every week, Giovanni's bank wired money to an offshore account that belonged to the Vizzini crime family. Did the Vatican know what was going on? Who knows?

The man Giovanni sent to New York to replace the comptroller gave Wade a weekly report summarizing the activity for the week, plus a pro forma profit and loss statement. Wade only saw the figures that Giovanni wanted him to see. Although Wade could never verify the information he was given, he knew the firm was making a lot of money. Being the CEO, he should have questioned it. But he didn't.

The chophouse kids were earning a special kind of money: money they threw around like it had no meaning. Some of them blew thousands of dollars every month at the casinos in Atlantic City; others were into costly drugs, and they were all into expensive partying. One of the kids paid some guy $100 a week just to bring him coffee and a piece of pastry every day from a bakery he liked three blocks away. They were fucking crazy. And Bobby Kane was no better. He was older, maybe smarter, but that was how he had grown up, and he wasn't going to change now, but with all that, he was a task master. You could do all the shit you wanted, but you had to produce or you were out on your ass.

Some of the licensed brokers downstairs in AA got wind of the kind of money the kids were making in the boiler room operation and wanted in. Bobby would meet with them to see if they were qualified. That was like saying, "Do you know how to lie and cheat?" He asked them questions like, "Would it bother you if some nice old lady like your grandmother lost her life savings on a stock you sold to her?" If you passed that kind of test, you had a shot at moving up to the boiler room.

They had been operating almost nine months when Jerry told Wade they needed more room.

"Them-a-guys they-a-packed up there like . . . how you say . . . sardines."

There was an insurance broker who owned the building next to AA Financial. Wade sent Bobby Kane to see him. He thought if anybody could get him to sell the building, Bobby could. Wade still didn't know Bobby worked for the Vizzini crime family. If he knew that, there would be no doubt in his mind that Kane could convince them to sell the building. In any event, two months later, AA bought the building next door, and three months after that, the renovations were completed, and AA had doubled their space. By this time, there were forty kids selling chop stocks as well as other phony stock schemes that Bobby introduced.

That eventually would be his downfall. There is nothing illegal about cold calling; most, if not all, of the brokerage houses on Wall Street do it. And most of the chop shops employ at least some brokers with clean records, as did AA. However, when Bobby Kane began having his crew unload penny stocks that AA secretly owned on unsuspecting investors, his future in the securities business was doomed. The sad thing was Wade didn't even know what Bobby was doing. The Vizzini crime family had all but taken over AA Financial without Wade knowing it.

Someone who did know, or at least had strong reason to suspect what Bobby Kane and the Vizzini family were doing was Tom Franklin, the chief of the organized crime section of the F.B.I.. Although it was taking him a lot longer than he anticipated, he was beginning to close in on AA Financial, the Vizzini crime family, and the Roman National Bank. Although he felt he had enough evidence to prove the illegal actions of the bank, both the State Department and the ambassador to the Vatican constantly warned him that he could not do anything that would damage the relationship this country had with the Holy City. He had to find a way to get around that.

While all of this was going on, Wade continued to work with different municipalities, helping them find a place to park their money after a bond issue. He had become very proficient at doing this. He also developed personal relationships with the banks and the middlemen who were rigging the bids and was beyond questioning himself as to whether or not what he was doing was legal. What he did know is that it was profitable.

During this time, he tried several times to get in touch with Albert Kline but was unsuccessful. He finally called Brenda, who told him her father was suffering from deep depression. She told him her mother had left him. She couldn't handle the media attention and the constant legal maneuvering that had seemed to consume their life. She was living in their condo in Palm Beach, and Brenda said she would not be surprised if her mother filed for divorce. Brenda was angry at her for not standing by her father. Her mother said, "I paid my dues" whatever that meant.

Before moving to Palm Beach, she was asked to give a deposition. The prosecution wanted to find out what she knew, if anything, about the Mexicans growing marijuana on their property. She resented it and was less than cooperative. Wade didn't know what to say other than he felt badly for her.

He did manage to speak with Angelo several times about Albert. He told him he didn't know anything about the vineyard when they did the deal with the bank. All he knew was that when Albert learned the bank was trying to sell it, he said if he could make a deal for him to get the vineyard, then he would sell his shares of AA. Of course, that was not true.

He went on to say that Giovanni called to tell him Albert's lawyer asked him if he would fly to California for a deposition, at their expense. Giovanni told him no. Then the lawyer said he would fly to Rome for the deposition, and Giovanni refused. He told the lawyer he didn't know how his deposition could help Albert.

All he could tell them was the bank owned the vineyard for a very short time, and he didn't know anything about the Mexicans growing marijuana on the land. The only thing he knew was the original owner had allowed the Mexicans to use the land to grow fruit. Once again, it was not true. However, Wade had no reason to disbelieve him.

Wade tried to find out when Albert's case was going to trial, but nobody seemed to know. Every so often, there was something in the media about the case; however nothing about the date of the trial. When he asked Brenda, she said she didn't know anything more than what she read in the papers or heard on TV. "It is impossible to talk to my father about it," she said. "He really is in terrible shape. I have never seen him like this."

Angelo was having his revenge.

CHAPTER EIGHTY-SIX

WADE AND KATRINA decided to spend a quiet night at home on New-Year's Eve and welcome in 2003, just the two of them. As they watched the giant silver ball descend on Times Square where throngs of people cheered, kissed the person next to them, and tried to get their face on TV, Wade leaned over and kissed her and said, "Happy New Year, baby. What say you and me get married?"

It was almost two years since that time in Rome when she had proposed to him. However, when they returned from Rome, neither of them talked about it again.

"Why now all of a sudden?" she asked.

"I don't know. I think I always wanted to, but for some reason or other, we just never got around to it."

She looked at him for a minute and said, "When?"

"What do hyou think about doing it tomorrow?"

"Tomorrow you mean the day after today?"

"Yeah, we can fly to Las Vegas. I don't think there is any waiting period there."

"Wade!"

"What?"

"That's crazy."

"Why?"

"I don't know . . . it's just crazy."

"Come on, baby. It's about time we did something crazy."

"I don't know . . ."

Wade drew her close and said, "I love you, and I want to marry you. What else is there to know?"

So on January 1, 2003, they flew to Las Vegas, and the following day, they were married by a justice of the peace. Wade had no idea the wedding present he eventually would receive when they returned to New York.

CHAPTER EIGHTY-SEVEN

TOM FRANKLIN'S STRIKE force had managed to place an undercover agent in Bobby Kane's boiler room at AA Financial. He was a young agent, twenty-five years old, who had worked at Smith Barney as a trainee while still in college. When Tom recruited him, he suggested he get his brokerage license. That way, he had a better chance of being hired by AA Financial, which was one of the targets of Franklin's crusade against the Wall Street criminals. However, his youth and inexperience prevented him from coming up with anything concrete. Worse than that, he began to enjoy the lifestyle of the other kids in the boiler room and eventually became one of them as opposed to one of the good guys.

The bureau was continuing to pressure Franklin to get enough evidence for an indictment against AA Financial. Some members of Congress thought the bureau was spending too much time and money on this singular part of their investigation. He needed to make a significant bust, and there would be none better than AA Financial. The NASD and Securities and Exchange Commission's highly visible campaign against small-stock abuses and the recent spate of criminal prosecutions had failed to have a significant impact on chophouses. Although Franklin's group had shut down a handful of cold-calling powerhouses, the vast majority of questionable firms, totaling over two hundred nationwide, remained untouched.

Unfortunately, officials of the NASD downplayed mob infiltration of Street firms, not wanting to admit their presence on Wall Street. At the NASD and SEC, officials kept telling the media that they were hard at work addressing the problem of small-cap fraud, trying to reassure investors that their money was safe on Wall Street.

While Tom Franklin and his strike force were hard at work trying to get the bad guys, NASD Regulation's head of enforcement testified before a senate subcommittee and said "that he would readily acknowledge there are some dishonest individuals and firms in the securities business, but they have been systematically minimized at this time." Who was he kidding?

What was helping Tom to continue to receive support from the bureau was the bust he made shortly after he formed his task force. He had put together a sting operation that led to charges by the U.S. Attorney for the Eastern District of New York against Mario Ambrosia, a reported Colombo crime family associate for conspiring to commit securities fraud. The indictment against him was he offered Tom Franklin's F.B.I. undercover agent posing as a money manager, a kickback of 25 percent in exchange for the agent's purchasing $2.5 million of a penny stock he was touting to investors. The Colombo family was allegedly manipulating the stock.

But as far as the bureau was concerned, it was the same old story. "What have you done for me lately?" What he was doing now had almost become routine with the bureau; they wanted something bigger.

On December 10, 2002, as a result of Tom Franklin's efforts, the U.S. Attorney in Brooklyn had charged thirteen people—brokers, mob associates, and officials of two brokerage firms with manipulating the prices of thinly traded microcap stocks. On the same day, in New Jersey, federal authorities announced a similar indictment. Two days later, ten people were charged with multiple counts of racketeering and securities fraud. Among the accused were six stockbrokers, three alleged mobsters, and a corporate official of a public company. But with all of this, the bureau wanted more. They wanted Tom Franklin to come up with something against AA Financial. The bureau resented other government agencies telling them to tread softly with respect to the Roman National Bank because they were owned by the Vatican.

"Forget those bureaucrats," the head of the bureau told Franklin. "This is my agency. They don't tell me how to run it. You get me something to hang my hat on, and we will fry those bastards."

Finally, on January 11, 2003, Tom Franklin got the break he needed. A man by the name of Martin Kelso called the F.B.I. and said he had information about a brokerage firm that was committing securities fraud. When the agent taking the call asked the name of the firm, Martin Kelso said, "AA Financial."

When the agent put the information into the computer to run a cross-check, Tom Franklin's name came up with the notation that anything pertaining to AA Financial was to be referred to him.

CHAPTER EIGHTY-EIGHT

MARTIN KELSO HAD worked at AA Financial for almost two years. He graduated Boston College with a business degree and decided he wanted to be a stockbroker. He went to New York and got a job as an intern at AA while he applied for his broker's license. After he got his license, AA hired him as a broker. He was a hardworking man and didn't mind making cold calls or follow-up calls that some of the other brokers in the office considered not worth the time. He was sort of a loner and as such didn't associate with the other brokers after hours. About six months before he made the call to the F.B.I., one of the brokers in the office somehow discovered that he was gay. At first, it was no big deal, but as time went by, Carl "Packy" Packman, the floor manager, began to give him a hard time.

Packy was a wiry five feet, six inches tall. His prematurely balding head was shaved; his eyes were a mean shade of green, and his lips were always curled in a sardonic sneer. He was not a nice man.

He began to refer to Martin Kelso as "the fag." He would make fun of him in front of the other brokers and was constantly embarrassing him. It got to a point where Packy stopped giving him sales leads. And for no other reason than to be mean, he would shortchange him on his commissions. If Kelso hadn't gone down the path of becoming a disgruntled employee, and then as so often happens to disgruntled employees, getting fired and becoming a disgruntled former employee, Tom Franklin would never have gotten the break he needed.

After interviewing Martin Kelso, Tom Franklin was convinced that his testimony would help build an airtight case against AA Financial.

When Franklin realized his undercover agent had been compromised, he knew he needed some other way to get inside the AA offices. He had to find some way to place a bug there. With the help of the telephone company, he was able to do that. After getting a court order, they were able to tape calls made to prospective clients by brokers, making false promises. It would be up to the government prosecutor to get these admitted into evidence.

Franklin thought the nail in the coffin would be the tapes the F.B.I. had in their file from two years ago when they were taping a bank suspected of conspiring with brokerage houses in unlawful activities. The tapes revealed that AA Financial was working with them in rigging bids on the interest paid to different municipalities on money they invested from municipal bond offerings. Franklin couldn't understand why the bureau had never followed through on that.

Now he was finally ready to present all of the evidence to the federal prosecutor so that he could take it to the grand jury.

Ten days after Franklin gave the federal prosecutor the files, the grand jury issued an order to prepare an indictment against AA Financial et al. In part, the indictment read as follows:

> "It is alleged that AA Financial has engaged in unlawful acts as defined by the Securities and Exchange Commission. AA Financial has also conspired with members of the Vizzini crime family in operating a boiler room engaged in fraudulent schemes to sell securities to the public on the basis of false and misleading statements and omissions.
>
> AA Financial, along with one Gerardo Jerry Costello and Robert Bobby Kane, hired and supervised unregistered brokers and cold callers in a boiler room set up solely for the purpose of conducting an illegal enterprise selling microcap stocks, most of which had little or no value.
>
> Attached as exhibit A are the names of those unlicensed and unregistered brokers who participated in these unlawful and criminal activities. The parties named in this indictment are also charged with securities fraud in connection with a vast pump and dump manipulation that involved at least 17 OTC Bulletin Board and NASDAQ small-cap stocks. The defendants are also charged with money laundering and income tax evasion.

> Separate from the charges listed above, one Wade Simon, CEO of AA Financial, and the three banks listed as exhibit B are charged with secretly conspiring to rig the public bids on municipal bonds and also lowering the interest rates that towns earn on these investments, thereby systematically stealing from schools, hospitals, libraries, and nursing homes—from virtually every state, district, and territory in the United States."

The indictment continued on in this manner for twenty-three pages.

The next step was for Franklin to get arrest warrants for Wade Simon, Robert "Bobby" Kane, Gerardo "Jerry" Costello, and forty-eight AA Financial brokers, some licensed and some not. He was disappointed the Roman National Bank and Giovanni DeLuca were not named in the indictment, but the director had made a deal with the State Department, and Franklin couldn't do anything about that.

The F.B.I. also made a conscious decision not to name Albert Kline. Since he was no longer involved with AA, they didn't want to cloud their case by including him, plus the fact he was in enough trouble with the drug charges that were pending against him. They could always charge him at a later date.

CHAPTER EIGHTY-NINE

ON MARCH 10, at 8:30 a.m. in a coffee shop two blocks from AA Financial, Tom Franklin, along with seven other F.B.I. agents, all in dark coats and wearing bulletproof vests were waiting for the other members of their team. The other members of the team included four New York state troopers, three New York City detectives and three NASD security people. Everyone was armed. The raid at AA Financial was scheduled to take place at 10:00 a.m.

Not sure if Wade, Bobby Kane, and Jerry Costello would be at the office this early, Tom Franklin arranged for three agents to be at each of their homes at exactly 10:00 a.m., the same time they planned to enter AA Financial.

By 9:30 a.m., the full team was assembled in the coffee shop. The owner had no idea what was going on other than the fact he was told, "We are here on government business, and we will be out of your way shortly." "*That's just great,*" he thought, "*a bunch of freeloaders taking up space and scaring away my regulars!*"

At 9:45 a.m., the team of eighteen men, all wearing bulletproof vests and carrying automatic weapons, left the coffee shop and walked swiftly the two blocks to AA Financial. Oddly enough, only a couple of people took notice of them and assumed it was some sort of publicity stunt. Those who paid no attention to them were either on their cell phones, walking and reading the *Wall Street Journal*, or so caught up in a conversation with someone that they were oblivious to anything else. After all, this was Wall Street!

When they entered the offices of AA Financial, the receptionist was aghast. She didn't know what to say. Tom Franklin handed her some official-looking papers and then made a very short speech explaining who they were and what they intended to do. He instructed her not to answer the phone if it rang and in no circumstances attempt to make any calls while they were there. She was so frightened that she could hardly breathe let alone talk on the telephone.

The team of eighteen quickly circulated throughout the offices of AA Financial, instructing everyone to stay at their desks and away from the telephone. Ten agents stayed on the main floor while two went upstairs to the executive offices, and the remaining six went up to the boiler room.

On the second floor, only Jerry Costello was in his office. Wade had not yet arrived, and Bobby Kane was on the top floor in the boiler room. When Jerry saw the agents, he started to come out of his office. However, one of the agents drew his weapon and told him to stay put. At first, Jerry thought this was a robbery, but as soon as the agent identified himself, and told him why they were there, he simply returned to his desk sat down and said, "Please, be-a-my guest. I'm a not a citizen of this a country, so . . ." One of the agents interrupted him. "Just sit the fuck down and shut your mouth, you guinea bastard!"

Jerry got crazy. He jumped up and started toward the agent, cursing in Italian. The other agent quickly came to his assistance with his weapon in hand. He stopped short of the office, spread his legs, held his gun in both hands with his arms outstretched, and yelled, "On the floor, now or I'll blow your fucking balls off!"

Didn't these guys know this was a Wall Street bust, not a raid on a Mafia stronghold?

On the top floor in the boiler room, there was loud music playing, and a bunch of young guys in street clothes with their feet up on the desk, some already on the phone with prospective clients, others still drinking their coffee out of Styrofoam cups. Bobby Kane was at his desk in the front of the room, sorting out the sales leads for the day. When the six F.B.I. agents walked into the room, Bobby quickly looked up from his desk and murmured, "Holy shit!"

The lead agent held up his badge and identified himself, giving the same instructions as the agents had done on the main floor. One of the agents who recognized Bobby Kane from his picture in the F.B.I. file called him by name, telling him they had a warrant for his arrest. Kane started to pick up the telephone, but the agent told him he could not make any calls at this time. He would have plenty of time after he was booked.

"That's not how it works," Kane screamed, "I'm entitled to one call now." By this time, two of the agents were face-to-face with him, instructing him to turn around so that they could handcuff him.

"How about my one fucking phone call?"

"Yeah, how about that," one of the agents said.

It took almost two hours to identify all of the people named in the indictment, handcuff each one, and read them their rights. With the exception of two brokers, the rest were told to go home. Franklin knew he would need a couple of clean brokers to work with the court in sorting out whatever securities and cash that AA had that belonged to clients. That was not going to be easy. A lot of people were going to lose a lot of money, but Franklin was not responsible.

In the meantime, one of the agents called the F.B.I. field office and told them to send over the vans they would need to transport the prisoners and all of the files they intended to pack up and take. They told the receptionist that AA Financial was no longer in business. They had an order from the court closing them down. At 3:30 p.m., the last agent left AA Financial, locking the door behind him when he left.

Forty-three brokers had been arrested.

Bobby Kane had been arrested.

Jerry Costello had been arrested.

Carl Packman, the floor manager, had been arrested.

Salvador Gori, the accountant Giovanni sent from Rome, was arrested.

Fifty-one boxes of files had been confiscated.

Eleven guns were seized in the raid. No one admitted ownership.

Sixty-three computers were also confiscated.

A box of porn CDs were found in the storage closet. No one admitted ownership. The F.B.I. took them.

In Bobby Kane's desk, the F.B.I. found $165,000. He said he had no idea how it got there or who it belonged to. The F.B.I. confiscated the money.

The agents found enough marijuana, cocaine, uppers and downers, and other drug-related material to warrant a drug bust under any standard. The state police and Franklin discussed how they should handle this. Franklin called the judge who had ordered the search warrant and asked his opinion. He suggested they take all of the stuff they found, mark it, and keep it separate from the other evidence.

"You may decide you want to file separate drug charges against some of the defendants," the judge said.

Before the police vans left with the prisoners, two young brokers from the boiler room told Franklin they wanted to cooperate with the F.B.I. One of them was almost crying. All of the bravado and

I-don't-give-a-shit attitude was gone. Franklin simply took their names and said he would think about it.

"We have enough evidence to put all your asses in jail without your help," Franklin told him. The reality was it is never as easy as one thinks it will be.

CHAPTER NINETY

THREE F.B.I. AGENTS showed their badges and their arrest warrant to the doorman at Wade's condominium at exactly 10:00 a.m. They told him to open the door and escort them to Wade Simon's apartment. At first, he hesitated, but when the agent opened his jacket and the doorman saw his bulletproof vest and the gun sticking out of his shoulder holster, he quickly opened the door.

It was 10:06 a.m. when the three F.B.I. agents knocked on the door to Wade's penthouse apartment. Wade and Katrina were having coffee. This happened to be one of the days when Wade decided to sleep in. Neither of them could imagine who would be knocking on the door. The doorman always announced any visitors.

"Maybe its Carlos the maintenance man," Wade said as Katrina went to open the door.

When she opened the door, the three agents quickly and politely entered the apartment, the lead agent holding his badge high above his head.

Wade got up from the table and said, "What the hell is going on? Who the hell are you guys?"

The lead agent said, "I am agent Joseph Donavan." Then pointing to the other two, he said, "And this is agent Walt Holland and agent Barry Hendricks. We have a warrant for your arrest and a search warrant that gives us the right to search your apartment. I must warn you that anything you might say at this time can be held against you in a court of law."

Katrina turned pale, and she started to shake. Wade put his arms around her.

Agent Donavan said, "Are you all right, ma'am? Why don't you sit down?" This was much different from the way the agents acted at AA Financial. Maybe it had something to do with being in someone's home and imagining, God forbid, this was happening to your wife.

Wade helped Katrina to the couch then turned to agent Donavan. "What the hell is going on? Are you guys crazy coming here like this? What is going on?"

The agent explained to Wade what had just occurred at AA Financial and told him they were here to remove his computer and any files that had to do with AA Financial and place him under arrest.

"I don't fucking believe this. This is like a nightmare," Wade said. By this time, Katrina was in tears. Then regaining his wits, Wade said, "I want to call my lawyer." Unlike what happened at AA Financial, the agent told him to go ahead and call him.

Fortunately, Wade was able to reach his attorney Charley Phillips. He was a corporate attorney and had absolutely no experience in criminal cases. He asked Wade where the F.B.I. was taking him. The agent told Wade he was going to be arraigned at the courthouse in Manhattan, and then most likely he would be sent to the Hudson County Correctional Center where he would spend the night. There would be a bail hearing in the morning. Charley Phillips told Wade he was going to call Sidney Kramer, one of the best criminal attorneys in the country whose office was in New York. He promised Wade that he would be at the bail hearing in the morning either with Sidney Kramer or someone from his office.

Also at 10:00 a.m., four F.B.I. agents and two security officers from the SEC entered the Empire Bank of America, one of the nation's largest banks. The lead agent showed his badge to the guard and said they were there to see Jonathan Abrams, Morris Leary, and David Scott. These were the three Wall Street finance geniuses that had spent the last decade taking part in the breathtaking scheme that skimmed billions of dollars from virtually every state in the union. They not only worked with brokerage houses like AA Financial, but with almost every other major bank and investment banking firm in the country. They were the core of the scam.

CHAPTER NINETY-ONE

SITTING IN HIS apartment in San Francisco, Albert Kline was watching the eleven o'clock news on TV, pretty much the same old stuff. A woman gets mugged downtown, the stock market keeps swinging back and forth, the Lakers win again, and then suddenly there was a special news report. The news anchor announced that the F.B.I. had made a major bust on Wall Street. He went on to describe how the F.B.I. joined forces with the state police and NASD in closing down a brokerage firm, AA Financial that was operating an illegal boiler room. He also reported the arrest of Wade Simon, CEO of AA Financial. They showed file pictures of Wade as well as pictures of the AA building. Then they showed pictures of the three executives of the Empire Bank of America.

Kline broke out in a cold sweat. Did this mean they would be coming after him? He couldn't handle something like that. He just sat and looked at the TV, waiting to hear his name. Finally, when the news ended, he picked up the remote and turned off the TV. A thousand things were racing through his mind. "*What was going to happen with the drug charges that had been filed against him? Was he going to be implicated in the AA Financial scandal? How much more of this could he take?*"

He got up from the couch and walked into the bedroom. He took a gold-plated Smith and Wesson revolver out of the closet, checked to make sure it was loaded, sat down on the edge of the bed, and committed suicide.

The following morning, his lawyer, William Goldenberg tried to call him but received no answer. He wanted to tell him that he had made a deal with the prosecuting attorney handling his case to drop all charges. Goldenberg had been able to get the Mexican that Angelo bribed to recant his story. Kline had never accepted any money from him, and he was sure Kline didn't know anything about the Mexicans growing and distributing marijuana on his property. Goldenberg had found out about the new house the Mexican had moved in with his family, plus the new used car he bought. Goldenberg also found some local people who worked with the man that Giovanni had sent from

Italy to run the winery until he was able to get rid of it. They were willing to testify that Giovanni's man knew about the marijuana, and that is why he was so anxious to get rid of the winery.

He also was able to prove that the Mexicans had been growing marijuana there for many years, and as a matter of fact, it was Giovanni's father who helped finance them. He also found some memos in the file that Kline's attorney had from the sale of AA Financial to Roman National Bank. There was no doubt that Kline's getting the vineyard was Angelo Santino's idea. He was also able to have Judge Lenore Madison removed from the case. After numerous meetings with the prosecutor, he was able to convince him that there was no case against Albert Kline. Had Albert waited another day . . .

CHAPTER NINETY-TWO

THE BAIL HEARING in New York was more like a circus than a legal proceeding. Lawyers, defendants, F.B.I. and NASD agents, and DEA agents crowded the courtroom. There was even a representative from the State Department there. The judge allowed only one reporter from The *Wall Street Journal* in the courtroom with the understanding he would be the go-between for all of the other TV and print media. As promised, Charley Phillips, Wade's lawyer, was there as was Sidney Kramer. When the judge saw him, he gave him a look as if to ask, "Who are you representing?" Sidney Kramer looked at Wade and smiled. The judge nodded his approval.

In order to expedite the proceedings, the judge suggested to the prosecutor and the defense attorneys that there would be just one reading of the charges. Since each one of the defense attorneys had a copy of the indictment, they could determine what specific charges were being levied against his client.

At this initial hearing, everyone entered a plea of not guilty. The judge placed bail at $10,000 for each one of the stockbrokers. Bail for Giovanni's accountant and Carl Packman, the floor manager at AA, was set at $50,000 each. The three executives from the Empire Bank of America had their bail set at $1,000,000 each. Initially the judge did not want to grant bail for Bobby Kane since he was a three-time loser or for Jerry Costello for fear of him leaving the country. However, after their defense attorneys agreed Kane and Costello would both surrender their passports and driver's licenses, the judge granted them bail at $750,000 each.

After a lengthy argument between Sidney Kramer and the prosecutor, the judge agreed to release Wade on his own recognizance.

Sidney Kramer then made a motion that there should be a separate trial for those defendants charged with bid rigging. He presented an argument that lasted almost thirty minutes. Initially the prosecutor strenuously objected. His thought was that if Kramer wanted something like that, it must give him some advantage. However, after listening to all of the arguments, he finally withdrew his objection, and the judge said he would take it under advisement.

Before the judge adjourned the hearing, he said, "Over the years, the public has become immune to news of financial corruption, partly because too many of these stories involve banker-on-banker crimes. Who cares if a hedge fund billionaire rips off a couple of European banks however the charges of rigging bids and scamming innocent investors out of their hard-earned money is another matter. It is like stealing money from innocent Americans and turning that money into sports cars and other luxuries for the already rich. It's the equivalent of robbing a charity to pay for a lap dance."

Sidney Kramer made a note to remember what the judge just said. It was definitely biased, and he wanted to make sure it remained in the record. Who knows, somewhere down the road, it might be helpful if he wanted to file for a mistrial.

As the judge was walking back to his chambers, he instructed the bailiff to ask the person from the State Department if he had time to visit with him for a few minutes.

The State Department representative got to the judge's office just as he was removing his robe.

"How do you do, Your Honor? You wanted to see me?"

"Yes, thanks for sparing me the time, I know you fellows are busy over there at the State Department."

"You could say that. By the way, my name is Samuel Gross. I am an aid to the secretary."

"Sounds interesting, Mr. Gross, do you mind if I ask you why the State Department is interested in these proceedings?"

"Not at all but as you know, one of the main defendants in this case is AA Financial. And they are owned by the Roman National Bank. The bank is owned by the Vatican."

"I see," the judge said. "And is that why there were no charges filed directly against the bank?"

"Well I can't answer that, but the reason we are interested is because the pope is planning a visit to New York within the next eighteen months or so."

The judge looked at him. "And so…?"

"Well we that is my boss wanted to get a feel for how long the trial might take."

The judge had a stern look on his face. "Tell me why that matters."

"Well, Your Honor, the pope's trip to New York could mean hundreds of millions of dollars for the city. If the trial was still going on, he might not want to make the trip."

"And why is that, Mr. Gross?"

"Your Honor, the fact that the Vatican owns the bank that owns a firm under indictment might cause him some embarrassment."

"I see," the judge said with a smirk. "I hope it is not the intent of the State Department to intercede in any way in these proceedings, Mr. Gross."

"Absolutely not, your honor I am here just as an observer."

The judge grinned and very quietly said, "And the dog ate my homework."

"I beg your pardon," Gross said, a little confused by the remark.

"Just a little bit of dry humor, Mr. Gross."

CHAPTER NINETY-THREE

IT WAS TWO weeks since the F.B.I. closed down AA Financial, and Wade's world had been turned upside down. He spent most of his time during these past two weeks with Sidney Kramer, the criminal attorney he hired to defend him. Wade explained to him in detail about the bid rigging. He was almost ashamed to admit that what he was doing was so incredibly common on Wall Street that you began to believe yourself that it was not illegal.

"Everybody was doing it," Wade said. "I mean Bank of America, Wells Fargo, Chase, even GE Financial . . . Jesus, if all these guys were doing the same thing how it could it be illegal?"

But the fact of the matter was it was.

Although Wade refused to admit it to himself, stripped of all the camouflaging financial verbiage, what he and all those others were doing was virtually indistinguishable from the same kind of thuggery practiced for decades by the mob, when they manipulated public bids for things like garbage collection and construction contracts.

Sidney Kramer knew he had his work cut out for him. Wade had knowingly taken part in bid rigging. Now it was his job to find some loophole, some minute piece of evidence that would help him make a plausible defense.

He finally came to the conclusion that it would make no sense to argue against the tapes and the cooperating witnesses the prosecution would probably use to help convict his client. He couldn't change any of that. He had to find another strategy. And then it came to him. Despite the fact the bids resulted in lower rates, wasn't it true that the cities and towns still technically speaking, received the highest bid? If a town received a 5 percent return on a $219 million bond instead of 5.04 percent, who is to say that wasn't a good price? The more he thought about it, the more he liked it.

Bobby Kane and Jerry Costello had also been meeting with their defense attorney, Dominick Esposito, the lawyer who represented the Carmen Vizzini crime family. Esposito told Carmen that he was very concerned about Bobby Kane. I know he won't do jail time, and I'm afraid he might turn. It wouldn't be a bad idea for you to talk to him. Carmen met with him the following day.

"I'm a three-time loser, Carmen," Bobby said to him. "I can't do jail time again. I know they will throw the book at me if I'm convicted. You gotta tell Dominick he has to make some kind of deal for me. I mean, you know I would never give you up, but maybe I can lay some shit on Wade Simon. You know, let him take the rap for everybody. Whatta you think, Carmen?"

Carmen told him not to worry. He would think of something. The something he was thinking of was how he was going to have him disposed of.

Three days after he had his meeting with Carmen Vizzini, Bobby Kane was on his way home from the liquor store. It was about six-thirty in the evening. He lived in a town house in the Bronx. He parked his car in the driveway, and just as he was about to get out of his car, two men came out of the shadows, holding automatic weapons. Before he had a chance to react, they shot him four times in the face and in the chest. Then they took his wallet and left. Vizzini hoped the police would think it was robbery. Who was he kidding?

CHAPTER NINETY-FOUR

THE CHURCH IS rich, but its finances are also bafflingly complex and utterly lacking in transparency. At the center of its archipelago of financial institutions sits the Institute for the Works of Religion or as it is more commonly called the Vatican Bank. It handles the money of many religious orders, but it also acts like a little piece of the Cayman Islands on the western side of the Tiber River, which is what makes it attractive to people who want to keep their wealth away from the prying eyes of the law.

Vatican insiders admit that a system aimed at quickly getting money to difficult places around the world is an invitation to abuse by tax cheats and organized crime. "The issue is that once you start doing opaque transactions in an institution, people don't know where to draw a line and stop." The Bank of Italy called that a poor excuse.

For years, the pope's bedroom was two floors above the Vatican Bank. The entrance to the private elevator leading up to the pope's quarters is next door to the back door of the bank. Debate about what the pope knew about who came and went through the bank's doors has occupied generations of Vatican watchers.

In 1982, the Vatican Bank was implicated in the fraudulent bankruptcy of the Banco Ambrosiano, whose president and chairman was found hanging under Blackfriars Bridge in London. His murder, or suicide, remains unsolved. Prosecutors in Rome concluded that he was killed by the Sicilian Mafia. The rumors that he was laundering drug money for the Cosa Nostra were never proven to be true or false.

For years, many have suspected that the Mafia has been concealing money under the noses of bishops and cardinals, and the Vatican condones this. That is one of the reasons why more modern-day pope's are anxious to bring the Vatican Bank in line with international standards of transparency and probity.

Now with the scandal involving AA Financial and the Roman National Bank, the Vatican was concerned it would once again be implicated unless they could distance themselves from those directly involved.

This was the reason Don Dominico Cleranzio, head of a Sicilian crime family and one of the richest and most powerful men in Rome was summoned to the Vatican for a private meeting with one of the pope's closest advisors.

"We have a very serious problem, Dominico."

"And what is that, Your Eminence?"

"I recently received word from the States that a man who indirectly worked for us was murdered."

"I too heard that, Your Eminence."

"Word travels fast, Dominico."

"In our circles, it does. Why is his death a problem for you?"

"Well it is not just his death that bothers us. There are some other factors that give us concern."

"And they are?"

"You, of course, know Giovanni DeLuca?"

"Yes I do very very well."

"Yes . . . and of course, you know he is the president of the Roman National Bank, which we own."

"I know that also."

"Last year, Giovanni purchased a brokerage firm in the States without first getting permission from the council at the Vatican."

"I heard about that. How was he able to do that without your approval?"

"Ah, my friend, Giovanni is a very clever man."

"And now that is a problem for you?"

"Not just that alone. The man who was murdered worked for our friend Carmen Vizzini, who placed him in the brokerage firm that Giovanni bought at his request. The F.B.I. has closed down that firm and indicted a number of people. The man who was murdered was one of the people named in the indictment."

"That sounds complicated as well as very costly to your bank, Your Eminence."

"You are right. It will be costly. The bank will lose a considerable sum of money, but that is not our immediate concern."

"Oh."

"We have discovered that Giovanni, while operating the bank for us, has gone in business for himself."

"Oh I didn't know that your Eminence."

"You may recall the Italian police arrested a priest several months ago in Rome and charged him with corruption and fraud?"

"Yes, I remember."

"The police have alleged that the priest, who was formally head of our accounting department at the Administration of the Patrimony of the Apostolic See, was moving money for some known members of organized crime in the States. They also charged that he was doing this with the help of Giovanni."

"That I didn't know, Your Eminence."

"Fortunately, nobody knew. We were able to convince the chief of police that Giovanni had nothing to do with it, even though the priest insisted he did."

"It was good you were able to do that, Your Eminence."

"Yes, and as it turned out, the priest committed suicide in prison before the case came to trial."

Dominico smiled. He knew about the suicide; at least that is what was reported.

"Giovanni continues to put the Holy City and the Holy Father at risk. We recently learned that he has been working with the Vizzini family for years without our knowledge. The F.B.I. is bound to find out about that, which will be more than just embarrassing. Fortunately, we have friends in the State Department in America who will do everything possible to see that we are not involved in any of this. But we can't allow Giovanni to continue putting us in these kinds of situations."

"Have you spoken to him?"

"I have. This is not the first time we have had issues with him. But he is a stubborn man. He has become very rich and influential. Although he says he respects the Church, I don't believe him. I think he only respects the almighty dollar."

This brought a smile from Don Dominico.

"And so you want to use my family, Your Eminence."

The priest simply nodded.

"If Giovanni would happen to have an unfortunate accident, Your Eminence . . . ?"

Before he could finish, the priest said, "I would pray for his soul, Dominico."

CHAPTER NINETY-FIVE

IN THE WEEKS that followed his meeting at the Vatican, Don Dominico Cleranzio assigned two of his people to track all of the movements of Giovanni DeLuca, his habits, where he ate, what time he left his office, pictures of him entering and leaving his home. Don Dominico was very strict and very thorough. He told his people, "We want this to look like an accident." His men didn't ask why; they simply did as they were told.

After a week of surveillance, Dominico received all the reports his men had collected on Giovanni. There were some photos of him and photos of his car showing the license plates. Although he had a chauffeur, there were times he chose to drive himself in his Porsche. Included in the report was a map of the road he traveled along the side of a mountain from the bank to a house in the country. His men were able to establish that this is where his mistress lived. She was a former model whom he met three years earlier. He convinced her to leave the modeling business and be his mistress. He bought her this house in the country, and as long as he wasn't traveling, he would go there every Tuesday and Thursday night. As far as his wife knew, these were the nights he played cards or had business meetings.

Dominico saw that the road Giovanni drove to see his mistress was very curvy and had very little lighting. He decided then how Giovanni was going to die.

One of Dominico's men managed to get into the garage where Giovanni parked his car. The man was an expert automobile mechanic. He knew how long it would take Giovanni to drive from his office in the bank to the curves in the road to his mistress's house. He was able to do something to the brakes that would cause them to lock at just about the same time that he reached the curves in the road. Since the stretch of curved road was almost three miles long, he had plenty of leeway.

The following Tuesday, when Giovanni was driving to see his mistress, he attempted to slow down as he approached one of the more treacherous curves in the road. Instead the brakes locked, and he lost control of the car, causing it to hurtle off the side of the mountain and crash fifty feet below on a bed of rocks. He was killed instantly.

When the priest who had met with Dominico heard the news of Giovanni's accident, he went to the chapel and said a prayer for his soul.

CHAPTER NINETY-SIX

DURING THE MONTHS leading up to Wade's trial, he spent a lot of time meeting with Sidney Kramer and Charley Phillips, his two attorneys. The prosecutor had subpoenaed him twice to give a deposition, each time trying to trap him into admitting that he knew bid rigging was illegal. It didn't work.

Wade often thought about what had happened over the last year. Albert Kline committed suicide the day before his lawyer called to tell him the charges against him were dropped. When he spoke to Brenda, she said that her father was suffering from such depression that it might not have mattered.

And then there was the murder of Bobby Kane. Although Carmen Vizzini hoped the police would write it off as a robbery, they called it a mob hit. First of all, that sells more newspapers, and second, it allows the city to further condemn organized crime.

Of course, the accidental death of Giovanni DeLuca came as a real shock to him. Here was a guy who had the world by the tail. Money, a good family, everything going for him, and then he drives his Porsche over a cliff. How sad if Wade only knew the truth?

And of course, there was AA Financial. He remembered the first day he went to work there. The main floor was filled with brokers on the telephone, the runner taking orders to the floor manager, and Albert Kline sitting up in his office like the king on a throne. Now the offices were locked shut. The telephones had all been disconnected. Whatever files the F.B.I. didn't take were strewn around on the floor after being examined by them, the SEC, and NASD.

But that was all in the past. Now he had to concentrate on his upcoming trial. Katrina had been a real rock for him during the past months. She spent every day in the courtroom, and most nights, they simply had dinner in the apartment and would either watch TV or talk. They both were anxious to get through the trial and move on with their life, if that was possible.

As Sidney Kramer had requested, there were two trials as a result of the raid at AA Financial.

The first trial involved the boiler room cold-calling operation and fraudulent sale of microcap stocks. Of the fort-three brokers who had been arrested, four pled guilty and made a deal with the prosecutor before their trial began. Five brokers who had previous arrest records were each sentenced to a year in jail and had to pay a $15,000 fine. Thirty received fines and suspended sentences. They all were ordered never to be able to work in any financial institution in the future. The remaining four were held over for the second trial.

Jerry Costello was sentenced to five years in jail and fined $100,000. His attorney made a deal with the F.B.I. and the State Department for him to serve six months in jail, pay a fine of $50,000, and be deported back to Italy. He was glad to leave.

Tom Franklin was disappointed in the sentencing. He was looking forward to the second trial. Hopefully the sentences would be more severe in that trial. Of course, the defendants had to be found guilty first.

Prior to the start of the second trial, there was a meeting between the prosecuting attorney, the defense lawyers for the four brokers held over from the first trial, the accountant Giovanni had sent from Rome, and Carl Packman, the floor manager. It was decided there was not enough evidence to include them in the second trial, so the charges against them were dropped. The prosecutor discussed this with Tom Franklin, telling him that including them could weaken the case against Wade and the three bankers. Franklin agreed.

However, they all were suspended from trading by the SEC and required to pay fines in varying amounts.

CHAPTER NINETY-SEVEN

March 10, 2004; the Trial

THE TRIAL WAS finally here. Wade and Sidney Kramer went over every detail time and time again. They were as prepared as they could possibly be.

Over two years in the making, the federal prosecutors now felt they could make public for the first time the inner workings of Wall Street and organized crime. The defendants in the case were Wade Simon and AA Financial, and Jonathan Abrams, Morris Leary, and David Scott of Empire Bank of America. The federal prosecutors intended to show the world how the Mafia was now operating not out of Little Italy or Las Vegas but out of Wall Street. Those kinds of headlines made for good press.

The prosecuting attorney concluded his opening remarks. It was time for Wade's attorney to address the jury. The attorney representing the three bankers would make their opening remarks after he was finished.

When Sidney Kramer walked over to the jury box, he had an engaging smile as he looked at each juror. His face was suntanned, and there was not a hair out of place. He was well over six feet tall and looked like he might have played football in college. Before he started to speak, Wade turned around and looked at Katrina, who was sitting in the back of the courtroom. He smiled, made a pistol out of his index finger and thumb, pointed it at the prosecutor, then snapped down his thumb and mouthed the word, "Click." She smiled and gave him a thumbs-up.

Sidney Kramer put both of his hands on the railing in front of the jury box and stared into the face of one of the two black women jurors and waited until she smiled at him before he began his opening remarks.

"The prosecuting attorney said this case is about right and wrong. He said it is about lying and cheating. With all due respect, I must disagree with him. This case is about being fair." He smiled at the woman he was staring at and asked, "Do you understand what being fair means, my dear?"

The prosecuting attorney stood up. "your Honor!" Sidney Kramer raised his hand as if to say, "Okay." Then he continued.

"This case is not about right and wrong. It is not about lying and cheating. And it is certainly not about good versus evil. This case is simply about being fair. What does being fair really mean? It means that you are satisfied.

"If your washing machine breaks down, and you call a repairman, and he comes to fix it, and charges you $25, is that fair? I don't know. I would have to ask the lady who couldn't do her wash until the washing machine was repaired. I guess she would tell you that it was fair. And if she thought that was fair, she would do business with that same repairman again."

He walked to the other end of the jury box and looked at one of the other women jurors and said, "My mother once told me the only thing in this world that is fair is blue eyes and blond hair." It took a moment for it to sink in, and then she smiled back at him.

"So what did really happen here? What did my client, Mr. Wade Simon, do that was so terrible that it took dozens of F.B.I. agents, the state police, and security people from NASD to bring him into court?"

The prosecutor wanted to object but decided to let that remark go.

"Did Mr. Simon cheat some poor old lady out of her life savings? Absolutely not. And although the prosecutor will lead you to believe that, it is nothing more than a fairy tale.

"Did Mr. Simon lie to any of the communities that asked him to invest their money Absolutely not. And the prosecutor will admit that. When Mr. Simon told a municipality they were going to get 0.05 percent interest on their money that is exactly what they received. If he told them they would receive 0.0525 percent on their money that is exactly what they received. If you were permitted to ask the prosecutor if that is true, he would have to tell you it is. Mr. Simon never lied!

"And were these municipalities forced to accept Mr. Simon's offer? Of course not they could have gone out on their own and invested their money wherever they wanted. Maybe they would have received a better return or maybe they would have received a lesser return. However, they accepted the offer from Mr. Simon because they thought it was fair.

"Did Mr. Simon benefit from this transaction? Of course, he did. That was his business. Does a car dealer make a profit when he sells you a car? When you buy an insurance policy, do you think the agent who sells you the policy makes a commission? Of course, he does. This is America. This is the American way of doing business.

"If you ask any investment banker how he determines what the fair rate of interest should be, his answer would be, 'I don't determine the fair price. The market does.' The market does. So how can you say that Mr. Simon was responsible for lowering the rate of interest on a bond when it is the market that makes that determination?" The jurors looked totally confused, which is what Sidney Kramer intended.

"Mr. Simon," he said, pointing to Wade, "is a product of the American system. He came from a blue-collar working class family, went to college on a basketball scholarship, and graduated with honors. He was a star basketball player in college, and as a matter of fact, he played for UNLV when they won the championship in 1990. After college, he had several jobs and then moved to New York to go to work for AA Financial. Over the years, he helped grow that firm and eventually was made the CEO. We intend to have several former clients of Mr. Simon testify. They will tell you how Mr. Simon helped them with their investment portfolio.

"The prosecuting attorney is going to attempt to prove that Mr. Simon was responsible for the manipulation of interest rates, something he will call bid rigging. The truth of the matter is Mr. Simon was doing nothing different than every other investment broker, banker, and stockbroker on Wall Street was doing and had been doing long before Mr. Simon got into the business.

"The real culprit in this case is Wall Street and the complicated double standards of the financial system itself. I like to compare it to the game of basketball, which Mr. Simon played in college. For those of you who are not sports fans, let me point out that the referees will often call a 'foul' on a player for something that all the other players have been doing the entire game. In other words, it's up to the discretion of the referee as to whether the play is legal or if it is a foul. That is what this case is about. The F.B.I. has decided to call a foul on Mr. Simon for something that has been going on for years on Wall Street, and as a matter of fact, continues to go on.

"The prosecutor is also going to try paint a picture of Mr. Simon as part of the mob, the Mafia, like something out of the movie The Godfather." Sidney Kramer hunched up his shoulders, looked at the jury, and said, "Stick 'em up!" The jury laughed. The judge said, "Mr. Kramer!"

"I apologize, your Honor."

Sidney Kramer walked up and down in front of the jurors then stopped and looked at one of the two elderly black men and said, "Mr. Simon has not broken the law. He has never even had a traffic ticket. He has been doing his job as he was trained to do, and that is get a fair rate of interest for municipalities around this great country of ours. Was there ever a case of a school not being built or a highway not being able to be extended or a library that could not be built because the rate of interest that Mr. Simon negotiated for a municipality was not fair? The answer is no.

"The Honorable Judge Walter Hodges and the prosecutor both made a point to tell you that you would be subjected to a hellishly dull maze of convoluted and boring and tedious financial transactions over the course of this trial. They were absolutely right. You are going to hear words, phrases, and terminologies that will be difficult for you to understand." He smiled. "They are difficult for me to understand. The prosecutor will try to coach you into understanding all of the financial gibberish that you will hear from the government's witnesses, but there is only one thing that you need to understand, and that is the municipality's received a fair rate of interest. How it came about is not the issue."

Sidney Kramer continued on for almost an hour with his opening statement. When he finished, he looked at each juror, waited a minute, and then said as he started to walk back to his seat, "I know you will be fair in your verdict."

The three bankers had a team of four lawyers representing them. The lead attorney was a very attractive woman. She was tall and had a nice figure that was not hidden by her two-piece wool suit. She had long black hair and dark eyes. If the jury had been made up of a group of young males, all of this would be important. However, to this jury, it didn't mean a thing.

She spent almost two hours making her opening statement. She hit on some of the same points that Sidney Kramer did, but her main thrust was on the legality of the charges.

She talked about Wall Street and the extreme complexity of the infrastructure within which these supposed crimes were committed. She pointed out that the government intended to present witnesses who themselves had dubious resumes regarding trading on Wall Street. The prosecutor objected; the judge gave her a warning, but the jury had already heard her attempt to discredit some of the state's witnesses.

She said, "The government is going to want you to believe that investors should receive some sort of permanent protection from the ravages of the market, from one another's competition. That, ultimately, is what this case is about: capitalism. The prosecutor will lead you to believe that companies like competition. That is a lot of baloney. One of the biggest lies in capitalism is that companies like competition. They don't. Nobody likes competition."

"Who are the real losers in these types of cases?" she asked the jurors.

"I will tell you who, me and you and the average taxpayer who see millions of our hard-earned dollars spent on bringing cases like this to court that should never have made it past the front door."

Unfortunately, a lot of what she said went completely over the heads of this jury.

At 4:00 p.m., Judge Walter Hodges adjourned the proceedings until 10:00 a.m. the following day. That is when the prosecution would present its case.

CHAPTER NINETY-EIGHT

The Prosecution's Case

HOW AND WHEN the government was able to produce the taped conversations of the three bankers was initially a mystery to the defense lawyers. However, once they began to put on their case, it became clear what had happened.

The government's first witness confusingly was a young executive from the Empire Bank of America by the name of Herman Waxman. Almost all of the other witnesses the prosecutor put on the stand from the bank were like Waxman, absurdly young. Many were just out of college.

Right off the bat, the prosecutor had Waxman explain that while he was working at the bank, he had routinely helped the "cream" of Wall Street rig bids on municipal bonds by letting them take a last look at other bids.

The prosecutor then proceeded with some direct questions:

"Who were some of the people you gave a last look to?

"There was a whole host of them. You name them, some of the biggest banks and brokers in the country."

The prosecutor insisted he give the specific names, which he did. It sounded like the "Who's Who" of Wall Street and the New York financial community.

On cross-examination, Sidney Kramer was able to find out how the government was able to get the recorded conversations of the bank executives, some of which implicated AA Financial, and how they were able to build their case. One after another, a bunch of young eager beavers were led up to the stand by the prosecutors, and on cross-examination by Kramer, they recounted how they'd been snatched up in an F.B.I. raid, separated from one another and blitz-interviewed by F.B.I. agents and then plunged into months of nut-crushing negotiations, resulting in almost all of them pleading guilty. Then they went to work for the F.B.I., planting bugs and collecting information. Sidney Kramer did his best to make the bureau look like the bad guys.

One of the government witnesses, also a former employee of the Empire Bank of America, testified that he and Wade rigged a bid involving a $200-million bond for Dade County, Florida. On cross-examination, Kramer asked him to explain how they did that.

"Well I told Wade that we, Empire, was willing to pay 0.52 percent on the $200 mil."

"And what did Mr. Simon say to that?" Kramer asked.

"Well I don't remember his exact words but something to the effect that he was going to give the deal to First Columbia Bank in New Jersey. He said we would get the next one."

"Did he tell you how much First Columbia was going to pay?"

"Yeah, 0.05 percent, and they were going to split the difference."

"When you say split the difference, what do you mean?"

"The bank in Jersey was going to give AA 0.001 percent."

"Wasn't that the fee that AA charged?"

"You could say that."

"I did say that. Would you say that?"

"Yeah, I guess so."

"Isn't it customary for a broker to get a fee when he gives a bank a large piece of business?"

"Yeah, I guess so."

"You do a lot guessing, don't you?"

"Yeah, I guess so."

The jurors laughed, as did most of the courtroom with the exception of the prosecutor.

"Tell me, weren't you on the receiving end of these types of transactions sometimes?"

"Yeah sure. We all got a piece of the business. That's the way Wall Street works."

"That's the way Wall Street works," Kramer said, looking at the jury.

"Let me ask you one last question," Kramer said, leaning against the jury box. "Was the 0.05% a fair rate of interest?"

The prosecution objected. "That is speculation. The witness can't say if that was fair or not."

Kramer loved that. "Do you mean to tell me this witness was negotiating million-dollar deals for the bank, and he can't say if the rate was fair or not?"

The judge overruled the objection and told the witness to answer the question.

With a big smile, the prosecution's witness said, "Yeah, I would say that's fair. Hell I'll take 0.05 percent on $2 mil all day long."

Kramer smiled at the jurors and said to the witness, "Thank you very much. I guess that will be all for now." He got a smirk from the judge and a giggle from the jurors.

The government took two full months to put on their case. They put more than thirty-five witnesses on the stand, each testifying to the same thing. Over and over again, the jurors heard them attempt to translate the tapes that been placed at the bank and at several brokerage firms. It was the same story; the bids were rigged, and that was illegal.

To do that, officials of a municipality hired a middleman firm known as a broker to set up a public auction and invite bids for the town's business. For the $100 million they invested, money raised on the elementary school bond or library, one bank might offer 5.0 percent interest. Another bank offers 5.25 percent. A third bank might offer 5.50 percent. It didn't make any difference; the broker and the banks secretly divvied up the business. Sometimes a bank and the broker would make phony bids. It was a scam of tremendous proportions.

But on cross-examination, the same witnesses testified that they didn't think what they were doing was illegal. "Everybody on Wall Street is doing it," became the theme song of the trial.

The lawyers who were sitting in the courtroom in hopes of getting information that would allow them to file class action law suits against some of the country's richest banks were beginning to lose interest. There was too much gray in the government's case, not enough black and white.

When prosecutors tried to explain the taped telephone auctions during the trial, projecting the transcripts of the calls on a huge movie screen set up across the courtroom from the jury, they could see the sheer bewilderment on the juror's faces. The men on the tapes seemed to be speaking a foreign language, using financial jargon that was insanely dry and boring. One of the jurors, an older black man, spent the first few days of the trial yawning repeatedly, fighting back a heroic battle to stay awake in the face of all the mind-numbing jargon about guaranteed investment contracts, interest rate returns, and market price.

"Who needs Lunesta," joked one lawyer who attended the proceedings, "when you can hear a lawyer talk about GICs right out of the gate?"

At one point in the proceedings, the judge took a recess and asked the prosecutors and the defense lawyers to come to his chambers. It was right after one of the government's witnesses finished testifying about the "dizzying array of methods for rigging deals," as he called it. When asked a question, the witness got so caught up in his own version of bid rigging that the judge had to continually remind him he was there to answer questions, not make a speech.

The judge wanted to remind both sides that the people in the jury box were average American citizens who had little or no knowledge of the banking system. He didn't want to prejudice either side but made it very clear that both sides should make an attempt to present their case so that the jury would understand it. He also told them that he was not going to allow a mistrial if either side felt the jury didn't understand the proceedings. Sidney Kramer liked this judge.

CHAPTER NINETY-NINE

The Defense's Case

THERE WERE TIMES some of the lawyers sitting in the courtroom wondered, *"How did this case ever come to trial?"* What defense attorney would look at hundreds of recorded phone calls, the parade of cooperating witnesses, the stacks of falsified documents, and conclude that airing all that in court would be a smart play? But as the weeks passed by, they got a feel for the defense strategy, which made kind of demented sense to them. Sidney Kramer spent very little time trying to argue the facts of the case. The tapes were what they were; he couldn't change that. He did spend some time attempting to discredit a number of the state's witnesses, but that was more for show than anything else.

What he did do in one cross-examination after another was keep hitting on the same theme. Despite the fact that the rigged bids possibly did result in lower returns, wasn't it true that cities and towns around the country still received, technically speaking, the highest bid? If there was a higher bid somewhere out there floating around in space that they never received, then technically they did receive the highest bid. If a city or town received a 5 percent return on a $200-million bond instead of 5.04 percent, which by the way was never offered to them, who is to say that is not a fair return?

Sidney Kramer put ten of Wade's former clients on the stand. The jury heard them tell the same story. Wade helped them make good investments. Kramer asked each and every one of them the same question at the end of their testimony.

"Suppose there was a stock or a bond or a CD that Mr. Simon could have found for you that paid a higher dividend? Do you think you were cheated because he didn't do that for you?"

And of course, the answer was always the same "absolutely not."

One elderly man said, "Mr. Kramer, did you ever hear the expression Cows go to pasture and pigs go to slaughter?" Sidney smiled and thought *"That's close enough."*

The pretty lady lawyer representing the three bankers spent a little more time on the legality of the charges. She challenged the way the F.B.I. bugged the bank's phones and questioned the government's witnesses in depth about the deal they made in order for them to testify.

The defense spent less than a week putting on their case.

The state's closing argument was long-winded and boring that even the judge almost dozed off.

He started with, "This marks the first time we actually have incontrovertible evidence that Wall Street has moved into this cartel-type brand of criminality. It also offers a disgusting glimpse into the enabling and cynical role played by politicians, bankers, and other members of the financial community who we thought we could trust. Wall Street trials almost never make it to court, and when they do, the offending banks usually escape with no admission of wrongdoing. Let us not allow that to happen here today. You twelve American citizens have the opportunity to make a statement. This case has finally dragged the whole ugly truth of American finance out into the open, and it was a hell of a show. Let's not let it go to waste."

When he finished, Wade looked over at the jury. Two of the women had actually fallen asleep.

On the other hand, when Sidney Kramer gave his summation, he had the jury eating out of his hand. He was smooth. He was eloquent. He was like a surgeon. Even the lawyers attending the trial were impressed. When he finished, they had to restrain themselves from applauding.

To say the least, the trial was a rare and somewhat confusing spectacle: high-octane lawyers working to rip the lid off Wall Street corruption in open court. The prosecution's case was almost surreal, spending an inordinate amount of time eliciting as much detail as possible about what they called "the grotesque corruption scheme" perpetrated on the American public. And all the time, the defendants cringed in a corner, seemingly taking a gratuitous ass-kicking, but in reality waiting for their turn to retaliate.

Now it was up to the jury.

CHAPTER ONE HUNDRED

The Verdict

THE JURORS WERE instructed by the judge to weigh the evidence presented by the prosecution and disregard any of the antics and showmanship by either the prosecution or defense lawyers. He thanked them for their patience and told them not to hesitate to let the clerk know if during their deliberation they had any questions. He concluded his instructions by saying, "The bottom line is even though many aspects of municipal bond financing are very complex, the sole question here is did the defendants commit fraud? If you conclude they did, then your verdict must be guilty. However, if there is any reasonable doubt in your mind that there was fraud on the part of the defendants, then your verdict must be not guilty."

And with that, the jury retired to a room on the floor above the courtroom to start their deliberation. They voted to make the elderly black man who had trouble staying awake to be foreman. Hopefully he would be able to stay awake during their deliberation.

To the credit of the jurors, they all understood the charges very clearly. However, they admitted to one another that they weren't sure they completely understood what constituted fraud. One of the women said, "I really don't understand who eventually got all that money they were talking about. The prosecutor said we were being cheated. Cheated out of what? No matter how much interest was paid, we ain't gonna see any of that money." That set the tone for the deliberation.

The elderly black gentleman, the foreman, said, "That is not what we are here for. We are here to decide if these men are guilty or innocent. Now I think the first thing we need to do is go around the table and each person . . ." He was interrupted by one of the matronly-looking housewives. "I think that lady has a good point. Who does get all that money?"

The foreman again said, "Ladies, please let's talk about the case."

Another lady spoke up. "I think they're all guilty."

A different lady asked, "Why?"

The matronly lady said, "Before we talk about who is guilty, I want to know who gets that money if the interest rate is higher."

The hearings finished at 3:00 p.m. on a Tuesday. The judge told the jury they would be sequestered until they reached a verdict. At 6:00 p.m., they had not come to a decision. They decided to have dinner and talk about it some more after dinner. As it turned out, they made their decision during dinner.

In the end, they found the three bankers guilty. They didn't buy Wall Street's ludicrous defense.

However, at the sentencing, it was nothing that resembled real censure. The bank got off with a slap-on-the-wrist fine and was allowed to retain its preeminent position in the municipal bond market. In the year following the hearing, the Empire Bank of America clocked in with over $10 billion in bond issues. That was after they had paid the slap-on-the-wrist fine of $50 million. Peanuts! You get busted for welfare fraud even once in America, and good luck getting so much as a food stamp ever again. Get caught rigging interest rates in fifty states, and the government goes right on handing you billions of dollars in public contracts.

AA Financial lost whatever license they had and were ordered out of business. Since they had not been in operation for well over a year, it was really academic.

Wade was found not guilty. The jury did not feel the government had made its case against him. The jury said they thought he was a victim of circumstances, and although he did make some poor business choices, he was not guilty of fraud. No fine, nothing. The judge simply said to him, "Mr. Simon, you are dismissed. Good luck."

However, the NASD and the SEC were not that compassionate. They stripped Wade of his broker's license and imposed a lifetime ban against him. He would never again be able to trade on Wall Street. They also fined him $100,000 for allowing the chop-shop operation to continue at AA Financial. Sidney Kramer argued unsuccessfully that the lifetime ban was unfair.

The following day the *Wall Street Journal* ran these headlines on the front page.

"The Bank Three Go Free"

The article went on to criticize the puny punishment, given that the bid rigging exposed in the trial was an entrenched system that affected major bond issues in every state in the nation. The article went on to read, "Truly commensurate penalty would be something like televised stonings of the top executives of every bank involved in bid rigging. Maybe better yet would be the forcible resettlement of every banker and broker in Lower Manhattan to some uninhabited wasteland—anything that would address the systemic nature of their crimes."

They concluded the article with the following statement:

"The end result of this (at least) more than a decade-long conspiracy was that towns and cities systematically lost, while banks and brokers won big. Lowering a bid by just one-100th of a percent could cheat a town out of tens of thousands of dollars it would otherwise have earned on its deposits."

Unfortunately, the average blue-collar worker in America does not read The *Wall Street Journal*. They read the sports page in their local newspaper. They are more interested in point spreads in a football game then they are in interest rate fractions.

CHAPTER ONE HUNDRED-ONE

IT WAS SIX months since the trial had ended. The media had finally stopped calling Wade, asking him to tell his side of the story. The TV shows "60 Minutes" and "20-20" also gave up asking him to appear on their show. Brenda called him from California to explain how badly she felt. "I feel partly responsible," she said. "After all, it was my father who hired you." He told her he was a big boy; nobody twisted his arm to make him work on Wall Street.

She told him she was engaged to a screenwriter she met six months ago. Wade was very happy for her. He asked her about her mother. Brenda laughed, "She is the Pearl Mesta of Palm Beach," she said. "One thing about my mom, Wade, she is a survivor." Then out of the clear blue she said, "How would you like to come out to California and talk about a book and a movie deal?"

"Are you kidding me?"

"Absolutely not, Wade. I know it hasn't been easy for you with the trial, and I am sure you would like to put it all behind you, but what the hell it would make a great movie. I spoke to an executive at Paramount who would like to meet with you. We could be talking about a million dollars up front Wade. I am sure you could use the money after all of your legal expenses."

"That is very considerate of you, Brenda, but I don't think so. Right now, I'm okay financially."

"Would you at least think about it?"

"Okay, I'll think about it."

A couple of days after he spoke to Brenda, he received a call from Louie. They had spoken several times since the trial. Louie told him how sorry he was that his father ever got him involved with AA Financial. Wade told him the same thing he told Brenda.

"I'm a big boy; nobody twisted my arm to make me work on Wall Street."

Then he asked him if he could come to Chicago. His father wanted to meet with him.

"Do you have any idea why he wants to see me?" Wade asked him.

"Don't know, pal."

Wade thought about it for a couple of seconds. "I guess I could, Louie, but I would like to know why."

"Wade, you know my father. If he wants to talk to you, it must be about something important."

"Yeah, I guess so. Tell you what, let me talk to Katrina, and I'll get back to you."

Katrina was preparing for a concert she was giving in three weeks at Carnegie Hall. She told Wade it would be too difficult for her to go with him to Chicago, but she encouraged him to go.

"If he is asking you to come to Chicago now after all that happened, well I think you should go see what he wants."

Three days later, Wade was in Chicago. Louie picked him up at the airport. "You're staying at the house," he told Wade. "No arguments."

"No arguments," Wade answered.

It had been a while since Wade was last at the Santinos' house, but nothing had changed. It was as if everything there were in a special time zone. Whatever happened in the world outside of the Santino mansion seemed not to affect Angelo or his family. Louie's mother was not there; she was visiting relatives in Italy. It was late in the day on a Wednesday when Wade arrived. Louie told him his father wanted to have breakfast with him at nine o'clock on Thursday morning if that was convenient. It was convenient.

Louie did not join Wade and Angelo for breakfast.

Initially the conversation was very light. Angelo asked about Katrina, and Wade asked about Louie's mother. After a while, Angelo began talking about what had happened during the past year. He was easy to talk to. Wade told him how the F.B.I. had arrested him at his apartment, about that one night in jail, and about the trial. To his surprise, Angelo thanked him for never mentioning his name. Wade told him there was no need to. But Angelo considered it to be a true sign of friendship. He said to Wade, "I believe in your religion they call that being a *mensch*."

Wade was embarrassed.

Finally, Angelo told him the reason he wanted to see him.

"You have been very loyal, Wade, both to me and to Albert. I am sure that was not easy trying to please us both." Wade simply nodded.

"And through all of that, you did a good job managing AA Financial. Unfortunately, things didn't work out the way we thought, but that is life."

Wade didn't have a clue where this was going.

The old Italian went on for about ten minutes, complimenting Wade on the way he handled himself after being arrested. The way his lawyer handled his defense, each time reminding Wade how much he appreciated the fact that he never once mentioned his name. Then came the shocker.

"Wade, I have deposited $20 million in your name in a bank in Bermuda in an offshore account." Then he handed Wade an envelope.

"In the envelope, you will find all of the information you need. The name of the bank, the access code numbers, the routing information, everything. The president of the bank is a man by the mane of Andre Lepoint. He is a very good friend of a good friend of mine. He will be expecting you to contact him in the next few weeks. He will be at your disposal to help move the money wherever you want."

Wade was speechless.

"I don't understand," Wade said, looking at Angelo, who finally managed a small smile.

"What don't you understand?"

"The $20 million . . . what do you want me to do with it?"

"It's yours. Do with it what you want."

"Mr. Santino . . . Angelo . . ."

"Wade, a long time ago, both Albert and I promised you that you would be a rich man. It was our plan for you take over and run AA Financial for many years, but like I said, that was not to be. You have befriended Louie, and you have respected my privacy. By no fault of yours, AA Financial is no longer in business. I was very lucky. When we sold it to the Roman National Bank, I made a lot of money. Now I want to reward you for your loyalty."

"Mr. Santino . . . I appreciate what you are doing . . . I mean, what you are doing is more than generous, but I can't accept that kind of money . . . I mean, $20 million . . . "

"Wade, come with me to my den. I need a cigar."

Wade followed Angelo into the den. He watched as Angelo took a cigar from a large box on his desk, looked at it as if it were a work of art, nodded his approval and then began the ritual of lighting it. First, he smelled it, then he bit off one end, finally, he lit it and then gently took a first puff. Wade wondered if he did this every time or just when he wanted to make sure he had your attention.

He motioned for Wade to sit in one of the large leather chairs by the fireplace. He sat on the one facing him.

"Wade, this money is not charity. It is repayment."

"Repayment for what you don't owe me anything." Wade answered.

"But I do. We haven't talked about it, but I understand that Albert's daughter has offered you a movie deal."

How the hell did he know that? He just spoke to her about a week ago.

"You seem surprised, my friend."

"To tell you the truth I am, she only called me last week."

"And…?"

"And nothing, she told me one of the studios was interested in making a movie about what happened to me."

"I appreciate that you chose not to do that, Wade. It would be embarrassing to me."

Wade had not even thought about that, but the old man was right. If there were a movie, they would make him out to be the "Godfather."

"Well to be perfectly honest, Mr. Santino, the little I know about the movie industry leads me to believe they would not give a fair and honest account of what really happened."

Santino said with a smile, as if he knew what he was going to say would hit home, "Who is to say what is fair?" These were the same words Sidney Kramer used in his defense. "Who is to say what is fair?"

"Mr. Santino, you are putting me in a very awkward place."

"Not at all, Wade. Take the money, start a business, travel around the world, buy your wife a diamond bracelet, enjoy yourself, you deserve it. And, Wade . . . trust me . . . I can well afford it."

On the way to the airport, Wade replayed in his mind all the things that happened over the last ten years, so many little things that turned into big things.

He thought about his father's gambling debts and how Angelo helped him.

He remembered the first day at AA Financial. Would he have stayed if he knew what they really did? And if he hadn't stayed, where would he be today?

He always knew he would be successful, and he assumed that also meant he would be financially secure. And $20 million was a damn good start.

He called Katrina from the airport in Chicago.

"So what was so important that he had to have you fly out to Chicago?" she asked him.

"Oh nothing really he just wanted to make sure I got all of my holiday and vacation pay from AA."

"What? You are kidding, of course."

"No, really, baby."

"What in heaven's name did he think your job was at AA, the janitor or something? You were the CEO. CEOs don't get holiday and vacation pay. Wade!"

"What can I tell you, baby?"

"Okay, I'll go along. How much did you get?"

"I think he said twenty."

"He gave you $20,000?"

"No, he gave us $20 million."

Sitting in first class on the flight from Chicago back to New York, Wade picked up a copy of Newsweek magazine. On the cover of the magazine was a picture of a bull with sunglasses, smoking a cigar, and wearing a dark hat. The headline was, "Crime on Wall Street Pays." He flipped open the magazine to the story and began reading.

"Crime on Wall Street, in banking, and in corporate America is alive and well, and it pays. One neither admits nor denies it, instead the government simply allows the white-collar criminals to pay their fines and continue. These are today's untouchables who steal billions and get away with it. Financial institutions are too big to fall, as are the corrupt top executives who run them. This is not fair to the average American stockholder who buys stocks and bonds from these firms in the hopes of retiring one day."

Wade put the magazine back in the seat pocket. He reclined his seat, closed his eyes, smiled, and thought to himself, "*Who is to say what is fair?*"

The End

EPILOGUE

AS 2004 ENDED, investors had plenty to think about, and at the same time plenty of reasons to breathe a sigh of relief.

On the down side of course the war in Iraq raged on. The Federal Reserve began raising short-term interest rates; oil prices topped $55 a barrel; the presidential election went down to the wire; and the stock market spent most of the year in the doldrums However the three main market gauges finished up for the year at the highest levels in over three and a half years creating billions of dollars for thousands of Wall Street investors.

And the F.B.I., the SEC, and the NASD were still chasing the bad guys. All of the arrests, the convictions, and the fines had not slowed down white-collar crime and the mob's infiltration on Wall Street.

Part of the problem is that the SEC, CFTC, and the Justice Department aid and abet these crooks in order to keep harmony in the system. They make no bones about it they come right out and tell you this.

Although this book is a work of fiction and there is no AA Financial, no Roman National Bank, or Empire Bank of America, or Angelo Santino, or Albert Kline, or Wade Simon, the story and the characters are based on my research into what actually has been taking place on Wall Street for decades. What is not fiction is the fact that Wall Street continues to this day to have more than its share of chopshops, boiler room operations, an infiltration of organized crime, and scam artists.

I can't honestly say if the regulatory bodies are doing the best job possible to eliminate crime and/or fraud on Wall Street. However, public opinion is that to many rich and influential people get off with just a slap on the wrist (a fine), and then go back to doing the same thing.

It is almost a comical dimension in allowing wealthy financial institutions to fork over hundreds of millions of dollars (in many cases), neither admitting nor denying that they have engaged in wrongful conduct. Allowing the rich and powerful banks, brokerage firms, and investment bankers to buy their way out of trouble exemplifies the unequal justice in our society. Government prosecutors and regulators have defended this practice on the grounds that these settlements allow for effective monitoring of future compliance by the firms involved and avoid the risk of destroying a business that employs large numbers of innocent people. Bullshit!

Wrongdoing on Wall Street was long believed to be deterred—at least in many cases—for the fear of harming one's good reputation. However, Yale University law professor, Jonathan R. Macey, argues that the transformation nature of the financial markets in this country has dramatically diminished the importance of a good reputation in order to have a successful financial business and I am inclined to agree with the professor.

People often ask the experts to explain the stunning number of financial crimes that we have witnessed over the last twenty years, and as a matter of fact continue today. It is not easy to grasp why financial institutions like Bank of America, Citigroup, UBS, and JP Morgan, and a bevy of giant hedge funds become involved in questionable transactions and then sweat their way through the demand for fines in the tens of billions of dollars.

Unfortunately, the prosecution of a financial crime usually occurs many years after the crime itself. By that time, the public has forgotten about it.

Bankers and stockbrokers are swept up by their success, which can be measured by money, and money is power. That is the reason organized crime has invaded Wall Street. It is really very simple; it is all about money. I repeat, when they asked Willie Sutton why he robbed banks, his answer was, "Because that's where the money is." Ask Wall Street criminal the same question and I am sure you will get the same answer.

Law enforcement should not rest on their laurels. Organized crime will always be attracted to easy money, and Wall Street offers that. The mob will continue to scam investors both on Wall Street and the Internet, whenever the opportunity presents itself.

During the nineties, it has been documented the six New York crime families took a heavy piece of the nearly $10 billion a year trade in grossly overpriced microcap stocks. By the year 2000, Wall Street had become a Mafia cash cow. What makes anyone think organized crime is just going to walk away from that kind of money?

Americans tend to like their crime stories simple: The good guys catch the bad guys, and the bad guys go to jail. Unfortunately, financial crimes are not that simple. Wall Street is confronting a vexing problem, call it what you will: Organized Crime, the Mafia, or The Wise Guys. It all sounds like stuff of tabloids and gangster movies. To most Americans it sounds like all of that has as much to do with Wall Street as the other side of the moon. And then you have the other side of the coin: the Bernie Madoffs and all of the other white-collar criminals. For some strange reason, the American public seems to separate them from Organized crime, I find that hard to understand. Is there really any difference?

Don't misunderstand me. Wall Street has been good to millions of people all across this great country of ours, and America is the greatest country in the world, and our financial system is probably the best in the world. And I would venture to say that most of the people who work on Wall Street and in banks and other financial institutions are hardworking, honest people. However, that doesn't alter the fact that thousands of investors fall victim to some sort of financial scam or fraud every year.

If the government and regulators are serious about undertaking the formidable challenge of demanding Wall Street firms admit to any wrongdoing they engaged in that will definitely be a step in the right direction. In addition, the powers-to-be, must continue their efforts in ridding Wall Street of organized crime once and for all.

Then maybe we can change the title from, "The Money, the Mob and Wall Street, to simply, "The Money and Wall Street."

Other Books by Harry Brooks
Published by Xlibris

A Family Secret

All In

Everybody Does Business

29990582R00224

Made in the USA
Middletown, DE
09 March 2016